#1 LOVE

USA Today Bestselling Author
T. GEPHART

#1 Love
Published by T Gephart
Copyright 2019 T Gephart

ISBN-13: 978-0-6483959-2-8
ISBN-10: 0-6483959-2-8

Cover by:
Hang Le

Editing by:
Nichole Strauss, Insight Editing Services

Interior Design & Formatting by:
Christine Borgford

#1
LOVE

DEDICATION

To all the people who not only tolerate
my crazy but encourage it. I love you all.

And to Skarsgård, because clearly no one
expected the insanity to turn into 6 books.

CHAPTER #1

FOR AS LONG as I could remember, I'd been in love with a Larsson.

First, it was Eric.

Long before he was a Hollywood superstar, he was my super-hero. Older and wiser than me and both of my brothers—or his for that matter—he'd always seemed so strong and larger than life. It was him we all turned to when we got into trouble. And man, did my little heart adore him.

Next came Roman.

Gorgeous—just like his older brother—but with a cockier attitude. He was smart and mischievous and had a smile that could charm almost anyone. He had the ability to get exactly what he wanted, and I so desperately wanted to be just like him.

Of course, when I got a little older my attention turned to Dave.

The man was a huge teddy bear, so caring and sweet, he never made me feel like the annoying little girl I no doubt was. He was beautiful and kind and gave the best hugs.

But Nick—sigh—Nick was the Larsson who made my teenage heart explode in my chest.

He was a GOD—good-looking beyond comprehension—with

confidence for days. Able to melt polar ice caps with little more than his amazing smile, he knew exactly what to say in order to turn any girl into a puddle of mumbling mush.

Especially this one.

Oh. God.

My heart still skipped a beat whenever I thought of him, and it had been years since I'd seen *any* of them.

He—like the rest of his family—were an amazing footnote in my past. A memory of happier times in my childhood when life was simple and all I had to do was go to school, be a kid and decide which Larsson I was going to crush on.

There had been only one who had escaped my infatuation. And not because I didn't love him—because I think I loved him most of all—but because the feelings I'd had for him had been different.

Alex.

He had been my best friend since I could remember, knew all my secrets and I'd known his. I'd even helped him score his first date when we were fourteen, coaching him on exactly what to say to win Lola's heart. He never once made me feel stupid, or small, and even tolerated my overdramatic crushes on all his older brothers.

God, they were beautiful. Each and every single one of those boys, genetically blessed with gorgeous perfection as well as being sweet, kind and wonderful. And while three of them had become superstars—Eric, Dave and Nick, famous actors—I'd been lucky enough to know the other side of them.

My dad, Glenn, and Jensen Larsson—the papa of those fine Larsson boys—had been friends since college. They both married their college sweethearts around the same time and impregnated their wives to add to their ever-expanding broods.

Unlike the Larsson family, my mom and dad decided to stop at three with me being the youngest. My brother, Jordon was nine years older than me, and the same age as Roman. Ben—my other brother—shared a birthday with Nick—literally thirty minutes apart. And I was two months younger than Alex.

Our families had been tighter than blood. Spending vacations and holidays together, with Alex and I being inseparable. He didn't even care I was a girl, happy for me to tag along despite the protests of both of our brothers. Not going to lie, I was probably five before *I* even noticed I wasn't one of the boys, able to do whatever they did without breaking a sweat.

When I turned thirteen, and suddenly it was obvious I wasn't one of them, Alex was great. He ignored my growing breasts and my loved-up feelings for Nick, treating me as he always did—as his best friend.

But like all good things, my picture-perfect childhood and idyllic adolescence came to a screeching halt right after my sixteenth birthday. My parents—and the Larssons—got divorced, throwing my world into a tailspin. And where Jensen and Kate's divorce had been amicable, Mom and Dad's was not.

Shame, embarrassment and a whole lot of reality landed in my lap, my mom taking us away from the scandal—and California—to go live with my grandparents in Carson City. Guess that's what happens when your father ends up being a major player in a Ponzi scheme. Of course there was the gambling addiction and the mistress we didn't know about either, which didn't help the situation. My mom was hit with a one-two punch, finding out the bank was foreclosing on our family home on the same day my dad's other woman announced she was pregnant. Surprise!

Oh, and he'd managed to swindle a couple of Gs from his old college buddy, Jenson Larsson as well. And because my dad didn't give a shit about *his* BFF, I'd also lost mine.

I'd been devastated, not only at the reality of losing my home, my father—the bastard skipping town and going on the run with his lover—but also at the loss of my best friend.

Sixteen was hard enough to navigate, let alone starting over in a new state and school. The only good thing my father ever did was make sure my mother was never implicated in his crimes. I'm sure his motives weren't honorable, more like wanting to keep the cash out of her reach should it have worked out and he hadn't gotten caught, but it was one time I was thankful for his greed. So while we'd lost *everything* at least we still had her. And even though my mother worked her ass off to make sure we had the most perfect life she could make it, it was never the same.

I hated high school, never really fitting in to any of the cliques, biding my time until I could graduate and leave. But there was one benefit to the lack of friends, my time spent studying earning me an amazing scholarship to Yale.

Then it was goodbye Nevada, hello Connecticut and the start of my new life.

No one knew me—or the piece of shit who was my father—and I finally found my feet. I flourished, came out of my shell and nailed Law School. All that blood, sweat and tears—a lot of them—finally paid off. And a year after graduating, I landed a prestigious job in a big-time law firm in L.A.

I was going back, baby.

"Oh, Maya." I could hear the tears in my mom's voice. "I am so proud of you."

"Mom, don't cry," I warned, the thirtieth time I had to remind her in the last five minutes. "I'm just excited I get to have my dream job and be closer to home. I miss you and the boys."

"Oh sweetie, they miss you too. It will be so good—" her voice warbled, "to have my babies all together again."

"Mom," I laughed. "Jordon and Vanessa have two babies of their own now, and Ben and Natalie won't be far behind them. Safe to say, your babies have all grown up."

"You'll *always* be my babies."

I didn't bother arguing, grateful that while I had enjoyed my time on the east coast, I was finally going home.

Especially since I didn't get to see my brothers, their wives and my two nephews nearly enough. And I really did miss them.

The boys had taken after my dad. While he was shitty at being a father, his genetics were pretty good. Tall and athletic, they had hazel eyes and sandy colored hair. I, on the other hand, looked like our mother. With the same emerald green eyes and light brown hair, the family connection wasn't immediately apparent. And while I would have liked the strong, toned limbs they seemed to be able to achieve without much effort, they would have looked out of place on my petite, curvy frame. Or at least that was my excuse for not working out.

"So . . ." My mother paused, the change in subject one I was anticipating and expecting. "Have you connected with any of your old friends and told them you're coming back?"

It wasn't the first time she'd mentioned *my old friends*, dancing around the subject ever since I'd been given the job offer.

"Nope," I answered, shaking my head with a grin. "I figured once I move into my new apartment and start at my new firm, I'll make new friends." *You know, like a regular person*, I didn't add.

Hesitation in my mother could only mean bad things. Which was why when she didn't immediately answer, I was worried.

"Why don't you call Alex and tell him you're coming, I'm sure he'd love to show you around?"

And there it was. Ever the optimist—probably how my father was able to cheat and swindle every cent we had without her noticing—I was wondering how long it was going to take before she brought it up. She'd been hinting at it for weeks but had stopped short at the suggestion. But with tomorrow's departure looming, she probably figured it was situation critical and she needed to toss it in.

"Mom, I haven't seen or spoken to Alex since . . ." *How long had it been?* At least ten years, maybe even longer. "Since forever. I can't just call him completely out of the blue and say, hey, I'm moving to Los Angeles, can you be my friend until I find a suitable substitute?"

I wasn't sure if it sounded ridiculous or pathetic saying it out loud, but it sure didn't do me any favors.

"Honey, but you *are* friends. You grew up together and cried every night for a month straight when we moved to Carson City. You swore that as soon as you were old enough, you were moving to Los Angeles."

"Yeah, I said a lot of stuff when I was younger too." My head shook as I reminded both of us of my wide-eyed dumb love. "I was going to marry Nick Larsson and make gorgeous Larsson babies. Pretty sure his wife might have something to say about that."

The only saving grace to the whole tragic conversation was that I was still in New Haven and my mom was on the phone. It was bad enough that my return to the west coast had stirred feelings and curiosity in me. And fine, I did happen to glance online at a picture of Nick with his gorgeous wife, but it was hard to avoid. It was news, and they were famous and it wasn't like I was cruising past his house and stalking him like I was a crazy ex girlfriend.

And no, I wasn't delusional in believing we still had a chance. Our love story had been completely one-sided—mine—with Nick not once showing any interest in me other than being an honorary little sister. Still, didn't mean I didn't feel a pang of jealousy.

Thanks a lot, Dad.

Who knew what might have happened between us if he'd been a decent person, kept his dick in his pants and the money of other people out of his pocket.

But if nothing else, all of that turmoil made me who I was today, and that had to count for something.

"Besides, pretty sure Alex, or anyone else in his family, doesn't want to hear from us." I sighed into the phone.

"Oh, sweetheart." Her voice warbled again. "You know that you had nothing to do with what your father did. I should have been stronger and kept in contact with all our old friends, but I was just so embarrassed and—"

"Don't you dare blame yourself for him," I fired back, unable to keep the edge in my voice at bay.

Even after all these years, it still stung, and was without a doubt the reason why I went into law. I wanted him to pay, to suffer like we had. I didn't have the stomach for blood so becoming a hitman and hunting him down to exact my revenge wasn't an option. Instead, I would do whatever I could to make sure men like him wouldn't get away with ruining people's lives. "Sorry, I didn't mean to snap. I'm just tired."

Not to mention nervous, excited, elated and about a million other emotions. I was going to be a junior associate at one of the best law firms in Los Angeles which meant all my time and energy was going to need to be spent being the absolute best.

"You know, Maya." Another pause. "I found Kate on Facebook. And we've been chatting."

Oh help me, Lord, my mother was on social media.

My mother had undergone a renaissance of late, trying new things she'd otherwise been unable to do when she was working two jobs and raising three kids solo. Making her own cheese and studying Feng Shui was a little out there but harmless; Facebook did not give me the same lack of concern.

While I applauded her leap into the digital age—making my time away at college easier when she got a handle on Skype—the access it had given her was downright scary.

"Kate?" I asked, knowing exactly which Kate she was referring to.

She blew out a breath and I could hear the smile in her voice. "Don't be mad."

Goddamn it.

It was Kate Freaking Larsson.

"It was so good to talk to her, and we're both grandmothers now. You know Eric has two children too."

I shook my head in disbelief, the effort wasted because there was no one else to see it. "Mom, the whole *world* knows Eric has two kids. I doubt the man could take out his trash without it ending up in the tabloids."

She laughed. "Okay, okay, point taken. Anyway, I mentioned you—"

"No." It shot out of my mouth before I even knew I had said it.

Dear. God.

NO.

I was happy for her to hang mirrors in corners and tie red ropes around doorknobs. Ecstatic that growing herbs and churning enough butter to make an Amish person proud gave her solace. And I was even glad she was able to reconnect with the matriarch of what was an astoundingly beautiful family, a woman who had once been her friend.

But I drew the line at having my mother intervening. I didn't care if her intentions were pure, I was twenty-six for Christ's sake.

"I'm fine. I told you, I'll make friends, I've been living on my own and—"

"Maya." She cut me off not letting me finish the sentence. "Just call him. I'm not saying you're going to end up being best friends again, but don't you owe it to yourself to at least tell him you're back in town?"

Usually I liked logic.

Except when it was used against me.

The pit of my stomach twisted in an uncomfortable knot. It

had been so long, and we weren't the same people we once were. And I didn't need to ruin what had once been a fantastic memory of a person on the chance of indifference. Or something worse.

"Aren't you even going to ask what he's doing now?" she baited, and I sensed her smile.

"Let me guess, he's a fireman." I rolled my eyes, wondering if she'd hoped the promise of a hot, toned first responder would tip the scale in her favor.

It wasn't that wild of a guess. Alex had wanted to be a fireman for years, loving the idea of running in to danger when everyone else was running away. I'd even entertained the idea of joining him until I decided my talents would be better used elsewhere.

"He's a lawyer." She laughed, with zero prelude.

"Whoa, what?" I felt the air rush out of my lungs, his change in career direction shocking the hell out of me.

He hated paperwork and research, bribing me with candy to do his English homework when we were in eighth grade.

"Yeah, Roman is too."

See, now that made sense.

He'd been studying law when we'd left and if history was anything to go by, Roman would slay in a courtroom. He could talk his way into or out of anything, but Alex . . . well, he was different.

Alex hated the idea of being confined to an office and thought people who wore suits and ties to work every day were suckers. We'd actively laughed at them, insisting we'd never be slaves to the grind. Instead, we'd vowed to remain misfits forever. Guess I wasn't the only one to break our promise.

"Where did he study?" I held my breath, waiting for her to answer. Of course I knew he hadn't been at Yale like Roman, but wondered if he'd come across to the east coast too. My skin tingled at the thought he might have been close all those years without me ever knowing.

"Well, if you call him, maybe you can find out."

She wasn't giving me shit.

"Mom," I protested, wishing I could stomp my foot on the floor to get my way like when I was a kid. Not that it did much good then, I imagined it would be even less effective now.

"Maya," she mimicked, followed by a laugh.

Ah. Damn. It.

"You know cruel and unusual punishments are an indictable offense," I deadpanned knowing my threats would get me nowhere.

She sighed, and while I couldn't see the look she was wearing, it was no doubt the very same I'd been on the receiving end of when she wanted me to concede. It was like her super power. Just a head tilt to the side, and a well-placed "Maya" and poof, the feeling of disappointment engulfed me so much I'd agree to whatever.

I sure hoped it was a skill I'd inherited, would come in handy when I came up against a jury.

"Just call him. Have one conversation with him and then if you don't want to talk to him again I'll drop it. Do this for me."

And there it was.

The final nail being hammered into my indecisive coffin.

Do this for me.

Seriously—a superpower. What ministers were able to do with scriptures and sermons, Anna Zaveri could manage with four little words.

"Shit." I cursed inwardly and outwardly. "Fine, I will *call* him, but if he even seems the slightest bit weirded-out by the fact some blast from the past is burning up his phone line, I'm tossing you under the bus."

Or pretend to be a wrong number.

National survey.

Shit.

Mom laughed, her objective achieved as she tried to sound

innocent. "Baby, you would do that to your own mother?"

"Yes, yes I would," I responded, sounding convincing even though I probably wouldn't. "Just promise me you will not tell Kate, and the two of you don't get involved in some shady intervention. Alex and I *were* friends, Mom, but a lot of time has passed. I'm sure he has a roster full of friends now, and I'm not really needed."

It was how it should be.

We served a purpose, but that time was over. And now I had a small—but carefully curated—group of people I would easily walk through fire for, who also had my back. It was just too bad they were all going to be on the east coast.

But going back to California was just something I needed to do. It felt right, even if it meant starting over.

"I promise you, sweetheart, you will get no interference from me." Her voice was sincere and I believed her. And if there was one thing more reliable than Anna's powers of persuasion, it was her bond to a promise. She hadn't broken one yet.

"Well, I better finish packing, I have an early flight."

"I love you, baby. And in case I haven't told you enough, I am so proud of you."

"Thanks, Mom. I'll see you soon."

CHAPTER #2

TRANSCONTINENTAL FLIGHTS WERE the worst.

It didn't matter how many times I'd flown from Connecticut to Nevada, every single time it was misery with a side order of chronic fatigue. And flying to Los Angeles was no different.

But for the first time since I'd been playing tag with the coastline, I didn't immediately want to shower, go to bed and give myself a day to adjust. Instead, I was buzzing, bouncing off the plane like a woman on a tampon commercial. So full of positivity and radiance that I was concerned it might be manic induced. *For both of us—me and the tampon girl.* No one was that happy to be bleeding out of her vagina, I didn't care how upbeat you were.

Capitalizing on my mood—or trying to do as much as possible before I crashed and burned—I'd picked up the keys to my apartment and unpacked my suitcases. I'd traveled light, electing to get rid of most of my college-life acquired furniture and was looking forward to starting fresh with a clean slate.

A clean slate.

How desperately I'd wanted that the last time I had been in L.A.

"You sure I can't help you out with something?" My landlord knocked on the door, checking in after seeing my underwhelming amount of luggage and lack of furnishings.

She seemed sweet, even with the Elmo-red hair that stained her scalp. Leathery skin hinted she'd spent a little too much time baking in the sun, only hidden by the housedress that looked from the 1950's she'd poured herself into. Creepy. "I can give you a foldout cot, maybe a chair and a table until you get on your feet?"

"Thank you, but I'm fine," I assured her, looking around the empty space. "The delivery truck for my bed should be arriving this afternoon, and if not, I'll camp on the floor for a night. I'll have everything else set up in a day or two."

"Well, if you need anything, I'm on the ground floor." Her leathery forehead receded into that bright red hair. "Welcome to Primrose Apartments." And with a curt nod, she shut the door and left me alone in my new home.

Wow.

It hadn't seemed real until that moment, looking around and seeing the sun still peeking through my living room window. And suddenly I felt emotional, like the cork had just been released from my bottle and all the feelings bubbled to the surface. My eyes watered as I glanced around the empty room.

Next week I would be walking into a new job and starting a whole new chapter, and I was excited for all of it.

Using the time I had productively—still waiting for the come-down—I caught a cab to the store and picked up a few basic supplies. I even managed to sneak out to the mall and grabbed a set of sheets, a few pillows, and a comforter, making it back just as my new bed arrived.

Lucky for everyone concerned, my apartment was only on the second floor. With no elevator, I had already been up and down the stairs a few times so it was nice to get the bed set up in my bedroom and collapse on top of it the minute the deliveryman had left.

And that was when it happened.

All the energy and euphoria leeched out of me like a virus and robbed me of consciousness. My body fell into a dreamless slumber Sleeping Beauty would be jealous of as I snuggled under my new comforter on the sheetless mattress. Pretty sure the plastic was still on the pillows too, but I didn't care. I was gone.

When I finally woke up from my nap/coma, it was dark outside. With no lamps or nightstands yet, I reached around on the floor to locate my phone, hoping I hadn't run the battery flat.

"Shit." I blinded myself with the brightness of my screen as I brought it to my face. It was only eleven o'clock but it felt like two in the morning. Of course, it was two a.m. in my old home, which was why I felt like a zombie despite my nap.

Apart from the fatigue—my tampon girl advertisement cheer missing in action—I was acutely aware of another part of my body giving me the middle finger. My stomach growled, announcing its displeasure at skipping dinner and threatening to cannibalize itself if I didn't feed it pronto.

So, with not much to work with in my old-mother-Hubbard cupboards, I managed to order some Chinese food before they closed, avoiding the dreaded fate of convenience store burritos which would have been Plan B.

I showered while waiting for my food, pretending that some H_2O and strawberry-scented body wash was going to make me feel less of a corpse. It was only once I was dressed in my pajamas and sucking down lemon chicken and fried rice that normal Maya seemed to return.

Or so I thought.

Because *normal* Maya would not have picked up the phone and flicked through contacts, finding the number that had been sent by her mother a day earlier. Bored by the lack of television, light, or basically anything gifted to us by the modern century could be the only excuse. Even so, if normal Maya was still running the show, she would have given those digits a cursory glance, and then called one of her friends, Jackie or Lisa even though it was ridiculously late where they were. But instead of being *normal* Maya—because that would have been too easy—she decided to be *abnormal* Maya, deciding that the right time to call a man you hadn't spoken to in like ten years was almost midnight.

Oh, and she didn't even have alcohol to blame, so her only argument would be stupidity.

And yet . . . She dialed.

Shit.

Oh, I also needed to stop talking about myself in the third person because I was starting to weird myself out.

I heard the phone ring as I swore under my breath. "Hang up, hang up," I chanted out loud, trying to convince my hand to do what clearly my brain wasn't capable of.

There was a click, my breath held as a voice answered. "Hello?"

"Hang up." The reflexive chant stuck on repeat as I tried to recover. "Shit. I mean, hello."

It was a disaster, like my mouth, hand, and brain were all on separate pilgrimages, and every single one of them intent on ruining my life.

"So, which is it?" he asked, his voice cool despite the hot mess he was clearly talking to. "You want me to hang up, swear or say hello?"

Say it's the wrong number.

Tell him you are calling to find out his views on recycling.

Ask if he's welcomed Jesus into his life.

"Ummm . . . hi?" *Fuck you, mouth.* "Hi," I said again, without the indecision and hopefully not sounding like a candidate for a lobotomy.

"Hey yourself," he chuckled, with all the finesse I didn't possess. "You want to keep going with the greetings or should we graduate to whole sentences?"

My heart squeezed, the charming sarcastic voice I'd remembered from all those years ago was almost identical, except perhaps more manly. And even though I'd been given the number from my mother—who had gotten it from his—there was no denying that the man on the other end of the phone was Alex Larsson.

"Sentences are so overrated," I volleyed back, hoping I had a chance at salvaging the conversation. "I was thinking we grunt syllables and see if we can't communicate on a higher level."

"Maya?" The hiss of surprise threw me off guard, not expecting him to guess who I was so soon.

So much for not weirding him out.

"Surprise." I waved my hands in the air even though he wasn't around to see them.

"Maya *Zaveri*?" he asked again, making me ponder how many other weird Mayas he knew who called him in the middle of the night.

"Aww, you remember me. Hope that is a good thing and not because you're still emotionally scarred from when I flushed your Ninja Turtle down the toilet."

Who the hell was I right now? My hand flew to my mouth, not convinced the voice that had spoken had been mine.

"Jesus. Christ. I can't believe it's really *you*." He breathed out, the confidence he'd had when he answered slightly rattled as he continued. "I haven't spoken to you since—"

"I'm sorry." It wasn't what I'd intended to say, the apology surprising me as I blew out a breath. "I'm sorry it's been so long."

And whatever my intention had been, it had been superseded by my thoughts, my mouth saying exactly what I was thinking.

I *was* sorry.

Even if the circumstances hadn't been my doing, I could have found a way to stay in contact.

Email, phone calls—anything, but I didn't.

"Yeah, I'm sorry too." His apology surprising me more than my own.

"What are you sorry for?"

He barked out a laugh. "Because I was a dick and didn't call you either. You know communication works both ways. I knew you were living in Nevada; you didn't move to Mars."

I hadn't considered him reaching out to me, assuming his family hated mine for what my father had done. Or assuming we were cut from the same cloth and therefore untrustworthy. It was the reason I had never even tried to find him, happier to live in oblivion than the reality of possible rejection.

A silence fell between us, years of unsaid words hanging in the air just waiting to open a Pandora's box of emotions. And I wasn't sure how many of them I could deal with in my jet-lagged state.

"Well, that got more serious than I intended." I laughed, my chest feeling heavy as I desperately tried to change the subject. "How did you know it was me?"

"Are you kidding? You tried to create your own language when we were seven, convinced that if we could communicate with grunts no one else would know what we were talking about." It sounded like he was smiling.

Which made me smile. "Well, we couldn't take over the world if everyone knew what we were going to do. Eric would have tried to stop us, Roman would have tried to usurp our power and Jordon would have created a flow chart detailing how impossible it would have been."

"And Dave, Nick and Ben were too busy playing computer games to be of any value to us," he added, remembering my original argument.

I chuckled. "Amateurs."

"So is that why you're calling me? You looking to take over the world?" I heard the curiosity in his voice, probably wondering why I'd picked that exact moment to pick up the phone and say hello.

"Umm yes, if you can write it in for Thursday that would be good."

"Thursday? But it's," there was a pause. "But it just clicked over to Tuesday morning. You're going to sit on these plans for domination for a whole two days?"

"I have to buy furniture or I won't have a table to unfurl my plans upon." I laughed.

God, it was so easy to talk to him. Even after all that time, it was like picking up exactly where we'd left off. I felt like a kid again, completely and utterly devoid of worry.

"Where are you living now?" he asked, breaking from our little walk down memory lane.

I took a breath and held it before finally letting go. "Here."

"*Here*, as in California?"

"Los Angeles. I flew in today. Well, yesterday," I corrected myself, the day melting into tomorrow already. "I've moved back."

Talking to me on the phone from an undisclosed location was one thing; being told I was back in town was something entirely different. And while I hoped our happy reminiscing would continue, I genuinely didn't know how he'd react.

Did he want to see me?

Did I want to see him?

Was there too much water under the bridge?

Too many questions for a Tuesday morning when my brain was still in another time zone.

"Well then." He pushed out a breath and I had no idea whether it was annoyance or happiness. "Lucky for you, I'll let you use my table."

What?

That told me *nothing* as to where he sat on the issue of being happy I was back. "Huh?"

"*My* table, Maya. For our plans of world domination. No reason to wait until Thursday when I have a perfectly good table lying around. You have a car, or do you want me to come get you?"

My eyes flew down to my pink and white bunny sleep shorts and tank top and I immediately started to panic. "Errr, it's the middle of the night."

It was a feeble response but all I had, his invitation throwing me completely off guard.

"Not now, wiseass." He laughed, the sound zipping up my spine and making my skin pebble. *That laugh*, even if I'd been gone a hundred years I'd have known it *and* him in an instant, able to pick it out of a lineup from a million other laughs. "Let's say seven o'clock?"

"Alex." His name felt so weird in my mouth after years of not saying it. "You don't have to do this."

Of course I was curious, who wouldn't be? While fame had guaranteed I'd seen dozens of pictures of his three brothers—and boy, had time been good to them—I hadn't even dared to search for him online.

Not even once.

It would have been too hard. To see him and know that everything had changed. Instead I chose ignorance.

But I wasn't a charity case either, and the last thing I wanted was for him to see me out of some sense of obligation.

"You're right, I don't. But when have you ever known me to do anything I didn't want?"

Well, I wasn't about to argue with that.

"Okay, seven sounds good. Text me your address and I'll see you then."

"Maya." His usual cockiness missing from his voice. "I'm really glad you called."

"Yeah, me too. Goodbye, see you tomorrow."

"Today," he corrected me. "See you *today*. Don't be turning up on Wednesday and wasting twenty-four hours of scheming time."

Annnnnnnd the cockiness was back.

"Right, today. Bye."

Awesome, nothing like jumping headfirst into the unknown.

Shit.

CHAPTER #3

AFTER CURSING MYSELF out a few hundred times and over-analyzing to the point of insanity, I eventually fell back asleep. And while I didn't feel great when I woke up—I seriously needed to make up my bed so I didn't feel like I was sleeping in a Serta showroom—my moments of stupidity were minimal.

I washed my sheets in the laundry room on the ground floor, trying to let mundane tasks quell the butterflies in my belly. Besides, I had no time to think about my evening, too busy heading to the mall and buying home wares so my apartment didn't look like it had been robbed. A lamp was the first thing I bought, along with a matching nightstand and dresser. I did some serious damage to my credit card at Target, it was a wonder I didn't get a call from the fraud department. Pretty sure I was also going to need to sell a kidney to cover the bill, but I'd deal with that next month.

It wasn't until five that realization set in.

"Hello, traitor," Jackie answered, her voice laced with venom even though I knew she didn't mean it.

We'd gone through law school together, vowing to be badass attorneys and even better friends. But in what seemed to be my MO, I had left her behind. While her job offer had taken her to

New York City with our other friend Lisa, I had defected back to the west.

"You attending Shopping Anonymous meetings yet? I heard they give you the number when you buy your first pair of Manolos." I laughed, happy just to hear her voice.

She snorted. "Ha, more to the point, have you bought a pair of boobs to go with your microbrew and avocados?"

"My boobs are still my own, *Jenny from the Block*."

"Well, *Gwen Stefani*, you'll be happy to know the only meetings I'm attending are the ones for my new co-op. Oh, and I think someone is peeing in our elevator."

I laughed out loud, unpacking the many boxes and bags I had bought while I spoke to her. I needed to multi task, too worried if I stopped and thought about seeing Alex I'd possibly freak out.

"God, it's good to hear your voice."

"Fine," she conceded. "It's good to hear from you too. I was spoiled when you didn't immediately move after college and hoped we might bring you across to the dark side."

"Yeah, well the only reason I didn't move right away was because I couldn't get a job. Then I had to sit for the bar, find an apartment and all that fun stuff. You know you got me to stay longer in Connecticut than I'd planned."

"Whatever, I'm still going to be bitter and curse you out for leaving us. So tell me, what's got your mind twisted in such a knot you need to call me at eight p.m. New York time on a Tuesday?"

What made Jackie a good friend were the same things that made her a good lawyer, she had a killer gut instinct and was rarely wrong. Oh, and she was one of the few people in the country who could read me like a book. Alex used to be one, but the jury was still out on whether he'd retained the skill.

"You remember that guy I told you about?" I had always been

vague about Alex, referring to him only by first name and never mentioning his family connection. Partly to protect him, and partly to protect myself.

"The dude with the hot brother you wanted to marry and make babies with?" she asked, her mind remembering every detail like she would be called to give testimony at any minute.

"Yeah, that guy. So, I called him and we're meeting up in a couple of hours." I stopped unpacking boxes, the distraction no longer enough.

"Is his hot brother going to be there? If so, wear the red dress. Even with your natural and regular-sized boobs, it still makes them look impressive," Jackie added, prompting me to roll my eyes.

"The brother already has a wife. I'm not trying to get married, have babies or seduce anyone. But I do feel stupidly nervous." The hand that had previously been occupied putting away my five billion purchases from Target was white-knuckling a throw pillow I didn't need.

"Babe, it's normal to feel weird. You've been gone a long time. But my advice is to treat him like you would a client. Smile, be polite and retain your judgment. And wear the red dress anyway. It will be good practice for when you find someone you do want to seduce."

"Other than your directive to flash my boobs, your advice is perfect as always, counselor."

"That's why you called me instead of Lisa. She gives you feels while I give you the facts." She chuckled. "And by the way, I want a transcript of this meeting after it takes place."

"Sure, I'll take notes. Oh, and one other thing, he's a lawyer too."

I took a breath.

"Wait a minute, you can't just drop that bombshell on me

right when you're about to hang up. What is he practicing? Where did he go to school?"

"All important questions which I intend to find the answers to tonight."

"Transcript. Do not forget to send me details."

"Yes, yes. And thanks for the pep talk, I needed it."

"Thanks for the ego boost, *Rodeo Drive*, but you know you don't need me as much as you pretend to."

"That's bullshit, *Fifth Avenue*, I'll always need you."

As the call ended, I felt better about my impending meeting. The conversation had gone great last night, and if nothing else, seeing him again would give me closure. Who knew, maybe we'd even see each other occasionally or even less likely, work a similar case.

It was still hard to believe that of all the professions in the world we had both ended up in the exact same one.

Not that it mattered at that moment, with the need to get ready and not freak out breathing down my neck. It would be okay, I reasoned, trying to quell nerves that had taken up residence in my gut. I had no idea what he thought about me or my family, or how any of that affected him. Time. Distance. And the deceit of my father might have been all too much. All of that was true, but I'd never remembered him to be vindictive.

Things might have changed between us but underneath it all, he'd always had the most amazing heart.

That *wouldn't* have changed.

It would be okay.

And it was ridiculous how much I was worrying about it.

There was no need to worry at all.

None.

Fine, there was maybe a little reason to worry.

Gah!

I needed to get ready.

THE UBER DRIVER stopped in front of a duplex in West Hollywood. It was a hell of a lot nicer than my apartment, and in a way better part of town. But since I wasn't there to give him a real estate appraisal, I stepped out of the car and continued up the stairs to his front door.

Wonder if he had a roommate? No first or second year associate in the country would make enough cash to cover that kind of rent.

I pressed the buzzer, pushing my shoulders back, straightening my ponytail, and applauded myself for not wearing the red dress. I instead went for a casual jean/V-neck combo that was more suitable to visiting someone at their home, and didn't show the kind of skin that might tempt him to slide in a dollar.

Oh.

My.

God.

I wasn't sure what opened wider, his front door or my mouth.

If *that* was Alex Larsson, then the years had been good to him. Jesus.

He had always been tall, sporty, and blond, with a pair of blue eyes that could make the Mediterranean Sea jealous. But somewhere between then and now he had taken a right turn at *cute* and drove straight into *hot*.

Six-foot-OH-MY-GOD-how-tall-is-he? My eyes roamed from his toes to his head like they were inspecting a Picasso at *Christie's*. And Lord, that body—all of it toned and delicious—I almost felt the need to genuflect as I stood there in front of it. His face didn't help either, a perfect blend of story-book-prince and every-hot-guy-ever.

His perfectly mussed blond hair and seawater-blue eyes double barrel assaulted me. He'd gotten hotter than any Larsson—or man for that matter—I'd ever seen. Even his stubble was hot, the smattering shadow across his flawless jaw taunting me to touch it. There was nothing "old childhood best friend" about him. He was a work of art; my hands wanting to run over him like a piece of modeling clay and get dirty.

"Maya?" He smirked, looking me up and down as he stood barricading the door. Lord, he had muscles. *He would have made an amazing firefighter.* "Are you Maya Zaveri?"

I swallowed, my throat feeling like sandpaper as I found my voice. "That depends. Are you trying to serve me?"

He chuckled, his sea blue eyes twinkling with mischief. "Exactly how many outstanding warrants do you have, *possible* Maya?"

"None in the state of California, but I only moved back yesterday."

Oh.

My.

God.

Was I flirting with Alex Larsson?

Before I had a chance to give my conscience a good shake and banish any sexual thoughts to friend-zone, he pulled me into a hug. So instead of just thinking inappropriate things about his body, I was touching it with mine, and gathering evidence that proved Alex worked out *a lot.* Gone was the soft boyish body I'd seen a million times, and in its place was a work of art with the hard curves of a man. I swear to God, if there was ever a way to get pregnant fully clothed, it was wrapped around me creating an embryo. Sure made me grateful I'd taken my birth control *before* leaving my apartment.

"Hey, how are you?" My hands decided to gather their own reconnaissance, moving up his back like I was giving him a pat down. "It's so good to see you." My voice was about two octaves higher than it needed to be.

"Good, *really* good." He pulled back briefly, flashing me a cocky smile that was on the wrong side of platonic. "Come in."

As much as I wanted to continue to hold him—my hands unsatisfied as they hadn't felt his abs—I untangled myself so we could shuffle through the door. He led and I followed, letting my eyes study his ass with great detail. Not because I wanted to, no. It was for the transcript I needed to compile for Jackie and Lisa.

It was weird.

My body and mind confused with feelings they should absolutely not be having. Yet, no amount of argument did me any good as I stood there gaping at him, trying really hard to imagine what he'd look like with his clothes off.

I needed to stop.

Think of something else, and stop acting like I was in his house for anything other than friendship. Hell, even *that* hadn't been certain, so being annoyed I hadn't worn the red dress served no purpose.

"Wine?" he asked, not taking his eyes off of me for a second. "It will be the first time we've drunk it together and haven't had to steal it from my mom or yours."

"Oh, I stole the bottle from my mom. I only had beer in my fridge and didn't have time to go to the liquor store. And because I had to work late, it is either drink the wine I pilfered from her last weekend or forgo the shower. And I remember how much you hated man-stink."

Lies, if the stink came from a man who looked like him, I'd potentially bathe in it.

I laughed like an idiot, throwing my head back like an airhead, and immediately started wondering when I turned into one of *those* girls.

"Ha, well then as two respectable attorneys, we should definitely dispose of the evidence."

Damn it.

I was still fucking flirting.

"You're an attorney?" His eyebrow lifted in surprise.

SHIT.

Not only was I acting like a dumbass but I had inadvertently revealed I knew more about him than he did about me.

God, I hope he didn't think I'd been stalking him all these years.

"Yes, and my mom mentioned you were too. Our moms apparently have been chatting," I added, not sure if I was making it better or worse.

"Hmmm, interesting." He stroked his chin, not giving anything away. "Sounds like I need to have a chat with my mother then."

Making a silent vow I would stop behaving like a moron, I nodded when he gestured to his leather couch. I figured there was less trouble I could get into sitting down and used the time when he disappeared into the kitchen to get a handle on myself.

He was not some hot guy.

Oh, yes he was.

Fine, he *was* hot. But that wasn't what I was there for, and I needed to remember that.

Ignoring that I was trying to demote him from his hot-man status and put him in the friend-zone, he strode back in with a bottle and two wineglasses, looking just as delicious as when he left. His sexy little smirk wasn't helping either, and I was beginning to think drinking was going to be a serious mistake.

"I hope you like reds." He rolled the bottle in his gorgeous, large—seriously, when did he get so huge—hand and showed off the label. "Because this baby is from my mom's hidden stash."

A quick glance at the bottle proved he hadn't been kidding, the blended Cabernet from Bordeaux a little flashier than the wine we used to thieve.

"So, did you steal it with intention? Or did the bottle have another purpose?" It was a dumb question to ask because I really didn't care about the wine.

No, the *wine* was irrelevant.

But, by his own admission he'd taken the bottle last weekend when I had still been part of his very distant past. Which begged the question.

Was the wine for someone else?

Another woman perhaps, who liked dry reds from France?

"Didn't realize I was on the stand, counselor." A playful grin hooked at the edges of his mouth, watching me the entire time. "But if you must know, I take a bottle a month. I set myself a little personal challenge to see if I can successfully get it out of the house and whether or not she notices."

I swallowed, suddenly needing a drink of that wine pretty damn bad. "How's that working out for you?"

"I haven't bought a bottle of wine since last September."

He was smoldering.

He didn't used to smolder.

That had been *Nick's* specialty.

Taking those good looks and making my insides twist was not something he used to do. But as his agile fingers worked the corkscrew that was exactly what was happening.

And if I didn't turn the conversation around really quickly, I was going to say a lot of things I didn't mean. Or maybe I meant them but it sure as hell wasn't appropriate.

"Your poor mom. She probably needs that wine, not sure that raising the five of you wouldn't have given me a dependency. And there you are, taking it for sport."

He laughed, his gaze dropping briefly so he could pour the wine into the glasses. "Oh, so now you're calling my mom an alcoholic? I think I'd prefer you just call me cheap. And to think she used to like you, that will probably change when I tell her."

"I didn't mean . . ." I snapped back defensively, not meaning to imply anything even close to that. "Just give me the damn wine." I snagged the glass from the table and took a swig.

It was great wine.

"And you'll tell her nothing, because if you do you'll only be implicating yourself."

"Well, you have a point there so I guess your secret's safe with me." He smirked, taking a slow mouthful from his glass. "So, talk."

He'd always been to the point—neither of us having time for bullshit—but I had hoped we might paddle in the warm end of the pool before diving into all that was my past.

I pushed out a long steady breath. "My dad was a criminal—"

"I'm not asking about your father." He cut me off, his eyes steadying themselves on me. "I don't give a shit about him, I want to know about you."

"Me?" I asked, his interruption surprising me. Surely he had questions, or at the very least whether I had suspected something.

"Yes, you Maya. What happened after you left?"

The cocky smirk was gone, but his voice hadn't hardened. He lowered his glass, giving me the full weight of the attention his beautiful blue eyes could give. I'd never been able to lie to him, and tonight wasn't going to be the day I started.

"I tried not to fall apart, it was all I could think about for a while. I hated Nevada, I hated high school, I hated . . . well just about everything." The laugh that made its way up my throat sort of ironic. "But hate didn't get me very far, so I decided to channel the emotion into something more productive—ambition."

I settled into the couch, telling him all about growing up and then moving off to college, both of us filling in the blanks of the time we'd spent apart.

Time seemed to evaporate, the conversation flowing between us way more easily than I'd expected. Almost like I'd never left.

I felt lighter, the weight that had been pressing on my chest lifted as the words flowed freely. Of course, it was entirely possible that was because of the wine but I didn't want to waste time analyzing either.

"Yale, huh? Roman is going to *love* that." He chuckled, swallowing what was left in his glass before pouring some more.

"Why?" I asked, holding my glass out for another refill. "Berkeley is a great school."

While I knew his second oldest brother had attended Yale, all of the others had stayed on the West Coast for school. Alex had chosen Berkeley, and had stayed there for law school as well.

He laughed, shaking his head in amusement. "You almost sound convincing, but I know you Ivy Leaguers all stick together."

"I don't follow." I was the last person on the face of the earth who was going to pull some elitist bullshit. If I had sounded condescending, it had not been in any way intended.

"Roman went to Yale," he deadpanned. "Didn't hear the end of it when I decided to stay out here for law school. Not that I gave a shit," he chuckled. "But I have a feeling the knowledge that you went to his alma mater is going to give him some new material. In case you're wondering, he's still a conceited dick."

"Roman was never a dick." I scoffed, remembering him to be assertive—and probably the cockiest of the bunch—but not someone I'd class as a dick.

"Wow, you didn't mention the head trauma." His eyes widened, as did his wicked smile. "When did that happen? And other than memory, what else has been affected?"

My hand reached out and playfully shoved his arm. It was a *fine* arm too, corded muscles that hadn't been there before. "Stop it, I remember him fine, and he wasn't *that* bad." I pulled my hand away, not giving it a chance to explore.

He smirked, pointing his finger in accusation. "Didn't I tell you all you alumni stick together? Case in point. You're defending him right now."

"Something tells me Roman doesn't need anyone defending him." I rolled my eyes.

"Yeah, you're right about that." Alex nodded. "Don't tell him I said so but he is one of the best lawyers I've ever seen. Watching him in a courtroom is pure fucking electric. He is so controlled, no mistakes, it's almost poetic."

"That why you went into law? Because of him?" I leaned in closer, hoping to learn more about his past.

While he had shared details of the years we'd spent apart, the conversation had been more slanted in my favor. And truth be known, I was more interested in talking about him than I was about me.

"Honestly, yeah. Seeing what he did, it got me excited. And there was no way I would ever consider being an actor—preferring slow torture rather than having to appear in front of a camera." He relaxed into his seat, the fabric of his shirt stretching across his chest as he leaned his arm against the back of the sofa.

I fought the urge to lean back into it. Not because I wanted him to wrap his sexy body around me, no. It was about wanting to regain some of the familiarity we'd once shared. Sure, let's go with that.

"I thought you wanted to be a fireman." I moved closer, not enough to be touching him, but minimizing the inches between us. Hey, I wasn't going to squander the opportunity.

"I'm still putting out fires, Maya, just a different kind."

Yeah, no shit.

He seemed pretty good at starting a few too. I swallowed, bringing my glass to my lips and then realizing it was empty.

Without asking he leaned forward, reaching for the bottle on the table and refilled my glass. It was my second refill, and between us, we'd drained the bottle. "Sounds like something they'd put on a corporate flier." I smiled, savoring the last of the wine.

"Well, if this law gig doesn't work out for me, I'll go into advertising." He gazed down at me with amusement.

And I *gazed* back because, gee he was mighty fine to look at.

My stomach picked that exact moment to remind not only me, but possibly the surrounding neighborhood, that it hadn't been fed since earlier in the day. The primal growl echoed in the silence as my eyes widened. Oh Jesus, I wasn't sure if I was just hungry or I'd drunk so much wine I'd swallowed a freaking bobcat and not noticed.

He laughed, breaking the silence as he glanced down at his watch. "Shit, Maya, it's nine and I haven't even offered you dinner. Sorry, let me order something before your stomach goes on a rampage and terrorizes the neighborhood."

If it were any other hot guy, I would have probably been mortified, but with Alex, it just didn't seem so bad. "Well to be fair, I'm still on East Coast time and it is probably closer to breakfast now." I laughed, only the slightest bit embarrassed.

"So am I ordering you pancakes or pizza?" He slid the phone out from his pocket. "We need to do something quick, a family with two small children just moved in next door. Wouldn't want to put anyone in danger."

"Pizza, you ass." I elbowed him teasingly. It wasn't just my hunger making itself known, the wine also reminding me that it was sitting front and center. "And make sure it has extra—"

"Cheese." He nodded as he dialed. "Yep, I remember."

He stood, walking towards the kitchen as he rattled off an order and took the empty bottle of wine with him. And while he was busy getting us food, I decided it was a good opportunity to find a bathroom. All that wine, it had to go somewhere, and at the moment, that *somewhere* was heading south.

Asking for directions would have been smart, but as I stood with the confidence of Bordeaux's finest pulsing through my veins, I decided I didn't need his help. It was a bathroom, not a pot of gold, and I could find it all on my own.

I giggled as I ventured down the hall, opening a door and finding a bedroom. I wasn't sure if it was his, or he had a roommate, but it definitely belonged to a guy.

It wasn't messy—the room in order with the bed pristinely made—but the air had a distinctive manly smell—woodsy with a hint of soap. Like someone had spliced the scent off the Y chromosome and spritzed into the air as fragrance. I breathed in deeply, feeling slightly more intoxicated while I was standing still.

Ignoring the breach of personal space, and the lack of invitation, I moved further inside to explore. The assumption that the owner of the space being male was further confirmed when I almost tripped over a gym bag beside the closet. I resisted the temptation to snoop further, finding a door ajar beside the closet, which—*thank you, Jesus*—happened to be the bathroom.

Probably should have wandered further and found the main bathroom instead of violating Alex's—or possibly someone else's—bedroom. But the niggling *probably could go* had intensified to *definitely need to pee.* My hands managed to get the door closed before I pulled down my jeans. I collapsed onto the seat, giggling as I breathed a sigh of relief.

If the man smell had been strong in the bedroom, it was more intense confined in the small space. My eyes closed as I braced myself and took a deep breath.

Two things, if I could bottle whatever that smell was, I'd be a millionaire, *and* I was thankful for the second time since leaving my apartment I had taken birth control.

Jesus.

While I wasn't drunk, my inhibitions were waaaay lower than

I would have liked them to be. And if I didn't want to blow what had turned out to be a touching reunion, I needed to stop acting like it was a date.

No more drinking.

Stolen French wine or not, the only thing passing through my lips was going to be water or—probably wisely too—coffee. And I needed to eat.

Yep, and remember that getting ga-ga over Larssons was in my past, not my future.

If only God had made them less irresistible.

CHAPTER #4

FINISHING WITH THE bathroom, I washed my hands and resisted the urge to peek in the bathroom cabinets. It was a hardship, and one I was able to overcome by reminding myself I'd already breached the acceptable boundaries for a guest.

We might have been besties once, but we'd barely become reacquainted.

Giving myself a stern internal talking to and splashing some water at my neck, I looked at myself in the mirror. Two sparking green eyes stared back at me as I pulled out my ponytail and let my brown curls fall loose. It made me feel less giddy, nodding my head in firm resolution that I was going to behave as I opened the bathroom door.

"You lost?" Alex's delicious arms were folded across his chest as he waited on the other side of the doorjamb. "Or you just doing recon?" He chuckled.

Behave, Maya, I reminded myself as I forced the smile. "I needed a bathroom, and look," I game show waved my hands around the space, "I found one."

"That you have." He nodded, an amused look on his face. "Pizza is on its way. Anything else you *need*, or do you want to go back to the living room?"

There were a lot of things I needed, and I was positive he was more than capable of delivering.

Shit.

No.

I wasn't sure if it was the wine or his tone had been intention-ally suggestive. His face gave nothing away, no hooded eyelids or sexy smiles helping me to decipher.

"No, no, all good now." I opted for safe, unable to actually leave the bathroom because his large, sexy, and very distracting body was in the way. "Happy to go back to the living room."

He eyed me suspiciously, hesitating a minute before stepping to the side and allowing me room to pass. "Good, you can finish telling me about where you're living and which firm you work for."

"Great, I can do that," I confirmed for my own benefit, as well as for his, as I strode back to the couch. "I'm at Palmer and Loft," I volunteered, the conversation safe as I settled back into my seat. "You?"

"Young, McMillian and Walker."

"Impressive."

"So I'm told." He smirked.

What the hell was that?

Was he flirting? In all the time I'd known Alex, he'd never flirted with me.

NEVER.

Not even when we were both single with raging hormones— which would have made sense—and yet, still nothing.

But those words were far from innocent, and there was that moment in his bathroom, which was also questionable.

"Everything okay, Maya?" He looked down at me as my breath quickened and my heartbeat raced. I'd never been speechless around Alex, but as he gazed at me—his intentions not known—I was having a hard time finding words.

"I'm just a little hot." I pulled at the neckline of my top, hoping to God I wasn't flashing my boobs. Or maybe that *was* what I was hoping for; my mind a bowl of mush as I tried to work out what I wanted to happen.

His eyes flicked down to my shirt before meeting mine. "You want to take it off?"

Oh.

My.

God.

I moved so fast, I almost head-butted him, leaping off the couch in an effort to either strip like he was suggesting or put some distance between us.

Okay, to be fair, he had only suggested removing my top, but we all knew where that led.

"Jesus, Maya." He laughed, joining me on his feet. "What the hell has gotten into you? I don't remember you being this jumpy." His hands settled on my shoulders, looking me in the eyes.

Interesting, not a seductive technique I was familiar with, but I'd been out of the playfield for a while.

"If you're hot, you're more than welcome to take off your top and change into one of my T-shirts. It wouldn't be the first time you've worn my clothes." He chuckled. "You already know where my bedroom is, go ahead and make yourself more comfortable."

Ohhhhhhhhhhh.

Shit.

"No, I'm fine. I think it's just the wine and the climate change." I fanned my face hoping he couldn't read my thoughts.

Not sure if I was more surprised by my own shock and disappointment, or if it had been so long since a man had flirted with me I'd forgotten what it looked like. And thank God, I needed to work it out before I did something stupid, like take off my top on the condition he removed his.

"Well, if you change your mind . . ." He left his sentence trailing, side-eyeing me like a stray animal that might spook. Clearly, my behavior hadn't gone completely unnoticed, we could only hope he chalked it up to jet lag or I was just generally crazy.

"Thanks." I smiled, locking my fingers together and shoving them in my lap where I figured they'd keep out of trouble. "That's really kind of you to offer, you have been . . . really kind."

Lord.

I was so lame.

So, in addition to never being at a loss for words around Alex, I had never acted like a swooning idiot either. That kind of behavior had been reserved for his older brothers, something he'd teased me about.

Please, God, don't let him piece it together. There could only be one of us acting weird, and currently that had been me.

His hands dropped from my shoulders, and he lowered his head to mine. At a foot taller, it wasn't a subtle move either, bending as he searched my eyes. "Something else going on, Maya?"

Busted.

Yeah, because hoping he'd be clueless was too much to ask, especially when he'd never been dense in the past.

"This is just weird," I answered honestly, feeling heat creep up my neck. "Being back here, seeing you, remembering . . ." I swallowed hard. "It's just a lot."

Without asking—and like it was the most natural thing in the world—he wrapped his arms around me and brought me closer. "I did miss you, you know. But I'm so glad you're back, I didn't want to waste time dredging up all that stuff. And I haven't brought up you leaving or your dad because I don't want you to feel like you owe me an explanation. You were just a kid, Maya, we both were. But if you want to talk about him, I'm happy to listen. I didn't even think about what seeing me and bringing those memories back might mean for you. You must think I'm such a heartless and thoughtless bastard."

God, I was irritated.

Not at my shithead father—who was the usual source for anger and all things bad—although he was in no way off the hook. But my current state of agitation was wholly self-inflicted. Because I was allowing Alex Larsson to comfort me, and I was enjoying it.

Instead of telling him the truth, that my off kilter behavior had nothing to do with my dear daddy or the memories of what I'd left, I nodded, easing into the warm sanctuary his chest was providing. I was so relieved that I had an excuse to touch him, and that I also had the perfect cover for acting like a fruitcake, my past a reasonable and rational excuse on why I was being weird around him.

Worst part was, I only felt a little bit bad about it, agreeing to take whatever penance for my lie. I didn't even care that the hug was tendered under false pretenses, too busy enjoying those strong masculine arms around me and breathing in that heady, intoxicating man scent.

He doesn't like you that way, my subconscious rationalized.

Who the hell cares, let me just enjoy all that fine body pressed against me, I argued back.

"Hey." He pulled away from me way too soon, my arms remaining around him in protest. "You forgive me?"

My chin tilted toward him and I answered honestly. "Nothing to forgive. And for the record, I don't think you have the capacity to be heartless or thoughtless and sure as hell didn't think it."

Perpetuating the misunderstanding in order to accept comfort was one thing, making him feel like he'd done something terrible was something else entirely. And I wouldn't do that, even if it did mean he might remove his hands all together.

His smile was fucking radiant, his hand giving my arm a platonic rub. "But if I do something that freaks you out, just let me know, okay? Promise?"

Jesus, take the wheel.

Not only was he worried about my current well-being but he was concerned about the future of it as well. He was so sweet, so charming that I had to seriously question *why* I had never had feelings other than friendship for him. Sure, he'd been cocky and slightly arrogant—traits I was almost positive he hadn't totally outgrown—but he'd always been so kind and considerate. He'd have made the most perfect boyfriend.

Why hadn't I ever seen it?

Maybe, it wasn't too late?

"I promise as long as *you* promise to tell me if I start acting weird. I'm still adjusting to all of this, I need someone who will be real with me."

He scoffed, his eyes lighting up with mischief. "Babe, it will be my pleasure to point out when you're being weird. And, as an added bonus, I'll even be your safe place. Any time you feel the need to weird out, you call me. No one will ever know."

"Still my holder of secrets after all these years?" I leaned in closer, despite the danger I knew that came with it, watching the smile twist on his lips.

"Of course."

I WASN'T SURE if it was the pizza or time I had to thank, but the heat from my body was no longer blasting like an out-of-control furnace as we ate. I was even able to keep my mind and mouth in check, chatting amicably about our respective families and keeping the conversation in friendly and safe territory. Not that I had suddenly stopped appreciating the fine specimen he'd become, or didn't notice how seductively his shirt seemed to caress the bulges of his chest, I'd just focused on other things.

Non-sexual things, which threw water on the heat simmering in my belly.

"So, both your brothers are married? I thought it would be a cold day in hell before Ben would walk down the aisle," he said, shaking his head in disbelief.

"Preaching to the choir." I laughed. "My mom thought he was high when he announced his engagement. Seems like even a serial ladies man like my brother is able to be tamed if he finds the right woman. And Jordon and Vanessa have two boys."

It wasn't just the Larsson boys who had played the field, the Zaveri brothers more than held their own.

"It's like an epidemic, everyone is getting married. Nick just got hitched a couple of months ago. It was small, low-key but it was kind of cool. Dave went before him, and Roman and Eric aren't only married but are dads too."

While I didn't say it out loud, Eric joining the ranks of fatherhood wasn't news. Everything the man did ended up in a magazine, especially when he knocked up his wife. Roman was another story.

"Roman is a father?" My eyes widened in shock. "He was a control freak who was wearing tailored suits at eighteen and doesn't like a mess. How the hell does that work out?"

Not to say I didn't think he'd be a great dad, but I just never thought it would be in his wheelhouse.

"Yeah, well like you said with Ben, the love of a good woman. Lauren is awesome, she's a lawyer too and probably the only one who can put Roman in his place. They had a little boy, Lucas, a couple of months ago."

"Wow, it's like the twilight zone. Roman has a kid."

It wasn't that I hadn't expected life to go on without us around, it was just startling how much things had changed. Not only growing up, but getting married and having kids also. And while neither of us had said it, Alex and I were the only ones left who hadn't followed the trend.

As we relaxed on the couch, there was a comfortable lull in the conversation. Alex turned to face me, his easy smile making me feel more at home than I had in years. "Hey, I have an idea."

The sentence had launched a million adventures in our time and its resurgence filled me with so much excitement I had to try to contain myself.

"I'm in," I agreed without even asking the particulars.

He threw his head back, his throaty laugh making its way to his delicious mouth.

"I love how you're game for anything, Maya. I swear, I've never had a better wingman." He leaned in closer, spilling the details of our latest adventure. "My mom is having a get together this weekend at the house. Ever since the grandkids, she likes to have us all together at least once a week. It's not fancy though, completely casual, and friends are welcome. How cool will it be if you show up?"

What?

That wasn't an adventure, it was a goddamn nightmare. It was bad enough facing one of them, but seeing all of them. *At once.* It was going to take more than a few glasses of wine to get me to agree.

"What?" My head shook, giving him the "hell no" my mouth had yet to say.

"Come to Mom's. It will be great, you'll get to see everyone, and they'll get to see you. Besides, you already said our mothers have been talking, and yet your call was the first I'd heard about you moving back. Think of this as payback for mine withholding information. It will be crazy." He laughed, his eyes brimming with mischief.

Crazy was exactly the right word for it. I'd been in L.A. for all of a couple days and I'd barely dipped a toe in. And Alex was expecting me to go to his mother's house and see them all?

Even putting aside my father swindling the cash from their dad, that wasn't a family you could just casually toss yourself into.

There was something about those Larssons that made them seem . . . godlike. Too good-looking, too smart, too brilliant at everything—and that was before any of them had become rich, famous or successful. One on one was hard enough, but to throw yourself in there with all of them? Last time I checked I wasn't a lion tamer and I'd already donated my gladiator sandals to Goodwill.

"Are you insane?" I choked out, not even pretending I was considering it.

His smile didn't dissipate, still living in denial that it was a good idea. "Oh come on, aren't you even a tiny bit curious? I'm sure they'd love to see you, and you know my mom loves you. Her house is like neutral territory."

Neutral territory?

Switzerland was neutral territory, not Kate Larsson's house.

"I can't." The excuses came thick and fast. "I start work on Monday and I still need to get my apartment in some kind of order." *And you know, I still hadn't had that lobotomy.* "I have a mountain of paperwork to go through."

All of it completely plausible, and not entirely false.

His perfectly formed lips pulled into a pout, making him look adorable because just being sexy had obviously not been enough. "Come on, it's Tuesday. You have three whole days to get your shit together. Give me an hour. Sixty minutes to see everyone, and then if you have to go, you can leave."

Next came the eyes.

Wielding those incredible crystal-blue pools for evil as he did his best to look sorrowful. Even though I knew it was an act, I was helpless to resist them.

Damn it.

Not sure why I'd bothered, that puppy dog look of his was irresistible. There wasn't a woman alive—including this one—who was immune. Those baby blues had been getting him out of trouble since he was five years old. If he ever needed help trying to convince a jury, all he'd have to do is unleash that look and he'd have them eating out of the palm of his hand.

"Fine!" I huffed out in exasperation, followed by a pointed warning. "An hour, and then I swear, I need to go."

He dropped the pout, his lips curling into a victorious grin as he nodded. "If that's what you want, I promise I won't stop you."

Lord, what the hell had I agreed to?

"And on that note, I should probably get going." I made a show of shuffling off the couch and standing. "Since you've commandeered part of my weekend, I should really get back to my apartment. Lots to do." *Like freak the hell out in private.* "But thanks for the evening, it was great seeing you."

He joined me on his feet, pulling me into the hug I'd been hoping for as he gave me his goodbye. I nuzzled closer, figuring I deserved the enjoyment of the well-toned chest of Alex Larsson considering the hot mess the weekend would be. It was the least he could do, and since he'd been the one who'd initiated most of the hugs I didn't feel guilty either.

Slightly pervy possibly, but guilty—nada.

"You park out front?" he asked, my reward taken away as he pulled back. "I'll walk you out."

"No, I don't have a car. I can grab an Uber though, no big deal." I slid out my phone from my jeans and swiped on the app.

He grabbed my phone, stopping me before I could enter my location. "You're not getting an Uber. I'll drive you, give me a second to get my keys."

"You've been drinking," I tried to argue.

He scoffed, turning and grabbing his keys from a bowl on the coffee table. "Two wines, hours ago, hardly DUI material. Besides, you can show me where you live. I'll need to know for when I pick you up on Saturday."

Well, he had a point there. As much as I hated the idea of him needing to chauffeur me around, my car situation wasn't going to change by the weekend and I had no idea where Kate lived.

"Okay, thanks."

He didn't even have to unleash those baby blues, my agreement coming completely of my own volition.

He lead me outside to a silver BMW i8 parked near the curb, a press of his fob confirming it was his car.

"Fancy." I eyed it up and down, the car worth more than most junior associates made in a year.

"A gift from Eric." He shrugged. "He had it for a few years and then got bored with it. I was more than happy to take it off his hands."

"Yeah, if he has any other cars he's looking to get rid of, let me know." I slid into the soft leather seat, the inside just as flashy as the sleek exterior.

Alex laughed, moving to the driver's seat before hopping inside. "You can tell him yourself when you see him on Saturday."

Awesome, because I needed the reminder in the ten minutes it had taken from agreeing and getting into the car that I was going to see his whole freaking family. One of which who was ridiculously famous. "I was kidding, I am not asking your brother for a car."

"Suit yourself." He shrugged, pressing the ignition and firing up the engine.

His face lit up like a little boy as the engine roared, his foot tapping the accelerator again before shooting me a sideways glance as he pulled out into traffic.

God he was gorgeous.

"Now, tell me where we're heading." His voice rumbled, pulling me from my thoughts.

I literally have no idea.

Oh, he meant where I lived.

"Primrose Apartments." I rattled off the address. "The place is still sort of a mess."

It was my precursor, the warning that I wasn't going to let him in. Not because I actually gave a shit about the mess, but because I needed to get my head together before we spent any more time together.

"Noted, I'll hold off on doing my inspection." He laughed, not at all fazed.

He handled the car like he'd handled the evening. Cool, calm and collected—not at all like the hot mess I'd seemed to be.

I didn't know if it was extreme confidence or he just wasn't as invested as I was. Living under the shadow of my father had made me feel like I'd constantly needed to prove myself. And damn if that chip on my shoulder made me push harder than I probably needed to for acceptance.

I hated it.

And yet, I couldn't stop myself either.

We made small talk on the drive, Alex asking me more questions and me reciprocating. It was all rather benign, nothing of any substance, but it felt safe.

"This must be you." He stopped, pulling up to the faded pink stucco building, the front iron gate left ajar.

"Yep. It's me." My lips tightened as my hand went to the door handle. "Thanks for the ride."

He reached across and squeezed my knee. "Come on, Maya, it's the least I could do. Call me if you need anything between now and the weekend."

"Yep, sure. Thanks." I nodded, stepping out of the car and onto the sidewalk. And as much as I would *love* to call him, there wasn't a chance that would happen. Not because I didn't trust him or thought he had ulterior motives. Nope, the lack of trust was on my part, needing to make sure I didn't make a fool of myself.

And with an awkward wave—on my part, he looked incredible—I turned and walked through the open gate to my apartment. The night hadn't gone as I'd planned it.

And I wasn't sure if I was happy about my latest Larsson infatuation or I was annoyed at my predictability.

Oh well, it wasn't like anything was going to change. Maybe when I saw him next the initial shock will have worn off and I could go back to acting like a regular person.

After all, I'd lost interest in all of his brothers in the past.

But, damn, I wasn't sure I wanted that either.

Shit.

CHAPTER #5

"ARE YOU A drug dealer?"

I laughed, hoping to God I didn't look like one. It wouldn't do well for me when I finally went up in front of a jury. "No, of course not."

She peered around the room, looking at the transformation that had taken place, the inside of my apartment resembling a Target catalog. I was nothing if not motivated, and while I hadn't had a chance to even look over my induction folder for work yet, the apartment was something I could get a handle on. The kitchen wasn't finished yet, but she couldn't see that from her eagle eye position.

"Never seen anyone work so fast. Especially when they haven't had a delivery from a moving truck. All of this looks new." Her nose sniffed, like the air might reveal some alternate truth. "You better not be doing any kind of drugs, I know this place isn't fancy, but I won't tolerate any of that nonsense here."

Prim—my landlord—had some mail which, apparently—not likely—had gotten mixed up with hers. As tempting as it was to point out that mail tampering was a federal offense, I knew she was harmless and just probably looking for an excuse to snoop. It wasn't like I had anything to hide, so I opened my door and humored her. Besides, always good to get the landlord on your side. Never know when you're going to need a repair expedited, and judging by the old pipes in my bathroom, I was probably going to test the theory sooner than later.

"I promise you, no drugs." I nodded, hoping my sincerity might convince her. "I'm a lawyer, trust me, it would be bad for business."

Not that it had stopped some other members of the legal faculty before, but I sure as hell wasn't about to point that out.

Her halo of bright red hair swung wildly as she shook her head. "A lawyer? Why the hell are you living here? Aren't you people supposed to be rich?"

If I had a dollar for every person who had that misconception . . .

"Yeah, well, I fell in love with the view," I lied, wondering how much longer I needed to be polite.

Her eyes narrowed not believing me for a second. "Hmmm, well I guess I should go then. I'll be seeing you around."

I didn't doubt she would, I finger waved to her as she disappeared down the stairs while my attention was redirected to my ringing phone.

It was late afternoon and I'd already spoken to my mother forty-two times. Okay, maybe that was a slight exaggeration, but it had been at least ten and there were no signs of her letting up. So I was fairly confident I knew who it was when I answered it.

"Yes, Mom." I didn't bother checking the caller ID.

"How many times has she called?" My brother Ben laughed in my ear. And as much as I loved my mother, it was great hearing from him for a change.

I closed my front door and leaned against the wall with a huge smile on my face. "Close to a dozen. I stopped keeping score after seven."

"Well, she's itching to come visit you. You haven't been this close in years, and I think she expected you to ask her to help you get settled."

My mother had not so subtly hinted that she would happily take time off work, come to L.A., and help me adjust to my new home. But as much as I appreciated all she had done for me in the past, I worked better doing things on my own. I didn't want to fight with anyone about where the proper place was for the salt shaker. It was beside the tequila, of course. So, delicately I hinted I would happily welcome houseguests later.

Much later.

Like give me a month or two at least.

"Ben, I know she means well, but I want to do this on my own. She'll have her chance to hover and visit, but for now, I'm finding my feet."

I knew he got it; he had been instrumental in convincing our mother I would be fine when I shipped out to the other side of the country for college. Out of the three of us, I was the only one who'd left. It hadn't helped that I was the youngest.

He chuckled. "I know, squirt, I'm just checking in on you. Besides, I heard that you've been spending time with Alex Larsson. Seems to me you don't need any help at all in *finding your feet*."

"You've *heard* have you?" I deadpanned.

"Yep, check your messages." He could barely hide the amusement in his voice.

I lowered the phone and flicked to my text messages. There it was—a group message no less—from my mother, both my brothers and their wives.

Mom—Have a great time with Alex Larsson, Honey. He was such a nice boy, make sure you give Kate my love.

Ben—Alex Larsson? As in, Nick's kid brother?

Mom—Yes. He and your sister have been talking. Isn't it wonderful?

Jordon—Didn't I give that kid a wedgie?

Ben—Didn't you give us ALL wedgies?

Jordon—It was character building. Look how awesome everyone turned out. Hey Sis, tell Roman he owes me fifty bucks. I left my porn DVDs in his room when we left.

Mom—WHAT porn DVDs?

Jordon—I meant history book. It definitely wasn't porn.

Vanessa—Chemistry maybe Dr. Zaveri? Pretty sure you never studied history. Unless you had changed your major before we met? ;-)

Jordon—Why is this even a discussion? We should be talking about Maya and Alex. Not my major.

Natalie—Oh, is he as hot as Eric? His brother is smoking.

Ben—Hello? Have you seen your husband? I'm way hotter than Eric Larsson.

Natalie—LOL

Vanessa—LOL

Ben—Why is that funny?

Mom—Both my boys are handsome, but those Larsson boys are quite easy on the eyes.

Jordon—Yeah, could have gone the rest of my life without hearing that, Mother.

"Jesus Christ." I pulled the phone back to my ear. "A group chat? Seriously? She couldn't have just sent a private message directly to me? Someone needs to take away Mom's smart phone."

Ben laughed, thoroughly amused. "She said it's the easiest way to share the family news. Just like a family dinner."

Ironically, it was a lot like family dinners before I went away. And despite being annoyed at the start, it warmed me to know that we were still close. "So you think you're better looking than Eric, huh? Delusional much?" I laughed.

"Not you too," Ben warned. "Bad enough my wife laughed at me."

"Probably because Natalie isn't blind."

"Yeah, well let's just wait and see, shall we? When we come visit, we'll get together with all of them too. Let's see how good looking the guy is without Photoshop."

Ben must be high.

Sure, if I looked at him objectively, he was handsome. And out of the two of my brothers, he was the one the girls all chased. But, he wasn't in the same league as the Larsson brothers.

And, in what universe did he think we were all going to get together? Did he miss the memo that most of them were famous?

High.

Only explanation.

"Yeah, let's worry about that later. I should go, Ben. Tell everyone I said hi."

"Or you could just tell them yourself in the group chat." My pain in the ass brother laughed.

"I hate you."

He chuckled. "Love you too, sis."

Maya—I'm going to start a cult. Calling it Larsson-ism. We meet at dawn in Death Valley where we dance naked and chant to the Larsson Gods.

Vanessa—I'm in.

Natalie—Me too, sounds like fun.

Mom—Bring a coat, baby. The mornings can be cool in the desert.

I shook my head, laughing as I tossed my phone in my handbag.

They were a crazy bunch, but they were *my* crazy bunch, a smile still on my face as I went to my bedroom and finished getting dressed.

I slipped out of my jeans and T-shirt, and grabbed the dress that had been lying on my bed.

Unlike Tuesday night where I'd dressed down, I'd decided to wear the red dress that did good things for my boobs. I mean, it was important to look my best, right? And what was the point of having nice things if I couldn't wear them? Of course, it was probably slightly overdressed, but things were always fancier in L.A.

Besides, if things got super awkward, I'd just tell them I had other plans. The dress would be my coconspirator. It was actually pretty smart, or at least that was what I rationalized as I applied a layer of matching red lipstick.

As I slid into my heels, there was a knock at my door, my heart pounding in my chest as I walked from my bedroom to my front door. God I hoped it wasn't Prim again, I really didn't want her to see me all dressed up and assume I was involved in prostitution instead of narcotics.

"Hey." I tried to sound casual as I opened the door, a smiling Alex Larsson standing on the other side.

Dressed in dark jeans that had no business looking that good, a button down he'd rolled at the sleeves and a pair of shades, he looked beyond edible. His blond hair was tousled with just the right amount of edge, still promoting his polished look and hinting at the rebellion underneath.

Maybe the idea of a cult hadn't been a bad one after all. I'd have no problem spending my days worshiping a man who looked like that.

He peeled off the dark aviators that had been hiding his crystal-blue eyes. "Hey yourself." His eyes traveled along the length of my body.

It was tempting to tell him my fake excuse, that *I had a thing later and it would be easier to already be dressed than to have to come* *home.* Or run back into my room and change into something a little less flashy.

But I didn't do either.

Instead, I kicked up my chin and pretended it was business as usual. *Nothing more to see here, folks.* Fake it until you make it . . . and all of that.

"I'm ready to go, if you are?" I grabbed my keys, pretending that my heart didn't feel like it might explode. It also didn't help my pulse to see his Adam's apple bob as he swallowed hard.

"Very ready."

I shouldn't care that he seemed to be affected.

But I did.

My smile beamed as we walked down the stairs to my courtyard, careful not to catch my heels on the metal stairs as we made our way down to where he'd parked his car.

Alex stalked over to the passenger side door, waiting until he was beside me to hit the key fob to unlock it. His hand reached for the handle, opening the door for me and stepping aside.

"After you." He smiled, watching me as my body sunk into the low seat of the sports car. My change in position had me eye level with his crotch.

Well. Then.

I bit my lip trying not to grin like an idiot.

He closed the door and went across the other side, sliding into the driver's seat in a swift, sexy move. I probably needed to stop noticing all the ways he was sexy considering we weren't on a date and on the way to his mother's house. But I was having a hard time with the argument.

It had been my hope that between seeing him the last time and now, that I'd be able to recalibrate my brain.

We were not going to date.

He probably wasn't interested.

I just hadn't dated in a while, and like water after a drought, I was just thirsty. *And boy was I ever.*

But as he put the car into gear and looked over at me and smiled, all that common sense seemed to disappear.

Damn it.

He didn't immediately talk, which was interesting, waiting until we were on the main road before he spoke.

"Have you seen your new office yet? You start Monday, right?"

His voice was a calm lake—not a throat clear, or a stutter, not a ripple out of place—nothing to indicate that the sexual tension I thought I'd felt in my doorway was anything more than my imagination.

"Yes, Monday. And I haven't had a chance to go in yet. I guess I'll see it Monday." Everything his voice had been, mine had not.

Putting aside I'd said Monday twice like an idiot, I hadn't dissolved into a complete disaster. The question had just been unexpected, even if it did make sense that he'd ask.

"You've already been at your firm a few months, right? How's work been for you?" I figured it was the polite thing to do, assuming we were doing small talk.

He nodded to himself, a smile creeping across his lips as he turned to face me. "Pretty good actually."

I had no idea if the smile on his face was because of his love affair with the law or if he'd gone back to flirting.

He gave nothing else away.

"Great," I offered, wondering if we should graduate the conversation to the weather or sports.

Screw that.

"So, your mom doesn't know I'm coming, does she?" I assumed when he'd convinced me to come, he might have mentioned it to her. You know, since it would be the polite thing to do. But then I remembered who I was dealing with, my surprise visit restitution for her not telling him I was back in town.

He grinned with no apology. "That would be a negative."

"And your brothers?"

His head lolled to the side, an eyebrow rising in question. "What do you think?"

"Probably not."

"Then you would be correct."

Honestly, I probably would have been more surprised if he *had* told them I was coming. He'd always enjoyed a good-natured prank, especially at the expense of his brothers. It was their thing—or at least it had been—all of them super competitive and taking irrational satisfaction over getting one over on the others. Hell, I'd even participated, Alex's excitement contagious.

"I guess I'll just have to be content with being used then." I pretended to be bored, looking at my fingernails.

If it was anyone else, I probably would have been annoyed. But it was different with him. I didn't know why, but it just was. I knew there wasn't a malicious bone in his body, and he'd be the last person on earth to use anyone. Or at least, the guy I had known in the past wouldn't.

He turned his head slowly, his smile not as sure. "Is that what you think I'm doing?"

"Isn't it?" I shrugged.

He pulled a hard right, my seatbelt holding me in tight as he moved to the shoulder of the road and stopped the car. There was a crack in his cool, calm veneer, his eyes fixed on mine. "I'd never use you. Maybe I haven't been clear, but I'm glad you're back, which is why I wanted you to come with me. Because I know they'll be glad too. And sure, not telling them you're coming gives me a stupid thrill because I like knowing something they don't, but you aren't a punch line, Maya."

God he was sweet.

My hand reached out, touching his arm and giving it a squeeze. "Thanks."

It was never an actual consideration he had nefarious motives, but I couldn't help but feel good to hear him say it.

"So, you still want to go to my mom's?" He had yet to put the car into drive, and I had no doubt if I said no, he wouldn't push it.

It was my turn to smile. "Oh, we're going. Apparently Roman owes Jordon fifty bucks for some porn DVDs he left behind."

"Who the hell pays for porn?" He screwed up his face in confusion.

"Right?" I nodded in agreement. "That's what I thought. I don't even have a DVD player."

We both laughed.

He had a *great* laugh.

I'd forgotten how much I'd loved hearing it.

He nodded to the windshield, putting the car into gear and getting back onto the road.

Ready or not we were going to his mother's.

And at that moment, my biggest concern wasn't seeing all of them again. It was the undeniable feelings of attraction that went way beyond friendship.

Well.

Shit.

CHAPTER #6

WHEN I DECIDED to move back to L.A. the plan had been to be kickass at my job, find some friends, and live a good life. I would be closer to my family, could enjoy the warmer weather and I'd hopefully feel like I was home.

Of course, I had wondered about Alex and his family. And sure, maybe briefly entertained the fantasy of seeing him—and them—again. But that was way down the track.

Like after a few months, or a year . . . who knows, if it was fate, maybe we'd just run into each other at the farmer's market or something as equally unlikely. Okay, I was being ridiculous. But I imagined it would be in the distant future.

Yeah, that theory went right out the window as we pulled up to a house I didn't recognize. It was actually a relief she didn't live in the same neighborhood we'd grown up in. I wondered if their dad did. Not like I knew what happened to any Larsson who wasn't in the press.

I took a deep breath, running my hands down my thighs as I looked at the front door. Lord I hoped this didn't suck. Last thing I needed was for all of them to hate me, blame me, or even worse, see that I was making ga-ga eyes at Alex. I hadn't even been in L.A.

a full week, shopping for a therapist to *share my feelings with* was too cliché for words.

Alex—apparently oblivious to my internal ponderings—opened his door and walked around to mine. Not sure if he was being polite or was wondering what was taking me so damn long.

Not that it mattered; I had still yet to open the door.

"Ready?"

"Yep," I answered, not even close to being convinced. I guess therapy wouldn't be so bad.

He waited as I stepped out but didn't touch me. There was no subtle arm hold, or hand pressed to my lower back, instead allowing me to move on my own. It was poetic in a way, because it was something I had to do on my own.

I swallowed a silent breath, moving with confidence I wasn't sure I possessed to the door, not asking for permission as I pressed the buzzer.

Wasn't exactly sure where the surge in bravery had come from, but I wasn't going to question. Instead I stood up straight, affixed a broad smile to my face, and hoped I didn't look like I was trying to sell them Jesus. It was entirely likely that no one would recognize me, especially since no one knew I was coming.

Alex stood beside me, his smile matching mine. He didn't say a word, just shooting me a quick sideways glance that used to mean trouble.

The door swung open, revealing a tall, attractive blond. Standard, considering the Larsson family had cornered the market on tall and attractive.

Except this one was female.

And, unless Kate had some major experimental regeneration surgery, it wasn't her either.

"Alex, you're here." The tall, good looking, non-Larsson female threw her arms around Alex, allowing the rest of her body to follow suit. Not that he probably felt it, her lithe figure, while vertically impressive, had to weigh less than a hundred pounds. And that was including her fancy fluffy jacket, glittery tight pants, and her ridiculously large earrings.

She looked Nordic, Scandinavian—the kind of place where the beautiful people roamed free and had weird circle-like accents above vowels in their names.

"Hey, I didn't know you were back." He seemed genuinely surprised, but not all that annoyed. The familiarity between them was obvious.

Fluffy jacket giggled, snuggling in closer like she was trying to bury herself into his chest. Clearly she hadn't seen the movie *Alien* or she would have known being in someone's chest wasn't romantic. Pretty sure that didn't have a favorable outcome either.

"I wanted to surprise you, and your mom told me you were coming over."

It was strange. While they both towered above me, I knew I hadn't evaporated into the atmosphere. I was *still* there in front of the doorway, wearing my kick-ass red dress that showed my natural yet impressive cleavage, representing the brunette minority in our little threesome. And yet, apparently I needed to remind them they weren't alone.

"Hi." I didn't wait for the introduction, the latent bravery I'd been feeling still with me, thank God. "I'm Maya."

I didn't bother sticking out my hand since hers were otherwise occupied. Pretty sure they'd wandered down and were getting acquainted with Alex's ass.

"Astrid, this is an old friend of mine." Alex spun around, wearing tall-and-pretty like a scarf as she dangled from him. "Maya and I grew up together."

"Oh, that's so cute." Astrid grinned. "You can tell me more stories about what he was like as a kid. I bet he was a hellraiser."

Astrid.

No weird accent, but I was close.

"Yeah, something like that," I coughed out, wondering when Alex was going to mention he had a girlfriend.

Oh, I wasn't sure if they were doing the labels thing, which was probably going to be his excuse. But I wasn't an idiot, and could tell just by looking at them he and Ms. Fancy Pants were more than passing acquaintances.

The signs were all there. The lingering hand on his chest, the adoration in her eyes, her reluctance to let him go. Not that I blamed her, given half a chance I might have done the same. Except she was Astrid and I was the "friend."

Not that it was any of my business, it wasn't like Alex had given me any indication he'd wanted anything but friendship. In fact, he'd repeated it numerous times about wanting to be friends.

Friends.

The kind that didn't kiss or get naked.

Damn it.

And it was probably at that exact moment when I finally admitted to myself that more than part of me had been hopeful. Hopeful that we *wouldn't* just take up where we'd left off, but actually graduate to something more.

My bad.

I should have known better.

Well, at least I was no longer worried about being overdressed. Disco ball pants trumped the red dress for sure.

"Alex, what are you still doing outside—" She didn't finish her sentence, the kind blue eyes I'd know as a child stared at me as her mouth remained open.

Yeah, I wasn't sure I was capable of much talking either.

Kate Larsson must have done a deal with the devil.

Her skin, while not completely wrinkle free, was smoother

than her age should have dictated. Her blonde hair was the right mix of casual chic, with her tailored pants and linen shirt doing nothing to hide what excellent shape she was in. And forget she was old enough to be my mother, she'd given birth to five boys who were giants, how the hell was that even possible?

"Maya?"

Arms grabbed me and pulled me to her chest before I had a chance to answer. "Oh, Maya, Anna told me you were back. Why didn't you call and tell me you were coming?"

She pulled back to look at me, her eyes misting in sincerity.

It was Alex and Fluffy Jacket's—yes, I knew her name was Astrid but I was still bewildered someone actually dressed like that—turn to stand around and look decorative.

"We wanted to surprise you." I smiled, looking over at Alex.

Kate shook her head, glancing over my shoulder to her son. "I guess I should have expected that." She turned her eyes back to me. "Look at you, you're beautiful."

It was weird hearing the compliment considering the company I was in. My five-foot-four petite but curvy frame, green eyes, and brown hair might have been "pretty" but it sure wasn't beautiful. "Thank you." I hoped to God I didn't blush.

"Okay, everyone in the house." She waved her arms, motioning me, Alex and Astrid into the entranceway.

Her home was stunning, soft hues and pretty fabrics—feminine and soft, just like her. She took my hand, leading me through the hall to her living room where not even pastel colors or silk organza could soften the noise.

All her sons—ALL of them—were squeezed into what should have been a decent-sized room. They were all involved in various conversations, some with their equally attractive counterparts, others with their genetically blessed offspring.

It wasn't a family gathering; it was a double-page advertisement in a *Condè Nast* publication. How all that perfection was allowed to exist in one place was astounding. That it belonged to one family—grossly unfair.

"Uh-hmm." Alex cleared his throat so blatantly loud there was no mistake he was angling for attention.

Guess he'd been able to tear himself away from his fangirl for a minute, the few seconds between the door and the room allowing me time to forget I'd arrived with Alex but he'd quickly become preoccupied with someone else.

Heads turned.

Eyes followed.

All of them landing on me.

Silence.

Shit.

"Well, that was a party trick I didn't know I was capable of." I smiled, waving lamely at my audience. "Hi."

"Really?" Roman was the first one to speak, raising an eyebrow as he stepped forward. Just like the rest of them, the years had been more than generous. Gone was the cute college kid I'd remembered, in its place an incredibly handsome man who exhaled confidence instead of carbon dioxide. "I'd have assumed you'd be used to it given your last name."

"Roman," Alex hissed, his eyes shooting to his older brother.

I shook my head, knowing it was too much to expect the whole reunion to be a cakewalk. Eric, Roman—they probably remembered the scandal all too well being older, I had no doubt they'd discussed it with their father. "It's fine. It's nothing I haven't heard before." I didn't lower my gaze.

He might have been intimidating, but I wasn't backing down that easily.

Roman moved closer, everyone watching as he stood in front of me. "See Alex, she doesn't need you to coddle her. Unlike you, *she* went to Yale." His megawatt smile beamed as he pulled me into a hug.

"Jesus Roman, you're crushing her." Alex yanked me out of Roman's arms before whispering in my ear, "I did try to warn you."

Apparently Roman had seen my name on the graduate list in an alumni email but failed to mention it to anyone, something that earned him a death stare from Alex. And after meeting his wife Lauren and their adorable little son, it was Eric's turn, giving me a hug while he juggled his two kids and then introduced me to his wife, Tia. "Maya. Jesus, I had no idea you'd moved back."

I hadn't even had a chance to answer his question when Dave took over, giving me a hug and introducing me to Jessica, his beautiful smile making me feel more at ease as Nick stepped forth.

And yes, he was still thirty-five shades of fine, but it was probably the first hug he'd given me when I hadn't tried to absorb every second. *Weird.* His embrace was warm as was his smile, his wife, Claire, just as kind.

Ironic how I'd always imagined myself in her place, and now that I was looking at him, it suddenly didn't feel right anymore.

Maybe I'd been cured.

Healed from my obsession with the brothers, which meant my current feelings for Alex were nothing to worry about. But I didn't have time to evaluate or enjoy it, a perfect red fingernail tapping me on the arm.

"And I'm Astrid. We already met at the door and like you, I'm with Alex."

Not sure why she felt the need to issue me a reminder, I probably could have worked it out all by myself. I passed the bar in two states, would have definitely clued in that the man she was trying very hard to drape herself across like a jacket was attached to her in some way.

"We're . . . friends." He hesitated over the word, their

relationship status a little more complicated than she probably would have liked.

WOW.

There was that word again and somehow I didn't think he meant it in the same context as he meant for me.

Her hand on his ass was my first clue, her other one edging to his crotch was a very clear second. She didn't even care that his whole family was watching which made it clear they were probably used to it.

Astrid laughed, "Yes, we are *good* friends."

Again, probably could have worked that out without her commentary.

Alex managed to tame her spaghetti arms, sparing the children in the room from what no doubt would turn into a hand job with a flick of Astrid's wrist. Had to hand it to her—pun intended—she knew what she wanted and wasn't afraid to go after it.

There were two types of ambitious people.

One who took adversity and rose above, not stopping at anything to get to their dream.

And the second kind, who preferred to step over people rather than do the work.

I wasn't sure which one of those Astrid was, but I was positive I knew her endgame.

As Kate shuffled me into a chair, Alex disappeared with Astrid in tow. Maybe it was so she could finish what she started out of the view of minors, or maybe he had some explaining to do as to why he arrived with another woman—me.

I didn't feel guilty; after all, I had no idea he'd been spoken for, and realistically we had done nothing to even feel guilty for. Still, I could understand why she'd be pissed. I was annoyed I was unwittingly dragged into the drama. And after what my father had done to my mother, there wasn't a chance in hell I'd be someone else's sidepiece.

And while the two lovebirds had disappeared, I was left to fend for myself.

That was something I hadn't done before. That was sarcasm in case you didn't catch it.

I fielded all sorts of questions from where I was living, what firm I was going to be working at and what the rest of my family was doing. Like a speed round reunion, the rapid-fire information shot out of my mouth with zero hesitation.

Alex had returned right around the time I was telling everyone about my two nephews, his "date" no longer with him.

"Astrid go home?" Kate turned her head, noticing the absence of the Scandinavian fairy princess and her ABBA-inspired wardrobe. I'd seen *Classic Hits* on VH1, and I knew my pop culture references.

"Yeah, she did. She sends her apologies."

Wow, he must be great in a courtroom. Not a hesitation, the lie passing through his lips like he had said, the whole truth and nothing but the truth so help him God.

She might have left, but I was almost positive it wasn't "apologies" that were uttered from those perky pink lips.

Alex took a seat beside me, offering no further explanation and I tried not to recoil. He wasn't the only one who had a good poker face, my mixed feelings stuffed down deep as I laughed about something insignificant.

It was a talent, pretending I wasn't silently seething as I carried on a normal and rational conversation. It was something I'd had to learn pretty quickly, and had served me well facing the ethics committee of the California State Bar when they grilled me about my feelings about my father.

I wasn't mad because Alex had a girlfriend. I mean, he looked like *that*, it made sense he wasn't sitting around single flicking through options on dating websites. What annoyed me was that he hadn't even mentioned her, shuffling her off like the dirty secret while he returned as if she hadn't even existed.

He wasn't allowed to be *that* guy, like my father—I just wouldn't allow it.

Or at least I wouldn't stand around and witness it.

Kate had just announced that we should move to the dining room for the big family dinner when I made my excuse. *That I'd love to stay but unfortunately I had plans. Thanks, but some other time. It was great to see everyone and we'd do it again sometime soon.* I used them all, not even feeling the slightest bit of guilt as Alex eyed me with suspicion.

The hypocrisy.

So, with the grace of a world leader at a peacekeeping summit, I circled the room making sure I said thank you and goodbye while maintaining my smile. After all, it wasn't their fault I was angry, all of them being incredibly kind and welcoming despite the circumstances surrounding my absence.

Alex followed me to the door, as did Kate—Mama Larsson giving me another hug and making me promise to call her soon before she'd let me go. I agreed, fully intending to keep my word and waited until she'd returned to the bustle of her dining room before I let my smile drop.

"You're seriously going?" he asked, his gaze flicking between my hand on the doorknob and my eyes. "Why are you leaving?"

Lord.

He had to be a smart man, surely they didn't give out law degrees to morons. And yet, he was asking the question, fucking bewildered as to why I was saying goodbye.

Don't make a scene, I reminded myself. *No good will come of it.*

I ignored that he had been my ride to Casa Larsson and plucked out my phone from my handbag. While the chances of hailing a cab weren't great, there were about a hundred Ubers just waiting to take me home. "I told you I had things to do. I only promised to stay an hour and it's been closer to two. I really should get back."

And while it was partially true, it wasn't a boldface lie either. I did have things to do, like give myself a good shake and remind myself that sometimes people change.

"Back to where? Your apartment? Or you have other plans?" He watched as I flicked through my phone. "Tell me where you want to go and I'll drive you."

"Alex, you're here with your family. It would be silly to leave." Besides, I didn't want him to. "I didn't mention it before but I had promised to meet a friend for a drink before I agreed to come here. I don't have many friends in L.A. and I don't want to be rude."

His eyes rolled down the front of my dress, like he was seeing it differently. Perhaps assuming the effort hadn't been for him. "You have a date?"

"No. Not a date. I haven't got time to date." There was no need to lie; I wasn't trying to make him jealous. And romance was the last thing on my mind.

"Then let me drive you home. My mom will have my balls if she finds out I left you to find your own ride."

He looked genuinely sincere, those puppy dog eyes doing their best to convince me I didn't really want to leave by myself. I had to look away, worried that if I stared too long into them I might say yes.

"Alex, I know you have no problem omitting the truth from your mother, you've been stealing her wine for God's sake. Just tell her I got a ride from a friend." My eyes dropped down to my phone, hitting the button to accept the Uber driver. "My friend Roger." I flashed the phone and showed him my new *buddy's* picture.

He wanted to argue, but he really didn't have grounds especially when he'd already set precedence. That was the problem with lawyers, everything counted. He couldn't sneak out a bottle of his mom's red and then say he felt bad because he told a tiny white lie. Nope. Couldn't do it. Which was why he shoved his hands into his pockets and looked at me instead.

"Is this about Astrid?"

I laughed, actually laughed because I had not ten minutes ago been convinced of his intelligence. "She seems like a nice girl, but I'm not leaving because of her."

I was leaving because of him.

"Okay, well I'll call you and we'll catch up later in the week." It wasn't a question, more like telling me about what he was intending on doing.

I tossed the phone back into my bag. "Not sure I have the time, it's my first week at work but I'll let you know."

Giving him a quick hug and a casual goodbye—again, precedent had been set and I didn't have time to explain why I was suddenly hands-off—I decided to go wait for my ride further on the street.

Thankfully, he didn't follow, going back to his amazing genetically blessed family and gorgeous girlfriend.

Ugh, sure I wasn't bitter.

Which just went to show, sometimes, the past was best left in the past.

CHAPTER #7

GOING BACK TO my apartment was too depressing. I was wearing my red dress that did favorable things for my boobs and I still hadn't worked out what I was going to tell my family. My phone had been vibrating silently in my handbag, the group chat no doubt responsible for the activity.

So instead I had Roger—my friendly Uber driver—take me to The Grove. A bar would have made more sense, but drinking on my own seemed too tragic. I wasn't going to allow one little hiccup in the road to derail what was supposed to be the most awesome comeback of all time. So, I probably wasn't going to be hanging out with Alex Larsson any time soon, that hadn't been my initial plan anyway.

Nope, I was going to become a kickass attorney and live an amazing life in the city that I loved. And maybe it took me a little longer to make friends, who cared? What was important was quality, and enough time had passed so my last name no longer raised eyebrows.

It probably would have been easier to change it, but for some reason my mother didn't. I never understood why, and didn't want to ask questions about it to cause her any more hurt than she'd already suffered. Now I was kind of glad she hadn't, made me feel defiant, fighting that little bit harder because of it.

I wandered around the fountain, deciding which store I was going to go into and pretend to be interested. Even if I wasn't on a shoestring budget, and trying to ration out my savings until I started earning a paycheck, I wasn't in the mood to shop.

But after fighting off bright-lipped ladies in Sephora—and assuring them I didn't need any help—I decided it was safer just sitting on one of the park benches and talking to someone who cared. Ignoring the ridiculous thread in my text messages, I instead dialed Lisa.

"Hey," Lisa huffed into the phone, sounding like she was out of breath.

"Hey yourself. Are you okay?"

Not that I could do much from almost three thousand miles away, but I could be moral support.

"Yeah, I bought a treadmill. I'm running," she panted. "I stupidly told my boss I was a runner and he signed me up to the race. I might have oversold my ability."

"The race?" I wondered if the law office didn't sponsor some cheesy team-building Olympics like some other firms tended to do.

Nothing like a bunch of sweaty, half-clothed bodies, heavy breathing together to get everyone to be more professional. I was positive whoever started the craze was laughing their ass off at the irony.

"New York City Marathon, some of the other people from the office are doing it. I," pant, pant. "Couldn't say no."

"Jesus, Lisa. A *marathon*? The most you've ever run is like three miles, and I was about to tell you my problems. Sounds to me like you're the one who needs counseling."

She laughed, causing her lungs to heave into a coughing fit. I heard the whirl of the treadmill stop as she struggled to catch her breath. "Nah, I have a few months to train. Think of how great my butt is going to look, and I'm the only newbie doing it. Even got a smile from one of the partners. If I die, it will totally be worth it. So talk to me, it must be bad if you're calling me instead of Jackie."

I cringed into the phone. "Why would you say that?"

"Come on, Maya, we both love her but it's no secret I'm more sympathetic. So you tell me, I help you through your feelings and then we call Jackie to help plan the attack. I'm assuming this is about your date?"

"It wasn't a date." I was quick to answer.

"Well then, your time spent together with mutual consent at a place you both were present at the same time," she said with a laugh.

"Well done on the redirect."

"Thank you, now stop avoiding."

I took a deep breath, my eyes roving over all the people who were ignoring me and had no interest in my conversation. "Okay, so I went. I wore the red dress."

"Interesting wardrobe choice considering—"

"Yes, yes, I know. Sue me." I cut her off knowing full well that my dress didn't speak of the platonic get together I had alluded to. "So, he picked me up and I was looking forward to seeing him again. Sure, I was a little nervous about his family but he'd been so great, it put me at ease."

"Go on," Lisa urged, no doubt wanting to get to the good parts.

"And they were all there, looking fucking ridiculously gorgeous. It was fine, I mean, I'm not sure how it's possible for so many good looking people to be assembled in one spot, even their wives were stunning. It was like I'd stumbled into a secret meeting for the beautiful people."

She laughed, as did I. I might have been joking but I wasn't exaggerating, no wonder I'd been in love with them most of my life.

"Anyway, it might have been an enjoyable experience if the girlfriend hadn't shown up."

"Girlfriend?"

"Oh yeah, not just any girlfriend either. She looked liked she belonged with them, all blond and blue eyed with willowy long limbs that don't fit in regular size pants. Probably trolls alleyways looking for Dalmatian puppies so she can make a nice coat."

"He's dating Cruella De Vil?" She chuckled.

I sighed. "No, I'm just being catty."

"I don't remember you saying he had a girlfriend when you went to his house."

"Funny that, I don't remember it either. Who knows, maybe they have an open relationship? Or he just didn't feel the need to bring it up when we were literally spewing out all our personal details? Or maybe he figured why bother even telling me? Not like he had an obligation." I summoned the drama Gods, whispering in a hushed voice as I tried to smile. *"I am no one."*

"Maya, you're not *no one.* And regardless of what your relationship was, wasn't or used to be, any regular man would mention his girlfriend. That's on him. So what happened next?"

"He shooed her away and she left. He has her well trained that's for sure, we had a Golden Retriever who wasn't as obedient." That wasn't a lie. Even Ben struggled and it was *his* dog. Only way to get Buddy to do anything was with a very enthusiastic shove and some treats.

"Did you ask him about it?"

"No, I made an excuse and left like a coward." I sighed, slightly disappointed in myself. "I just didn't want to make a scene when everyone else in his family was being so nice to me."

"Well, you should definitely ask. It's suspect and should have come up."

She was right about that, we'd talked about college, our time apart from each other, our new jobs, what our siblings were doing. Hell, I'm almost positive we spoke about how funny it was that everyone was married—some even with kids—and neither of us were. Or maybe I'd thought I'd mentioned it? Either way, the time we were talking about the relationships of other people would have been a perfect time for him to let me know, hey, I'm dating someone.

"Yeah, I'll get to it eventually. At least I know now." And saved myself from any further embarrassment.

I'd give myself a day, and then try to get back to being a regular friend to him. And whether he had a girlfriend, or even tells me about her, will have no consequence.

Or not.

There were like four million people in the city of Los Angeles, it wasn't like I didn't have other options.

A couple walked past during the beat of silence, both of them firmly entangled in each other's arms, looking at each other with adoration. The guy obviously said something funny, the woman squealing in delight. It had been a really long time since a guy had made me feel like that.

Not that I wanted to *squeal in delight* but . . . I should have just gone to a damn bar.

"What was that?" It wasn't just me who'd noticed the couple, Lisa obviously hearing them too.

"I'm at The Grove. I should go eat dinner and then head home. When you see Jackie, you have my permission to tell her everything. It's probably easier if you do it." Because no amount of recounting the story was going to make me feel any differently about it.

"Will do. Although I have to warn you, she's probably going to want a debrief of her own."

Lisa was probably right, but that interrogation would have to wait until I wasn't so . . . I'm not even sure what I was feeling.

Annoyed? Hurt? Just generally pissed off?

So he didn't disclose his relationship, I hadn't exactly asked either. And he hadn't inquired about my relationship status. For all he knew I could have ten boyfriends I rotated through like underwear, one for each day of the week and extras for the weekends and holidays.

Why was I acting so crazy?

"Yep, I'll expect her call." Maybe she could work out why I was acting like a moron.

We ended the call and I walked to a pizza place hidden in the corner. It looked good and smelled even better and enjoyed my dinner as the sun set.

No questions.

No pressure.

And I felt myself take a big breath.

Sometimes the past was just better left in the past, I told myself as I enjoyed a second glass of wine. And while Alex Larsson had been an amazing part of my past, he didn't have to be part of my future.

ALEX CALLED ONCE and left me a voice message I hadn't bothered to listen to. Not because I was avoiding him or anything. Pfft, I was just busy.

He also sent a text message I hadn't bothered opening, again not for any other reason than I was slaving away unpacking, assembling the rest of my furniture and meticulously bringing order to my apartment. Granted it took me almost nine hours to put together two kitchen chairs—the instructions included were for a canoe and written in every language *other* than English—but eventually I got there. Not that I would be signing up to moonlight as a furniture assembler at IKEA, but I was pretty confident if I was dropped in the middle of a flat-pack jungle I'd survive. Oh, and I was also sure I could build a boat too if I ever found panels C and D.

It was reassuring that despite my blistered fingers and the obscene amount of cardboard boxes, I was finally—and complete-ly—moved in.

That was it.

I was done.

My kitchen chair project hadn't just distracted me from Alex and his gal pal, but also that I was about to start my new job. I wasn't so much nervous as I was excited, Palmer and Loft something I'd only dreamt about with a healthy dose of cautious pragmatism. They only took Ivy League graduates, had a brutal recruiting system and expected a level of excellence that was almost unachievable.

Almost.

Lucky for them and for me, I had no problem taking a shitty hand and turning it into a fist full of aces. Which was why even though I should have been peeing my pants at the prospect of my first day, I couldn't wait.

I'd barely slept—the constant buzz in the family group chat thread only half the reason for my lack of Z's—waking up well before my alarm.

I finally caved last night and told them about my time with Alex and his family, but I'd escaped a full-blown inquisition by giving them just enough details for them to drop it. *It had been fine, everyone was really nice and I was too busy to give them a play-by-play.* Then I redirected their attention to the fact I was excited about my new job and how cool it was going to be. Their late night/early morning messages had been encouragements instead of questions.

So after assuring everyone I was fine, I used the extra time to take a leisurely shower, draining the hot water heater before I finally stepped out. Then it was dry off, a light breakfast, coffee, and finish getting ready.

The bus schedule was something I'd studied before I moved, checking out the times and connections so I knew exactly which bus and what other options there were so I wouldn't be late. But for my first day I was going to splash out and pay for a ride. Who wanted to turn up a hot mess when you were new? Not me. Which was why I opened the Uber app on my phone, grabbed my handbag and walked downstairs to wait.

My finger hovered, just about to confirm my driver when I saw a sporty BMW parked out front. Not just *any* fancy BMW, it was a silver i8, the same kind of car Alex drove.

Huh.

And if I believed for a second that the exact make, model and color was just obscenely popular and it was a coincidence, then I wasn't as smart as I gave myself credit for.

"Hey." Alex cracked open his driver's side door and stepped out, his beaming smile present despite the early hour of the morning.

My eyes washing over him like a tsunami, following every curve of his incredible body wrapped in a suit that was possibly stitched by angels. Casual Alex was hot, but suit-wearing Alex needed a warning label and fire extinguisher. He was sexy as hell, bending the laws of physics in such a dirty way that would make Albert Einstein blush.

"What are you doing here?" I didn't move closer, gripping my phone as I ogled him from my place on the sidewalk.

For all he knew my wide-eyed expression and lack of movement was caused by surprise, which was partially true. The other reason was I still couldn't get used to seeing Alex as a man who made me want to touch myself. *To think we'd slept in the same bed so many times when we were younger.*

Girlfriend, I reminded myself.

"Our mothers." He rose a brow as he walked over to me when it was clear moving wasn't on my agenda. "Not sure whether it was yours or mine, but between you leaving my mom's on Saturday and yesterday afternoon, they chatted. Heard you were going to be getting a ride this morning because you didn't want to deal with the bus on your first day." He stood in front of me but didn't touch. "So, here is your ride." His hand casually waved to his waiting car.

First of all, the wave was the only thing *casual* about him and it had nothing to do with his suit. The laid back attitude had taken a backseat, and in its place was all business. Ironic how I hadn't been able to imagine him as a lawyer before, but at that moment, there was no place I could picture him other than a courtroom.

Okay, maybe there was *one* other place.

My hand waved my phone while I tried to ignore the intoxicating scent of his cologne and the sexiness radiating off his body. I was all ready to tell him that I was about to call an Uber and his help wasn't required. But when I went to open my mouth and execute the argument I'd prepared, I found I no longer wanted to give it. Instead, had some other things to say.

"I don't remember you always doing what your mother told you." I put my hand down, tossing my phone into my bag.

He didn't break eye contact. "She didn't *tell* me to do anything. I'm here because I want to be, not out of some obligation."

"Good, because I don't want obligation," I fired back, taking care to moderate my tone.

I wasn't sure if it was because I was inappropriately turned on, annoyed he had a girlfriend and hadn't told me, or if it was because our mothers were playing puppet masters, but my emotions were all over the place.

His chin tipped toward the car still parked at the curb. "And you'll get none from me."

"Fine." I strode past him, not having the time or inclination to argue. I still had to get to work and if driving me gave him some warped sense of pleasure then so be it.

I opened the car door, slipping into the passenger seat while he walked around to his side. Both of us buckled in and ready with neither of us saying a word. He started the ignition and drove, a small smile creeping on his lips. "You always this feisty in the morning?"

"Yes," I deadpanned, trying to stop my lips from doing the same.

He laughed. "Well then, my morning drives are going to be interesting."

"Wait a minute." I turned to face him. "You're not driving me every morning."

He chuckled, enjoying himself at my expense. "Jesus, Maya. Have you checked out the location of our firms? Palmer and Loft is around the corner from Young, McMillian and Walker. So I figured we could drive together until you get your own car."

"You *figured* huh?" I rolled my eyes, wondering if he was even going to bother asking or turn up on my doorstep every morning. "Thanks for the offer but in addition to obligation, I don't want to take advantage of you either."

Sure it would be great to have a ride, it would save me dealing with the Los Angeles transit system and not to mention some cash. Would mean I'd get my set of wheels a lot sooner.

But.

"Advantage? Really?" He laughed. "For a second back there I thought I was going to have to beg you to get into the car."

I rolled my eyes. "You wouldn't have begged. It's not in your repertoire." I was fairly sure I'd never seen Alex beg for anything. Cajoled—sure, charmed—definitely, begged—never.

"Maybe it is, maybe it isn't. Guess you'll have to find out." He winked before returning his eyes back to the road.

And that's when the silence hit, and not the comfortable kind where no one has to fill the space either. It was tense, the weight of the quiet hanging between us like a pair of wrinkly old testicles no one wanted to acknowledge.

"So, how was your drink on Saturday night? You have fun?"

He was the first to speak, rolling his head to the side while we were stopped at a light. His lips were pressed into a hard line, an eyebrow rose as he waited for my response.

"Yeah, it was great," I lied, not willing to admit it had been dinner and I'd been by myself. But what would have been my reason for leaving his mom's if I *hadn't* had plans? Yeah, a drink with my fictional friend was definitely the better option. "How was dinner?"

His smile returned as he leaned toward me.

Shit, why was he moving closer? My heartbeat quickened as he brought that hot, sexy body closer to me, the Lord testing me in a way I wasn't ready for on a Monday morning after only one coffee.

"It was excellent." His arm moved behind my seat, bringing his mouth inches from mine. "And since you missed out, I got you a little something to remember it by."

He was so close, his sexy man scent right *there* as I remained still, waiting for the surprise. Didn't even know if I should want it, but I did, curious what he had stashed behind the seat and why he wanted to give it to me.

The light had changed with cars moving in front of us, his arm and the rest of him shifting back as he pulled away from me and took his delicious body with him. In his hand was a wine bottle, angled towards me as he grinned.

"You stole *another* bottle of wine?" My eyes widened as my gaze dropped to the contraband. "I thought you took one a month, and you already got one last weekend."

"I was feeling inspired. I was hoping to have had a coconspirator, but you bailed early. So, I had to take one for the team. Take it." He waved the bottle in his hand. "Might as well, you're already an accessory after the fact, you should enjoy the spoils as well."

I snatched the bottle, shaking my head as I read the label. His latest lift was a white from Napa. "You sure you don't want to take it home to replenish your supply of hijacked alcohol?"

"Nope, I got it for you. You can owe me."

"How do you figure I owe you? I didn't *ask* you to take it, so realistically, I am helping you by disposing of the evidence. If anything, you *owe* me." I had to admit while I wasn't pleased with his wine-stealing habit, it had managed to break the weird tension between us. I guess sometimes, crime does pay.

I placed the precious bottle down by my feet, deciding to leave it in the car for safekeeping.

His smirk widened. "You're right. I do *owe* you, so you should let me take you out to dinner as a thank you."

Was he joking?

It was one thing for us to share dinner before I knew he was in a relationship—or whatever it was he was calling it—with a leggy blond with an 80's glam wardrobe. But it was something else to go when I had seen the evidence with my own two eyes.

"What about Astrid? She cool with you going out to dinner with other women?" I asked, because I wasn't going to pretend I hadn't put two and two together.

He shook his head, biting his lip as he tried to hide the smile. "So you *did* leave because of her."

I had no idea why the hell he thought that any of it was funny, the urge to shove him too great as I reached out and punched him in the arm. Lightly, of course, he still had his hands on the steering wheel and I didn't want to die on day one of my new job. "No, I left because you didn't tell me about her. A girlfriend is something I'd assume you'd have mentioned."

"*Girlfriend?*" He laughed, even more amused despite my annoyance. "Astrid is a lot of things, but she is not and has never been my girlfriend."

I scoffed, seriously not believing he'd become one of those guys. "Does she know that? Think you might want to let her in on your secret because her behavior seems to indicate otherwise."

"Listen, she has lived next door to my mother for the last three years. We're friends, we aren't in a relationship. She likes to pretend it's more than that, but it isn't. She is just in "love" with my family, you know what my mom is like. When she found out Astrid was on her own, she took her under her wing and Astrid loves the idea of having people around her who care. I just happen to be the only single one around. Trust me, if Nick was still available it would have been him. In fact, it *was* him up until he got married."

Well then.

Guess Astrid and I had something in common. Who knew? Not that I blamed her, the Larsson family was easy to fall in love with. And as for moving from Nick to Alex . . . yeah, I wasn't touching that at all.

"I assumed." I shrugged.

He rolled his eyes, not nearly mad enough considering. "Yeah, I figured. Maybe next time just ask me, okay?"

"I didn't feel like it was any of my business." Vulnerability wasn't something I was used to showing, especially not recently. But with Alex, it seemed to come naturally, to let down my defenses even after all that time. "Look, I don't expect you to tell me everything about your life but there are things that just . . ." I stopped, trying to find the right words. "I just don't think I could deal with it if you turned out to be a lying asshole like—"

"Your dad," he finished for me. "I get it, Maya. And I'm not. Not saying I'm perfect, but I'm not ever going to lie to you."

His eyes shone with the same sincerity they'd always had, and deep down I knew I could trust him.

"Jesus," I cursed under my breath, shaking my head. "I swear I'm not some basket case with daddy issues." Or at least I hoped I wasn't.

He just laughed, shifting his eyes back to the road. "Well, let's discuss it over dinner just to be sure."

I didn't argue, no longer feeling like I had a valid excuse to say no. I *wanted* to go to dinner with him, and now that I knew he wasn't involved with Astrid, it made it that much easier to say yes. "Fine, I could probably use someone to help me decompress after my first day anyway."

"Oh, so now you're using me?" He chuckled, shooting those perfect blue eyes in my direction.

"Yep, now I'm using you." I eased back into the seat, and for the first time since slipping into his car, relaxing a little.

A *little*, still slightly on edge at the thought of making small talk right before heading into work. While some people loved chatting in an effort to help them relax, I preferred to let things roll around in my head and go through a million scenarios instead. And since I had no idea what it was going to be like at my new law firm, I needed to flip through alternates in my thoughts. Which was why I prayed Alex didn't suddenly feel the need to discuss the weather or the some other bullshit I didn't have the mental capacity to concentrate on.

Like he read my mind, he didn't ask any more questions. Instead choosing to turn up the stereo and tapping his hand on the steering wheel as we made our way through the traffic.

By the time we'd pulled up to a stop, we'd barely said anything else. My head craned back as my eyes looked over the grey high-rise.

"I'm round the corner." Alex left the car idling as my hand went to the door handle. "Call me if you need anything."

I turned, giving him a final smile before stepping out. "Thanks, I'll see you later."

And with as much confidence as I could muster, I pushed my shoulders back and walked to the front door. I didn't need to turn around to know he was watching me, I could feel the weight of his stare. Not that I had time to work out why. Nope, I had more important things to worry about, and with one foot in front of the other, I headed right through the door that would hopefully change my life.

CHAPTER #8

"WE HAVE A hot desk situation, just take which ever cubical is open, but make sure you take your laptop and stuff when you leave. You aren't assigned to any one senior associate, so work will come in from different sources depending on what needs done. Unless there's a big case, and then you might be asked to work alongside someone."

Leah Throne seemed like she could talk while barely taking a breath. She'd been with me all morning, showing me the ropes and taking care of my induction. Most of the associates had come in straight after graduation and had been there awhile, but some had already decided to move on—read, couldn't handle it—so they needed to replenish their supply. Add fresh meat. I was one of three new faces, the other two both guys who'd graduated from Harvard.

"Any questions?" Leah spun around, making sure to connect with each of us before waiting exactly three point five seconds and moving on. "Good, there's a kitchenette down the hall for tea and coffee but make sure you wash your own dishes, there's no maid service here. There are some energy bars and snacks in the cupboard as well so feel free to help yourself if you're working through lunch. No one is a preschooler here so take your break when it's most convenient, just make sure someone is aware in case we're looking for you, and you're not checking out when you're on a tight deadline. Sound good?"

One.

Two.

Three.

"Great, let's move on."

Eyes followed us as we moved through the hall, accompanied by either polite smiles or impassive indifference. I could tell at least a few of the staff had wagers on how long we were going to last, their calculating gazes not going unnoticed as we took the elevator back to the lower level. It's where they "penned" us, the concentration of cubicles and desks not unlike most law offices in America.

And with a folder each, and another brief pause, Leah Thorne left us to find a desk and wait for someone to "give us assignments."

"She's a hell of a trial lawyer." One of the new guys, Mike, leaned in and whispered, tipping his chin to a departing Leah. "I can't believe they've got her showing us around."

"Well, they aren't going to trust us to just anyone. Only the best for the best will do." Harvard graduate number two, Stefan, winked.

It would be easy to dismiss Stefan as arrogant, but it was exactly the kind of attitude that had gotten him through the doors in the first place. Questionable self-esteem had no place where we were, it was either be great or fake it so much you convince everyone including yourself.

I dropped my purse on the closest desk and slid my company-provided laptop out of its bag. "You're both right. Leah is fantastic in the courtroom, but is also head of the associates as well. They want us to shine, and they aren't going to risk that to an office manager who doesn't know what it's like to be where we are."

Stefan took the desk closest to me while Mike grabbed one

three cubicles over. The place was full of activity, men and women too busy with files or computer screens to concern themselves with the new kids. They looked up sure, but no one really made an effort to come over and introduce themselves. It was like the first day of a new school all over again; only this time I didn't care what they thought. I was too excited to worry about the court of popular opinion.

"Yale?" Stefan asked, watching as I continued to unpack.

I stopped, placing my phone on top of my laptop as I turned to him. "How did you guess?"

"It's a gift." He laughed. "I once convinced my neighbors I was like that TV guy who can connect with the dead. I'm just really good at picking up cues and reading people." He reached across and picked up my coffee mug that I'd placed on my desk, ready for my first cup. "And the Blue State Coffee cup is a total giveaway. More like a study hall for you guys, wasn't it?"

"Something like that." I looked at the cup in his hands, the same cup that had been with me through every midterm, exam and test since I'd started at Yale. "I'm originally from L.A. though."

His brow rose as the smile spread. "Me too. Tarzana. My folks still live there. You?"

"Encino," I answered, not used to needing to be so specific.

"Wow, we were practically neighbors. See, I knew there was a reason I liked you." He grinned, pleased to have found a connection.

I was just about to tell him I didn't live there anymore when Mike wandered back over. "You guys already forming an alliance? You aren't muscling me out that easily."

"We're just chatting, dude." Stefan leaned back in his chair. "You shouldn't look so scared though, lawyers can smell fear."

"Yeah, well I won't be now you've included me in your circle of newbies." Mike grinned. "Now, tell me what you guys have been "chatting" about."

Stefan was just about to open his mouth when a senior associate handed us folders with our assignments for the day. All three of us were on research duty, banished to the paperwork hell to crosscheck and review case studies to be used by other attorneys.

There was a pecking order, and it was going to be a while before any of us saw any real action. Though it did mean we got to work in the records department and library. Our "hot desks" abandoned as we camped in the windowless room under the glow of artificial light.

"So, your parents still live in Encino?" Stefan asked, our earlier conversation of being neighbors not forgotten.

"No, my parents are divorced. I moved to Nevada with my mother when I was sixteen." I'd delivered the sanitized explanation so many times I didn't even blink as it spilled from my lips.

I had no doubt the real version would eventually come out, but I wasn't shining a spotlight on it any sooner than I needed to.

"Nevada, my apologies." He grimaced and laughed. "Still, you're back now."

Deciding he'd been left out of the conversation for too long, Mike interjected, saving me from needing to volunteer any more. And I would have kissed him if it wasn't completely inappropriate or if I was attracted to him in any way. Unlike Stefan and I, he grew up on the other side of the country in Rhode Island. His dad was a county judge back on the east coast, and his mother, brother and sister were all lawyers.

Both guys were different sides of the same coin. Tall, good-looking with dark hair and brown eyes and looked like they still rowed crew on the weekends. They came from upper class white families who probably posed for Christmas portraits in matching sweaters. But to their credit, neither of them were jerks, or at least if they were, they were hiding it extremely well. Which was good enough for me.

Not sure if it was Mike or Stefan who decided we were going to be friends, but throughout the course of the day the motion was raised, seconded and passed. And unless you counted Prim—which I didn't—I was severely deficient in the friend department in the city. The Larssons were a grey area, so for the sake of collecting data, I hadn't counted them as "friends" per se. The last thing I wanted to do was go down the rabbit hole, analyzing everything about what each member of that family was and wasn't. And if I was really honest, I wasn't sure I wanted to be just *friends* with Alex anyway. Lord knew what he wanted.

Gah, it was all so confusing.

So, while I wouldn't be cutting my palm and swearing a blood oath to Stefan or Mike, there'd be at least two people who'd report me as missing within twenty-four hours if I was kidnapped. That was of course assuming my mother didn't beat them to it, she who used the "group chat" like a roll call every morning.

"Shit." Mike rolled his head from one side then the other. "It's like studying for the bar all over again."

Stefan glanced at his watch as he raised a brow. "It's also six o'clock and we've been sitting here since lunch."

"Lawyer hours, boys." I yawned, stretching my arms above my head. "You really didn't expect to finish at five like a *regular* job did you?"

We all laughed, knowing nine-to-five wasn't going to happen for us any time soon. Instead, we packed our folders neatly, filing information appropriately for each associate, and then dispersed so we could drop off all the important files at the corresponding desks. I got a smile and a thank you from Louise, while Mike and Stefan got grunts and hand waves from Jarrod and Bill. And with our deliveries completed, our first day had come to a close.

Mike had decided he needed a beer or two, telling us he'd discovered a sports bar not far from work. Plans were made, with

Stefan agreeing to join him, the bonding of the newbies set to continue after hours.

"You coming?" Stefan asked, watching as I grabbed my handbag and slung it over my shoulder.

I wanted to say yes but the words stalled in my mouth before I agreed. "I can't tonight. Maybe next time?"

He nodded, turning his attention to Mike. "Guess it's just the boys then."

"Don't worry, Maya. I'll save anything important for when you are around." Mike winked.

Stefan grinned, pretending to look disappointed. "You know I only agreed to come to be polite, it was Maya's company I was hoping for."

My eyes widened, surprised that I had been sitting next to him all day and he hadn't even hinted he was interested. Or if he had, I had been really bad at reading it.

"Jesus, Maya. I meant you would be more interesting than him." Stefan laughed, totally reading my expression. "I'm not hitting on you. I don't date people I work with. And by the way, you looking so horrified isn't doing wonders for my ego."

It would have been easy to be embarrassed, but I wouldn't allow myself to be. Pushing myself out of my comfort zone with people I didn't know all that well was going to be happening a lot in my future. It was time I started getting used to it.

My lips spread into a cheeky grin as my eyelids fluttered. "I was only horrified because I thought you'd been reading my secret lusty thoughts all day."

It was his turn for the wide-eyed stare, a cough making its way up his throat.

"Gotcha." I laughed, pointing at him with amusement.

"How come no one is thinking I was hitting on them?" Mike narrowed his eyes, his hands firmly on his hips as he looked between us.

"Which one of us would you hit on?" I asked, not sure if it was inviting trouble.

He took a minute, considering his answer. "Neither. I don't date lawyers."

Stefan grabbed his chest, trying to look hurt. "Twice I've been injured."

My phone buzzed with an incoming message, my eyes cutting to the screen and seeing Alex's name in the preview. My finger flicked across the glass and my heart kicked up a beat as I pretended the message didn't excite me as much as it did.

I'm downstairs, ready to be used and abused after your first day.

My smile was automatic as I quickly typed my response.

How did you know I was done? Are you spying on me?

Yes. I slipped the security guard a hundred and he gives me hourly reports.

I knew he was kidding but I laughed out loud as I responded.

Creepy. But I like it. Be down in five.

CHAPTER #9

STEFAN AND MIKE were also ready to go so we took the elevator down to the ground floor together. It made me strangely nervous, to know they were going to see him, but it wasn't like I could barricade my arms against the door and not let them out. It would probably raise more eyebrows, besides both of them had pulled out their phones and seemed more interested in their screens than me or our journey. With any luck neither would even look up, tossing me a goodbye as they went to their sports bar.

I saw him the minute the metal doors parted, a floating buoy in a sea of gray, white and glass. He had his back turned, looking out the floor-to-ceiling windows to the noise of traffic and people. I took a moment just to appreciate him, the muscular perfection of his frame in his designer suit. I was guessing it was designer, he could have picked it up from a thrift store, but the way it looked on him made it look like a million bucks.

He turned and smiled, and suddenly his spectacular body faded to the breathtaking glow of a cheeky Larsson grin and the most amazing blue eyes. I could drown in those eyes, literally take my last breath looking at them and not have any regrets.

"How was your first day?"

He spoke first, giving me a minute to gather my thoughts that had scattered. Mostly about how blind I must have been in my youth.

"Great. It was great," I answered with a smile.

"Good, I want to hear all about it. My car is over here." His head tipped to the door.

Without saying goodbye to my newfound friends I followed Alex out of the door. His car was parked at the curb, the lights flashing as he hit the fob.

His eyes twinkled and I knew it meant trouble. "Let's go. I've got a surprise for you."

"I hope it's to further our plans of world domination?" A nervous laugh bubbled up my throat. "We didn't really get to it the other night."

"Trust me, you're going to love it." He held open the door and waited for me to get in.

I wasn't usually big on surprises—hello, my father saw to that—but if it was one thing I could do, it would be to trust him. Especially when he was wearing the same look he wore when we stole Nick's car and drove to Malibu. He instinctively knew exactly what do or say, and it had been one of the best nights of my life. Ironic considering I had a boyfriend at the time and hadn't shared any of those feelings with him. Guess that's how I knew what we had was special. It had been one of the last times we'd been together, and one of my favorite memories. Something I'd carried with me for years after. Maybe we'd be going to Malibu? This time without the grand theft auto.

We talked as we drove, him telling me about getting to assist one of the partners of his firm and me filling him in about my day. The air was warm and the windows were down, the breeze blowing into the car as tension and unease blew out.

It wasn't until we got to a rundown hotel in Lynwood that I

started to have questions. We definitely weren't going to the beach.

If surprising me was the objective of the evening, he'd well and truly done that. My eyes peeled open wide as I surveyed the burned-out building across the street. The windows had been boarded up, the bricks charred black with a homeless person camped out on the stoop.

A helicopter flew overhead while a siren blared in the distance, and I was positive the group of men standing around on the corner were not part of a barbershop quartette.

"Um, I thought we were going out for dinner?" I looked back to the hotel, its flashing sign advertising vacancies, and suddenly eating was the last thing on my mind.

He reached across—the calmness in his eyes matched by his smile—and squeezed my knee. "Just trust me."

And so help me, I didn't have a choice.

We could be walking into a drug den, looking to turn some pseudoephedrine into meth and I'd have followed him in. Although, I really hoped that *wasn't* what we were doing. Apart from the legal implications, I hadn't been great at chemistry.

He exited the car first but I wasn't far behind, our strides even as we walked to the door of the hotel while I tried not to freak out. I'm sure there was a plausible explanation why he'd taken me to a cheap hotel in a shady neighborhood. I knew it couldn't be to make all of my dreams come true and have sex. With both of us living alone, we didn't need an alternate venue. Which meant it had to be something else. Pity most of the things I imagined would need an industry-strength drop cloth and five gallons of bleach.

Jesus, I was being stupid. This was *Alex Larsson*, someone I'd trusted for more than half of my life. He knew my family, and I knew his, surely if he'd had hidden serial killer tendencies I would have seen them.

Of course, that was what they always said in the news grabs.

"He was such a sweet man, I never would have suspected it." Meanwhile the "sweet man" had three dismembered bodies buried in his backyard and a hard drive full of hard-core snuff porn.

He put a hand around my waist and I involuntarily jumped. Too busy thinking about how hot his mug shot would be to notice how close he'd gotten. "You okay?"

"You've never lied to me before." I turned and put my hands on his chest. "So I need you to answer a question before I go in."

Not sure standing in the parking lot was a hell of a lot safer, but I took comfort in the added witnesses. Even if their testimonies would probably never stand up in court.

His eyes glanced at my hands on his chest. "Okay, what do you need to ask?"

"Are you going to kill me?"

It didn't sound any less absurd coming out of my mouth than it did in my head, causing him to laugh loudly. "Do you think if I was going to kill you, I'd admit it?"

He had a point, and God help me his smile wasn't helping. I shoved him roughly, feeling even more ridiculous for having thought it in the first place. "Maybe you'd have a moment of integrity, feel like you owed me. You know, for old time's sake?"

"Is that why you are coming so willingly to your apparent death? Nostalgia?" He grabbed my hands and held them to his chest as he grinned. Yeah, he was capable of a lot of things, but killing me wasn't one of them.

"I was curious."

"Well, *curious*, let's go inside where I promise I won't kill you." He led me to the door and we walked inside.

His hand was still around my waist as we breezed right past reception. The lady behind the counter looked up, gave him a smile of recognition and went back to whatever she'd been doing before. He clearly knew where he was going, strolling down the hall like he'd done it a million times before. And just before we reached the exit, the sad empty pool visible through the glass, he pointed to a door.

"Through there."

I didn't bother waiting for him to turn the knob, my hand twisting it as I took a breath and pushed the door open.

It was a function room, or at least that was what it had probably meant to be, the faded walls and carpet almost an identical shade of brown. It was filled with people, waiting around in lines that snaked up and down while their faces wore what was possibly worry or fear. At the far end was about six card tables, the kind you'd find in your grandmother's basement that was brought up at Christmas time so the kids had somewhere to sit.

Only two of the six tables were occupied, a man and a woman both wearing business attire, busy in conversation with the people who were sitting opposite them.

I felt him behind me, his hands on my waist as he leaned in closer. "It's a legal clinic. I started volunteering when I was in law school in the summers when I was home, but I stayed on after I graduated. Most people can't get to the office during business hours so they rent out the conference room here. At the very least we can give them some advice and emergency intervention if needed, and then refer them to one of the clinic's regular staff if they require more than that. Sometimes all they really need is help filling out forms."

Wow, and I'd been worried he was a murderer.

Pretty sure he was at the opposite of that spectrum, and if anyone was the monster it was me.

"Alex, this is—" I wasn't sure what I wanted to say, emotion getting stuck in my throat. "You're amazing."

He beamed, pleased by the adulation. "You might want to hold off on the praise. I brought you here with ulterior motives, we've been short staffed the last couple of weeks and I was hoping I might be able to sweet talk you into helping out. I promise I'll feed you later."

"Sweet talk me? I'd been ready to commit a class B felony in the parking lot and then willing to walk into my own demise. I'd say using the law to help the people who needed it most is not going to take any kind of convincing. How can I help?"

He snorted, my earlier suspicion revealed in its entirety. "Jesus, Maya. What the hell goes on in that head of yours? What class B felony?"

"Making meth, can we focus now?" I rolled my eyes, hiding the grin. "Where do you want me?"

We were greeted by a man who looked to be about forty, Alex handling the introduction. His name was Don, and when he found out I was there to help, you'd have thought he'd won the lottery, giving me some forms and showing me where I could set up.

Alex took the desk beside me, shooting me a wink as he sat down with his first client.

We worked together, side by side, tirelessly without saying a word to each other. And though it had only been a few hours, I'd discussed everything from unlawful evictions to custody disputes. It was nothing like I'd experienced at my firm earlier, my research work, while necessary, not as exciting as actually making a difference in someone's life.

When it was time for the clinic to end, there was still a bunch of people who hadn't been seen. Their protests not quelled by the promise that they could return next week. I guess for some of them next week was too long to wait.

I felt terrible, wishing there was something I could do as they were ushered outside. The lawyers were left alone in the room to process whatever paperwork they needed, the guilt of my fantastic life almost eating me up alive.

"It's hard the first few times. Don has been doing this for years, man can be a hard-ass but even he's struggled closing the doors a few times. I've even offered to stay back by myself in the hope of getting through everyone. But you can't and it doesn't help anyone if you end up burnt out." Alex rubbed my back while my eyes stayed on the closed door. "Come on, I promised you dinner and I am becoming really terrible at delivering on my promise."

"So we just go?" I asked, wondering how I could walk past the people who would no doubt still be in the hall.

His hand laced in mine, it was oddly familiar and yet I couldn't remember holding hands like that before. "Yeah, and then we come back next week. I know it might not feel like it but we made a difference tonight."

"I want to come back," I said with zero hesitation.

He squeezed my hand a little tighter. "I knew you would."

DINNER ENDED UP being tacos from a food truck and a couple of sodas. I hadn't realized how hungry I was until I scarfed down my food like an animal. I didn't even care how unattractive it might look, too focused on feeding my stomach.

When it was time to go home I was oddly disappointed. It was late and we both had to get up early the next day, but I just wasn't ready for it to end.

"You want me to walk you up?" Alex asked, stopping in front of my apartment building.

I was tempted to say yes, and not because I was worried about walking around on my own. But I knew that would be selfish, and he was probably tired. "No, I'm fine. My landlord, Prim, has a pair of binoculars and sits by the window day and night, pretty sure she doesn't sleep. If there was anything to worry about, she'd have already called the cops."

"Prim sounds like my kind of lady." He laughed.

"What, creepy with a tendency to spy on other people? She's probably in her 50's but has a rather fetching housecoat. I can introduce you if you'd like?"

He shivered, raising his brow in what was quickly becoming his signature move as he lowered his voice to a sexy rumble. "Baby, you had me at housecoat."

Those words should not have been arousing. Sure, he'd called me baby, but it had been in jest and not as a tool in seduction. Yet for all my smarts and common sense, that one word vibrating between his lips was enough for me to press my thighs together.

I had waited too long.

Too long without having sexual contact and now I was in the danger zone. So desperate for it I was about to leap across the center console and rub myself against him like a cat.

Meow.

Jesus. I really needed to get out of the car.

"I should go." My hand couldn't work fast enough to open the door so I could eject myself from my seat. "Thanks so much for everything."

I all but threw myself out on to the sidewalk, desperate to get into my apartment before the thirst took real hold and I'd be forced to chain him to a chair and use him as a dildo.

Pretty sure that was illegal.

"Maya, wait!" he called out after me, forcing me to turn back.

My heart thumped, almost hopeful he was going to tell me he didn't want the night to end either. Or needed to touch me. Or kiss me. Or make me come so hard I forgot my own name. Fine, I was being optimistic, but it had already been a super strange night.

"Your wine." He held up the bottle he'd stolen over the weekend and given me earlier in the day. "You forgot it. If I didn't know better, I'd say you were reneging."

I'd completely forgotten about it to be honest, and it wasn't wine—stolen or legitimately bought—currently on my mind either.

I reached back into the car and took the bottle, not really wanting it but because I had already agreed. "Fine, but next time I'm implicated in a crime, I want to at least have participated in it." It wasn't exactly what I had in mind when I wanted him to make a dishonest woman out of me, not that I could admit that to him out loud.

"Something tells me that won't be a problem." His low husky voice was back and I was in serious trouble.

"Okay, bye." I turned around, forcing my feet to move. His car continued to idle, only driving off once I'd disappeared from view.

It was a relief when he was gone, my body pressing against the stairwell, needing a minute before I climbed. I never understood why women in old black and white movies threw an arm across their eyes while breathing rapidly like they were going to faint, but I was quickly finding out.

It was so you didn't have to look at yourself when you dissolved into a white-hot mess over a man.

But no amount of hiding was going to save me.

CHAPTER #10

IT HAD BEEN a miracle I'd been able to sleep at all, but thankfully exhaustion did its thing and biology took over. Not that closing my eyes stopped me from seeing him or thinking about him, my dreams flicked from one Alex-filled dream to the next.

Heels and a pencil skirt stopped me from racing down the stairs to see him the next morning, but he was rather amused by my animated shuffle.

Like the morning previous, he came bearing gifts. Instead of stolen alcohol, this time it was two coffees and two doughnuts from the shop in Encino my mom used to go to.

"You went to Hole-In-One?" My eyes lit up at the brightly colored box. "I can't believe that place is still open."

He nodded, taking a sip of his coffee. "I figured it might have been a while since you had one, and I didn't have time for breakfast so figured we could eat in the car."

I narrowed my eyes in suspicion. "You didn't have time for breakfast, yet you had time to drive to Encino before coming here?"

"I know, I'm a saint." He smirked.

I didn't disagree.

The drive seemed to end too soon, his sainthood and my love

for doughnuts only a fraction of what we discussed.

It *wasn't* like how it used to be.

It was better.

As I waltzed into work—floating on a cloud of happiness, sugar and caffeine—I was in a pathological good mood that had no business in a law office that early in the morning. All I needed were those obnoxious cartoon birds whistling around me, and an urge to skip.

"Looks like someone had a good night." Stefan lifted his head, already working at one of the desks, his smile dripping with suggestion.

Mike cleared his throat, not bothering to look up. "Can't say that, dude. Sexual harassment."

Stefan rolled his eyes as he swiveled his chair to Mike. "All I said was it looked like she had a good night, it's not like I asked if she got laid." He rotated back to me. "And I wasn't asking. It was an observation, I'd have said the same thing to Mike if he walked in here with a big grin on his face."

"It's fine." I lowered myself onto the seat next to him, maintaining the big grin I was allegedly wearing. "Besides, I want to hear about *your* good night."

Their evening had been different to mine, the two of them falling in love with some dive bar that had awesome food. I promised I'd tag along some other time and we went about our day.

And when the day was over, Alex was waiting downstairs as usual. I tried to act casual, when really I just wanted to leap into his arms and kiss him. My stomach and heart doing weird aerial gymnastics in my body that I was sure wasn't good for either of them but I managed to keep the craziness contained.

He suspected absolutely nothing when we stopped at a bistro on the way home and ate dinner, my hands, mouth and body kept to myself the entire time. I may have—not confirming or denying—given him a playful hug when we made an extra stop for ice cream before he took me back to my apartment. But that was gratitude and therefore allowed. Him reciprocating didn't help things though—encouragement would probably be my downfall.

Again, our goodbye was bittersweet.

"Hello?" I answered my phone, a smile still plastered on my face as I closed my front door.

"Oh, you're alive," Jackie deadpanned. "I'd already picked out the black dress for the funeral."

"Har-Har, I sent you a text yesterday." I kicked off my shoes, stripping off clothes as I made my way to the bedroom.

"You mean the thumbs up emoji in response to my message? Sweetie, last time I checked, you spoke in whole sentences so I assumed some asshole must have stolen your phone from your dead fingers."

I knew she was being sarcastic, but I had been quieter than normal. Between work, Alex, and overanalyzing everything, it didn't give me a lot of time to check in. "I'm sorry. I've been really busy."

"You've been busy or you've been *getting* busy?" she asked. "Did your blast from the past become your blast of the present? Come on, Maya, I'm an information girl and you're not coming up with the goods."

I sighed, flopping onto my mattress as I stared at the ceiling and proceeded to tell Jackie every last detail. Not that there was much to tell, we seemed to be spending a lot of time being in the car, eating and talking. The law clinic was kind of special and the doughnuts. And maybe it was all just really "nice" and that was all it would ever be.

She listened but thankfully refrained from offering unsolicited advice. And when I was done, we switched our focus to her and how she was enjoying New York.

When she was satisfied I hadn't been taken over by an alien

life form, we said our goodbyes. It was late in L.A. and her wake up time was a hell of a lot earlier than mine considering the time difference.

"Uuughhhhh," I groaned loudly into my empty room.

It was going to be another long, sexually frustrated night.

THE DAYS THAT followed didn't deviate from the routine, every morning and every evening, my days made infinitely better with Alex being in them. Work was great and I was really starting to find my feet, but spending time with him was a cherry on top of a delicious brownie sundae. Ironically I wanted to lick them both—Alex and the sundae—having to be content with touches and hugs that weren't overly sexual.

I was dying.

Wound up so tight inside that when I did finally give up—let go of the fantasy and sleep with someone less perfect—I would pass out. They wouldn't even have to be very good at this point, just be a human man with a hard-on. It was probably better they didn't talk too, then I could keep indulging in my fantasy.

Oh, God. I seriously needed help.

"Drinks. Sports bar. Food that isn't anywhere close to being good for you." It was Stefan's turn to try to convince me, he'd oscillated with Mike extending the invitation every night for a week.

And every single time I turned them down.

But it was Friday, and everyone was getting ready for the weekend and my excuses were starting to sound lame. I didn't *need* to spend every single night with Alex, but like a drug addict with a coke habit, I couldn't make myself stop.

I was just about to give my usual excuse of "sorry I have plans," when Stefan stopped me. "We've survived our first week, something that definitely needs to be celebrated."

"I know, and I agree that celebratory drinks are required. Maybe we can go tomorrow night?" I offered. "Then we won't have the early morning to distract us."

"It's *Friday*, we don't have an early morning tomorrow." Mike grabbed his satchel. "But okay, Saturday it is. No more rain checks, your position in the crew depends on it."

Stefan shook his head. "Relax, Maya, I won't let him kick you out."

"I promise. Saturday. No more rain checks," I assured them, crossing my heart in a show of commitment. At least I wouldn't be sitting at home on a Saturday night alone, there was a positive.

They followed me into the elevator, Mike pressing the down button while he checked emails on his phone. Stefan's cell was still tucked away in his pocket, looking at the closed metal doors as we descended to the ground floor.

While limiting screen time and interacting with humanity was usually commendable, I didn't need that kind of attention at the moment. Especially not when I wasn't sure if Alex was already waiting downstairs.

I needed him to check his Twitter.

Or text that girl he'd been flirting with since Wednesday.

Or develop a temporary blindness that miraculously disappeared the minute I did.

Anything would do, I wasn't fussy.

"Something wrong?" Stefan asked, my concentrated effort to *will* a distraction causing my forehead to wrinkle.

I shook my head, trying to look casual. "Nope, just thinking. The Clayton merger."

He shrugged, either buying the lie or deciding he didn't want to get involved in my crazy and continued to stare at the door that would open at any second.

Please let him be circling the block, I prayed. *Let the entire block be filled with vehicles, not a vacant space for at least a mile.*

The metal doors opened revealing my prayers had gone unanswered, Alex Larsson standing in the foyer with his hands in his pockets, waiting.

Shit.

He looked amazing, his jacket from the morning MIA with his cuffs rolled to the elbow. His blond hair was slightly ruffled, sticking out in sexy angles that just made him more alluring.

And he was looking directly at us.

Short of some seismic activity courtesy of the San Andreas Fault, there wasn't a distraction big enough to divert from that view.

Pretending if I walked fast and got out of the door I could remain inside my bubble, I accelerated my pace to almost a jog, reaching Alex and grabbing his arm.

"Hey, how are you? You parked out front? We should go." My hands yanked, pulling him toward the exit.

It was like moving a tree; his big feet rooted to the floor while he looked at me like a lunatic, probably wondering what the hell was the rush.

"Maya, are you okay?" His perfect face tilted down to me as an amused smile played on his lips. "Did you have a good day?"

There was a time and place for chitchat and in the lobby of Palmer and Loft was not it.

"Great. Fantastic. So good." I nodded, hoping if I answered the question we could go.

Turns out, we couldn't.

I heard the laugh come from behind us, reminding me that I hadn't magically turned on my invisible juice when I'd power-walked to Alex. Anyone who happened to be around was able to bare witness to my crazy, and currently that audience consisted of Mike and Stefan.

"She's exaggerating. It was boring and long." Stefan appeared beside me not bothering to wait for an introduction. "And now I see why Maya is continuing to blow us off. I'm Stefan, and this here is Mike." He thumbed over his shoulder to the guy who was no longer interested in his phone. "And you are?"

Dead.

Not Alex of course, but me. And not for the reason most people would have suspected.

I wasn't worried about them assuming he was my boyfriend— please, that little rumor could only give me street cred. Plus I'd glanced at my mom's emails about manifesting bullshit into reality. And if *Janine from Ohio* could *manifest* herself a shiny new Range Rover then getting Alex to consider a relationship—where we kissed—didn't seem like that big of a stretch.

No, my concern was about something else and sadly didn't just affect me. If they found out *who* he was—and about his collection of famous siblings—then I had no doubt the sideshow would follow. Or at least that was what I guessed happened whenever he mentioned his last name and who his family was, we'd been strangely immune to it in our ride/chat/eat bubble.

I didn't want that for him, to become a *thing* that people saw as a commodity. And as weird as it sounded, I wanted to protect him, keep those speculative eyes and curious glances away from him. And I sure as hell didn't want to be the reason for it.

"This is my friend, Alex." I deliberately left off his last name. "He works around here too and is giving me a ride home."

As far as explanations went, that one sucked. Not only did it sound like the words of a five-year-old, but it made me look even more suspect than if I'd just introduced him like a normal person. Oh well, too late for that now.

Stefan gave me a sideways glance, picking up the weird vibe immediately as he threw out his hand. "Hey *friend* Alex, nice to meet you."

It wasn't only Stefan who was looking at me strangely, Alex was too, his mouth hooking in a grin as he reached for Stefan's hand. "Likewise. Now tell me about Maya and her *blowing you off*."

It sounded dirty, and I knew it was probably intentional. Not because I thought Alex was flirting with me, oh hell no. He just liked to watch me squirm, probably wondering why since walking back into his life I was acting like an extra from *American Horror Story*.

"We invited her for celebratory drinks all week. She told us she had plans. Rain checked us every night, but failed to mention a boyfriend," Mike added, joining in on what seemed to be a united effort to make me feel awkward. He was grinning too, and here I thought he was the nicer one.

I laughed, trying to sound casual but failing miserably. "Alex isn't my boyfriend. We're just friends. We grew up together. When we were kids."

It was ironic that I was trying to convince them of the same thing I had been trying to convince myself. We were just *friends*, no chance of him ever being my *boyfriend*. Blah, blah, blah—Lord, I hoped it didn't sound as lame as it did in my own head.

With zero time to even process what was happening, an arm wrapped around me and pulled me closer. The full length of Alex's delicious body was pressed against mine—or was it mine against his?—as he grinned. "Come on, Maya. Don't lie to your friends. It's totally fine to tell them how much you *love* me."

If it was possible for a heart to dislodge itself from its place in a chest and catapult into a throat, I was sure mine would have done it. Even knowing how impossible it was, I was positive mine was trying to attempt it, my lungs feeling like they were on fire from the effort.

I was about to demand to know how he'd suddenly developed mind reading abilities, or deny it and accuse him of having severe narcissistic tendencies—I hadn't decided which—when he laughed.

"Which is probably the only thing stopping her from tearing my balls off right now. She is right though, we're really good friends."

Relief and disappointment both filled me, because as glad as I was he couldn't see into my brain, he had confirmed friends was probably all we'd ever be.

"Interesting." Stefan grinned. "Well, offer stands and you're welcome to join us as well."

The words were already in my throat, ready to assure Stefan that I'd—singularly, without my friend—happily grab that drink tomorrow as we'd planned. Hell, I'd even meet them in the morning, start the day with mimosas and then move to liquid lunch before drinks in the evening assuming they didn't think I was encouraging them to become alcoholics. But my "thanks, some other time," was halted by Alex's "Sure."

"We can grab a drink with your friends before dinner tonight." Alex turned to me, his hand remaining on my hip. "Unless you don't want to."

The grin forced its way onto my lips. "Nope, I just don't want you to feel weird drinking with people you don't know. I'm fine with drinks."

I couldn't be any less fine.

"Well to be honest, does anyone really *know* anyone?" Stefan picked that moment to dabble in philosophy, funny he'd never shown an interest before. "Aren't we all just friends we haven't met yet?"

If he started quoting Maya Angelou, I was going to throw up.

He was enjoying it, flicking his eyes between Alex and I, trying to gather evidence while I retained my 5th Amendment rights.

"Stefan and I both graduated the same year and barely spoke, I thought he was an arrogant asshole," Mike added, clearly no longer believing that to be true as he "backed up" his buddy. Both of their points of view were extremely unhelpful.

"Gee, thanks Mike. Sounds like you are joining us after all." Stefan smirked. "Meet us at Bar Six. You need directions?"

Alex shook his head. "Nope, I know where it is."

With my fate sealed, the objective had shifted. Fall out had to be minimized at all costs.

"Great, we'll see you there then." I grabbed Alex's hand and hoped this time when I tugged he'd move.

Praise Jesus, a miracle.

His feet unglued from the floor, the forward motion continuing as we walked to the door. We didn't talk, Alex moving his hand to my lower back as he guided me towards his car.

He'd clearly made a deal with the devil. If looking good wasn't bad enough, he'd managed to secure a parking spot right in front of the building every single time. "Wow, what do you have to do to keep getting prime parking? It's like they know you're coming and clear out a spot." I chuckled, sliding into the passenger seat of his BMW.

"I sacrificed a virgin at midnight. It's a little extravagant I know, but it's working out well for me so far." He grinned, waited until I was settled and then walked around to the other side of the car. "Were one of those guys your friend from the other night?" He threw out casually as he buckled in.

The other night?

It took me a minute to work out he was talking about my fake friend drink commitment, and the excuse I'd used to get out of dodge when I thought he might be part of a pair. And while it was tempting to validate my lie, using one or both of them as my alibi, it was pointless and would only lead to trouble.

"No, we just met this week. The three of us all started together and just sort of clicked. Amazing how quickly you bond when you're down in the trenches."

He nodded, starting the car and heading onto the main road.

He didn't plug in coordinates into his GPS, seeming to know exactly where the bar was. "So," he eased in casually. "Is there a reason you don't want me around your friends?"

I scoffed, choking back the panic. "Of course I want you around my friends. I just didn't want to make it weird for you, have them asking questions about your brother?"

"Which one?" He cocked an eyebrow, his question valid.

"Eric I guess. I mean, they'll all pretty famous now."

He laughed, no hesitation as he answered. "You'd be surprised how many people don't even make the connection. And when they do, they get over it pretty quick. I've had a lot of time to get used to it so it's no big deal. Trust me, it's easier for them to be impressed by Eric, Nick or Dave, than find out Roman is my brother. Why do you think I kept *Larsson* and didn't do *Pierce* like he did? The man is a litigation machine. Trials, depositions—you name it, there's nothing he doesn't kick ass in. Harder legacy to live up to if you ask me."

"Makes sense." I nodded, thinking how weird it must be. "Guess it just really hit me about how hard it must be for you. Everyone wanting a piece for one reason or another, and all because of who you're related to."

He laughed, his wicked grin turning toward me. "You feel sorry for me?" The look on my face obviously giving him the confirmation he needed. "Tell me again how hard it must be for me?"

"Only you would think that is a good thing." I rolled my eyes, biting back a smile.

His gaze returned to the road. "Hey, I'll take what I can get."

And there was a sentiment I could get behind.

CHAPTER #11

ONE DRINK TURNED into two and our plans of leaving and getting dinner elsewhere were shelved in favor of ribs and wings and draft beer.

"So all of those guys are *your* brothers?" Mike's eyes were wide, the family connection finally being discovered two hours in.

Alex slapped his hand dramatically over his chest. "Yep, it's just my cross to bear."

"And you grew up with all of them." Mike's attention turned to me.

It was my turn for the drama. "Yes, guess that was *my* cross." I laughed, slapping my hand on his chest and liking the excuse to touch him.

Stefan swallowed his beer, picking up a wing and pointing it accusingly. "And you didn't go into acting like the rest of them? What a waste of that pretty boy face." He chuckled as he took a bite.

Alex didn't even break a sweat, taking the good-natured jab. "My face didn't get me a 179 on my LSATs or help me graduate in the top five percent of my class at Berkeley Law."

"*179?* It wasn't his face he wasted. Berkeley? Really?" Mike looked horrified.

Alex groaned, looking up to the ceiling. "My God, you people are all the same."

Stefan shook his head, wiping his mouth with a napkin. "You mean *smart* people? If so, yes, we're all the same."

"Well, I think it was fantastic he did what he wanted to do." I took a sip from my oversized mug. Cheap beer always went right to my head and I needed to remember that before things started getting blurry. "And clearly it hasn't hurt him. Just look at him."

I meant his job.

His position at Young, McMillian and Walker.

I'm sure he was kicking ass and taking names, earmarked for a fast track to greatdom. But as I gazed dreamily at him—my decision to stop drinking a touch too late it seemed—it was obvious to me he was successful in all areas. Currently, he was *successfully* wearing the absolute hell out of that suit.

"Yeah, yeah. He's fantastic." Mike rolled his eyes before looking back at me. "But just so we're clear, he's not part of our crew."

Alex raised a brow in interest as his fingers picked up a delicious looking BBQ rib.

Its saucy goodness dripped down his fingers.

I involuntarily licked my lips.

"Your crew?" he asked, bringing the rib to his perfect mouth and I had to force myself not to stare at the man while he ate.

"Mike decided we needed to start a gang, makes it harder for them to pick us off one at a time if we're looking out for one another." I laughed, the idea sounding more like prison survival under my beer haze. "But you don't work with us so you have to find your own back up."

Stefan raised his palm, seeming to give the idea some thought. "Now let's not be too hasty. Always good to have someone in another firm. Never know when you're going to need a favor, or a lookout on another cell block." He laughed, on the same wavelength with my earlier analogy. "Let's call him an alternate."

Mike wasn't convinced, but he was outvoted, Alex victoriously holding up his hands as I decreed him officially included.

We finished the rest of our dinner, the conversation easy between the four of us as they switched from beer to soda. I wasn't driving which meant I was free to continue to drink, careful to keep myself sober enough so I didn't do something stupid but loving the soft edges the cheap beer gave me.

It wasn't just my mind and my mouth that loosened, so had my body. My head had rested on his shoulder at least three times and my hands had staged their own revolt, roaming with reckless abandon.

Alex didn't seem to mind, not moving the fingers that had inexplicability become attached to his thigh under the table. Not sure how they got there, it had definitely *not* been premeditated.

He was just so . . . everything. The unrelenting assault of his body and his face just really unnecessary, there was no one on earth who could forget he was hot.

There was a flutter in my stomach, a tightness I couldn't explain as I looked at Alex. He was so relaxed, at total ease around people he'd met a few hours ago and a woman who had been undressing him in her imagination for at least a week. Yeah, I should probably not admit that, saving that little nugget of information for myself as my skin heated unnecessarily.

Must be the booze.

I excused myself, shuffling out of the booth on my quest to find the bathroom. Not that I had any idea where it was but I was confident I could find it.

Alex's body blocked my exit as I pushed up beside him, waiting what seemed like an eternity before he stood and let me out. His hands steadied me as my heels dug into the crunchy carpet underfoot. I didn't bother inspecting it more closely, fairly sure I'd be finding Hepatitis C in between the synthetic fibers.

"You good?" he asked me, his fingers lingering around my waist. I was tempted to tell him that I wasn't and insist he act as ballast until I made it safely to the stall.

Not sure I'd ask him to stop when I got there either.

Lord.

I wasn't even really drunk, just looking for a convenient excuse.

"All fine." I nodded, resolving for my thoughts to be cleaner than the carpet.

My body pushed through the crowd of mainly men, their attentions on brightly lit large screens that covered the walls and hung from the ceiling above the bar. I ignored them, both the men and the screens, as I found a flashy red sign that advertised the bathrooms. It was loud like the rest of the place, its big letters pointing the way in a shouty abrasive font.

The low ratio of females in the bar did have some perks. Apart from not having their unwanted glares on Alex, it also meant there was no wait at the bathroom. Not that I had plans to spend any quality time inside, the sepia colored walls not having seen a dust cloth since the turn of the century.

I was in and out like a member of SEAL team six, washing my hands and using tissues from my purse rather than touch anything else. My mind still muddled as I made my way back to the booth.

Mike was tossing some cash onto the table as Stefan chatted to Alex—the crew had decided to disband while I was gone.

"Hey, I'm going to bail." Stefan tipped his chin to me. "See you bright and early on Monday."

Mike nodded as well, shoving his wallet back into his pocket. "Yeah, me too. This was fun though, we should do it again, even with the ring-in." His eyes went directly to Alex.

"Yeah, it was pretty fun. Let me just cover the rest of the check. " My hand reached into my handbag, ready to pull out some cash.

Mike shook his head, looking pleased with himself. "Nah, I took care of it. I had to fight the other two off but I was successful."

"I'd say threatening to get your Judge Daddy to report us for suspected illegal drug use was a little extreme to be honest," Alex scoffed.

Stefan agreed. "Yeah, more a shakedown than us actually agreeing."

"It got the job done." Mike waved his hand, ignoring them both.

They said goodbye, disappearing into the sea of people as I stood beside Alex.

Alone.

Well, other than the hundred or so people in the bar but they didn't count.

"You ready to go? Or do you want to hang out a bit longer?" His hand pressed against my back as he leaned into my ear. The move was totally unnecessary, I'd been able to hear his regular modulated voice perfectly. But I loved it, absorbing each point of contact and letting his breath tickle my neck as I turned toward him.

"We should go," I answered, not even attempting to be considerate and offering to call a cab so he wouldn't have to drive me home.

I *wanted* him to drive me, wanted to spend more time with him—that the two of us would be alone while we were doing it was even better.

He nodded, lifting his head away as he guided me to the door. Thankfully, he kept his hand in place, the heat of his palm spreading through the fabric of my dress as he pressed. It was good, but not even close to what I wanted.

To save myself from admitting any of it out loud, I pretended to be tired on the way home. Resting my head against the side of the door and closing my eyes as he drove me to my apartment.

The thoughts festering along the way, growing inside of me until I could hear them inside my head as clear as my own voice.

Kiss him

Just once.

What's the worst that could happen?

Reason wasn't really part of the equation, the idea of kissing someone whose feelings for me I wasn't sure of, was risky at the very least. Not to mention that while he clearly stated he didn't have a girlfriend, he didn't say he was going to bed alone, saying his prayers and vowing celibacy either. And lastly, there was the option that he possibly didn't even want to be kissed, the idea of my lips on his might repulse him. I mean, I hadn't sent a man screaming into the night yet, but I was only twenty-six, there was still the chance it could happen.

On and on the warring thoughts tumbled, stretching out with each mile with no clear resolution as we weaved through traffic. It was only after we'd stopped that I peeled an eye open, rolling my head to the other side of the car to look at him.

I shouldn't have done it.

The streetlights only amplified what was already a ridiculously attractive face. His blue eyes darker in the shadows, his perfect jaw cut through the light in a symmetry that didn't seem real. He was so fucking beautiful I wanted to weep at the unfairness of it all.

He cut the engine, not asking whether I wanted him to walk me up as he moved out of the car and walked around to the passenger side. The door opened, reaching for me like a wingless angel in a tailored suit as I blinked back at him.

Oh hell, I was going to need to kiss him.

Stepping out onto the sidewalk, I strategized my plan as we walked to my front door. I'd get him up to my apartment, kiss him and then if it was totally terrible, push him out the door. It wasn't a good plan, but I figured it was all I had. What I didn't have was a contingency for a good kiss, something I wasn't even daring to hope.

It would almost have been easier if it were bad, able to push those feelings of longing and wanting to the side with a reality that it wasn't that good.

A good kiss?

A kiss that he reciprocated?

I might combust just thinking about it.

"You still on east coast time?" He finally broke the silence as we climbed the stairs to my apartment, his hand on my back graduating to an arm around my waist.

If tone had a grin, those words would have been wearing it. Oh, I'm sure he was asking me something, but it had nothing to do with my circadian rhythm. More probably, *why are you acting like a weirdo?* But I wouldn't take the bait.

"Possibly." I fake yawned, fumbling with my keys as I tried to open my door like an axe murderer was in pursuit.

It was a race against time, not wanting to lose my nerve or spook him at the last minute so he said goodbye to me on the threshold. No, I needed him inside so I could kiss him, and the longer I took the less chance that had of happening.

The worn wooden door finally gave way, making me stumble inside into the dark. Under the guise of being clumsy, I pulled him in with me and shut the door behind us.

I didn't bother with the lights; it would be easier without them.

It was now or never.

I just needed to—

What the hell?

His mouth was on mine but I hadn't moved, my eyelids peeling back in surprise as I tried to make sure I hadn't hit my head when I fell through the doorway. It was *really* dark, and it *might* have happened.

Nope, I was not only conscious, but getting kissed like hell by Alex Larsson.

Oh my God, I was going to die.

My back hit the wall as his hands traveled roughly up my body, his mouth exploring mine as the shock wore off and I started to participate.

In my dreams, it hadn't been as amazing. The feel of him—all of him—pressed against me, made me feel like champagne was coursing through my veins.

My skin—electric.

My core—about to explode.

"Yes." The word bled out from between my lips as my fingers threaded themselves into his hair. My tongue met with his, our breaths shared as we consumed each other.

It wasn't slow or romantic, teeth clanged and lips were bitten as we played a kissing game of to-and-fro. Robbed of our sight, every touch so intense I wasn't sure if I was dreaming or awake.

He groaned, a heavy breath pushed out of his mouth as he pressed against me. Of course he was bigger, his frame not only a foot taller than me but he had more than eighty pounds on me too. The two of them combined made me feel like a Hobbit, minus the hairy feet.

Pushing him outside the door was no longer an option, the idea buried with my other bad ones like stopping my mouth from being on his.

I couldn't.

I wouldn't.

Arching into him as the hard ridge of his pants pressed against my hip, his lips moving down my neck.

"Oh my God." It came out of my mouth, as I reached down between us to touch him. "You're kissing me."

My fingers palmed the front of his pants as best they could, hindered by material they really didn't care for as they stroked his impressive length. He was big all around it seemed.

"You're kissing me back." His teeth nipped at my collarbone before his mouth moved back to my lips. "And did we want to go into what your hand is doing or are we done with commentary?"

He didn't get an answer, the hunger ravishing us both as we rubbed up against each other like an ancient mating ritual while we stayed fused at the mouth. Pretty sure we were going to leave an imprint in the drywall like a prehistoric fossil, but it was worth losing my deposit over.

It felt so good, every receptor in my body igniting like he'd hit the master switch. I was turned on, hot, and so needy I couldn't remember the last time I'd felt so unhinged. I'd never begged to be touched, but there was a very real possibility I was about to start.

"Fuck, you're beautiful." His hands reached under my ass and lifted me up against the wall. The hem of my dress slid up like he'd commanded it, exposing most of my thighs and probably my underwear if there'd been any light to see it.

Turned out he wasn't interested in the color of my panties, the hard length of his cock pressing against my throbbing center as his hips rocked against mine.

Somebody groaned—probably me—his hard-on hitting me just right with every thrust of his hips.

I was going to come.

Come fully clothed while my childhood best friend dry humped me against the wall.

It should have been wrong—having feelings about him like that—but nothing had ever felt more right.

I wanted him.

And holy hell did it feel like he wanted me.

I couldn't even comprehend what was happening, the sensations too much as I wrapped my legs around his waist and kissed his neck. "God, you're so hot. How the hell did you get so hot?"

It was a rhetorical question, earning me a chuckle as his fingers teased at the edge of my underwear. They stayed on the respectable side of an invisible line, taunting me with each feathered touch.

"Do it," I moaned, "Touch me, please."

I didn't recognize my own voice—reed thin, weighted in desperation.

And then as quickly as the hurricane had engulfed me, it blew itself out. His hands, his lips, the press of his erection—all stopped as he stood in front of me panting.

"I need to stop."

He probably could have saved himself the words considering he'd already done that.

"Okay." I nodded, not really *okay* with it but not exactly sure how to argue with his reason considering I didn't know what it was. "Why?"

"Because I want to fuck you, Maya."

Jesus.

Christ.

His voice was so raw the words stroked me like he was already inside of me.

"O-kay." I nodded a second time, my body pulsing, ready to strip down and have sex right there on the floor.

His head dropped, what little I could see of his face lost in the darkness as he pulled away. "No, not okay. Not tonight."

"Don't you think I should get a say?" I started to protest, wondering why the hell not. "In case you were wondering, I was on board with that."

He chuckled, his arm reaching out to my arm and ghosting his fingers against my skin. "Trust me, you don't want it. Not tonight."

Excuse me? I didn't want it? Short of me stripping down and offering myself to him like a fucking—literally—canapé, I didn't think I could be more clear on my wants.

I wanted him.

Biblically.

"Um, trust me. I can tell you that I *definitely* want it. Especially tonight."

Tired of not being able to read his face, I fumbled along the wall for the light switch, the overhead globes illuminating the room so I could survey the carnage.

His eyes were darker, the pool-water blue consumed by inky irises as they stared at me.

They didn't look like they believed him either.

"You've been drinking." His hand fisted at his side, keeping himself contained as he stepped away.

None of it made sense to me.

He'd said with his body and his words that he wanted me.

I had done the same.

We were two consenting adults, neither of us in relationships. And we knew each other, it wasn't like I'd picked him up at a bar and brought some stranger home with me.

"A few drinks, I'm not even close to drunk," I argued. Was I begging? Probably. Did I care? Not really. "I'll take a sobriety test. Look, watch me." My finger extended to the tip of my nose, and then out to my side.

His eyes followed my finger, not impressed with my coordination. "Come on, Maya. You know those tests are bullshit. Which is why a drinking related charge needs substantiation with a blood test."

"Ugh, this isn't a trial. And I'm telling you I'm good." I didn't get what the problem was? Was he worried I'd later accuse him of taking advantage of me? There was a better chance that I'd call my landlord and ask *her* to make out than I'd ever do that.

He raked his hair in frustration. "No. Not now."

"Wait, this isn't like some weird bet with yourself just to see if you could, right?" I waited for his answer, mentally calculating the distance between us and the kitchen.

While I *probably*—most likely, but wasn't one hundred percent sure—wouldn't castrate him with that fancy serrated bread knife I'd recently bought, the thought had crossed my mind. Because kissing me, and working me up into a frenzy for the sole reason to prove that he could have me if he wanted, was not something I would easily forgive.

He cursed under his breath, shaking his head as he took a long, heavy breath and then blew it out. "This isn't some bet. With myself or anyone else. I should go, I'll see you on Monday."

If his annoyance was sexual frustration, then he only had himself to blame. After all, he still hadn't given me a good reason why we weren't getting naked, other than it wasn't going to happen.

"Monday?" I asked, both confused and disappointed that I wouldn't see him on the weekend.

"Yeah, when I drive you to work."

Work.

And no doubt the return to driving, talking and eating like we had the entire week before.

He was trying to reinstate the old terms.

"Don't go." I grabbed his hand, grasping—both physically and emotionally—for just a little bit more. "Stay."

He stood there a beat, his eyes rolling up my body before he moved closer and took my chin in his hands. I was still holding out hope he'd have a change of heart.

"My sweet Maya." He lowered his head, brushing his lips gently across mine. "So eager to do bad things?"

"Yes." My voice was hoarse, not even trying to hide it.

He closed his eyes, the gentle brush of his mouth turning into a slow kiss. "You're not making this easy for me."

"Good, if I have to suffer then so should you." I caught his bottom lip with my teeth, pulling gently before stepping away. I didn't usually have a mean streak, but if I was going to be horny and unsatisfied, then I wanted to make sure he was too. Maybe more so, because he was the reason for it in the first place.

He chuckled, not as annoyed as I would have liked. "Rest assured, there will be plenty of suffering. Night, Maya. I'll see you next week."

And with a quick kiss on the cheek, he walked out the door. My head followed, craning out of my doorway as I watched him disappear down the stairs until he was gone completely from view.

Alone.

The emptiness in my apartment only a fraction of what I felt inside of myself, the realization of what had happened hitting me with full force.

I'd kissed Alex Larsson, told him I wanted him, and gotten rejected.

No reason and no explanation, except that he thought I didn't want it.

But I had.

I'd wanted all of it, and all of him, and he must have wanted me too.

Those kisses weren't imagined, the touches—real, and his words, "*I want to fuck you, Maya*," they couldn't have been any clearer. It wasn't one sided.

Why?

None of it made sense.

But one thing was for sure, I would never do that again.

I'd already begged, so if there ever was a next time, it would be him.

CHAPTER #12

I WOKE UP feeling like shit.

Not because I was hung over, because for all of Alex's concerns, I hadn't even been close to drunk. Buzzed a little, with lowered inhibitions—sure. But I knew what I'd been doing and I remembered everything.

No, the seedy feeling that made my head pound had nothing to do with the draft beer and everything to do with the sleep I didn't get. Instead of closing my eyes, I tossed and turned like salad, unable to get any sleep.

I tried the usual things.

Warm shower.

Cold shower.

Reading.

But nothing quelled the feelings of emptiness and loneliness I felt, my body aching in parts that both confused *and* worried me.

Firstly, I was still horny.

Utterly ridiculous considering sex should be the last thing I wanted. But I could take all that common sense and toss it out the window with my sanity, because as much as I hated it, I still wanted him.

God, when I thought about him, my skin instantly heated. It didn't matter that he stopped and it may never happen again—my body didn't care.

I even tried to take care of it myself, but all I got was an empty orgasm and a tired hand. Nope, my body wouldn't be fooled, and closing my eyes and pretending Alex was the one touching me wasn't going to cut it.

I needed the real thing.

Hell, we wouldn't even have to have sex. I'd settle for his lips and his hands, and the sweet delicious press of his—

Ugh.

I was disgusted with myself.

Shaking my metaphorical fist. I had better self-esteem than that, and certainly more self-respect. So the only reason I could be feeling that way was clearly a temporary psychosis brought on by sexual deficiency.

So I wanted sex, it had been a while. I'd dated some guys in college but I didn't binge cock. I needed a connection; wanting there to be some *thing*—even if it was fleeting—before I let a man inside of me. And when I decided I was moving back to California, getting involved in a relationship seemed stupid. It had to have been seven months, maybe even eight—the fact I couldn't remember was telling.

It was the sex I was desperate for.

Not him.

But every time I did manage to doze off, my mind flipped me off. The darkness took me right back to there, where our bodies moved against each other, reliving every sweet inch of him, and that freaking kiss.

That *kiss*.

I could make myself come a million times and it wouldn't be enough.

When it became clear that my window for sleep had expired, I hauled myself out of bed. There wasn't a reason to get up—I had no place to be—but lying in bed was depressing the hell out of me.

I dropped into the family group chat, sending a selfie as proof of life and assuring them I was fine. I didn't expect anyone to be awake, but it made me feel less alone.

Mom—You're up early. What's wrong?

Maya—Nothing, just decided to get up and start my day. Think I might go for a jog.

Vanessa—Jog? You don't jog, Maya. Is this code for you're in trouble and need our help?

Maya—What are you doing up?

Vanessa—I have two children under the age of five. Who sleeps any more? So do I need to wake your brother? I can kick him really quick for you.

Mom—Oh sweetie, don't wake up Jordon, you know he's no good to anyone this early.

Vanessa—Mom, he'll still be able to read this when he wakes up. LOL

Mom—I swear this phone types its own messages, I have no idea what's going on.

Natalie—Why is everyone awake?

Mom—Maya can't sleep.

Maya—I slept. I slept plenty. Got all the sleep I needed. Which is why I'm awake. I just wanted to tell you all I loved you and that I was doing fine.

Mom—You should try tea. Tea helps me.

Maya—I'm fine. No need for tea.

Natalie—How's the hottie? I heard he's been driving you to work ;-)

Maya—Mother >:-|

Mom—Oh, look at the time. I'd love to stay and chat but I've got to go.

Maya—I should go too.

Vanessa—Don't jog.

Natalie—And email me later.

I hugged my phone, carrying it with me while I turned on my coffee machine and my computer.

Coffee had been consumed in such high quantities, my heart felt like it was shuddering in my chest. And I'd brushed my teeth at least six times before being satisfied it was minty freshness I tasted and not the memories of my *Keurig*. Nothing said pathetic than sitting in your living room at seven in the morning on a Saturday, with a resting heart rate of 120, and actually *reading* the affirmation emails your mother kept forwarding to you.

The power of positive thought, my ass.

But at least I had stopped obsessing about him, reminding myself that there was a time where I didn't think about Alex sexually and he wasn't the hottest man on earth.

If I thought it would help, I'd have called Jackie or Lisa. But talking about it wouldn't do any good. What would I even say? So I continued to sit on my sofa, staring at the ceiling, watching the minutes tick by agonizingly slow and hoping I didn't have a heart attack.

It was around nine when there was a knock at my door. I had been in a trance, lying on my couch in a black Marc Jacob's dress I wore to graduation because it made me feel pretty, contemplating whether Gregorian chants were actually still performed by Gregorian monks.

I didn't even bother asking who it was, rolling off the couch and ambling to the door, praying it wasn't Prim reminding me about the tenant in 4F who had *allegedly* jizzed in the pool.

She wanted me to handle the case.

I vowed never to go for a swim.

"Oh God." I clutched my chest, unprepared for the onslaught of an impeccably dressed Alex on the other side of the doorframe.

He was in his weekend clothes—jeans and casual Tee.

My thanks to a higher power weren't only because I didn't have to hear about my perverted neighbor and his semen. It was also because by some miracle I'd managed to remain upright and breathing.

How did he get *better* looking? His mussed up blond hair rebelled against the soft cotton of his T-shirt. His crystal clear eyes hinted at the trouble that played on his lips. All of him perfectly curated imperfection that made me want to devour him one painfully slow lick at a time.

"Expecting someone?" He raised that infamous eyebrow in question, looking down at my dress.

Even his eyebrow was sexy, the single part of his face worthy of its own fan club and possibly a parade.

Okay, so questioning my sanity was a little redundant, as was my hope that I stop thinking of him sexually.

No point arguing with human nature.

Deciding to use his surprise to my advantage, I grabbed his arms and pulled him in for hug. Oh, I hadn't forgotten I'd laid myself before him like a plate of naked sushi and he'd decided he was no longer hungry. That shit was still very much on my mind as I curled my arms around him and took a lungful of his gorgeous heady scent. So clean, and fresh, like waterfalls and pine-covered forests.

I hated that he smelled so good.

"No, I was just glad I wasn't having a heart attack."

Okay, I needed to lay off the coffee.

Alex unwound me from his torso and pulled back to look at me.

"Was there a danger of it happening? Or have I missed something?"

Oh he'd missed plenty, mainly the hours I'd spent sleepless wishing he'd touch me. But like my OD of caffeine, I didn't want to discuss that either. "Nope, it was just a weird night, strange dreams." I shook my head, gathering my thoughts together and wondering why the hell he'd come.

"Are you sure you're feeling okay?" The back of his hand tested my forehead, and it was a challenge not to lean into the contact. "You want to talk about last night?" He dropped his hand, satisfied my body temperature was normal. Sadly, that wasn't the part that was fevered.

"No, I don't want to talk about my dreams," I scoffed, looping my arm around his and leading him to my living room. "Just crazy, mixed up stuff—nothing worth mentioning." Because admitting to him I'd been having sexual fantasies all night wasn't happening.

Somewhere between getting into the Marc Jacob dress, putting on makeup and contemplating the Gregorian chant thing, I'd also decided something else. Last night didn't happen.

The kiss.

The rejection.

Throwing myself at him.

None of it.

Deny, deny, deny.

Despite my tugging, he didn't budge, standing still while I animatedly tried to yank him to the couch like a Great Dane who needed to sit. If I had remembered yesterday, I would have recalled I hadn't had much success in moving him against his will. But I didn't, which was why I continued to try.

He put his hands around my waist, stopping my efforts. "I wasn't talking about the dreams. I mean, *last night*."

So he wanted to talk about it, huh? It was my eyebrow's turn to rise, biting my lip as I played dumb. "Do you mean at the bar?"

His eyes narrowed, studying me closer. "No, at your apartment, after I drove you home."

"Oh, *that*." My hand waved casually followed by a chuckle. "Thanks, I probably should have offered to take an Uber. I promise buying a car is at the top of my to do list in the next few months."

He looked at me like I was insane.

But I didn't care.

I had made up my mind—plead ignorance and denial.

Partly because I was embarrassed. I'd practically begged him for sex and he'd refused. And it wasn't some random guy I'd never see again. He *knew* me, and I knew him. And as much as I tried to toughen up and get thicker skin, it still stung.

The other reason was my pride.

He'd kissed *me*.

Granted, I had plans to do the very same to him, but our first kiss—the only one we'd *ever* shared—had been initiated by him.

And then what?

He changed his mind?

Decided he didn't want to anymore and turn it around on me like he was doing me a favor?

No.

I had my own mind.

So if he wanted to pretend like it *wasn't* his rock hard dick rubbing up against my clit last night, then I was good to keep up the premise. Besides, after hours of slipping in and out of sex dreams, I'd began questioning whether it had actually happened or if it was my vivid imagination.

Seemed fair he'd do the same.

His brow furrowed, faint lines crinkled in his forehead as he opened then closed his mouth.

Speechless.

Satisfied I'd won the upper hand, I grinned and went into the kitchen. I was positive another cup of coffee was going to send me into a cardiac arrest but willing to take the risk. "Coffee?" I yelled cheerily over my shoulder, watching as he followed.

"I wasn't talking about the ride." He spun me around, his eyes stormy like New Haven in the fall, and if I didn't know any better I'd think he was going to kiss me. He didn't. "I meant *inside* your apartment."

"Oh? Something happen inside my apartment?" My hand adjusted my neckline demurely, his eyes drawn down to my cleavage.

And he thought his brothers were good actors, ha! I wouldn't be collecting any fancy statuettes on my mantle but I could definitely hold my own.

Pretending to be clueless wasn't fun for me, and not something I was in the habit of doing. But with an objective, I allowed it.

He shook his head, discounting whatever thought had presented itself and finally met my eyes.

"Everything okay?" I asked, vowing to not break before he did.

He kept his eyes on mine. "Yep." His mouth popping on the P.

"Well good." I spun around, turning my back to him as I reached for cups. "So what brings you here on a Saturday morning? Did we have plans I wasn't aware of?"

For all the lies I'd told, the truth had finally shown up.

I had no idea why he had landed on my doorstep after he'd promised me *Monday*, and I very much wanted to know. If it was a stupid sense of obligation to make sure I was "okay," then he could go fuck himself.

Of everything I wanted to be, his *obligation* wasn't it.

"Why are you wearing an evening dress? In the morning?" He ignored my questions, deciding to ask one of his own.

I spun around, rolling my eyes. "It's a cocktail dress. Some people think they are interchangeable but they really aren't."

He didn't answer mine; I didn't answer his.

"Cocktail dress then." He put his hands on me again, stilling my unnecessary movements.

I tried not to enjoy it.

I did anyway.

"Oh, this?" I looked down at the short black lace that curled around my body doing little to keep its secrets. "It's a *Yale* thing. We wear cocktail dresses to breakfast on Saturdays."

Lame.

I hoped my smile was more convincing than my words.

His eyes raked up my body. "Funny, in all the time Roman attended, I never heard him mention it. Sounds like something he'd have remembered."

"It's a secret society, like the Skull and Bones," I countered, wondering if adding something to their Wiki page was taking it a little too far.

"And yet, you told me?" His brow lifted.

Damn, that fucking sexy brow.

"Yes. But if you tell anyone I'll deny it." I jabbed a finger in his delicious chest, the vow real because there was no way I'd ever admit how crazy I was to anyone else.

He dropped his hands from my waist, folding them across his chest like he knew I was full of shit. Just daring me to continue. "So breakfast in cocktail dresses? You go alone?"

"Oh no, there's a group. We eat pastries, and on the first Saturday of the month we wear white gloves and pillbox hats."

Never surrender.

He didn't have a chance if he thought I was going to let it go.

"Well, then let's go to breakfast." He tipped his head to the door.

Shit.

While I was happy to continue the charade in my apartment, taking it public brought a whole new set of challenges. Plus, I had more lying on my couch to do, contemplating random shit that didn't matter. I couldn't possibly go out with him.

"We can't." I raised my chin defiantly. "You're *not* a member."

He leaned in closer, smelling better than was acceptable, and smirked. "Who's going to know? Do they have secret lookouts that report back illegal breakfast activities?"

Checkmate.

"Fine, let me get my shoes."

I stormed off into my bedroom and slid on a pair of black patent leather pumps. My feet were going to curse me in about an hour.

My light brown curls were swept up into a messy bun while I smoothed on a fresh coat of red lipstick. Freshening up my makeup was overkill, but I had already committed to the sham and didn't want anyone mistaking my odd breakfast ensemble as walk of shame kind of material.

When I came out my bedroom, he was waiting by the door. I didn't bother talking, grabbing my keys, handbag and phone and locking up after us as we both left.

With a confidence that was completely manufactured, I proceeded down the steps, my heels clanging noisily on the metal as I walked.

I might have finished the descent, but Alex wasn't far behind, his long strides reaching the bottom about a second after me.

His car was parked up front as usual, his ability to conjure up vacant spots still working as I stopped in front of his BMW. Given the choice I'd have preferred to have climbed inside. But the fob and all its power to unlock doors was safely inside Alex's hand, forcing me to wait until he came up behind me.

"You said we needed to eat pastries, right?"

He was so close, his body taunting me as it hovered inches away from mine.

I smiled sweetly, determined to see this through until the end. "Yep."

The lights flashed, the locks popping open and I said a small prayer of thanks. He opened the door, watching me fold myself inside while I tried to stop my hemline riding up.

I didn't try too hard.

His eyes flared, but he said nothing, walking around to the driver's side and getting in. He didn't wait, hitting the ignition as he latched his seatbelt, and then pulled out onto the road.

He didn't tell me where we were going, and I didn't ask.

Faced with the real probability there'd be questions during the drive, I instead launched into a barrage of small talk. I chatted about work, my new work friends and my crazy landlord—filling the time with a whole bunch of nothing. Then when I'd exhausted those topics, I talked about my family and his and how awesome everyone was doing. And when we still hadn't reached our mystery destination I launched into a detailed description about the kind of car I was planning on buying. Mentioning while I loved the idea of investing in something more environmental, I was probably going to have to go with a planet-destroying, gasoline guzzling machine instead. Nothing fancy, maybe a Toyota but I'd seen a Mazda that looked kind of cute too.

Not a word from Alex; letting me go on with my unending dialogue while he drove in silence, casually looking over at me while I tried not to pass out.

When we'd finally arrived in Marina del Rey, I was out of breath, my throat was raspy and I was breathing a sigh of relief that I could stop talking before my voice totally gave out.

Yachts bobbed on the waters, the sea catching the morning sun and making their hulls twinkle.

It was beautiful.

We opened our doors at the same time, getting out of the

car and stepping out onto the gravel parking lot. The loose stones were going to be a pain in the ass to navigate in my shoes, but I soldiered on as Alex took my hand and led us to a small café that was close to the water.

A hostess showed us to a table, handing us some menus and promising to be back while we shuffled into our chairs. Alex's eyes stayed on me as I glanced down at the offerings of breakfast food.

"Why are you looking at the menu?" he asked curiously. "Doesn't secret society cocktail dress law dictate we eat pastries?"

My smile peeked out from behind my menu. "Of course, it has to be pastries."

When a server arrived we ordered croissants and juice, and then stared out into the harbor until our food and drinks arrived. Thankfully it didn't take long, saving me from needing to make more small talk.

I pretended to be Audrey Hepburn as I took a bite out of my croissant, feeling strangely powerful as I sat there overdressed.

"Any weird ritual we need to perform? Or do we sit here in silence until we're done?" Alex took a leisurely sip on his juice.

"You already know too much." I threw him a dismissive wave. "I've broken the code and can't possibly disclose anymore."

"Maya?" He reached across the table, gently touching my arm. He wasn't playing anymore, his gaze softening so much it made my heart hurt. "You *sure* you don't remember last night?"

"You drove me home and I went to bed, what's there to remember?"

The game was no longer fun, and I wanted to go home.

CHAPTER #13

LEAH THORNE CALLED as we were walking back to the car and asked if I could go into work. She apologized, assuring me that weekend work wasn't the usual but she really needed the help.

I couldn't say no.

Not only did I need to prove myself at work, but I could also use the distraction. The added bonus of giving me an out with Alex made it even more attractive.

Even though I insisted he didn't need to, he drove me home and waited while I got changed. We didn't say much, letting the music from the stereo fill the silence as he drove me to work.

"You don't have to drive me home, you've already done so much for me," I offered, reaching for the door handle when we arrived.

He caught my arm, keeping me in the car. "I want to, besides I owe you a celebratory dinner to mark your first week."

"What do you mean, we had dinner last night." Pretty sure watching him licking sticky BBQ sauce off his fingers was what started the whole degradation of the evening.

He shook his head. "Mike paid, doesn't count. Just us tonight and *no* drinking."

Yeah, because that *had been the problem.*

I fought the urge to roll my eyes as my skin bristled with annoyance.

Not at him, but at myself.

Because as much as the situation was getting to be ridiculous, I couldn't make myself say no.

Even though I *needed* to say no.

"Look, I don't know what time I'm wrapping up. How about I just call you later?" It was as close to a no as I was going to get, but I was pleased I'd said it.

"Sure, whatever you want."

His grip loosened and I stepped out, waving goodbye as I strode toward the door.

"Maya." Leah had been waiting for me. She was sitting cross-legged at the table with some papers in front of here. "I've called Mike and Stefan in too, but I'd like a word before you get started."

My stomach twisted into a knot as I kept my strides even, and suddenly Alex Larsson wasn't my biggest problem. I'd heard those exact words so many times, I was almost positive I knew what would follow them.

Glenn Zaveri.

Proceeded by his rap sheet, his outstanding warrants, and a case study that would make an excellent teaching aid for any budding attorney. I should know, I poured over every single document I could get my hands on until I thought my eyes would bleed out.

The partners of the firm had all known my history, so had the Bar, the ethics board and probably everyone in the law profession in the greater Los Angeles area over the age of forty. It had been big news. And when I took the job I was assured the only legacy I'd have to live up to would be my own. Other firms hadn't been so generous. But no matter how you presented it, shit *always* ran down hill, and other people—who thankfully didn't sign my paycheck—might have something to say about it too.

"Of course." I gave her my rehearsed smile, dropping my bag on the table and sitting opposite her. "What can I do for you?"

It seemed a game I was playing a lot lately, trying to guess what someone wanted from me and not giving them any information until I was sure. It wasn't something I enjoyed, even if it had become necessary.

She tapped her neatly manicured finger on the papers. "It's about this file. The Clayton merger."

I didn't have time to temper my expression; genuinely surprised the conversation had nothing to do with my father.

"Is there something wrong?" she asked, seeing what I knew I hadn't been able to hide. "You looked like you were expecting me to say something else."

"I just." I took a breath, composing myself. "I had only put that file together yesterday and I wasn't done. I didn't even think you'd had time to look at it."

Leah opened the folder, flicking through the notes I entered and supporting documents. "Well I did, and it was really impressive. You seem to have a good eye for detail. Think you can wrap it up in a few hours? I have an meeting with opposing counsel first thing on Monday, they want to finalize ASAP."

"I'll have it to you in two," I responded, my stomach twisting again but this time for a different reason.

"That's what I like to hear." She stood, straightening her skirt. "Actually, you want to sit in on the meeting? Might be helpful to have you take an extra set of notes. Plus, I find I work better with an audience." Her lips spread into an unapologetic smile.

I rose to my feet, torn between wanting to shake her hand and give her a hug. "Thank you so much, it would truly be an honor."

"No problem. Just get the papers to me on time, okay?" Her eyes darted to the door, Mike and Stefan wandering in with a tray of coffee. "Gentlemen, great work yesterday. Keep it up." She walked past them on her way out.

"I thought we got rewarded for good behavior not punished." Stefan held out a coffee before smirking. "And what did you do to get sent to the principal's office so soon? Geez, Maya, it's only been a week."

I took the paper cup even though drinking it was probably not a good idea. "I'm going to sit in on a meeting for the Clayton merger on Monday."

"Oh really?" Stefan looked impressed. "Don't forget the little people when you're up there sitting with the grown ups."

"And don't break up the band," Mike warned, taking his coffee and moving to his chair.

I rolled my eyes, taking a sip of my latte against my better judgment. "Please, it's *one* meeting. I think I'm a long way from *breaking up the band*."

"You're on record." Mike scribbled down something on a piece of paper before turning his attention back to his work.

Stefan didn't have the same urgency, lowering himself down to his seat, his grin hiding behind his takeaway cup.

"What?" I asked, knowing he couldn't be more obvious if he tried. He had something to say, and the sooner I heard it, the sooner we could all get back to work.

"So Alex Larsson." He played with his cup, lowering it to the table.

I swallowed hard, almost choking on the stupid coffee I shouldn't have been drinking in the first place.

"We're friends, I told you last night." I tried to sound casual, wondering if it was written all over my face that I wanted it to be more.

Mike shook his head, obviously knowing what Stefan was going to say. "Dude, seriously, you just met the guy."

"Pipe down, nerd boy. I'm trying to work here." Stefan leveled Mike with a look before returning to me. "As I was saying, you and Alex are friends. Which means you will probably hang out again, right?"

"Yeah, that's usually how friendships work." I was still no closer to knowing what he was getting at.

He nodded, agreeing with me. "And possibly with some of his friends? Considering he came out with us, it would be logical you'd reciprocate."

Oh my God, was everyone in my life trying to make me feel like I was in a murder mystery? I'd had way too much caffeine, not enough sleep, had been through about fifty emotions already.

"Stefan, seriously. I haven't got time to go through the extrapolations. What is it that you want?"

"Alex knows Astrid. You know, the model who is so cool she only has a first name? Well, *your* buddy is *her* buddy. Not sure if they're dating—I didn't have enough time to do any real digging—but they've attended a couple of events together and I want an introduction. Even if they are dating, if I don't get to at least meet her, I'd never forgive myself." He anchored his hands behind his neck, looking off into space with a stupid grin on his face. It was how I imagined most men looked when in her presence.

"You looked him up?" I was horrified, the invasion into Alex's privacy not something I'd expected from Stefan. Not that I knew him all that well, but still.

"No, I *didn't* look him up." It was his turn to look offended. "She called him while you were in the bathroom and asked him if he'd go to some bullshit dinner with her. It wasn't like he was hiding it; he spoke to her right there at the table. After he was done he told us who she was, and that he helps her out from time to time. Now her, I definitely looked up." The mention of Astrid subsided his irritation.

Shit, she'd called him? Last night? I'd left his side for like ten minutes and in that time she'd gotten her meaty hooks in? Was she stalking him? No wonder he hadn't wanted to sleep with me, it all made perfect sense. He'd even gone through with the stupid charade, pretending to be honorable and not wanting to make a move on me while impaired. Ha! All he was doing was saving himself from looking bad if he slept with me and then went and did whatever he was going to do with her. He might have said they were friends but she seemed to believe different.

"Did he say yes?" I sucked in a breath, holding it as I waited for Stefan to answer.

He shrugged, shaking his head. "About what?"

My hands curled into fists, welded to my sides so I didn't reach across and beat out every piece of information he knew. "The dinner or whatever it was she asked him to?"

"Ah, that. Yeah, said he'd get back to her which is why I'm not sure if they're dating." He sighed. "A man has a woman like that, and there's no way he'd say no."

Yeah, I bet.

Wow, my morning had been one poor choice after another.

Guess there was no real reason to stop.

"Not making any promises, but I'll speak to Alex and see what I can do." If for no other reason than I wanted to know what the hell was going on too.

"Maya, you are a fucking rock star." Stefan's grin beamed on his face.

"Yeah, I'm freaking awesome."

Funny how I didn't feel it.

CHAPTER #14

AGAINST MY BETTER judgment—pretty sure it hadn't been good for a while—I called Alex and asked him to meet me. It was dumb, my mediocre show of keeping my distance from him earlier looking pathetic when I called him a few hours later.

Not that it mattered what anyone thought; I had a mission which apparently had me moonlighting as a matchmaker. From what Stefan said, Astrid had been using Alex as arm candy, inviting him along to events to help her look good. While she wouldn't have been the first woman to do that, I wondered how much of an "escort" she wanted.

Alex seemed surprised by my call—*yeah, you and me both, buddy*—telling me he'd be about twenty minutes. And the minute I ended the call, I started to have second thoughts.

There were so many things left unresolved between us, I wasn't sure if it was smarter to just get my own ride home. I still had the bus schedule in my purse and I'm sure Mike or Stefan would give me a ride if I asked. But running would be the coward's way out, and I was anything but a coward so I was just going to have to wait.

I was sitting on a bench in the lobby when I saw his car from the windows. It had been half an hour, my nerves starting to get a little frayed as I continued to wait. Not wanting for him to sacrifice another virgin to the parking gods, I walked out without waiting for him to come inside to get me.

"Hey, sorry, the traffic on Santa Monica was insane." He tapped his watch as I climbed into the car.

"Alex, it's only been ten minutes. I barely even noticed," I lied, the time ticking by so slowly it had felt like ten hours.

"Even so, I'm sorry." He put his hand on his heart, giving me a smile I hadn't realized I'd missed. "So what are you feeling? Any preference for dinner?"

Spending my evening trying to have a conversation in a busy restaurant wasn't going to work. I didn't want to have to yell over noise or fight for his attention with the wait staff.

No, we had a lot to discuss and we needed to go somewhere where we wouldn't be interrupted. And while his place was nicer, I needed whatever advantage I could get.

"Do you think we could just get something at my place and just hang out? I'm don't really feel like going out."

I didn't think how it might sound, until it had already left my mouth.

The fiend, wanting to take her prey home so she could maul him without an audience. Thank God, I was still playing ignorant to the kiss and everything that came after.

"Of course," he agreed, not questioning my intentions. "We'll pick something up on the way."

He waited, looking over to see if I had anything to add, his hand casually resting on the steering wheel.

"Sounds good." I folded my hands in my lap. "So how was your day?"

"I went and hung out with Nick," he responded, surprising me with his answer.

I'd half expected him to go see Astrid, and I hated how

irrationally glad I was he hadn't. Yes, yes—he said they were friends, but he'd said we were friends too and he kissed me last night. To say my mind was scrambled was an understatement.

"How is he?" I asked, trying to be polite.

"Yeah, good." All he was giving me.

We opted for burgers and fries, cruising through the drive thru around the corner from my apartment. His *no alcohol* stance from earlier made easier by the lack of alcoholic options on the menu. Two chocolate shakes it was, not bothering to remind him that I had his stolen bottle of Napa wine as he grinned at me smugly when he collected our order from the window.

He parked the car, and we got out, climbing the stairs up to my apartment with the food in my hand while he carried the drinks. To an outside observer we might look like a couple, coming home with takeaway, ready for a relaxing night in.

It was funny how that fantasy excited me, needing to remind myself that it wasn't what was happening.

When I got to my front door I could sense his gaze intensifying. Like he was looking to see if my key in the lock would spark the memory of what had happened the night before.

It did, the temptation to toss the food and the drinks aside and kiss him the minute we walked in so overwhelming I was positive I needed therapy. But not only did I not kiss him, I kept all those emotions locked in the vault.

He kicked the door closed behind us with a loud thud, his eyes following me like laser beams as I walked into the living room and put the food on the coffee table. We settled on the couch and I started my cross-examination.

"Hey, so Stefan was wondering if you could do a favor for him." I peeled back the wrapping on the burger, taking a small nibble from the bun. "I told him I'd ask but don't feel obligated or anything."

He mirrored me, stripping his burger of its paper shell but waiting to take a bite. "What's the favor?"

I chewed thoughtfully, making sure I maintained eye contact. "He wanted you to introduce him to Astrid. Maybe you can mention it when you see her for that dinner or whatever?"

It had been delivered casually, tossed at him like a bouquet at a wedding and I was just waiting for him to catch it.

"Sure, I can do that. I'm sure she'll enjoy the attention." He shrugged, taking a lazy sip of his chocolate shake.

"Ah-ha! So that was why you wouldn't sleep with me." I dropped the burger back onto the coffee table, pointing at him with accusation. "All your talk about me being drunk, when really the truth had nothing to do with me."

Playing it cool had gone out the window, along with the reasons why I shouldn't confront him. I might regret it later, but at that moment, I wanted to know why.

His eyebrow rose, taking a bite from his burger chewing thoughtfully before he responded. "I thought you didn't remember."

No pointing, no raised voice—complete lack of surprise, like he knew all along.

I bet he was fantastic at Poker, bluffing his way to winning the pot when all he had was a pair of deuces.

"I was mad," I fired back, the emotion making a come back. "I threw myself at you, and—"

"And I'm not going to be your drunken mistake." He cut me off, his eyes simmering.

"I *wasn't* drunk." My fingernails bit into my palms as I balled them into fists. Violence was never a solution. At least that was what I told myself as I fought the urge to lash out. "And I sure as hell don't need anyone else saving me from my mistakes. If I fuck up, I'll own it. I'm a big girl. What I won't have is you, or anyone else, telling me what I can or can't do."

I was a warrior princess on a hill, sword drawn, and ready to go to battle.

Power surged inside of me as my back straightened and I dared him to say it again.

He didn't.

It seemed he thought the *dare* was something else, reaching out for me, pulling me towards him in a heated rush as he put his mouth on mine. Our lips crashed as I wasted no time in kissing him back.

The conversation wasn't over, we'd just moved to an alternate method of arguing.

"Fuck," he moaned against my mouth, his hands moving to my ass as I shifted into his lap.

There was no resistance from me, my brain forgetting the argument entirely and my body grinding against him as our tongues and lips tangled. Kissing him, biting him—wanting more than what he was giving me as I rocked my hips. Feeling him already hard made me even more turned on.

"I want you. Jesus Christ, I want you." His mouth moved to my neck, sucking and biting as his hands explored my body. Desperately touching every inch as his lips stayed on my skin.

It wasn't only his hands on an explorative mission; mine had decided to do the same, my fingers rippling over his muscular arms and chest in a blind frenzy. "How did you have time for college? It feels like all you did was work out."

"I can multitask, something you're about to find out."

Unsure exactly how it was achieved, he lifted me—and himself—from sitting on the couch to a stand. My legs wrapped around him, my arms anchoring around his neck as his hands cradled my ass.

He didn't stop kissing, fevered and desperate, possessing my mouth like he needed it to be his.

I closed my eyes, absorbing it all and felt us moving. He was carrying me, kissing me, his impressive hard-on pressing against me, until suddenly we were in my room.

He wasn't kidding when he said he could multitask.

We went horizontal, both of us crashing onto the surface of my bed.

"You better not stop," I warned, pulling him down onto me. "We don't have to have sex if you don't want to, but you better not stop kissing me."

He lifted my knee, slipping into the space between my legs and ground his cock against my core. "Oh, I'm not stopping." The pressure against me was making me wet. "And it is going to be a hell of a lot more than just kissing."

My clothes were burning against my skin as I pulled at his T-shirt. "Get it off," I begged, needing less barriers between us.

His weight lifted, his hands moving from my body to his own as he tore the shirt off his body in one sexy maneuver.

Boom.

I had to physically stop, remove my lips from his neck and take a minute to appreciate it—his body was a work of art.

My fingers moved over the ridges, snaking up his torso to his solid pecs and strong shoulders. I explored with wonder, my hands sliding down his corded arms and then back up again, committing each muscle to memory as they returned to his chest.

"You happy with just the shirt? Or you want me to take something else off?" A sly grin hooked at his mouth, watching me as I ogled him.

He was no longer my childhood friend, that memory had been tucked away for safe keeping so it wasn't polluted by my dirty and very un-friend like thoughts.

"Take *everything* off." My fingers slithered down to the zipper of his jeans, tracing the shape of his hard length under it.

There was no going back.

He hissed as I squeezed him, rotating his hips underneath my hand as he tilted his head back. He gave us both a minute to enjoy it and then pulled my hands off.

Hands shouldn't be erotic, but as his got busy taking off his jeans I was mesmerized by the flex of each tendon. Strong and capable, they tossed his pants to the floor as he toed off his shoes and then lost his socks.

A pair of short black cotton trunks strained to keep his cock contained, his thumbs hooked into the waistband and hesitating for only a second until they were gone too.

My eyes flashed greedily at his skin, devouring each inch as I licked my lips. It wasn't just his torso that had been perfect, the rest of his huge toned frame was a mastery of human evolution.

Oh.

My.

God.

I was going to pass out.

My body was too warm, my skin itching underneath my clothes as my core throbbed. My nipples peaked, hardening against my bra as I sucked in a breath. I was dying for hands to touch me, preferably his, and right the hell now.

"Your turn." His voice rumbled as he brought all that beautiful perfection closer, his fingers moving to the front of my blouse and unbuttoned.

He wasn't going fast enough.

My hands competed with his as I yanked at my top and pulled it off over my head. Next was my skirt, the zipper ripped down as I shuffled it past my hips. I couldn't get it any further, the material bunched up under my thighs as my back arched. His attention had been diverted from undressing me, his hands palming one breast while he sucked the nipple of the other one through the lace of my bra.

"I need to taste you," he groaned, sliding the cup off the swell of my breast and returning his mouth. His tongue swirled around the peak, teething it gently before sucking it hard.

"More," I begged, lifting my butt and working my way out of my skirt.

My panties and bra would have to find their own way off, my hands no longer capable of resisting touching him.

Heels fell to the floor as I kicked them off, our bodies writhing together as my fingers wrapped around his shaft and stroked. "Maya." He breathed out my name, tearing at my bra until the metal clasp at the back gave way.

Tossed to the floor with everything else, he licked my breasts and sucked my skin while his fingers glided down my stomach, stopping when he reached the top of my cleft.

I didn't know what he was thinking, but if he was having second thoughts he wasn't showing it. Like I had stashed our history, so had he, touching me in a way he never had.

Pulling my panties aside, his fingers touched my core. I breathed out, the air hissing from my lips as he continued to explore, coating himself in my wetness while he circled my clit.

"You want me to fuck you, Maya?" He nipped at my chin, his hips pumping into my grasp. I wasn't sure if I was still jerking him off or he was fucking my hand but it was hot, my fingers doing their best to stretch around his girth and stay tight.

"Yes. It's what I want." My mouth found his, kissing him as he plunged two fingers inside of me.

"Ah, fuck," he cursed, moving his fingers in and out of me, my core tightening around him. "You feel so fucking good."

The mood changed, the lines of his face hardening as he slid his fingers out and pulled down my underwear, removing the last barrier between us. We'd crossed the line, the point of no return and I was sure he felt it too.

He unwrapped my fingers from his cock, and took it into his own hand, giving it a stroke. His eyes stayed on me, watching as I followed the glide of his fingers up and down and then squeezed at the base.

"There is so much I want to do to you." His voice raw as his gaze heated. "But right now I *need* to be inside of you, Maya."

He was in luck, because that was exactly what I needed too.

My moaned "yes" enough.

He leaned down to his pants on the floor and pulled out a condom, with the speed and precision of a bomb technician. Each movement practiced, efficient—tearing open the pack, rolling it down his hard length and settling back between my thighs.

He didn't waste time, kissing my lips as he rubbed the head against my opening, circling it twice before pushing in one fluid motion. I gasped, my mouth spreading across his as I arched into him, absorbing the fullness as I pulsed around him.

"So good." He growled, holding his hips still against mine. "You feel like fucking heaven."

"More, Alex." My body bucked underneath him. "I want more."

The first slide in and out was slow, and measured, my eyelashes fluttering at the sweet bite of pain as I stretched around him. But slow didn't last, his next thrust faster and deeper, my body taking every inch he gave me.

"I'll give you more." His hand hooked under my knee, using the position for more leverage. "So much you won't be able to walk for a week."

His hips rocked into me, delivering on his promise with each hard and fast thrust, our mouths alternating between kissing and biting.

I couldn't speak, reduced to mumbled gasps as he drove into

me, knowing exactly what to do to drive me crazy.

"I feel you wanting to come." His voice rough as his fingers slid between us and circled my clit. "Feel your pussy squeezing against my dick, wanting the release."

"Not yet." My fingers dug into his back, my body teetering at the cusp and desperate to hold on. "I don't want it to end."

"Let go, Maya." His teeth grazed against my shoulder. "I plan on making you come so many times, you'll be begging me to stop."

My body exploded, resisting my effort to prolong the feeling as I came hard around him. I shivered; a sheen of sweat covering my skin while my muscles twitched like defective Christmas lights.

He didn't stop, keeping up his tempo as my body pulsed. "Yes, baby. Just like that. Come for me."

Waves rippled through me as he shuffled to his knees and raised both my legs, anchoring them on his shoulders. "Heaven." He thrust, the sensation starting to build again. "Being inside of you is fucking heaven."

There was no time to think about what was happening, my brain checked out as every single cell of my body vibrated with him.

It had never happened before, the idea of coming twice nothing more than an elusive fairytale that women whispered about to each other over cocktails as they giggled. But I hadn't believed its existence.

"Oh my God," I yelled, overcome by the sensations, the crest taking me by surprise as I looked into his eyes. "Alex."

His name was both the question and the answer as my body found what it was looking for, splintering into a million tiny pieces.

"Maya." My name a benediction, as he followed me over the edge, pumping into me as he came too.

Breaths came out in hard, labored pants as my eyes widened. He was holding me in place, buried inside of me as the last little pulses ended.

"You okay?" he asked, his fingers feathering on the top of my legs as he lowered them onto the bed. "I know I promised you wouldn't be able to walk, but I was hoping it might take a few more times." His mouth hooking into a grin as he slowly pulled out of me.

"Fine. I'm fine. I could sprint two miles easy." I lied, my legs feeling like jelly as I shuffled onto the bed. I hadn't thought about the "after" and was hoping it wasn't going to be weird.

He leaned down, kissing me slowly. "Good. Give me a minute, I'll be right back."

The mattress moved as he lifted, shifting off the bed and striding to the connecting bathroom. It was still early evening, the light in the room bright enough I could see everything, which is exactly what I did.

Of course I'd seen his body when he'd stripped off his clothes, and it had been pretty spectacular. But I hadn't been able to appreciate all its wonder until my eyes followed him out of the room. Like wolfing down a meal when starving, I had gorged on him and not tasted how incredible my feast had been.

Stunning, every inch of him so devastatingly beautiful it almost hurt to look. I did of course, taking the risk of damaging my corneas when he returned with the condom removed and his glorious cock hanging half hard.

God, I hoped he was serious about doing it again.

"Something you want to say, Maya?" He stood at the edge of the bed giving me the opportunity to let my eyes linger.

He was so generous.

I shook my head, keeping my eyes right where they wanted to be. On him. "No, I just like looking at you."

"Well good, I like looking at you." He folded his arms across his chest causing his muscles to flex. "Now, are we going to talk about what happened, or are you going to let me make you come again? Since you don't like being told what to do, I'll let you make the choice."

So.

Fucking.

Generous.

My arms stretched out either side of me, offering myself to him like a gift. "Make me come."

"Good choice. We'll talk later."

CHAPTER #15

FORGET NOT BEING able to walk for a week, a month was likely more reasonable.

My body lay tired and languid, crumbled onto its side and sprawled on Alex's chest. He was asleep, the low whistle that blew past his lips as reassuring as the steady strong beat of his heart.

We'd had sex three times, only stopping because we'd run out of condoms. He'd had three tucked away in his pocket—the idea making me irrationally jealous, especially considering I'd been the beneficiary—while my recent sexual hiatus had meant I'd had none.

That would change though. The idea of me sliding out of bed, finding a convenience store and buying their entire supply, a consideration I was giving some serious thought.

He stirred, his hand brushing against my ass and then squeezing when he registered the contact. He'd done that a lot through the night, keeping his hands on me, even while he slept.

In my head, it was going to be no big deal.

I wanted him, he'd wanted me, and we'd had sex.

But we'd also reconnected in a way I hadn't expected, the friendship we'd rebuilt in a short week something I'd mourn with regret if I ever lost it. There were going to be repercussions, whether

I wanted to admit them or not.

We'd also run out of condoms, which meant that when he did eventually wake up we couldn't have sex. So the conversation I had been so diligently ignoring would probably happen sooner than later.

Unless I gave him a blowjob, that would distract him a little longer.

"What are you thinking about?" His voice rumbled as his fingers traced the length of my spine.

He was awake.

I turned in his arms, lifting my head to look at him and answered honestly. "About giving you a blowjob."

Hey, I said I was being honest, and it *had* been my last thought.

"Mmm, I like the sound of that. Except that I'm not sure I'm comfortable with the look of concern on your face when you're thinking about my dick in your mouth. Something I should be worried about?" Our eyes crashed, the ice blue of his melting against my green, thawing me from the inside with nothing more than a look.

I couldn't lie to him.

I wouldn't.

"I hate we have to talk about what we did, but I also can't make myself regret it." I rolled onto my stomach, forcing myself up onto my elbows. There was enough light in the room from the rising sun sneaking glimpses from between the curtains and I wanted to see him.

His fingers brushed the hair out of my eyes. "Good, because honestly, you regretting it is the only thing I was worried about."

It was the right thing to say but still didn't magically take away all my concerns either. And I was still unsure where we stood in all of it, and if he'd been considering seeing someone else.

I didn't care he didn't call it dating, I didn't want to share.

"Then why—"

"Why did I leave you on Friday night?" He stopped me, not giving me a chance to ask the millions of questions that were coming. "Because I needed you to be sure. Yes, you assured me that you knew what you were doing, and I wasn't trying to be an asshole and tell you what to do. But I needed to protect us. The first time I'd lost you, it hadn't been either of our faults. I wasn't going to chance losing you again because I couldn't stop thinking about sleeping with you."

"Wait a minute, how long exactly have you been thinking about sleeping with me?"

I mean, *I* had become a bag of raging hormones the minute he'd opened the door the first time at his place. Not even going to pretend I didn't want to climb him like a tree and cling to him like a baby koala. But I hadn't expected it to be the same for him, secretly hoping the dress that made my boobs look good was at least partially responsible.

"A while." His only answer, avoiding a more precise timeline. "But I would have kept my dick in my pants." He grinned.

My fingers wandered underneath the covers and found that he was hard. "Such a wonderful dick too, it would have been a shame if I hadn't seen it."

He laughed, the aforementioned *dick* jerking in my hand. "You and him seem to be on the same page. It took everything I had to leave you that night. And I had every intention of waiting until Monday to see you, made it until six a.m. before I realized that wasn't going to work." His eyes were clouded with regret.

I'd have assumed it would have made me glad to know he'd suffered like I had, but knowing the truth didn't make me feel better.

"Is that why you came back?" I asked, the mystery of his Saturday morning visit still unsolved.

He groaned, reaching down and unwrapping my hand from

around his shaft. "Yeah, it was either come see you or lose my balls. I'd been *hard* all night." The word vibrated on his lips, sending a shiver down my spine.

Which meant.

Hold on.

I stopped trying to seduce him as my attention focused. "You mean to tell me that if I had just admitted I remembered the night before—"

"I'd have taken you to bed that second." He didn't hesitate.

Well, that was annoying. Finding out after the fact of the wasted opportunity. We could have been screwing hours ago and possibly replenished our condom supply.

"So you want to tell me what you were doing in a cocktail dress?" His finger traced small circles on my skin. "And don't tell me it's a fucking Yale thing, give me a little credit."

I groaned, flipping over, throwing myself back against the pillow and covering my eyes with my hands. "It's dumb, but I put the dress on because it makes me feel beautiful. And I'd been feeling so hurt and rejected, I just needed something."

It was more vulnerable than I wanted to sound, but I didn't want to lie. I'd once trusted him with my most sensitive parts, been naked with him in everything except skin. And like a pair of old jeans, I slipped right back there with him. Laying myself bare, and knowing he'd keep me safe.

"I'm sorry I made you feel like that." He pulled my hands away from my face and dropped a soft chaste kiss on my lips. "Honestly, Maya, hurting you was the last thing I wanted to do."

I could be the biggest moron of all time, setting myself up for a heartbreak I might never recover from. But I believed him.

"Soooooo." I threaded my hands through his hair, holding him close. "Are we dating now?"

He kissed me again, moving his mouth slowly against mine—no

tongue—before pulling away. "Is that what you want?"

"Yes." Dying to say it fast enough.

He grinned, rolling on top of me and caging me in with his body. I tried to ignore his erection poking me in the hip. "Good, because you said you hate being told what to do, but I wasn't giving you a choice."

I shoved his chest roughly, giving him my best pout. "And what about Astrid?"

Oh yeah, I hadn't forgotten about the saucy ice queen who was annoyingly beautiful. As a couple, the two of them would look like they made sense. Both of them tall and stunning. Unlike me who was on the outside of the gorgeous Venn diagram.

"I told you, Maya, it's not like that." He shook his head before fixing his gaze on mine. "But in the interest of full disclosure, I have slept with her. Once. Over a year ago. And occasionally I'll be her date at an industry thing if I'm free. But I promise you, I don't want her."

While I appreciated his honesty, hearing he'd slept with her didn't make me feel better. Even though it had been a year ago, and only one time. It was ridiculous to even be jealous, but I was literally a green-eyed "monster." I could only fight genetics so far.

But what was I going to do? Lock us in a fallout shelter and live on canned food for the rest of our lives? If I was going to date him—or anyone—I was going to have to trust them. Not easy when the one man who you trusted with your life proved how misguided that faith had been. Just another thing to thank my dad for.

"I know I have no right to ask, and this is serious psycho girlfriend behavior. But please stop going on *dates* with her. I'm not asking you to stop talking to her, or even not to see her. It's just those events . . . it might mean something else to her than it does to you."

Had to admit, the fallout shelter was looking pretty attractive.

"If it makes you feel better, I had no intention of going. She called, and I just wanted to get off the phone before you got back. Not because I was hiding it, but there was no way not to give you my full attention."

"Yeah, well, Stefan will probably still want to meet her." I rolled my eyes, wishing I could forget about the promise I'd made. Maybe *they* could go live in the fallout shelter.

"It will be my pleasure to introduce them. Anything else you want to talk about?" He waited, his body pressed to mine, holding me captive.

"This could get complicated." I winced, thinking of almost everything that could go wrong. There were too many interconnections. Our families, our jobs, the memories of a perfect childhood friendship—all at risk if something went wrong.

He chuckled, kissing me on the nose. "Lucky for you, I *love* complicated."

AS MUCH AS I wanted to spend the day in bed with Alex, the condom situation hadn't rectified itself. I'd tried visualizing them and putting them up on a vision board, but no boxes of Trojans landed on my doorstep.

And while I was on the pill, and both of us had a clean bill of health, we'd—uh-hum Alex—decided that we needed to go out and at the very least, get food.

Other than one or two bites of our burgers, dinner had been non-existent. After the kissing had started, I'd even forgotten we were eating, leaving whatever had been in my mouth in favor of putting Alex there instead. It was a great plan, and I was happy with it. But my stomach didn't share the same feelings of gratitude. It growled in protest, demanding attention.

So, with Alex deciding we were going to be responsible, we

got out of bed and into the shower. Sadly, there was no shower sex but I had given him that blowjob and he'd done some magical things with his hands. Being creative was actually pretty awesome.

Alex left me to get dressed, heading back to his house to get a change of clothes with the promise to return. We were going to spend the day together, our first as a shiny new couple.

Not knowing our plans, I threw on a dress and a pair of flats, keeping my makeup simple. Then giving the family group chat enough information so nobody called, I was ready to ignore my phone and give Alex my undivided attention.

He arrived back in a clean pair of jeans, a fresh T-shirt, and generous dousing of that seductive man-scent he always seemed to wear. I didn't know if it was cologne, deodorant, or the tears of unicorns, but it was magical.

"Where are we going?" I threw myself at him the minute he'd walked through the door. Now that I could touch him, I wanted to all of the time.

He caught me, scooping me up and bringing me to his lips. "Where ever you want to go. I just need to go past Roman's house to pick up something and then we can do whatever we want."

"What about breakfast?" I asked, knowing that my stomach would not be pleased food hadn't been mentioned in our current agenda.

He looked at me with a sly grin. "It's Sunday, that means breakfast burritos from Los Rancheros. We can get them on the way to Roman's."

Los Rancheros had been a Sunday ritual when we were younger. I think it was probably Jordon who'd started it, being hung over and asked to babysit while my mom and dad went to visit my great aunt Louise. She was my dad's only family, but had dementia and scared me a little, so the kids would stay home while our parents went. Of course Jordon had spent his Saturday nights out, which usually meant coming home late. So in order to keep us happy, he'd call Roman to round up the Larsson tribe and we'd all go out for breakfast. I was positive Jordon had slept with the waitress at some point, which was why he stopped taking us.

"We should pick one up for Roman for old times sake." I laughed, grabbing my keys and locking the door behind us.

We ate in the car, enjoying the food as we drove to Santa Monica. Roman and his wife Lauren had a large double story, not far from the beach. It was modern, with clean architectural lines and a neat front lawn. I was sure the grass was probably scared to grow, keeping itself at regulation length at all time.

Alex parked in front, kissing my hand as we walked up the driveway. "Not in front of your brother." I glared at him. "The last thing we need is the third degree."

He rolled his eyes, holding up his offering housed in a white paper bag. "Then why did we bring him breakfast? I assumed it was to encourage him to be nice, like positive reinforcement."

"Not now, okay," I warned, just wanting a day to keep it all to myself.

"Okay," he agreed, kissing my hand again, then gently dropping it and ringing the doorbell.

When Roman answered I had to look twice just to be sure it was him. He was still gorgeous, but his eyes looked tired, his hair ruffled and he had a burp cloth draped over his shoulder. He was dressed casually in a pair of jeans and T-shirt, answering the door in bare feet.

"You ring that thing again and I'll kill you," he warned, his voice ice cold like a killer. "Lauren went out to get her hair done, and it's taken me an hour to get Lucas down for a nap."

"Maybe you need to make a sign for your door." Alex smirked. "You know, like *forget the dog, beware of owner*."

He mocked laughed. "You're hilarious. Now shut up and get

inside." His eyes floated to me, a grin that I didn't trust widening on his lips. "Hi, Maya. You helping Alex run errands?"

"Yeah, I don't have a car so your brother is being my chauffeur." I laughed, wondering if seeing us together was suspect. We'd shown up to his mother's last weekend and no one had assumed we were a couple, and they knew he'd been driving me to work. Surely, if anything, Roman would just assume we had just become close again.

"How nice of him." Roman smirked, stretching out his hand and welcoming us inside.

We followed him down the hall to a large living area. The baby toys on the couch and how-to-parent books on the coffee table were juxtaposed with law magazines and *The Wall Street Journal*.

"Sit," Roman offered pulling the burp cloth off his shoulder.

"Oh, before I forget." Alex held out the paper bag. "We got you a breakfast burrito from Los Rancheros."

Roman's eyes narrowed, taking a moment like he was examining some evidence. He didn't speak, looked at the bag, and then looked at each of us before chuckling. "Holy shit, you're sleeping together?"

"What?" I squeaked out nervously, wondering how the hell could he know that simply because we brought him breakfast. Was the man psychic?

"Sweet little Maya and moronic baby brother." He shook his head, assumingly. "You know, I've had about two hours of sleep and I didn't think anything was going to cheer me up but this is fucking brilliant."

"Roman," Alex warned, a concerned glance shot my way before continuing. "We just had breakfast."

Roman shook his head. "Oh? You just had breakfast? Please, save it for someone who'll buy that bullshit." He laughed. "Even if it wasn't written all over your faces, Los Rancheros is a dead giveaway. You aren't usually sentimental, Alex, which means you must have had a reason to be."

The more I thought about it, the more I knew Roman was right. Alex had never done things out of habit or emotional attachment. He hadn't kept old T-shirts until they fell apart like I did, or reread birthday cards, or gone back to the same place without good reason. While I hadn't started working straight out of college because of lack of opportunity, he had voluntarily taken the time off to go travel. He wanted to experience new things, see new places and create new memories. Where as I had been desperate to get back to the place I'd been happiest.

"You did it for me." It wasn't a question. The doughnuts, the breakfast, the reliving of your youth—all of it—not because he wanted to revisit any of it, but because he knew I did. To remind me of a time before my father tainted it. "Alex, thank you so much."

Forgetting I was all but confirming Roman's suspicion, I threw my arms around him and kissed him. "Thank you," I mumbled against his lips.

Alex's arms engulfed me, lifting me off the floor as he turned my sweet kiss into something a little dirtier. I didn't care who was watching, unwilling to sacrifice the moment.

"Still going to tell me I'm wrong?" Roman's voice came from behind. "Because your tongue down each other's throat would argue otherwise."

I reluctantly pulled my lips away from Alex as he lowered me. "You can't tell anyone," I warned, spinning to face Roman. "I mean it." I glared at him.

Roman smirked, my warning sliding right off him without leaving a mark. "Or what? You're going to kill me with your little death stare?" He laughed. "Have you met my wife?"

Alex might not be sentimental but he'd never been scared to stand up to his brothers. Even when they towered over him—not the case anymore as he matched them in height—he'd gone toe-to-toe without fear. "It's not Maya's death stare you should be worried about, Roman." He slung an arm around my waist, bringing me close to his side. "If she doesn't want you to tell anyone, you won't."

Roman lifted a brow in surprise. "I'm not saying a fucking word to anyone. You two want to screw each other's brains out, it's your own business but I'd work on your," he waved his hand between us, "interactions if you don't want anyone to find out. The hand on her ass, dead giveaway, and do something about that look on your faces as well, it's like happiness threw up on you."

We were interrupted by an ear-piercing scream. The noise loud enough without amplification, echoed through the baby monitor sitting on the end table.

"Fuuuuuuuuck." Roman scrubbed his hands down his face. "I swear he is a perfect angel for Lauren, she thinks I make this shit up. Give me a minute to go get him, I'll let you decide who gets to die."

He stormed off, taking the stairs two at a time as his son cried his little heart out not waiting for an answer.

"He's joking about killing us, right?" I heard the baby monitor click to static, the crying less muffled without the assist.

Alex shrugged as he looked at the stairs Roman had climbed. "Not sure. He knows how to get away with it and I'm pretty sure he could convince a jury he was innocent. It really could go either way. Maybe we should go before we find out?"

He might have been more convincing if he hadn't been grinning, or if he hadn't lowered his head and brushed his lips to mine.

"You're terrible." I pushed gently against his chest. "And we're not leaving."

Roman returned, a bright blue eyed little boy cradled in his arms. I wasn't sure at what age babies started to smile, but if I wasn't mistaken, little Lucas was wearing a grin. Almost like he knew he'd won that round. The taunting each other seemed to be a family trait, and while Lucas didn't have the Larsson last name, he most definitely had the DNA.

"Oh, he is soooo cute," I cooed, not having had a proper chance to see him at the gathering at Kate's. The room had been filled with so many people and emotions—there wasn't time for any real interaction. "He looks exactly like you."

"Poor kid," Alex laughed.

Roman shook his head, his eyes dropping to the precious bundle in his arms. "He might look like me, but he has his mother's temperament. I think he actually enjoys tormenting me."

The chuckle bubbled up my throat. "Babies don't know how to manipulate, Roman. He's just probably sensing that you're tense."

"Don't know how to manipulate?" He scoffed. "I'll bet you my Ferrari the minute Lauren walks through the door, he'll go right to sleep. Nothing she does is different."

"Pretty sure you aren't breastfeeding him," Alex unhelpfully added. "Ouch, Jesus, Maya." He grinned as I elbowed him in the ribs.

I moved closer, lowering my face to the little guy. The kid was literally blessed with out-of-this-world Larsson genetics, incredibly cute, no doubt able to charm the world like the rest of them.

"Aw, you're not a bad boy, you just can't tell us what you want yet. You're just misunderstood." My lips spread into a smile as Lucas wiggled in Roman's arms.

Roman grinned at his son. "Only a few months old and already making women fall at his feet. Definitely my kid. Now let me get that thing for you."

Without further explaining what that *thing* was, he disappeared into another room, taking his now content baby boy with him.

"What are you picking up?" It hadn't occurred to me to ask

before but suddenly I was curious.

Alex shook his head like it was no big deal. "Just some information I wanted to check out. Roman uses a private investigator for some of his cases, and I needed some extra help."

Lawyers used private investigators all the time; the practice wasn't new. Whether it was to help recreate a crime scene, check out an alibi or just do some extra digging—it could literally change the outcome of a case.

What wasn't normal was a lawyer not primarily involved in the case to help facilitate it. Sure, they were family, but it might be seen as blurring the line between privilege, and I knew both men had more integrity than that.

"He's helping you with a case?" I asked, the question not sounding right. "Isn't that risky?"

"Not *helping*. Just allowing me to use his resources. X is on his payroll, not his firm's, so it's not like it's a conflict of interest or anything."

"His name is X? Do you guys play James Bond in your spare time too?" I laughed. I still wasn't sure any of it was a smart move but I trusted Alex knew what he was doing.

"His name is Xavier." Roman returned, with a folder under one arm and Lucas in the other. "X for short. And since you're here when I'm handing this over, I'm assuming he wants you to know about it too."

My body twisted, looking at Alex, confused. "Why would I want to know about a file about a case you're working?"

He took a breath, pushing the air out of his lungs as his smile dropped.

"Because it's *not* a case I'm working on, it's about a job offer."

Job offer? Hadn't he just recently started working at Young, McMillian and Walker?

"You're already thinking about leaving?"

"I was headhunted." He paused. "By a firm in New York."

Well.

Shit.

CHAPTER #16

"NEW YORK?"

I hadn't meant to say it so loud but judging by the looks on their faces, I'd almost shouted it. "As in, on the other side of the country?"

"The very same," said Roman blandly.

Alex took the file from his brother, his fingers lacing with mine. "I asked Roman to help me investigate and vet the offer considering the size of it, but I wasn't going to tell you about it until I had a more solid idea what I was looking at. Now," he rubbed his hand against the back of his neck. "Well now things are different, and I don't want you to think I'm sneaking around behind your back."

Granted I had a tendency to draw incorrect conclusions—or at the very least think the worst of the situation—but I wasn't sure finding out at anytime was going to be easy.

"Investigate what? You're considering it?" I tried to keep the panic out of my voice. "You're going to move?"

The words sounded weird coming out of my mouth, partially because he was the last person on earth I thought would move to the East coast especially since he hadn't even considered it for college. And secondly, I wasn't expecting to talk about the possibility of leaving the morning after what had been the best sex of my life.

He kissed my forehead sweetly. "I haven't decided anything yet. But I'm not going to hide anything from you either. You're too smart for that."

I really wanted to be mad.

To yell and tell him to tear up the offer.

He'd hate New York. It snowed there, endless days below zero and Californians weren't built for that kind of cold. And his fancy car would probably end up neglected in some garage in New Jersey because it cost too much to park—assuming you could find one—in the city.

But how could I ask him to not even *consider* an offer if it was as good as he was suggesting? He deserved better than that, especially since he didn't even have to tell me about it.

We'd slept together once, the vague definition of our relationship never promised any longevity. He sure as hell didn't owe me anything.

"Won't you miss your car?" I asked, childishly hoping to use logic to convince him to stay. "And it's so cold there. I should know, I lived in Connecticut and I almost died the first year." Okay so I was exaggerating, but that first winter I had to buy what was basically a wearable sleeping bag just so I could get out of my dorm.

"Sounds like the two of you have things to talk about." Roman looked down at Lucas who had fallen asleep in his arms and dropped his voice to a whisper. "And you can do it outside because if this kid doesn't take a nap soon, I'm going to lose my goddamn mind."

We said our quiet goodbyes to Roman and walked back out to the car. I was unintentionally quiet, knowing if I was going to say anything, it should be supportive.

Alex didn't have the same problem. "Look, we can talk about New York and the job offer or not, but you have to say something."

"Do you want to leave? I thought you wanted to stay here?" I tried to keep my voice modulated like a reasonable person despite not wanting to be.

He gently lifted his shoulder; the tiny shrug not what I would consider enough of a reaction considering what we were talking about. "Honestly, it wasn't something I'd even thought about. I love L.A. and I love being close to my family. But it's a lot of money, and there's a provision to make junior partner in five years. It could take double that here. They came after me; I wasn't looking."

"When did you get the offer?" I heard myself asking.

"Three days before you first called."

Logic dictated that timing had nothing to do with it. That any serious offer that had the potential to inflate your bank balance and career aspirations needed to be considered regardless of when it arrived. But—there was always a but—I had to wonder if he would have been so eager to have the offer vetted if it had arrived now.

"When do they need an answer?"

I wasn't sure I wanted to know but asked anyway.

"They haven't said, but obviously I can't string it out either. They're giving me time to do due diligence. I figure I have one or two more weeks at most before I need to commit."

One or two weeks?

Shit.

But he would still give notice at his current firm, so that would be another two weeks. So all in all, we could still have a month.

That was assuming he took the job, which was more than likely since he was going to all that trouble.

One month of blissful happiness.

It wasn't a lot but it was more than I'd had in the past. Maybe it was for the best, letting me have the amazing opportunity to be with him without a possible messy breakup. There was no guarantee we would have lasted forever anyway, and then what? I lose my best friend all over again? We could stay friends, our split because of distance preserving all the wonderful things without the opportunity of anger or hurt.

And I'd still have a whole month.

"You said after we went to Roman's I could decide what we did all day, right?" My hand wandered across the center console and touched his thigh.

He glanced down at my hand, a confused smile curling on his lips. "Yeah, you have somewhere you want to go?"

"Yes, we need to go pick up condoms and then I want you to take me to bed." My hand edged higher, moving to the front of his jeans.

"You want to have sex?"

"Yes. Right now."

After all, if I only had a month, I was determined to make every single second of it count.

I WAS POSITIVE the cashier at *Walgreens* thought we were sex addicts.

Either that or I was a hooker and he was my pimp. Or maybe it was the other way around, women could do anything they wanted and I would look amazing in a stretch Cadillac and a fedora.

We'd bought enough condoms to have sex three times a day for six weeks and not run out. Which meant I had calculated enough for a variance if we exceeded our daily trifectas. Alex was pretty talented, and I didn't want the man restricted by a lack of latex.

He'd decided to take me back to his house and I didn't argue. I loved the idea of being in his bed, the way he had been in mine. There was no way I'd ever lay between my sheets and not picture him. I also had another purpose for which I needed access to his apartment which I wouldn't ever admit out loud and wasn't sure if it meant I needed serious help.

While shopping for condoms I'd secretly picked up a bundle of cheesy souvenir postcards at the *Walgreens* as well. I'd once read a study that found some women left personal belongings—like hair ties or tampons—at a boyfriend's house in a way to sort of mark their territory. That the reminder was aimed at warding off cheating or to serve as a sign to other women that he was taken. Not sure if it worked for cities—*I've got your back, Los Angeles*—but I wasn't willing to discount it. So either the postcards of the L.A. landmarks were going to subliminally convince him to stay as he discovered them hidden in strategic places *or* he was going to think some psycho tourist littered in his house. I was really hoping it was the first option or at the very least that he didn't discover the psycho was me.

"Wow, the rent on this place must be insane." The postcards safely hidden in one of the bags of condoms I was holding.

"It's Eric's, and he lets me stay out of the kindness of his heart." He chuckled clutching his own bag of condoms as he opened up the door. "Everyone except Roman has stayed here at one point or another. Nick left after he and Claire got together, so I moved in."

The door slammed behind us, finally allowing me to have him all to myself.

"Car and an apartment." I dropped the bag and wrapped my arms around his neck. "You have gotten all kinds of cool hand-me-downs."

He kissed me, dropping his bag so he could squeeze my ass. "Hey, I got *plenty* of uncool hand-me-downs too. Five boys, I pretty much wore everyone else's stuff until I was like twelve. I figure it's restitution for my previous pain and suffering."

"My poor Alex." My hand slithered down his chest, coming to rest on the front of his jeans. "Do you want me to kiss it better?"

His eyes hooded, glancing down to where I'd palmed him.

"Yes." An appreciative rumble traveled up his throat as he watched me unzip.

I wasn't sure when I turned into a fiend, but since discovering the clock was ticking, I didn't want to waste anymore time. I lowered myself to my knees, a wicked smirk on my lips as I tugged down his jeans. Next were his boxer briefs, pushed down just enough for his erection to spring free.

"Already hard." My tongue swirled around the tip as my hand grabbed him, watching him as he watched me.

"I'm finding it difficult to *not* be hard when you're around." He sucked in a breath as my lips covered the tip of his cock. "Maya."

His hands raked through my hair as I sucked him deeper into my mouth. My hand worked up his length, the tight lock of my fingers straining against his girth as I slowly moved them up and down. My mouth kept busy, licking and sucking him, my syncopated rhythm making him slowly unravel.

"Faster," he begged, thrusting his hips into my mouth.

Sliding up his hard length with my tongue it curled around the end like it was licking an ice cream cone as I shook my head. "You know I don't like being told what to do."

The blue of his eyes filled with black as I sucked hard and fast and then slow and deliberate, drawing it, teasing him as he got harder than I thought was possible.

My own body had its own protests; my nipples rock hard peaks inside of my bra while I felt myself get wet. Every part of me longed to be touched, the dull ache between my legs intensifying while I took him with my mouth.

Struggling to maintain control, his hands scraped my skull, the need to come biting at his heels while he was unwilling to give up my torture.

"Fuck this," he growled, pulling his cock from my mouth with a loud pop and pulling me off my knees. "You had your chance to make me come in your mouth, now it's my turn."

Without giving me a chance to ask what *his turn* entailed, he kissed me hard on the mouth while his hand lifted my dress. He didn't bother attempting to take it off, yanking down my underwear roughly as his hand went to what had been covered by soft cotton.

His fingers swirled around the edges of my pussy, feathering lightly across my clit. "So wet, and all from sucking my dick."

The smile was both sexy and possessive, and I liked it on him, his mouth closing on mine as he thrust two fingers inside of me.

I shuddered out a "yes" as my hand reached out for his cock only to find he'd angled himself out of my reach.

"No." He shook his head. "You're not the only one who doesn't like being told what to do."

Before I had a chance to argue, he spun me around and bent me over the back of his couch. My face was surrounded by cushions as his hand pressed against my spine. The hem of my dress was pushed up to my waist, the cool air hitting my bare skin replaced by the warmness of his mouth as he kissed my butt.

"I'm going to fuck you, Maya. If you have any objections, now would be the time to raise them." His hand moved along the crease of my ass teasing me as he waited for my answer.

I strained my head to look at him. "I thought you didn't like being told what to do?"

A firm smack landed on my ass as a chuckle rumbled up his throat. "Just so we're both clear."

His hands left me, the heat from his body taken away as I heard the rustle of the plastic bag. He returned, his hard cock bobbing against my ass as he tore open a box and ripped the foil wrapper. Without looking back and seeing it, I could feel every single movement. The anticipation was killing me, knowing he was rolling on the condom but having no idea what he was thinking as he looked at me bent over his sofa.

His knees edged my legs out further as the blunt head of his cock teased my entrance. It was the only warning I had, his thrust coming in a hard and fast rush. My body contracted, tiny pulses moving along his length as he slid out and then back in again.

My hands gripped the cushions either side of me as he increased the speed, my breasts aching against the fabric of my bra and dress, desperate to be free.

It was different being unable to see, to have myself completely at his mercy, with every single movement heightened by my loss of sight. His hands anchored on my hips as he rocked into me, our breaths panting in unison as he got harder and deeper with each drive.

One of his hands moved from my hip to between my legs and found my clit. His body was pressed against me, the weight of him keeping me steady as his fingers swirled. My muscles ached—the angle of my body awkward—but I didn't dare tell him to stop. The burn just made it sweeter, each twinge bringing me closer to the edge.

He circled my clit, teasing me as he took me from behind. "I don't think I'll ever get used to this," he groaned into my ear. "Or how good you feel when I'm inside of you."

It was too much, my body feeling like it was splintering apart as I came hard. He was right there with me, following me off the cliff as he pounded into me, his cock jerking inside of me.

Nothing could be heard over our labored breathing, his hands pulling me back toward him to ease off the pressure on me. "Did I break you?" His lips touched the back of my neck gently. "I promise that wasn't the plan."

He pulled out, turning me around into his arms and kissing my mouth. The kisses no less fevered considering we should have both been sated.

He still wanted me.

Even though he'd just come, his hunger was palpable as his mouth nipped and sucked my lips.

"We should probably get undressed." I looked at his pants and boxer briefs pooled around his ankles and my dress hiked up at my waist. "Anyone would think we're a pair of animals."

"Maybe we are." He kept his hands on me as he toed off his shoes and kicked off his pants and boxer briefs.

My hands ran across his chest, grabbing the T-shirt and lifting it over his head so I could touch his skin. He was so warm under my fingertips, each ridge of muscle contracting a little as I passed over it.

"I think the request was for you to take me to your bed." My head dipped down and swirled his nipple. "And while this was nice and all, you still haven't given me what I wanted."

He chuckled, his finger and thumb locking under my chin as he lifted it to catch his gaze. "Oh this was *nice*, huh?"

Releasing me, he stepped back, pulled off his socks and left them with his clothes in a pile on the floor. I watched as he picked up the opened box of condoms and turned it over to inspect it. "Eleven left, should be enough for now."

With the pack in one hand he reached for me with his other. "Let's not waste any more time and give you what you want."

I followed him into his bedroom where he undressed me. Unlike his own clothes that he'd torn off, he took care unzipping my dress, sliding it off my body as he kissed each new exposed piece of skin. When the dress was finally off, he cupped my breasts, kissing them through the cotton fabric before reaching around and flicking at the clasp. He let the material drop, stepping back and admiring my body as I stood naked for him.

"I love that you don't hide yourself from me." He moved closer, his fingers delicately traveling from the swell of my belly up to my breasts. "You are so fucking beautiful, Maya."

I closed my eyes, absorbing the touch for a minute before opening them to find his were flaming.

"Then take me to bed."

UP AGAINST THE couch had been hard and fast but in his bed he'd been slow and generous. I loved that he didn't ask me what I wanted, but instead looked for clues, noticing every time I whimpered and giving that part of my body more attention. He was a quick learner, and I was very vocal about giving my appreciation.

We showered together, got dressed and cooked frozen pizza in his kitchen, the hours slowly ticking away.

It was late afternoon when he went out to the car to collect something he'd forgotten to bring in. I used the few minutes alone to run to the shopping bag on the floor in his living room and grab the postcards. There would probably only be enough time to hide one, so the colorful picture of the Hollywood sign was stashed underneath the sofa cushions with the rest of the postcards being shoved into my handbag for later. The idea seemed easier when I dreamed it up inside of Walgreens, but having the time and the opportunity when he wasn't around and still have access to his apartment was proving more difficult than I thought.

I had just finished hiding the postcards in my purse when Alex walked back in, the folder Roman had given him in his hand.

Great.

Maybe I should have distracted him, broken into his car and stolen the stupid file instead. Probably would have been more productive than hiding postcards.

"You know, I took you with me to Roman's because I wanted you to know about the job offer. Did you want to help me go through it?" He laid it down on his coffee table.

I'd have preferred to drink Sriracha straight from the bottle than to read and discuss any of it. And I didn't even like hot sauce.

I shook my head and took a breath. Earlier he'd said that he loved that I didn't hide myself from him. Granted, I was naked at the time and that was what he'd been talking about but I wasn't going to hide myself now either.

"I need to recuse myself." I rested my hand on the file, stopping him from opening it.

He laughed. "Very funny."

"No, I'm being serious, I can't be a part of this." I shook my head. "And not because I don't care or I don't want the best for you. The truth is, I want the very best for you which means you need an unbiased opinion, which is something I can't give you."

He stopped laughing, moving my hand off the file and lacing his fingers with mine. "Why can't you give that to me?"

"Because whether you stay or go, it has to be what you want. Not because of something I said or did." *Or because I beg you not to go*, I finished in my head. "Whatever you decide, I promise you I will support you. Two of my close friends live in New York, so if you decide to go, I'll visit you all the time." I stopped short of telling him I'd be happy because I knew that would be a lie. Happiness might eventually come, but if he did go, it wouldn't be what I would be feeling.

He took my hand and placed it on his heart. "So why don't you think about coming with me?"

It wasn't something I expected him to ask, and hearing it just broke my heart.

"Alex, I can't. I *just* moved here, and unlike you, people aren't tripping over themselves to offer me jobs. I like where I work, and I like being back close to my family, I can't just leave."

"Apart from not wanting to pick up and move—yet again—I've signed a lease, I've made a commitment to the firm. Even if I could get out of those contracts legally, I need for my word to mean something."

My family name wasn't the best in the business and I knew that. I needed to be doing it better, more efficient, more precise than the next person, and personal integrity wasn't something I was willing to throw away. And even if I did lose my mind and forget all those things, and blindly follow him to the other side of the country, I'd always wonder why he asked. Whether it was because he felt the things I was starting to feel for him, or if he was just scared to lose me. It would be like marrying me just because I was pregnant, and I would never be anyone's shotgun bride.

"Yeah, I guess that makes sense." He visibly deflated. "So you want me *not* to talk about it?"

Yes, I wanted to say. Tell him to bury it away, for us to deal with later when I'd had more time with him. "That can be your decision too."

"Then we won't." He picked up the file from the coffee table, walked over to a bureau and shoved it in a drawer. "Poof, it's gone."

If only it were that easy.

"Anything else you want to recuse yourself from?" he asked, leaning up against the couch.

I shook my head. "Nope, that's it."

"Good, now let's go back to your place and pack a bag. I want you to spend the night with me and would rather spend the extra time in bed with you in the morning than drive back to your apartment."

That was a plan I could definitely get on board with.

"I concur."

CHAPTER #17

"HOW WAS THE rest of your weekend?"

I had barely made it in the door when Stefan's question flew across the room. It was early, with most of the junior associates not in yet, but they didn't have to impress the partners as much as the new kids on the block.

"Great, you?" I looked around, the third member of our three amigos missing in action. "Where's Mike?"

"Was called into a meeting. You happen to see Alex?" He handed me a coffee from his tray of takeaways, mine light on the sugar and cream, just the way I liked it.

I took a sip, the caffeine-y goodness making me feel more alert as I shot him a glare. "He picked me up Saturday afternoon when we finished, you *know* I saw him."

"Okay, Okay." He raised his hands. "I was just trying to be polite but if you don't want to do the dance, then we won't." He straightened his tie and grinned. "So did you talk about me?"

"You know you sound kind of pathetic, right? Do you want me to pass Alex a note and see if he wants to go to prom? You guys would make such a cute couple." I hid my grin behind my coffee cup.

"If it gets me a date with Astrid, I'll even buy the corsage." Stefan leaned back in his chair. "I'm secure enough in my own manhood."

The thought of Alex dressed in a tuxedo was mouthwatering. I had left, never getting the opportunity to see him all ready for prom. I didn't even know who he would have taken, or if we would have gone together just for the hell of it. I never did go at my new school, preferring to stay at home and study than be around a bunch of people who I didn't know and/or like.

"I did tell Alex about your request, and he said he'll mention it." I took a seat down at the vacant desk beside him and plugged in my computer.

He fist pumped, clearly pleased at the news. "So when we going to do this? The weekend? Friday night?"

"I said he'd mention it to her, I didn't say it was a done deal," I countered, not sure when Alex was planning on having the conversation with Astrid. We'd spent almost all our time together and I'd almost forgotten about it entirely. Maybe he did too.

"Make it happen, Zaveri." He gave me a pointed look. "I know you have the power."

I rolled my eyes as I scoffed. "I'm not a superhero, Stefan. I can't will something into existence." *Because lord knows if I did have that power I'd be using it for my own purposes.* "I'll remind him but after that, you agree to drop it."

He clapped his hands, rubbing them together. "I have every faith."

"Guess who gets to tag along this week in court?" Mike puffed out his chest strutting into the room like a peacock, the guess not needed as he sat down beside me.

I gave him a playful shove. "What happened to not breaking up the band? You were concerned when I mentioned getting to sit in on a meeting and you're going to court?"

"And he thought we should be worried about you." Stefan tsked, pointing to Mike. "A traitor to his own pact."

"Our bond remains intact." His fingers traced a cross over the left side of his chest. "And it's only to observe."

While we were pretending to be worried, both Stefan and I were happy for him. To be asked to observe was a big deal, especially given it was only our second week, we were all doing awesome in finding our feet so fast.

The day progressed as usual. Files, research, demands from senior ranking staff, but it was useful in keeping my mind off other things.

I also got to sit in Leah's meeting for the Clayton merger, and even managed to contribute to the meeting. Well, it was more passing Leah notes, letting her take all the glory as she brokered with opposing counsel, but it was awesome to see my work in action in front of me.

It was the end of the day before I knew it, my phone buzzing with a message that Alex was still in a meeting but would meet me in about half an hour.

"You heading out?" Stefan slid on his satchel and Mike grabbed his laptop bag.

"Alex is running late, I'm just going to hang out here for a bit." I put my bag back on the desk and sat back down.

Mike tipped his chin to the door. "I can give you a ride if you don't want to wait. I don't mind."

"Thanks, but I don't mind waiting." I smiled. "I probably should use the time to talk to my family, I'm in a group text and I'm already in double digits of unread messages."

Stefan winced. "Ouch. My olds need to be called once a week or I catch grief."

Mike snorted. "Consider yourselves both lucky. My dad has the police commissioner on speed dial. I don't check in every three to four days, I'll have a BOLO put out on my ass."

After commiserating on the reluctance of Mike's parents to let go of their boy, they left me in the office. I was far from alone, lights on in offices down the hall as lawyers pushed the envelope of the work-life balance in order to get ahead.

Maya—I got to sit in on my first negotiations today. I'm still super pumped. And yes, I'm doing great. No need to panic.

Jordon—Congrats Sis.

Vanessa—Yay, Maya! You should go out and celebrate.

Jordon—On a Monday night? :-o

Natalie—Well done, Maya. I agree with Vanessa, celebrate.

Jordon—Are you all illiterate? It's a MONDAY night.

Vanessa—She isn't an old man like you are, baby, she can go out on a school night and still be okay.

Ben—Ooooohhh burn, J-Dawg. From your own wife too. ;-)

Jordon—. . .

Mom—Oh sweetheart, that's fantastic. I'm so proud of you.

Maya—Don't get too excited people, it was one meeting and it wasn't even in a courtroom.

Mom—Not the point. Every step moves you forward, and look at how far you've come.

Ben—I bet she is crying. :-P

Jordon—100%

Mom—I am allowed to cry!

After a little more back and forth, we ended the conversation and I suddenly got a little choked up. For all their crazy, I really did love my family. I was glad I could call or message without calculating the time difference, or get on a plane and be next to them in two hours. While I knew I could never go back to living in Carson City, I didn't think I could go back to the East coast either.

When I got down to the lobby, Alex was there waiting. His hair was ruffled, his tie slightly askew but so heartbreakingly beautiful that I ran into his arms and gave him a kiss.

"Ooooooh kissing me in full view of security cameras," he taunted as the smile spread across his face. "Someone's living dangerously."

"I don't care if people at work find out, I'm more worried about our families."

I was positive that my dating life was of zero interest to most of the people I worked with. And as long as I didn't take Alex into a boardroom and screw him on the table, there would be more interest in whether granola or protein bars were in the kitchenette than any boyfriend of mine. Except for maybe Mike and Stefan, who would probably at this point be unsurprised.

"Good, because I hate keeping my hands off you." He pulled me closer, giving me a soft kiss on the forehead before leading me outside.

His deal with the devil had obviously expired, his BMW not parked out front like it usually was. We walked hand in hand on the sidewalk, looking like lovesick teenagers as we stopped after a few steps to kiss. Honestly I didn't care how tragic it looked, I was happy.

We drove first to my apartment to pick up some more clothes and then back to his place where we planned to spend the night. The law clinic had been canceled for the night since Don was sick so we had our evening free.

It was nice having a whole house to ourselves and not having to haul a basket of laundry up and down stairs to use the washer and dryer. Something I happened to mention when I emerged from my bedroom with not only an overnight bag, but a hamper full of my dirty clothes too.

Alex dropped me off at his house so I could get started on my laundry while he went out and picked up some groceries for dinner. Both of us were tired of eating out and him leaving gave me the perfect opportunity to hide the rest of my postcards. If I had known domestic chores would have gotten him out of the house so quickly, I would have asked to wash my dirty underwear yesterday. Clearly, my first hidden postcard was still undiscovered and I liked being able to finish the job.

One by one, I took pictures of Santa Monica Pier, The Farmer's Market, Grauman's Chinese Theatre and Disneyland and hid them in random places. Nowhere glaringly obvious but he wasn't going to need a compass and treasure map either. I was done by the time he got back, my clothes already in the dryer while I poured us a glass of the Napa Valley white he'd stolen from his mother's on my behalf.

He lowered the bags of food to the floor and leaned against the jamb looking at me in his kitchen, barefooted and wearing one of his T-shirts. "Well, well. Nice choice of outfit." His eyes rolled over my bare legs.

"It's laundry day." I handed him a glass of wine. "Figured I'd just wash *everything*."

His hand traveled up my thigh, stopping when it got to my ass, his brow raising in surprise. "I really hope this isn't how you do laundry at your apartment."

"Of course I do. I'm trying to give Prim a heart attack," I mocked, laying my head on his chest.

"Poor Prim, being terrorized by the likes of you." He squeezed my butt. "We should probably start dinner before you're a hazard to anyone's health."

He kissed the top of my head and then took a sip of his wine, using one hand to carry the groceries over to the counter.

I looked at the ingredients with interest as he pulled them out as there was no cohesion between them. He had ground beef and chicken breasts, taco seasoning and a jar of pasta sauce. It was like he'd randomly thrown some things into a cart with no real plan. "What are we making?"

"Tonight, my famous baked Mac N Cheese." He pulled out some elbow macaroni and two different kinds of cheeses out of his mystery bag. "I assumed we'd want to eat for the rest of the week so I got enough groceries so I didn't have to keep going to the store."

My. Heart.

I tried not to get too excited and read more into what was happening. He was just trying to be efficient. And he had to eat whether I was there or not. But I'd be lying if I weren't delighted that he'd factored me into his shopping expedition, punctuated by a loaf of cinnamon bread, which I absolutely loved and knew he couldn't stand.

"You bought me cinnamon bread." I hugged the plastic wrapped loaf, holding it close to my chest.

He stopped unpacking groceries, his eyes on the bread. "I will never understand how you can eat that stuff but I know you used to love it. I'm assuming you didn't come to your senses."

"You would be right, Mister." I poked out my tongue. "And thank you."

He chuckled a "you're welcome" while I helped him put everything away. Then I watched as he started making dinner, boiling the macaroni while mixing up a rue of milk and flour in a saucepan.

It was mesmerizing to watch, his hands working competently in the kitchen as he continued without the use of a recipe.

"I thought the only thing you knew how to make was scrambled eggs?" I pointed to the fancy baking dish he was loading the cheesy macaroni into. "Now you're making non-packet Mac N Cheese in *Le Creuset*."

"The lady in the Crate and Barrel said it was the best. Can't say I disagree." He put his expensive stoneware into the oven.

No Target for him, oh no.

He flicked me playfully with a tea towel. "And when most of the local takeout places recognized who I was by the sound of my voice, I knew it was time to learn to cook."

"Yeah, I feel your pain. By the end of college I had mastered making a three-course meal on a camping stove. Necessity is the mother of invention," I exclaimed proudly.

"Three-course meal? That's a big graduation from the chocolate brownies I remember."

I loved that even though we knew so much about each other, we were still learning new things. Not just filling in the gap between the years we'd been absent, but how we'd changed as people too.

"This the wine from my mom's?" He picked up his glass and took a sip.

I nodded, grabbing my own glass. "Yep, although I think your next challenge should be smuggling a bottle back in. Increases the degree of difficulty *and* you get to replace at least one of the bottles you stole."

He eyed me curiously, biting back his grin. "You want to join me on this mission?"

"Sure, I'll even go buy the bottle. Only fair since I partook in drinking two of them." I held up my glass and we toasted in agreement.

When our Mac N Cheese was cooked, we heaped it onto plates, brought them with our glasses of wine into living room and ate on his couch with the television on. It was blissful; spending time together doing something we'd done a million times but it was so much better. I felt so at ease, so completely relaxed, like I didn't have to keep proving myself. I could just be Maya, and I was enough.

With dinner done, we snuggled together on the couch. And for the first time since we started sleeping together his kisses and touches didn't dissolve into sex. It surprised me how much I loved just being held, especially by him.

"How was work?" He kissed the top of my head while some movie we were watching continued to play in the background.

I snuggled in closer, running my fingers against the strong muscular arms around me. "Good, it's a steep learning curve but I love it." I took a breath, wondering if bringing up Stefan's request would ruin the perfect mood we had going. "So, have you spoken to Astrid?"

Guess I was about to find out.

"No, wasn't really on my mind today," he said drily, punctuated by another kiss.

I hated how much I liked that he hadn't been thinking about her. I'd never been a needy woman, or jealous, or wanted to be the sole focus of anyone's attention. And yet with him, I could easily fall down the rabbit hole, end up on a talk show about how I cut a lock of some girl's hair and put a hex on her because *she looked at my man.* I was already doing the postcard thing, I didn't need to add anymore ridiculous to my bag.

"We should all go out," I unhelpfully suggested. *What are you doing?* my self-conscience whispered. You cannot be a bunny-boiling psycho without being her best friend as well.

"*You* want to go out with Astrid?" He used each word cautiously like even he knew it wasn't a good idea.

I spun around so I was facing him. "Well, Stefan wants to meet her and it might just be more comfortable for everyone if we just go out together. Make it seem less like a set up."

It had absolutely nothing to do with me wanting to see Alex and Astrid interacting together and read if she still had feelings for him.

No, of course not.

It definitely wasn't to collect a lock of her hair just in case.

Because even though the man was clearly committed to me, I still had a niggling feeling in my gut that I wasn't good enough. And maybe someone with fewer issues would probably be a better fit for him if I were honest.

And clearly obsessing over things and examining them from every angle is the smart way to go, right?

Jesus, I was one step away from a country song.

He shook his head with a smile. "Maya, you don't have to do this."

"You're right, I don't have to. I want to. It will be fun." I faked my excitement and hoped he didn't see right through me. He was a smart guy, and I wasn't sure how convincing I was actually being.

He shot me a cautious glance. "Fine, if you're sure I'll see what she has planned for the rest of the week."

"Great." The lie almost got stuck in my throat. "Can't wait."

Lord help me.

CHAPTER #18

THE GROUP DATE thing was set up for Friday evening. I'd have preferred for it to be on Saturday so I had time to properly obsess about how much prettier, taller and thinner she was but alas, Astrid had plans on Saturday. No doubt there was a convention or something where willowy blondes all gathered and laughed at shorter brunettes with green eyes and she just couldn't miss it.

It would have also given me time to talk myself out of acting like a possessive moron. *If he'd wanted her, he could have had her*, I repeated over and over in my head. It didn't help that he'd already *had* her and I knew about it.

I.

WOULD.

NOT.

BE.

THAT.

GIRL.

Work helped though, not only did it occupy my mind and distract me from my own crazy but things were *really* going well. Mike had been the first of us to go to court, but I had been asked to assist Leah on another case. And not just sit in on a meeting and pass her notes discreetly like a dirty little secret, but actually introduced to the client as an assistant. It meant my time with the guys was limited as I worked mainly on my own, but I loved focusing my energy and having the opportunity to shine.

Stefan of course was ecstatic, pleased beyond measure that he was not only getting to meet Astrid, but spending an evening with her. He didn't care that it was a group thing, telling both Mike and I that he could improvise and wow her even if we were in tow.

"We suiting up tonight?" Mike asked, nowhere near as excited as Stefan—who'd been counting down all week—for our outing.

"Dress pants, button shirt—open at the neck and rolled sleeves—no tie." Stefan instructed him with zero sarcasm. "L.A. girls are more casual than East Coast, they see you in a suit and they're going to assume you're there to serve them a subpoena. But also don't be scared to let them know you have some class."

"Wow, and I thought *I* gave my choice in outfits a lot of thought." I laughed, grabbing my bag as we packed up our desks.

Stefan puffed out his chest. "Nothing wrong with dressing right and taking care of yourself. You win people over first with your appearance, then with your personality. Give off the wrong vibe and you won't get a second chance. Like it or not, that's how the world works."

Of course he was right, which didn't help since we were going out with a woman who was gorgeous.

"So, what time are we meeting?" Mike packed up his computer as some of the associates waved goodbye for the weekend. They were ready to start their weekend early and weren't interested in waiting around for stragglers like us.

"Nine." I checked my phone waiting to see if there was a message from Alex. He usually texted during the day, his messages making me smile as I went about my work. But even if he was busy, he always let me know in the afternoon when he was finishing.

Stefan looked over my shoulder and grinned. "No news from lover boy?"

I had casually mentioned that Alex and I had started dating earlier in the week and was met with complete lack of surprise. Allegedly I was terrible at hiding how ridiculously happy I was, their suspicions confirmed when they saw Alex and I kissing out front one day after work. They were cool though, didn't make an issue about it or ask any questions. It was just as well because I hadn't told Jackie or Lisa or any of my family yet. And for all the no-big-deal I got from Stefan and Mike, I was going to get the Spanish Inquisition from everyone else.

"No, he must be working late. I'll just wait until he's done." I dumped my bag on the desk and sat back down. I was trying to not be disappointed, but I needed as much time as possible to get ready. Didn't Alex know I needed at least an hour to obsess *before* I even started to get ready? Geez, at this rate I'd barely have time to try on every outfit I own twice before settling on the first one I'd chosen.

"Why don't you let one of us drive you home and he can meet up with you when he's done?" Mike added, not leaving like I assumed he was dying to do.

"Are you sure you don't mind?" It was the first time I'd even considered it, my usual thanks-but-no-thanks almost automatic whenever one of them asked.

Mike shook his head. "Not at all. Just let the guy know so he doesn't file a motion of illegal detention and restriction of personal liberties. I like the guy, but something tells me he's not all that 'likeable' when pissed off."

"Yeah, I bet he's a fucking beast in the courtroom." Stefan laughed. "Hard to believe he's only a first year like us. He's got the chops of a third year at the very least."

They were right about that. While Alex had graduated the

same year as I had, he had presence that oozed confidence. I hadn't had the pleasure or privilege of seeing him in action, but I bet it would be hot.

"Guess it runs in the family," I said, not really thinking about what was coming out of my mouth as I gathered up my bag.

"Why? You mean because his brothers are actors?" Stefan looked at me confused.

"No, because his other brother is Roman Pierce." It slipped out of my mouth before I could stop it.

Silence.

It was as if we had floated out to space, living in a vacuum and sound had ceased to exist.

"His brother is *Roman Pierce*?" Stefan's eyebrows receded into his hairline as he stuttered out the word.

Shit.

"Do not say anything." I grabbed Stefan's arms. "Don't make it weird."

"Roman fucking Pierce?" Mike echoed in case Stefan hadn't made it clear enough. "As in the guy who is about to become a partner at Moss, Byrne & Carter?"

Stefan leaned in, his face covered in complete awe. "Bet his name is on the wall inside of a year."

"Yes, yes. That guy. Now don't make it awkward, he's still the same guy."

I would never intentionally disclose information about Alex's private life, but I'd become so close with Mike and Stefan, it just kind of . . ."Please don't say anything unless he tells you himself."

"We won't, will we, Mike." Stefan elbowed him in the ribs as he focused on me. "His secret is safe with us."

Mike made a show of pretending to zip his lips. "Not a word. But now I'm going to insist you tell him I'm taking you home. I might be worried about Alex, but I'm terrified of Roman."

I laughed, agreeing it was probably for the best and picked up my phone.

Guessing your day has been crazy busy, so don't worry about needing to rush. I'll just catch a ride with Mike, and will see you tonight whenever you're ready. I'll be at my place with an overnight bag and all my dirty laundry if you're lucky. Love you xxx

Shit.

I'd hit send before I realized what I'd written, the text flying off into cyber space as I was left staring at the bubble on the screen.

LOVE YOU.

Written for the both of us to see.

"No, no, no," I screamed at my phone, wishing I could recall the message before he had a chance to read it. Too bad my lapse in judgment hadn't been restricted to telling Mike and Stefan about his superstar lawyer brother. No, I had to go ahead and declare my feelings via text. I was literally the worst.

"What's wrong? Your phone not working?" Stefan tried to glance at my screen as I shoved it into my handbag. It was bad enough the first time I'd said those words to Alex it had been electronically, I wasn't going to let anyone else read them before he did.

"No. Just something I forgot to do. It's fine. We should go." I stalked to the door, desperate to get out of the office and get home as soon as possible.

Not that I could fix anything once I got there, but it would be easier to think. Shit. What if he freaked out, thinking it was too soon? Things had been going so well, I had even managed to keep my anxiety of him possibly moving completely under control. Not once breaking down and begging him to stay like I wanted to.

"Sure." Mike pulled his keys out of his pocket, shooting Stefan a quick concerned look. "Let's go."

I didn't dare look at my phone the entire ride home, preferring to live in blissful ignorant denial for as long as possible. I wasn't even sure how I wanted him to react, to read the message and confront me about it, or read it and ignore it. Either had their own pros and cons, but neither could change the fact I'd said it and he'd know.

Oh, I had pretended like I wasn't falling in love with him, like we had just evolved into some *really great* friendship where we had *really great* sex. But the truth was I'd always loved him, and the minute he reclaimed a place in my life, he reclaimed a place in my heart too.

Only this time around, it had been different. It wasn't just a piece, but the whole freaking organ.

Mike thankfully didn't ask any more questions about Alex or my phone, taking one for the team and filling the silence with mostly one-sided small talk. I was more grateful than I could ever tell him, even more so when he finally dropped me off at home.

"See you tonight." His parting words as he drove off, leaving me in front of the faded pink stucco building I hadn't slept inside of for a week.

I climbed the metal stairs up to my apartment, just managing to get my key into my door when I heard footsteps behind me. It was Prim, in her trademark housecoat with her fire engine red hair in rollers. "You're back. Was beginning to think you'd run off."

"Nope, just working a lot and spending time with a friend." I struggled with the key, wondering why the world seemed to be conspiring against me.

"A man? The one with the movie star face who I've seen leaving your apartment?" She tipped her head to my now opened door.

"Yes, my boyfriend. Thanks, got to go." I scrambled inside and slammed the door shut.

I did not want to talk to Prim, especially about Alex and my relationship. I locked the door behind in case she got bright ideas about following me in and pressed my back against the wood as I slid to the floor. I shrugged off my handbag, placing it gently on the floor in front of me, my fingers itched to pull out my phone while my brain told me I didn't want to look.

Carefully—like I was defusing a bomb—I opened my bag and extracted my phone. I moved it toward me, the screen angled to the floor as I prolonged my self-imposed torture.

Damn it, I cursed internally. *Damn it all.*

Knowing there was no way to avoid it any longer, I flipped the phone to the right side up and saw there was a message. Alex's name flashed across the screen, alerting me that the message was from him, and adding salt to the wound.

Shit.

I swiped my finger across the screen and held my breath, our text thread opening up and reacquainting me with the one I'd sent previously. And directly underneath it

Sorry, babe. Was getting slammed. I'll see you tonight.

That was it.

Three short sentences that told me nothing.

Maybe he'd been so busy he hadn't even read the message properly, seen that I'd gotten a ride home and ignored the rest. It was possible, especially if he was still at work. Which meant he would read it later.

Lord, I was going to throw up.

Heading back to my room and throwing myself on my bed, I allowed only thirty minutes for screaming against my pillow. Any more than that and it would cut into the time I had allocated to try on everything I owned and obsess in front of the mirror.

I forwent being sensible and made myself some dinner, choosing to eat ice cream straight from the tub with a soupspoon like a savage. My fall from grace had been rather epic, still shoveling mint choc chip into my mouth when I heard a knock at my door.

It was him.

I didn't even need to open the door, feeling it instinctively in my bones as my spoon froze halfway between the ice cream tub and my mouth.

"Shit."

I tossed the spoon in the sink, the ice cream back into the freezer and walked to the door like I was on a tightrope.

My palms were sweaty as I wiped them on front of my old faded college Tee—I had stalled in my plan to get ready—and pulled open the door.

Oh.

My.

God.

He never got any less impressive, standing on the other side wearing a pair of black dress pants, black button down shirt, and a smile that could convince me of anything.

His eyes rolled up my body, traveling over my bare legs to my faded Yale top. "Doing laundry without me?" He stepped inside without an invitation and shut the door behind him.

"I'm not ready," I said, stating the obvious as he stalked closer. "I need more time." I wasn't sure *what for* exactly, but I knew it wasn't just to get dressed.

We were racing against a clock, and it was ticking by so fast. I just need everything to stop, to be able to stand there in that moment with him and not worry about an expiration date.

His thumb grazed my cheek, wiping away what was probably some remnant ice cream and brought it to his mouth and sucked. "Mint."

I nodded like an idiot. "With choc chips."

He moved his hands back to my face, cradling my chin in his palms. "My favorite."

He kissed me with a desperation that defied logic. It was like he hadn't seen me in days instead of hours, pulling me close to him like I might disappear. In that moment I didn't care about the text, about Astrid, about him leaving—all of those thoughts completely insignificant.

It was just him.

And us.

And now.

"I'm sorry I was late," he mumbled against my lips. "I'm glad you got a ride home with Mike."

"It's okay, I'm just glad you're here now," I mumbled, smiling back at him.

It would have been easy to wrap my arms around his chest and stay in that moment forever. Or to drag him to my bed and have sex, which also was a good option.

But I couldn't.

"I love you," I said out loud for the first time as I looked into his amazing eyes. "I'm in love with you."

"I know," he smirked back. "I read your message."

I pushed roughly against his chest. "*You know*, what kind of response is that, you jerk."

Emotions swirled inside of me, wondering if he thought it was some kind of joke.

"Hey." He grabbed my hands, their pitiful excuse of an assault halted as he held them still. "You didn't let me finish. I love you too, Maya."

"You, you do?" I asked, sounding so vulnerable I winced. I didn't want to cut myself open and bleed in front of him, but my heart hadn't given me much choice.

His lips brushed against mine. "Yes. I do. And I'm not taking the job in New York, I'm going to stay here with you."

"What?" The word got stuck in my throat, oxygen burning my lungs as I struggled to breathe. "You're not going?"

"No, I'm not."

His thumbs swiped the tops of my cheeks and I hadn't realized my eyes had started to water. Tears of happiness and relief bled out of me as I hugged him close. "Please, just tell me that you didn't decide because of me. Tell me you want to stay here because of you."

It wasn't enough to know he wouldn't leave; I needed to know that he wouldn't hate me for it later. That me, and my refusal to follow him, wouldn't be the sore that would fester. I loved him too much for that, too much to be the reason he was held back.

"Maya." He tilted my chin, forcing me to look at him. "I can't tell you that."

And I knew, he was giving it all up for me.

"But you can't. What if this doesn't work? What if you end up hating me? What if—"

"What if you just let the future be the future's problem? And no matter what happens, I could never hate you."

I had to trust him.

Even if I didn't trust myself.

"Okay." I nodded, agreeing because I didn't have the energy to fight it. "We'll leave it up to the future then."

His mouth spread into a cheeky grin. "Now should we explore if you're wearing panties underneath this T-shirt or do you want to hear me tell you I love you again?"

I wanted him.

Selfishly I wanted him to touch me and make it feel more real. To hear him say those words to me, while he held me in his arms and both of us were naked.

Bare.

In every sense of the word.

My hands ran along his sexy black shirt and played with the buttons, looking at him from under my lashes and I shot him a cheeky grin of my own.

"I thought you said you could multitask."

CHAPTER 19

SEX HAD FOILED my initial plans.

Time allocated to outfits and obsessing was usurped by kissing and touching and sweet, sweet love.

I didn't even care, too full of sex endorphins to worry about whether I looked good in my dress or if Astrid was going to look hotter. Actually I didn't care about *anything* to do with Astrid, or Mike, or Stefan, or the fact we were running late to the stupid date Alex and I had put together.

Alex tossed the keys to the valet and kissed my hand as we walked in. The loud music and pink lights spilling onto the street as we walked up to the entrance. There was a line, but we didn't wait in it, magically waved through as Alex whispered to the pretty hostess holding a clipboard at the front.

It was a nightclub in Hollywood, but not the kind of place I'd have picked for myself. The inside was covered in candy pink walls, the glow of the matching pink LEDs floating over the crowd making sure everyone was color matched.

"It's like Barbie's dream house for over 21's," I screamed over the music. "Let me guess, it was Astrid's choice."

He nodded, guiding me through the crowd. "This is her favorite place to go. Figured letting her choose made the most sense."

I wasn't sure I agreed—or if the pink radioactive glow wasn't going to permanently damage my retinas—but I would try to not behave like a spoilt brat. After all, the man I loved had told me he loved me back, and we'd just had really awesome sex as well.

"Alex." Arms grabbed him and almost pushed me out of the way. "You're here."

She was dressed predictively in a pink glittery dress that most women would have worn as a top. Her lean legs poked out the bottom, her pretty pink toes housed in a pair of sky high sparklingly peep-toe stilettos that I would twist an ankle just looking at. But as much as I wanted to throw shade, she looked freaking fabulous.

"Yeah, sorry we're late." He deliberately tugged me to his side. "You remember Maya, don't you?"

"Ah, yes of course." She held out her hand, her smile spreading wide. "The girl you grew up with. How nice."

Instinct told me she was being sarcastic but her tone suggested otherwise. While it wasn't obvious English was her second language, her slight accent peppering words hinted that she'd grown up speaking something else.

"Yes, very nice." My cheeks heated as I looked up at Alex. "I'm very lucky."

Whatever her agenda, I wasn't going to let my good mood be affected by the Glitteratti.

Her eyes shone with excitement. "Well good, now let's go sit down and get some drinks. They have the most amazing cocktails here called Tickled Pink, you simply must try."

She led us to one of the rounded booths that lined the back wall, a big burly security guard doing an ocular frisk of her body as she floated by.

Mike and Stefan where already seated, both of them looking

like kids that had eaten too much candy, standing as they saw us approach.

"Maya. Alex." Stefan put out his hand but had trouble making eye contact. Astrid had shuffled past, her butt grazing his crotch.

"I've already made friends." She smiled at Mike and then at Stefan. "They've generously been keeping me company."

"Great, glad to see we weren't missed." Alex shook hands with Stefan and then moved to Mike, all of us taking our seat as a waitress appeared.

"Tickled Pinks for everyone," Astrid announced not giving the waitress a chance to speak.

"I'll have a beer." Alex pulled out his wallet and handed her some bills. "And whatever they want."

"Such a bore." Astrid pouted. "You used to be more fun."

I was positive she meant before he slept with her, when he was charmed by her pink—probably glittery—vagina. But I knew Alex hated cocktails, and there wasn't a chance he was drinking anything pink.

"I'll have one," I volunteered, interested to see how *tickled* it made me feel.

"Me too," Stefan offered, gaining an appreciative squeeze from Astrid.

Mike shook his head. "I'm team beer, guys, sorry."

Finalizing our orders the waitress disappeared, leaving us to make small talk over the blaring music.

Alex curled his arm around me and leaned over towards Mike. "Thanks for driving Maya home."

"Don't mention it, dude. Happy to do anything for Maya." He shot me a wink.

"You all work together?" Astrid asked, directing her question to Alex.

"Maya works with Mike and Stefan, I'm not part of their

awesome crew," he answered casually.

I beamed up at him, his firm one of the most formidable ones in the city. "Pretty sure you're *leading* your own awesome crew, not like you need us."

The waitress brought our drinks, three martini glasses filled with light pink liquid, rimmed with colored—pink—coconut, with sparkling glitter floating inside. There was a theme in case anyone didn't catch it.

"Looks interesting." Alex laughed, watching me bring the drink to my lips. It was sweet and fruity, but deceptive in its potency, the vodka hitting me like a truck.

"WOW." I swallowed, making a mental note to drink slowly.

Astrid shimmied as she gulped hers like it was fruit juice. "I know, right? So good."

Stefan followed Astrid's lead and drained half his glass while Mike and Alex enjoyed their beers. It was definitely a different dynamic from when we'd been at the sports bar, but no one seemed to mind.

Alex asked Mike and Stefan about their work, and they reciprocated without mentioning his brother. They were careful to include Astrid, asking her about her work as another round of drinks arrived.

I was intentionally quiet, doing my best to observe interactions and then interpret them every conceivable way. While I was sure Alex had no interest in her, her lingering looks at him didn't ease me, the urge to grab some of her hair just in case, fierce.

"You okay?" Alex whispered in my ear, his breath tickling my skin.

I nodded, laying my head against his shoulder. "Yep, all good."

A song came on that Astrid loved, making her squeal with delight. She demanded someone go dance with her and Stefan was only too willing to volunteer. The smile on his face was ridiculous

as she led him onto the dance floor; he mouthed a silent thank you
to Alex as he left.

"You want to dance?" Alex kissed my neck, my skin burning
from the heat of his lips.

I looked over at Mike who had remained in the booth with
us. "No, maybe later."

"Don't stay on my account." Mike raised his beer. "I'm hoping
if you leave that hot waitress comes back. I'm not as flashy as Stefan, and working with an audience gives me performance anxiety."

Alex laughed. "So how do you do in a court room?"

"Pretty good considering I'm not usually trying to get the
judge or the jury to sleep with me." He shrugged, taking another
swig of his beer.

"Well, on that note." I stood, straightening out my tight black
dress. "We'll leave you to do your best."

Alex followed me out onto the dance floor, his hands on my
hips as I walked in front of him. I let my ass graze across his crotch
a couple of times, deliberately slowing my stride so he'd press into
me. I could feel him hard in his pants, the tightening of his hands
warning me.

When we made it where other people were gyrating, he spun
me around and pulled me flush against him. While my movements
had been subtle, his had been deliberate, holding me against his
hard-on as he bent down and kissed me.

"You think you can tease me and I won't react just because
we're in a public place?" he breathed into my ear.

We were surrounded by bodies; the path we'd created to get
to the dance floor filling with people the moment we'd past.

"And risk a public indecency charge?" I laughed as I raised a
leg onto his hip and dipped like a Salsa dancer. "My, my, what will
the partners think?"

His hands went to my ass, traveling up my back as he bent

me back toward him. "I'll get you off and then clear myself of the charge. Don't doubt my ability in either of those things, Maya."

The way he rumbled my name gave me goosebumps, and if I weren't so worried of my own ability to clear myself, I would have risked it. Instead we fucked with our clothes on, our movements on the blurry side of decent as he kissed me without apology while we moved.

I wanted it to be perfect and in a lot of ways it was. I had not only fallen in love with one of the best men I'd ever known but I'd had the guts to tell him. And lucky for me he felt that way too. But I still worried about the job offer in New York he turned down for me. It ate at my happiness, trying to steal my joy as I lived in the moment, knowing that I could never just forget about it and let go.

"What's wrong?" He cradled my chin in his hands and he kissed me. "You went from smiling to that scowl you get when you're thinking too hard. And right now the only *hard* thing on your mind should be my dick," he chuckled.

He always seemed to know what was on my mind; it was both amazing and frustrating. "Not now. We'll talk about it later, after I've had your hard dick."

"Now this is something I can get behind." He squeezed my ass.

My hands ran down his strong arms. "Want to go back and see how Mike did with his waitress?"

He rolled his eyes, giving me an adorable pout. "Not particularly but I guess we should try and be polite since we're here with other people."

We wove back through the crowd to the booth at the back. Astrid and Stefan had returned—both wearing matching smiles— and Mike staring at his phone proudly.

"I bet it's not even hers," Stefan teased.

Mike shot him a sharp look. "It's hers. I texted her so she would have mine and she already responded."

"Sounds like we missed all the fun." I slipped into the booth, Alex shuffling in right behind me.

Astrid's eyes lit up. "Oh, I think the *fun* you were having on the dance floor was more enjoyable." She fanned herself gently. "It was very hot."

"You saw us?" I asked, not allowing myself to feel embarrassed. We hadn't seen either of them but to be fair, we weren't looking either.

Stefan coughed into his fist, hiding his grin. "Yeah, I think a lot of people saw you."

"Look how hot you are!" Astrid leaned across and angled her phone, the frame filled with a photo of me and Alex. He had one hand around my waist, while the other was holding my face, and his lips were on me in a way no one would be confused about what he was doing.

It was weird seeing us like that, and even weirder that she felt the need to take our picture, but I did have to admit it was pretty hot.

"You took a photo?" Alex asked, clearly annoyed.

Astrid huffed, folding her arms across her chest. "You know I document everything, people want to know what's going on in my life. I have three million followers on Instagram and six million on Twitter, this is how the world works these days."

"We're more the *not* documenting type." I tried to be diplomatic. "The world works a little differently for us."

While lawyers used social media as well, we had to be careful what we posted. There'd be no duck-lipped bikini shot on a beach in Cancun for me, or a bare chested, muscle flexing gym shot for Alex. At least not on anything public.

She gave a half-hearted apology I was sure she didn't really mean, making a show of deleting the pic before going ahead and taking a selfie she promptly posted for her hungry, waiting audience.

"So you're a model?" Mike asked, trying to change the subject.

"I model yes, but I'm more a social media influencer. People pay to have me try things or advertise their products knowing that my followers will buy. I still have a long way to go. There are some people who have ten times the reach I have, but everyone has to start somewhere."

Astrid then told us about all the parties and events she's paid to attend, her life sounding more and more exhausting the longer she spoke. There was a movie premiere she was invited to, not so subtly hinting she didn't have a date. Stefan very kindly offered to take her, shamelessly mentioning that because he was relatively new to the city his calendar was wide open and would love to meet new people.

Not sure if she agreed to because she didn't want to go alone or she if she liked the idea of someone falling over themselves to impress her. But either way Stefan had earned himself a date, sadly it wouldn't be just the two of them, Astrid's millions of followers bound to tag along.

Mike's waitress was getting off early and asked him if he wanted to go somewhere else for a drink. He barely said goodbye before leaving us. Which prompted me to decide it was time for us to leave too. Stefan and Astrid seemed to be having a good time and didn't need a chaperon which meant I could get Alex alone and hopefully naked.

While Astrid continued to talk, I leaned my head on Alex's chest and smiled up at him. "Take me to bed."

He leaned down and whispered, "I thought we agreed we wouldn't tell each other what to do? How about I take you back to my house and fuck you on my couch instead?"

I didn't answer, pulling him with me with as I waved to the others. "We're going to go, have a good night."

Alex laughed as we exited the club onto the street. "You're usually more polite than that."

"Well, I'm trying something new, sue me." My fingers moved in his as we waited for the valet to bring us his car.

The drive home was a challenge, while we didn't break any traffic laws, we bent them a lot. And when we finally got back to his house, we couldn't lock that door fast enough.

There was no sexy seduction, no slow and deliberate teasing as we kissed each other, stripping off clothes as we made the blind journey to his couch.

"I want you," he growled, backing me up until my ass hit the soft cushion of the sofa.

He followed me, falling to his knees, kissing me, as his hand roamed, filling the space between my legs. Every cell came awake on his command, the tingles traveled up my skin as little whimpers escaped my lips.

Oh. My. God.

It felt so good, *so* good, and I knew it was because it was him. Because it was us.

There was no part of my body left untouched, my hands finding his hard cock and giving it a stroke.

His fingers moved to my legs, pushing them out wider as he dropped his mouth to my center and licked. The change in position forced me to let go of him, my frustrated protest lasting only a second until he started to lap at me.

"I want, I want." I couldn't finish, *wanting* what he was doing to me more than my next thought.

His tongue swirled against my hot center, teasing me before he began sucking hard against me. Lick, suck, lick, suck—he alternated his movements as I rocked against his face. My toes curled against the floor as my back bowed, taking the pleasure while it slowly drove me insane.

While his mouth continued to dominate, he added in two fingers, their firm and rhythmic pumps sending me spiraling out of control as my hands tangled in his hair. Rivulets of pleasure echoed through me as I panted in the dark.

We hadn't bothered to turn the lights on, too desperate for each other to worry about that. But with his lips gently kissing my thigh and his fingers teasing the very last tremor from me, I wanted to see his face.

My hands fumbled to reach the lamp on an end table, knocking it over in the process. Alex lifted his head, chuckling. "You trying to trash my house?"

"No, I was trying to turn on the light. I wanted to see you."

I felt him move, lifting away from me as the heat of his hands and mouth left me. There was a pop, the overhead light illuminating as he walked back, his very hard cock jutting out in front of him.

My eyes rolled over his perfect body, my fingers curling around his length and stroking it. His eyes hooded, watching me as I moved his cock to my mouth and sucked.

His abs tightened as he swallowed a breath, my slow suck drawing him deeper into my throat as my hands pumped.

"Maya."

It was a warning, his hands threading in my hair as my tongue flattened against the underside of his erection while my fingers gently pulled on his balls.

His hips thrust, pushing himself deeper into my mouth while I fought the urge to gag. My teeth grazed him gently as he pulled himself out, repeating it over and over as his hold on my hair tightened.

"This is what I thought about on the dance floor tonight," he gritted out, his jaw tense. "About taking you and not giving a fuck who sees."

His hand went from my hair to his cock, pulling himself out of my mouth and giving himself a tug. "Stand up." He held out his other hand, helping me to my feet.

The height difference wasn't in our favor, needing to get on my toes just to kiss him. But he didn't share the same concerns, lifting me off the floor and holding me in his arms as I wrapped my legs around him.

Our mouths tangled, hot fevered kisses as the blunt head of his erection poked me. All I had to do was press down against it and he'd be inside of me. I wanted him to fill me, to feel the sweet bite against my skin as I adjusted to his girth.

My hips swiveled against him, using him for the friction I needed but not seeming to get enough. And then without thinking I pushed my hips down, the tip of his cock entering me.

His hands dug into my skin, holding me steady so I couldn't move. "Condoms are in the other room, Maya. I'm not wearing anything."

"It's okay, I promise it's okay," I begged, needing more of him.

He hesitated, probably having the same arguments in his own head that he'd shared with me the first time we got together and didn't have condoms. I was on the pill, we both had a clean bill of health—but was it really worth the risk?

"Fuck it." The argument was settled as he tilted his hips and pushed into me.

It felt so good, his skin bare against mine as he continued to pump. My hands adjusted their grip, feeling the strong muscles of his body flex with each movement, my ankles locked at his back.

My skin felt electric, the hard pebbles of my nipples teased by the firmness of his chest. I felt myself tense, the familiar wave of arousal flooding my body with the desperate need to come.

It was primal, fucking each other as we groaned and grunted, every inch of him spearing me deep and fast until I thought I was going to explode.

"Too good." He cursed against my mouth. "This feels too good. I need to pull out."

"Don't," I warned. "I want you inside of me." My hips rocked, praying he wouldn't stop. "Please don't stop."

He bit his lip as his eyes darkened, hips continuing to piston. I could tell he thought it wasn't a good idea but he wasn't going to tell me no.

I came with a shout, my body trembling as I held on as he continued to pump, his finish coming a few seconds after mine as he exploded inside of me. Our bodies pulsed as his load shot into me in hot bursts.

His lips kissed me gently on the shoulder as he smiled against my skin.

"You are such a bad influence."

CHAPTER #20

MY EYES OPENED at the sounds of incessant buzzing, followed by a low ring tone that wasn't mine. I groaned, shoving Alex roughly as I pulled a pillow over my head. We had been up late, moving to the bedroom shortly after the sex in the living room where I did my best to exert as much bad influence as I could. It was way too early to be awake, especially when we didn't have to.

Alex rolled to his side, taking me with him as he answered his phone. "Yeah," he bit out gruffly. He wasn't feeling the need to be awake either.

"Umm . . . yeah, why?" I felt his body stiffen as he spoken on the phone. "Okay, hold on."

His hand peeled the pillow I was holding against my head, and kissed me gently. "It's Roman, he needs to talk to us."

"Roman?" I shot back confused. What could he possibly want with both of us?

Alex shuffled up the bed, hitting the speaker button on his phone as I settled beside him. "Okay, you're on with both of us. What's going on?"

"Good morning, love birds." I could hear the grin in his voice, sounding too chipper for that time of the morning. "How's everyone feeling? Good? Great to hear. Now, I'm sure you already have plans for the day but they might want to include calling your mothers."

"I thought you agreed not to tell anyone?" Alex fired back, clearly annoyed.

Roman laughed, seeming to be thoroughly enjoying himself. "I didn't tell a soul, dipshit. But that photo of the two of you mouth fucking each other on Astrid's Instagram account is another story. Not very smart, little brother."

"SHE POSTED IT ON INSTAGRAM?" I screamed, suddenly wide awake as I grabbed for my phone and opened the app. I didn't even need to try to find her account, Astrid doing us both a favor and tagging us in the steamy pic. It wasn't the pic she had shown us, with this one taken a minute or two earlier. Her head was in the side of the frame, her mascara'd eyes looking dreamily as she covered her cheeky smile with her perfectly manicured pink nails. #Lovers #AlexIsOffTheMarket #LegalAffairs #SoHot #DebriefingNeeded

Oh.

My.

God.

My eyes widened at the number of likes and comments. She wasn't kidding when she said she had a following, her posse of "influentials" loving the steamy picture of Alex and I.

Alex grabbed the phone from my hands, his hand tightening around it. "Fuck."

"Yep," Roman answered. "Anyway, don't tell me I never do anything for you."

"Wait, what are you doing up so early?" Alex checked the time display on my phone as he handed it back. It was only five thirty.

"My son is a tiny terrorist who has a vendetta against sleep. I'm doing my best not to give in to his demands," he deadpanned.

"Thanks, Roman." I rubbed my temples, the idea of a lazy

Saturday morning with Alex swirling down the toilet.

Alex grabbed my hand as he shook his head. "Yeah thanks, Roman."

"Don't mention it, kids. Have a great day."

He hung up and was no doubt going to laugh at our carelessness. We weren't exactly hiding our relationship, I just wanted us to be in it awhile before my mother got any harebrained ideas and started planning a wedding. She'd always loved Alex and his family, it would be like Christmas coming early knowing we were together.

"Fucking hell. I'm going to kill her." Alex scrolled on his phone, finding her name and pressed call, it automatically diverting to voicemail.

While he tried again, I returned back to the post. Not only did it have thousands of hearts and comments, but I'd seemed to have picked up at least a thousand follow requests not to mention at least twenty direct messages.

So much for flying under the radar.

And if I thought Instagram was a problem, then it had nothing on my actual phone. It was still on silent, with about thirty missed calls from Jackie and Lisa combined and so many text messages I was surprised the thing hadn't dissolved.

"SHIT." The bubble of the family group chat was sitting at twenty unread messages. No need to guess what the topic of conversation was, my brother Jordon had his own little sleep terrorists so I was sure he'd seen it too.

"She's not answering." Alex pulled the phone away from his ear. "If I can just get through to her, I'll make her delete the post."

"Pretty sure it's been screenshot and regrammed a bunch already. It's been up for hours. And I'm almost positive my family already know too." I waved my phone, displaying its obnoxious unread messages.

And speak of the devil and he doth appear, the freaking thing started vibrating in my hands, the word MOM lighting up the screen.

"Well, this will be fun." I grimaced as I swiped and answered. "Hey Mom, what are you doing up so early?"

I was hoping it was a coincidence and she was awake because her micro herb garden needed watering or something. But the minute I answered, there was no doubt she knew. "Maya Louise Zaveri. Are you dating Alex Larsson and didn't tell me?"

It was clear she was pissed, and not because I was dating Alex. It was because I was dating Alex and didn't tell her about it.

"Mom, it's new. I just didn't want anyone to get the wrong idea or get too excited." I tried my best to talk her off the ledge.

"What wrong idea is there to get? I think from that photo it's pretty clear what is going on."

Well, she had that right. It was damning evidence to say the least, with random strangers weighing in on what songs were going to be on our sexual soundtrack. Had to admit, some of their suggestions had actually been decent.

Alex held out his hand for the phone, gesturing for me to pass it to him. My head shook as I continued to deal with my mom. "You're right, and I didn't want you to find out that way. But know that we are both happy and it's a good thing."

"Oh, Maya." I could hear her voice warble.

"Do not cry, Mom," I warned, knowing the tears were going to come whether I wanted them or not.

"I'm just really glad. He's such a good boy and well, I'm just so happy for you."

"Yeah, well I'm glad too. Now, can we maybe talk about this in a few hours when it's a more reasonable time?"

"Of course, baby. But you might want to talk to your brothers. Jordon is threatening to get on a plane and . . . wait a second, I need to read it." Her voice lowered as she moved the speaker away from her mouth. "Remove Alex's spleen through his nose if he hurts you." She brought the phone back to her mouth. "I know he's a doctor, but I don't think that is possible."

"No, it's not and I'll talk to him. And everyone else." I shrugged, knowing Ben and my sisters-in-law probably had their own ideas on what was happening. Not that it would change how I felt about Alex or persuade me I had made a mistake.

"Okay, sweetheart, call me later. And give my love to Alex." She chuckled on the phone.

"Will do." I hung up and tossed the phone onto the bed. "Just so you are aware, my mother is probably planning our wedding and naming our children. If you are as smart as you say, you should probably run now."

Alex kissed my shoulder and smiled. "I'm not going anywhere and I'm not afraid of your mother."

I shook my head, waving my finger. "You have no idea what you are dealing with. Run. Run away and don't look back."

"You don't think I'm going to be getting the same kind of heat from my mother? The same woman who had five boys and looked at you as a surrogate daughter? At least your mom lives out of town, we're scheduled to meet mine for brunch later today."

Ah crap.

I hadn't thought about that, our plans to smuggle in the bottle of Yarra Valley Shiraz taking a backseat since the evolution of our early morning drama. It was definitely going to add a degree of difficulty. Fairly sure the chances of the two of us sliding down to her cellar undetected were extremely low. Especially when we were probably going to be watched like hawks.

"Okay, divide and conquer." I sat up, not willing to let it spiral anymore out of control than it already had. "I'm going to call my brothers and deal with that and you see if you can get a hold of Astrid. While the damage is done, we still have clients and partners we need to answer to. Hopefully they don't mix in the same circles."

"On it." Alex moved from the bed and grabbed his phone. "I'm calling her agent. She might not take a call from me, but there is no way she'd dodge a possible booking."

He wandered into the living room to make his call while I called my brother, Jordon, first. He was angry, thinking Alex was using me as his new plaything, still seeing me as his kid sister he needed to protect. I assured him that no one was or would take advantage of me and I didn't need protecting. I know in a lot of ways he took Dad's departure a lot harder than us. He was forced to grow up sooner, and be the man of the house when most of his friends were out getting wasted and screwing girls. It was hard for him to see me as a woman who knew her own mind, which was part of the reason why I had to leave when I went to college. I promised him I was okay, and that I was happy and that I needed to live my own life. And that life included Alex Larsson.

Ben was easier to convince. He was happy for me as long as I was happy, but warned that if Alex ever hurt me, he'd make it so his body would never be found. Typically the kind of threat you'd expect from a brother, but as an engineer on a construction site, Ben actually had the resources to do it.

After an exhausting marathon of calls—which included another to my mother who had texted me three time while I was on the phone to my brothers—I pulled the phone away from my ear and collapsed on the bed.

Alex had been making some calls of his own, the post and photo of us miraculously disappearing after a heated call to her agent.

Part of me hated the intrusion into our personal lives, our relationship public fodder for people to weigh in on. But another part of me was glad, being pushed to say to everyone what I already knew in my heart.

I loved Alex Larsson.

"Well, Nick and Dave think it's utterly hilarious, while Eric tried to convince me that it might not be a bad thing. Apparently he knew or Tia knew, anyway, he thinks we should just do our thing. I haven't spoken to my mom yet; I figured she is probably sleeping. Jeremy, the agent for my three brothers, sent a group text to all of them when he saw it and asked if I wanted to work." Alex shook his head as he laid beside me. "I can't believe he woke them to ask, like law is just some hobby I'm doing to pass the time."

"Well, agents aren't exactly the most sympathetic of creatures. I hope they told him to fuck off." I turned to look at him, his blond bed hair so perfectly mussed it was grossly unfair.

"Yep. Although, Nick did threaten to remove my balls if I hurt you." His finger traced the edge of my ribs. "He's made it clear out of the two of us who is his favorite."

Years ago, hearing that Nick felt that way would have made my year. But as I hugged Alex, I realized that had just been a schoolgirl infatuation.

My lips brushed against his as I whispered, "Jordon says he'll remove your spleen through your nose."

"Well that sounds painful." Alex laughed. "Guess I better make sure I don't fuck this up."

"Likewise, and just so you know, none of what they say means anything." I grabbed his hand and rested it on my heart. "Because there's only two people we need to worry about. Me and you. I don't care what anyone else says."

JACKIE AND LISA were doubly pissed. A. Because I hadn't given them all the juicy details of my friends-to-lovers romance, and B. Because he was Alex *Larsson*.

Both of them were flabbergasted as to how I'd held on to that little gem for so long, not breathing a word to any of them, let alone growing up with intersecting families. They understood when I explained all of my reasons why—my dad and the disgrace affecting the Larsson family, and my need to protect them and feeling responsible—and they agreed to forgive me. But apparently that didn't get me off the hook for a future cross-examination from both of them.

It was a compromise.

And speaking of cross-examinations.

"Don't you think we should have called your mother and explain about the picture before she sees it?" I warned Alex, my hands clutching my handbag that weighed a ton thanks to the Shiraz I had stashed in there. The challenge was still on apparently, because we needed more drama in our lives.

"Trust me, I know my mom and it's easier if we just do it face to face. Like ripping a Band-Aid, right off. Then everyone will know and we can move on with our lives."

Alex pressed the doorbell and my heart was pounding. It had been hard enough going to Kate Larsson's house the first time when all I had been carrying was my father's bullshit, now a woman who used to change my diapers would know I was sleeping with her youngest son. Not sure how to make myself feel less awkward about it.

Kate answered, looking just as amazing as the last time, and smiled warmly at both of us. "Maya, Alex." She held out her arms. "Come in."

She fussed with Alex's hair telling him he needed a cut and complimented me on my cute skirt. If she's seen the picture or knew anything, she wasn't showing it.

"You two are the only ones stopping by." She sighed, showing us to the already set table. "Eric has an audition in New York so Tia and the kids are with him and staying in Brooklyn for the week. Roman and Lauren had a bad night with baby Lucas so decided to try and get a nap if he lets them. Dave and Jessica said they double booked and their other plans weren't breakable. And Nick—well, I haven't heard from him or from Claire to be honest."

It was decided—by Alex—that the rest of the crew sit out, and give us time alone with Kate. Roman had been the only one who'd protested, but was brought into line by his very persuasive wife. But of course that was all news to Kate who was wondering why her house that was usually bustling for brunch only had the two of us.

"Their loss." Alex leaned over and kissed his mother on the cheek and then sat down beside me.

He tried to grab my hand under the table and I kicked him. If we'd somehow caught a break and she hadn't seen anything, then she wasn't going to get a personal show at her dining room table. We were going to do something novel and *tell* her.

"Anything I can help you with, Kate?" I offered, standing while Alex grinned from behind his glass of orange juice.

"No, sweetie." She reached out and squeezed my hand. "I'm making a baked omelet that is almost done and the salmon is ready. Why don't you two tell what you have been up to?"

My eyes shot to Alex, encouraging him to take the lead. That was our cue if ever I'd heard one and dragging it out wasn't happening.

Alex cleared his throat, coughing to hide his laugh as I kicked him under the table again.

"Well Mom, so we have an interesting story."

"Oh?" she asked, collecting her juice and taking a sip. "Is everything okay? You're not in any trouble at work, are you?"

"No, nothing like that. We're just not sure how you're going to take it." His eyes glanced over at me in what was the biggest tell of all mankind.

She lowered her glass and looked at him with that momvision

that all mothers seemed to possess. Then her eyes moved to me, not sparing me of their scrutiny as she scanned.

"Alex, Maya, I may be old, but I know how things work." She shook her head, giving us a tight smile. "And as long as you're happy, I'm happy."

My heart raced, pole-vaulting in my chest as I breathed a sigh of relief. "Oh thank God," I whispered under my breath and reached for Alex's hand. "We are very, very happy."

She beamed at us both proudly. "Well good. It's still early days, but I'm sure you're going to make great parents."

WHAT.

THE.

FUCK.

DID.

SHE.

JUST.

SAY.

"Um, what?" I looked at Alex confused, releasing his hand like it had caught fire. "No. No. No I'm not."

"Are you sure?" Kate's brow arched, looking like she knew something I didn't.

"Mom, we've only been dating for a couple of weeks. There's no way Maya's pregnant." Alex laughed nervously, and I wondered if he was doing mental calculations in his head like I was to see if it was a possibility.

I mean, sure we'd used protection and it wasn't always a hundred percent effective. But even if I were pregnant, there was no way I'd even know yet. No skipped periods, no magical signs. And yet, even though I knew the chances were virtually zero, I wanted to run out and get a pregnancy test just to be sure. On the remote chance that Kate Larsson could sniff out an elevated hCG like a human EPT.

I went to Yale, people. YALE.

"Well, okay then." She smiled at us unconvinced. "Just to be sure, brunch is high in protein and folic acid. The first trimester is extremely important."

"Oh my God." My throat constricted, trying hard to breathe.

I was pregnant and didn't know it. She was able to look into my uterus with that momvision and see a tiny Larsson. How the hell could it happen? We'd been so careful.

"Maya." Alex looked at me concerned, probably because I was turning blue. Asphyxiation probably wasn't good for the baby but there wasn't a lot I could do. "Mom, we're not pregnant. We were just trying to tell you that we're in love with each other."

Kate laughed, shaking her head at both of us. "Son, it might be news to you, but it isn't to me. Of course you're in love with each other. I saw it the first time you came to the house. Look at the two of you, pretending like it wasn't a thing." She chuckled to herself, amused. *So that's where Roman got it from, interesting.*

"But if you keep kissing her like you did in that picture, you *will* get her pregnant." She playfully clipped her son over the head.

"You saw that?" I asked, still not sure if I understood what was happening.

"I think most of the country saw it, sweetheart." She gave me a warm smile. "Alex isn't the first of my children to be featured online kissing a woman. I just think the whole thing is hilarious and that you made this big show of coming to tell me. I am flattered that you think so highly of my opinion. And I meant what I said, I am genuinely happy for both of you."

"So this whole thing is a joke?" Alex narrowed his eyes at his mother, trying to hide the smile.

She shrugged innocently like she hadn't stressed me the hell out. "Don't be angry at your mother, Alex. I gave you life. Besides, I think it's only fair since you've been helping yourself to my wine collection." Her pointed look directed at Alex.

"You knew about that too?" Alex's eyes widened as she laughed.

Kate looked at us both, giving us a smirk. "Sweetheart, I know about everything. Maybe next time we can save the theatrics and save your brothers from having to make up excuses. You know how much I love having a full house and I miss my grandbabies."

Well, at least it was now all out in the open. As *out in the open* as sharing a picture with millions of people would make it at least. And with a huge sigh of relief, we ate our "pregnancy friendly" brunch, and I reminded myself that unprotected sex probably wouldn't be a good idea moving forward.

Alex leaned into me as we finished eating, a devilish smile playing on his lips. "I'll help with dishes and distract her while you sneak the bottle of wine into the cellar. She might think she knows everything, but she sure won't see that coming."

And with my mission clear, I excused myself to go to the bathroom.

Alex may have been discovered, but I'd spent *years* flying under the radar.

CHAPTER #21

THE WEEKEND HAD been perfect.

Astrid called us both to apologize, and I assured her that while I wasn't pleased about being publically outed, I was no longer angry. I didn't think the two of us were going to be close friends anytime soon, but I saw in a lot of ways we were a lot alike. Obviously not in looks or temperament, but in that we both moved away from our families and were trying to make it work. Neither of us had been alone, but it didn't mean that we hadn't been lonely.

So with all of that put behind us, I felt like it was time to jump another hurdle. Because clearly I just couldn't allow myself to be blissfully happy for twenty-four hours.

"Have you turned down the job offer yet?"

It was late Sunday night and we were lying on Alex's couch after dinner. Just casually relaxing, with no real worry. Which is exactly why I had to bring it up. Sometimes, I literally hated myself.

"You worried I'm going to change my mind?" He laughed as his hand strummed my back.

I shuffled up to face him. "No, but are you sure this is what you want to do? I know you said you wouldn't hate me or regret your decision. But have you really thought about what turning it down would mean for your career?"

He rolled his eyes, probably wondering—like I was—why I wouldn't leave it the hell alone. He said he was staying. Why couldn't I be happy with that? "Maya, it might take me a couple more years but I can achieve everything I could have in New York, right here."

"Have you called them yet?" I asked, ignoring his attempt to placate me.

He shuffled up too, knowing it wasn't going to be a three-minute conversation. "I was going to call tomorrow. Initially, I was going to fly to New York to turn down their offer since they flew to California to offer it to me. It seemed like the right thing to do and I just wanted to shake their hand, and assure them that the timing wasn't right but I was thankful for the opportunity. But it seems like over-kill, flying all the way over there just to say no."

Alex—like all of his brothers—had an extremely high level of personal integrity. It was something I'd always admired and a quality I fiercely shared. Which was why he wanted to turn down the offer face to face. It's exactly what I would have done, making sure I didn't burn any bridges I might have to cross one day. So I had my own suspicions on why he had the change of heart.

"Are you worried that when you get there they might try and change your mind? Or that if you see the firm, you might have second thoughts?"

He blew out a breath of frustration. "Maya—"

"No, wait. Just hear me out." My hand went to his arm stopping him from continuing. "When I was growing up, I thought I had the most perfect life. Honestly, it's stuff Hallmark movies are made of. But in a second, it all changed and the rug was pulled out from under us. I know I haven't spoken much about it, but like it or not, it's changed me and how I see the world. I can't be blindly optimistic anymore. I wish I could be, and as much as I know you have the best intentions. I have to ask questions. It's what makes me a good lawyer. And it's not about not *trusting* you, it's about believing enough in myself that my opinion has value. That I'm allowed to test a theory, and even if I'm wrong, you'll still love me. My mom never once questioned my dad, believing he had our best interests at heart. And as much as you aren't him, I am not her either."

He blinked, probably expecting an evening of mindless television followed by some hot and heavy making out. I had a bad habit of not keeping my hands to myself and he didn't seem to have a problem with it. Instead, he got a philosophical debate *without* a hand job. But if I'd been in his shoes, I knew it wouldn't have been an easy decision. Hell, he'd asked me to go with him and I had turned him down. Not because he loved me more, but because I knew our relationship had to be built on *more* than just love.

"So what are you suggesting? Because Maya, I know you sure as hell aren't breaking up with me," he warned.

"No, I am not breaking up with you." I shoved him playfully. "But I think you should go. See it with your own eyes and if you decide to turn it down, I will never bring it up again. But if you're there and you decide that you want it, I promise you we'll make it work. I don't want you to have to choose, Alex."

"Make it work how? See each other on weekends and holidays?" he scoffed in disbelief. "Maya, it's a five-hour flight. The time difference, the jet lag, how long you think that is going to last?"

"It will if we want it to," I assured him, knowing that as difficult as it would be, it would be worth it. "Maybe in a couple of years, things change all the time. Maybe a firm out here will try and poach you back or maybe I'll get an impressive offer of my own out there."

"Do you want me to leave?" He narrowed his eyes, probing

me with each word. "Are you worried this isn't going to work out and think it's just easier if you don't have to try?"

"No," I shot back. "I want you to stay. I want you to stay so badly it scares me." I grabbed his hand, needing for him to believe me.

"Then why are we fighting about this?" He asked the very same questions I asked myself.

"Because you said it yourself. You would have gotten on that plane and shook their hand to turn them down, and the reason you aren't now concerns me."

He opened his mouth like he was about to say something and then stopped. He couldn't argue with something he'd already admitted to me, which meant he knew I had to at least been partially right.

"Just go see them. Go see your brother and his family for a day or two, I promise you I'll be here when you get back," I offered, hoping Eric being in Brooklyn might sweeten the deal.

"I won't change my mind, Maya. Promise me this isn't some bullshit excuse because you're scared."

"I'm terrified." I laughed. "The idea of losing you is more than I can stand, but I promise you, that I'm not pushing you away."

I meant it too. Knowing that it would be easy for me to reconcile our breakup by him moving away rather than any failing on either of our parts. That I loved him so much I couldn't imagine my life without him. And what would that mean if we did eventually break up? But it wasn't an act of sabotage, and if he chose New York, I would do whatever I could to maintain the relationship. I'd fight to the death for it. Because we might have only been "dating" a few weeks, but I'd had him in my heart for years and there was no way I'd lose my best friend again.

He nodded, reluctantly agreeing. "I'll see if I can leave Wednesday, so I can be back in time for the weekend."

"Good." I put my arms around him and leaned my head against his chest. "I'll be here when you get back."

I THOUGHT ALEX'S trip would hang over us like a dark cloud, but it didn't. He agreed that declining the offer in person was the right thing to do given how big and generous it had been. And I felt like when he came back it would be for the right reasons. There were no guarantees either way, but I knew we'd survive it.

Leah and I were still working our case, putting in long hours as we mounted our response. It was exciting work but time consuming, which meant when I did see Alex, all I wanted to do was eat dinner and then fall into bed. Half the time we ate *in* bed, capitalizing on our time together as I refused to become distant. We even did our usual Monday night at the legal clinic, staying there until they kicked us out and promising to go back again in a couple of weeks.

And my heart was full.

The day of his departure, I kissed him goodbye in the morning and he caught a cab to the airport. He very generously let me use his car while he was gone, and I loved the feeling of driving again.

"Alex left?" Mike asked as I strolled in.

I nodded, handing out coffees I'd picked up since I had extra time. "Yep, he had an early morning flight to JFK. He should be back Friday night or Saturday morning."

"You need a ride?" Stefan asked, the two of them careful not to coddle me.

"Nope." I waved his key fob. "He's letting me drive his car. Crazy because I might not give it back when he returns."

Stefan smirked, taking a sip of his coffee. "You could argue abandonment. Squatter's rights? I'd be happy to be your second chair."

"Thanks, I'll check out precedent on my lunch break and we can discuss strategy." I laughed, checking the time and knowing Leah would be in at any moment.

Stefan shook his head. "Oh no, we are going out and taking a proper break today, Maya. Now Leah has you working that case, you haven't put enough hours into the trio. Mike checked the by-laws, and you are required to give us at least an hour of your time or you forfeit your position."

"And there is a new associate coming in next week who's a transfer from Minneapolis." Mike grimaced.

"You boys are such snobs." I laughed. "But lunch isn't going to happen, how's dinner sound? I'll even go to that horrible sports bar you guys love." Actually excited about going out to dinner and not sitting at my apartment by myself.

"That horrible sports bar has amazing food," Mike argued.

"Whatever, clock is ticking and you need to make your choice. Dinner or rain check." I tapped my non-existent watch as Leah breezed in through the door.

Stefan nodded his hello to her before turning back to me. "Fine, dinner. And no reneging."

"Not a chance," I said as I waved goodbye.

Leah pointed me toward her conference room as she went into her office. I figured I'd get set up, arranging the files we'd worked on last time on the boardroom table and strategically put my phone where I could see it.

It was on silent, but I wanted to be able to see when Alex landed. It might only be for a couple of days, but I was still going to miss him.

"Hey Maya, change of plans." Leah came in and smiled. "I'm going to need for you to go on the road and do some digging. Our client maintains that a memo was circulated by the company alluding that the airbags were faulty in May but didn't issue a recall until September. And of course, the only memo released in discovery is the mention of the recall."

"Does she have a physical copy?" I asked, knowing if there was one, she wouldn't be asking me to dig.

"Nope and the five people in the email chain have denied its existence as well. I still plan to question them when we take the deposition, but if we can get information from the importer, we might get a clearer idea if they knew or didn't."

I looked at my watch, it was nine a.m. and gridlock on the road. "It will probably take me at least a hour to get there, maybe an hour or more to get back. That's not even taking in question time. Are you okay with losing me for that long?"

"Take as long as you need. Check out the warehouse, talk to the person at the front desk, be personable." She smiled. "Most of these things were made in China and only assembled here, but something tells me if someone is going to take a risk, it's a big corporation and not a struggling import business."

"On it." I grabbed my phone and started to pack up the files.

"No, leave it." Leah shook her head. "I'm going to have Stefan do some fact checking for me today."

"Stefan?" I raised a brow, surprised.

Leah laughed. "Don't worry, you're not being replaced. Just get me what we need. Take the day, if you finish early then go home and spend some quality time with that hot boyfriend of yours. We'll go over findings tomorrow."

I stopped short of telling her my hot boyfriend was on the other side of the country, instead thanking her and grabbing my things.

"You're leaving?" Mike looked up from his desk.

"Yep, I'm on assignment." I winked. "Stefan is taking my place for the day and before you worry, I'll meet you both tonight for dinner. I'll call when I leave my apartment in case I'm running late."

"Short of a kidnapping, you better be there," he warned,

waving me off out the door.

I bundled up my bags and grabbed the keys for the car. "Cross my heart."

Stefan passed me in the hall also surprised to see me leave. "We sneaking out?"

"No, you're staying and don't mess up my files," I warned, waiting by the elevator.

"*Your* files? Have I been summoned?" He held his hands up dramatically to his chest.

I waved, pressing the call button and waiting for the car to arrive. "Yes. You can tell me all about it tonight."

THE I8 DROVE like a dream, and while I wasn't able to discover the missing memo, I was able to find out who the direct supplier was from China and an email from them advising to check their stock as there may have been a quality issue as early as March of the year in question. It wasn't a smoking gun and didn't admit fault, but it would strengthen our case.

Rather than going back to the office with mediocre news, I decided to take the rest of the day off and hope I was able to talk to Alex.

He'd texted earlier to let me know he'd landed but didn't have his meeting with the firm until tomorrow. So he was going to take the day, hang out with Eric and possibly play tourist for the afternoon. He also mentioned that he left a set of keys to his house inside the glove compartment and to feel free to use them if I felt the need to do any laundry.

The permission to go to his house and the keys did make me wonder about the postcards I had planted. Other than the day I'd hidden them, I hadn't seen them resurface. I'd have expected him to find at least one or two, their hiding places hopefully not so obscure that I wouldn't remember them myself.

Curiosity getting the better of me, I decided to take a detour to Alex's house and do some investigating for my own purposes. Maybe he'd found one, thought nothing of it and tossed it in the trash. It still seemed odd he hadn't at least mentioned it, wondering why there were unwritten postcards floating around his home.

I parked the car out front and let myself in. The air still smelt of Alex, the heady mix of soap and cologne wafting through the air like he'd left minutes ago instead of hours. God I missed him, ridiculous since he'd barely been gone and would have still been at work. But I knew he was miles away, and there was no reasoning with my stupid heart.

My hands started opening up cupboards, searching for a postcard. I was positive the Disney one had been stashed behind the sugar canister but when I moved things around there was nothing there. Maybe I'd been mistaken? So much had happened in such a short time and I had been in a hurry.

Next I moved the laundry where I knew for a fact I'd hidden the card of the Griffith Observatory. I distinctly remembered how the colors of the sky had matched his box of detergent, and assuming it would be the first to be discovered. Its hiding place was confirmed a few days later when I did laundry again, which meant it had to be there. But as I moved the detergent and stain remover on the shelf above the washer and dryer, there was nothing. It was as if it vanished.

So freaking odd.

With my resolve to find at least one of those stinking cards, I systematically went room to room opening closets, doors and rummaging through his personal belongings like I was a thief. If I'd thought about it I'd have been embarrassed and remorseful for invading his personal space but I was too involved in my objective to worry about all of that. Where the hell were they? Did I imagine the whole thing? Have some weird out of body experience brought on by stress where I visualized myself doing it but didn't actually follow through?

No. Surely I wasn't losing my mind.

I finished up in the bedroom, even if it had been the only room that hadn't hosted a hidden postcard. At the time I hadn't wanted to go through his things—something I'd clearly made my peace with—and left the room untouched by my silly attempt at suggestion.

Not sure why I felt the sudden need to lie on his bed, it was still early afternoon and I wasn't that tired. Besides, I still had to a job to do and unless I wanted to admit the possibility of a psychotic episode, or ask Alex point blank what had happened to them—which would bring up the why—I didn't have time for a nap. But as I kicked off my heels and crawled onto the comforter, I couldn't think of anything else than putting my head on his pillow and breathing in his scent.

I'd officially reached a new low.

Too bad I didn't care as I nuzzled against it and took my first deep sniff.

As my fingers slid underneath—to bring it closer to my face and expedite the crazed stalker behavior I was clearly demonstrating—something pricked my skin.

Like a snake had bitten me, I pulled my finger out quickly to examine it, my heart beating a million miles a minute. No skin had been punctured, which hopefully meant there were no creepy crawlies under there, but I wasn't going to put my hand under there again either.

Carefully, I lifted the pillow by the corners, pushing it away from the mattress towards the headboard. My eyes floated around the room looking for a weapon, if there was something under there I wasn't going to run from the room screaming without killing it.

And it was times like that where I was glad I didn't carry a gun.

"Oh, Alex." I gasped, tossing the pillow aside to reveal a pile of postcards tied up with a red ribbon.

My fingers fumbled as I pulled at the knot desperate to see if they were all there. And as I laid them out on the bed, picture side up, I could see that not even one was missing. He'd stealthily found them all—clearly being busy in the limited time we weren't together or I wasn't watching—and not said a word. Instead, collecting them and putting them somewhere he'd hope I'd find them. For a man who didn't do sentimental, it was incredibly romantic.

I lifted the picture of Santa Monica Pier and turned it over, there on the part that was supposed to be blank, was his familiar black scrawl.

First time we went there alone we ate at that Mexican place at the back. Best chips and salsa.

I brought the card to my chest, hugging it and remembering the memory. We'd been maybe fourteen and had hitched a ride with Jordon. We made fun of the lovers kissing on the pier and I'd confessed to having feelings for Nick. It felt like so long ago.

Next there was a picture of the Hollywood sign, I flipped over the card, hoping to see another message.

Went hiking up the trail when we were fifteen. Our moms freaked out when they found out, both of us were grounded for a week.

I laughed, remembering how mad both Kate and my mom had been. Of course they might have been more okay with it had it been during the day. But we'd snuck out, deciding that climbing it at night sounded like a better idea. *Hey, they always went up there at night in the movies, what was the big deal?* We had barely made it a mile before a park ranger found us and called our parents. It was the first real trouble I'd been in, my juvenile brush with lawlessness extremely limited.

Every card I turned over, he'd written a note. Either mentioning a time we'd been there or reminding me how cool our "backyard" was. I didn't disagree, every single postcard making me want to revisit every single one of those places with him. *God I hoped he hated New York.* I laughed to myself, holding the postcards in my hands like precious jewels.

Well, I guess if I'd been the subject of the experiment I'd have said it was a resounding success. But whether he felt the same way was another story. One thing I did know for sure, was if he took the job in New York, me staying back without him was no longer a certainty. Because for as much as I loved L.A., I loved him more.

CHAPTER #22

I'D SPOKEN TO Alex while I was getting ready for dinner. I hadn't mentioned the postcards, figuring we'd save that for when he got back. Plus, I wanted to hear all about his day, find out what he'd been up to.

He was still wide awake despite his early morning start, and told me at least three times he wished I'd been there with him. I promised we'd go visit together soon, and told him to go surprise Jackie and Lisa if he had time. Most guys wouldn't have even considered going to meet two people they didn't know, but Alex wasn't like most guys. No doubt he was going to turn up to their firm and mess with them in some way. I wish I could have been there to participate and to see the three people I cared about so much get to meet for the first time.

But instead I'd go spend the evening with two new friends, who while hadn't been around long, had become important to me all the same.

"Was beginning to think you weren't going to show up." Stefan rose to his feet and gave me a hug.

"I told him you would." Mike smiled proudly. "Should have put some money on it."

I shuffled into the booth and very maturely poked my tongue at both of them. "I had to go past Alex's and I got distracted."

"Ahhhhh yes, have you heard from lover boy?" Stefan flagged the waitress down, buying a round of beers.

Hiding the stupid grin on my face wasn't even a possibility as I answered. "Yeah, we spoke for a little bit before I left."

"Hence why she's late," Mike stage whispered.

Stefan stage whispered back, "And smiling."

"You two can knock it off already," I warned, picking up a menu and pretending to read it. Not sure why I bothered, there wasn't a chance I was missing out on the BBQ ribs, especially when they brought up such fond memories of Alex licking his fingers.

Tragic.

I was tragic and I needed help.

The waitress arrived with our drinks and we ordered food, and then proceeded to talk about work even though we weren't at the office. Stefan had told me about working with Leah and asked about my field trip and then Mike had talked about his case.

"So, when's your hot date with Astrid? The movie premiere?" I asked batting my eyes playfully. Hey, if he was going to tease me about Alex, then I could tease him about Astrid.

"Next *Monday* night." The emphasis on the day of the week like it was offensive. "Who goes out on a Monday? Anyway, apparently it's a thing so I've already dropped off my tux at the cleaners. Not sure how it's going to go, she hasn't really spoken to me since that night at the club." He shrugged, not seeming to be too disappointed.

"Well, she's a busy woman." It was strange times when I was defending her. "She's got influencing to do." I couldn't help but laugh.

"Indeed. Well for what it's worth it will be an experience. Give me something to tell my buddies back home." He winked as he took a swig of his beer.

We finished our dinner and our beers, deciding not to play too late on a school night. That morning alarm was going to come way too soon, and all of us had been putting in serious hours.

"I'm assuming you drove Alex's car?" Stefan paid the bill before any of us could argue.

I nodded, throwing in some money for the tip despite his protest. "Yep, I parked around the corner on the street."

"Let me walk you to your car." He put his hand on my arm stopping me from leaving. "There wasn't a question mark at the end of the sentence, Maya. I know you're good, but think of it as a favor to me. I'm parked about a block away and could use the ride."

While I was positive his car was neither parked that far, nor that he needed to be chauffeured to it, I agreed because I didn't feel like arguing. Walking around the streets in L.A. was no different than any major city—don't be stupid, stick to well lit areas, and don't go into shady neighborhoods. But as we said goodbye to Mike and strolled to Alex's car—the back half obscured by shadow—I was glad to have the company.

Something was off, the hairs on the back of my neck standing on end as we got closer, and I wasn't sure why I felt the panic.

"You okay?" Stefan asked, looking at me strangely. I hadn't realized I'd stopped, the car literally a couple of feet away.

With no good reason—and a very loud internal voice telling me I was ridiculous—I looked around with suspicion, my feet refusing to move.

Clearly, I'd watched too many crime shows, or horror stories because other than a streetlight that must have blown a fuse there was nothing that pointed to foul play.

See, there is nothing there, Maya. It's just another example of you trying to find problems when they don't exist. It's what I had done with Alex and what I was obviously doing with the damn car.

"Yeah, I'm just acting crazy." I laughed, trying to shake off the weird feeling in my gut and convince my feet to move.

Not sure he bought my stellar act of bravado, glancing at me and then the car before reaching out and grabbing my arm. "Maybe I should check it out."

I shook my head feeling slightly embarrassed. What the hell was my problem? There was no big conspiracy, no one was "after" me, and if someone wanted to steal the car, they would have done that already.

"No, it's fine. We'll go together." Instinctively I moved closer to him, my head swiveling to each side as I familiarized myself with the surroundings. I probably looked like a moron, but I preferred being alert and looking ridiculous than to end up as a corpse in the gutter.

It was with a sigh of relief when I reached the driver's side door. No one jumped out and mugged us and the boogieman hadn't appeared either, making me feel a little stupid.

"Too much caffeine." I laughed, holding my hand against my pounding chest as I unlocked and opened the doors. "And I need to stop reading police reports late at night."

Stefan laughed, waiting until I had the door closed before walking around to the passenger side. He rounded the front of the car and then stopped, lifting the wiper blade and pulled out a piece of folded paper.

Shit.

I thought all that stuff about notes on cars were urban legends or fodder for the internet chain, but I was wrong.

"Get in the car," I hissed, reaching across and popping open the door.

With the note safely tucked into his hand, he slipped into the car in a rush. Not sure if he was as spooked as I was or it was *me* that that was freaking him out.

While I hit the central locks and started the engine, he craned his head around looking for clues.

Great, he could do *that,* meanwhile, I didn't care if that piece of paper was a flyer looking for a lost pet or advertising for a new car wash, we were getting out of there.

"What the hell is it?" My voice as tense as my grip on the steering wheel.

He carefully opened what looked to be standard A4 copying paper. "It's a note that says." His eyes scanned down the page before reading it out loud. *"If you want to know more, meet me at Esmeralda's Coffee Shop.* And there's an address."

"More? Do you think it's about the case? The investigation? Do you think someone wants to talk?" I didn't dare take my eyes off the road, knowing it was taking all my concentration to not crash because my heart was beating so fast. Excitement overtook fear as I slowed down to the speed limit, the risk of trashing Alex's car lowering by the second.

Stefan laughed. "Relax there, Sherlock Holmes. We have no idea who this is from or what it even pertains to. It could be a bunch of kids pranking you, or it could be some asshole trying to lure you into the sex trade. Or this letter might not even be for you, this is Alex's car, right?"

He made some valid points and the letter didn't give us a lot to go on. But if there was a chance that someone did want to talk, I wasn't going to ignore it.

"So are you coming with me? Or am I dropping you off at your car?" I asked with no intention of letting it go. Maybe it was just a joke, or worse. But it could be a lead, and a vital piece to the case, and I wasn't going to risk throwing it away because I was unsure.

"Maya, you can't be serious," he tried to argue. "You know nothing about this, maybe we should call the police—"

"And tell them what?" I scoffed. "No threats have been made against me, no damage to property. And last time I checked there was no law against leaving a note on someone's windshield. So answer the question, are you coming?"

"Well, considering we passed my car about five minutes ago, I'd say I'm coming with you." He rolled his eyes, pressing his lips into a thin line to adequately convey his displeasure.

I grinned back. "Think of it as an adventure."

He read out the address and then put it into his phone, which read out directions. Turned out Esmeralda's Coffee Shop was a place in Burbank, right near the airport.

The parking lot was well lit and you could see the booths from the road. It was freshly painted, made to look vintage but too shiny to be authentic. The waitress visible from our vantage point dressed in 1950's diner appeal, complete with winged black rimmed glasses and curled up-dos. It wasn't the Beverly Wilshire, but it wasn't a shady dive restaurant with a line of Harleys out the front and a meat saw in the back either. And if someone was trying to lure me there under false pretenses, the bright overhung lights were going to be terrible for their plan.

"So now what?" Stefan asked as we sat in the car. "We just walk in there and hope the author of the note makes themselves known?"

I shook my head. "No, I'll go in there and you wait in the car."

"Maya—" The protest ready in his mouth.

I waved my hand, cutting him off. "If the both of us go in, we might scare them off. And if it is a source who wants to provide information, they will know me, not you. What if they think you are a cop and they get spooked?"

"This has bad idea written all over it." He swore as his fists balled in his lap. "Fine, but anything looks suspect you get the hell out of there. I don't need your boyfriend and his posse of Larsson brothers to deal with if anything goes wrong."

"I'll be fine. I'll pick a booth by the window so you can see me and I promise you I won't take any risks. I'll even have my phone in my lap with a pre-typed message. You get it, call the cops." The last thing I wanted to do was waste a good law degree by doing something incredibly stupid.

Knowing he didn't have a choice, he nodded as my hand went to the door handle. I slipped out of the car, looking around as I went to the front of Esmeralda's and walked inside.

It was quaint and neat, with stools at the counter as well as some tables on the side in addition to the booths I could see from the parking lot. There were people inside but it wasn't overly busy, and no one looked suspicious from my brief scan as I strode past them to a vacant booth. Sure could have utilized Kate's momvision, but I was going to have to make do with my own gut.

Careful not to look out into the parking lot, I sat at the table making sure I would be visible from the window beside me. I wasn't sure what else to do, so I picked up a menu and pretended to read it while I laid my phone casually in my lap.

The letter gave nothing away as to the identity of the writer or how to signal them, which meant I had to sit and wait and hope I didn't end up drugged with a posting on the dark web.

"Coffee, hun?" A waitress who couldn't have been more than twenty waved her coffee pot, speaking with the most atrocious New York accent I'd ever heard. "Or are you ready to order?"

"Um, just coffee thanks," I replied, watching her turn over my cup and pour in the steaming black liquid.

"Let me know if I can get you anything to go with that." She tipped up her coffee pot, adjusted her glasses and then moved to the next customer.

I had no idea how long to wait, or how long the note had been sitting on the car. It was feasible the person had already been and gone or they weren't coming until later.

Ten minutes passed, and then twenty, my phone kept buzzing

from messages from Stefan, which I chose to ignore. I could see him in my periphery, getting impatient in the car, but he had me in plain sight and no one had even sneezed in my direction.

It had been half an hour when I'd decided I was going to leave. Stefan had probably been right, and some asshole teenagers had written the note hoping to scare me. I was just about to wave the waitress and pay for my single, unconsumed coffee when a woman slipped into the booth.

She looked to be about forty, her blonde hair greying at the roots that curled erratically in different directions. Her face was free from makeup, showing deep lines around her hazel eyes that scattered around the room before focusing on me. She was nervous, her hands playing with the buttons of the coat she wore, odd considering it was over seventy.

"Maya."

It lacked a question mark, which made me curious considering I'd never seen the woman in my life.

"Yes, how can I help you?"

You're trained in law school not to get emotional. Not give anything away and ask questions rather than give answers. Never volunteer information and only tell someone as much as they need to know. Act calm, even if you weren't, and always maintain control. So, even though I was dying to demand who she was, how she knew me and what information she had, I remained cool and tried to be impassive.

"I have something for you." She lowered her hand, reaching into her pocket.

"Hold it." I reached across the table—dumb, but I was acting on instinct—and grabbed her arm. "Don't give me anything until you tell me what it is."

While I hope the lady didn't have a hard-on for Tarantino movies, I wasn't going to risk her pulling out a gun. Who knew if my questions earlier in the day hadn't pissed someone off, and this was their "Tony Soprano" way of scaring me off.

"It's just a phone. I promise." She moved her hand out slowly, revealing a black Nokia that you could probably buy at any Wal-Mart or Best Buy.

I knew the type, cheap, disposable, and easy to get without giving too much information. The kind that tourists got when they flew in or what criminals used when they didn't want to leave a trail. And apart from the coat, she didn't look like much of a tourist.

"Who are you?" I asked, my eyes glued to her hands as she placed the phone in front of us. "What's your name?"

"I'm . . ." She paused a second too long for me to believe whatever she said next would be the truth. "Lane."

"Well *Lane*, you still haven't told me who you are and what I can do for you? I'm assuming you have something to tell me?" Again I remained composed, committing to memory everything I could about her while we spoke.

"I am just here to give it to you." She pushed the phone closer just as it started to ring.

I'd watched enough movies to know how it worked. The decoy was sent to meet someone, a phone call directed the wait-ee—in this case me—to another location and then they killed them. That wouldn't be happening, my hands remaining in my lap as the phone continued to ring.

"You need to answer it." She looked at me with desperation. "Please, Maya. It's your dad."

There were a lot of things I was expecting sitting in a coffee shop in Burbank, hearing someone mentioning my father wasn't one of them. And considering being possibly shot was on the list, it proved how unlikely I thought the possibility.

The phone silenced as I raised my stare to her. "You're her, the woman he had the affair with."

I'd never met her or seen a photo, my mother shielding us from all of that before we left. After, I didn't care, preferring to not know who she was or what she looked like because she wasn't the one who'd ruined our family. Oh, she wasn't completely without blame, but the lion's share belonged to someone else. Apparently the man on the other end of that phone.

"Please, Maya, just answer the phone. I have a little girl too. You have a half sister. And this is my one chance to get her back." In an effort to try to gain sympathy, she'd confirmed her identity.

Dina—not *Lane*—was the woman my father impregnated, and who accompanied him when he went on the lam.

Of course I'd known she was pregnant but must have missed the birth announcement when she delivered. Guess taking out an ad in the paper or sending out cute cards with the details might have hindered their plight. You know, the one where they defrauded thousands of people out of their money and devastated the lives of his existing wife and children.

I wanted to walk out, to tell her I didn't want to hear from either of them and to go back to whatever rock they crawled out of. But as the phone started ringing a second time, my need for justice overrode every other emotion.

If there was even a chance I could find out something that could help locate him and convict him, I needed to do it. My fingers snatched the Nokia as I answered it, bringing it to my ear and spoke. "Hello."

"Maya." His voice hadn't changed, sickly sweet like you'd expect from Santa Claus, which was probably how he'd duped us all. "How's my baby girl?"

I wanted to throw up, forcing down the bile rising up my esophagus as my skin crawled. "What do you want?" I kept my voice measured, my emotions, a vault as I denied him the reaction he probably wanted.

"Now, is that any way to talk to your father? I saw something on the internet the other day, was *very* interesting to me."

Dina slid across the table a print out of the Instagram picture of Alex and I along with the stupid hashtags, some of the comments from posters visible underneath.

He continued, assuming his accomplice had shown me what he wanted me to see. "You've done well for yourself. A lawyer no less, and dating that boy you always followed around, Alex. Quite a catch, sweetheart. Those Larssons are loaded with cash. I definitely taught you well."

"I am nothing like you." The rein on my emotions cracked at the mention of Alex, gripping the phone tighter as the words fought their way out of my clenched jaw. "And you keep him out of it, you've done enough damage to their family and to ours. So why don't do you the first decent thing you've ever done in your life and turn yourself in."

I'd played my hand too early and I knew it the minute the words had left my mouth. If I had any hope of getting any information from him, that had left when I confirmed I wanted him in jail. Harder to convince someone you are on their side *after* you've told them you wanted them locked up. Totally my bad.

"Dad." The word was like acid in my mouth as I tried to salvage the situation. "Why don't you tell me why you are calling?"

He laughed, the jolly stomach shaking cackle I could never forget. "You know why I'm calling. It's been a while and I'm a little light on cash, so you and your hot shot boyfriend are going to wire me a couple of million to tie me over."

"And why would I do that?" I resisted my first instinct, which was to laugh at him and ask which fairytale he was living in. And then tell him there'd be a cold day in hell.

"Because you owe me. And because I never thought my own daughter would stab me in the back. It wasn't enough you became one of *them*, you had to go put your nose where it didn't belong. Besides, if it weren't for me, you wouldn't have even met Alex. You think I couldn't have ruined either of you by now? Try me, Maya, I still have friends in low places, could make things very difficult for you and him. And of course, we wouldn't want to upset your mother and brothers again, now would we? There are a few other people who might get hurt too."

Stab him in the back? I had no idea what he was talking about other than I'd become the very thing he resented. Honest, hard working, and vowing to bring men like him to justice.

My blood boiled, the asshole hitting every single button I had as he systematically mentioned every person I loved. I hated him, and there wasn't a chance he was hurting us again. But I wasn't going to be extorted either.

"And how am I supposed to get *a couple million* dollars?" I fought the urge to laugh at how ridiculous his request was. He couldn't even give me a figure; too fucking scared he'd low-ball himself. "Let me guess, small unmarked bills in a black briefcase left at an abandoned warehouse?"

"No, you'll wire the money to an account number I'm giving you. And don't even bother trying to go to the cops, they can't touch me."

The phone called ended without a goodbye, which was his style. Dina took the printout of Alex and I and handed me a small card. A random sequence of numbers written across it that I assumed was attached to an offshore bank account. "Just do what he says, Maya." Her voice strained, the look of coercion evident on her face.

"Where is she? Your daughter?" I grabbed her arm from across the table, knowing it must have something to do with her. "Maybe I can help you get her back."

On the list of things I wanted to do, helping Dina was second to last. The bottom spot was reserved for helping my father. But there was an innocent child in the middle of it and whether I wanted to accept her as my half-sister or not, I wasn't heartless either.

She bit her lip, shaking her head like she regretted having told me.

"You do this, and you might never see her again," I tried to reason, relieved that at least the child was safe, away from both of them.

"No, he *promised*." Her eyes misted. "He promised we'd get the money and I'd get her back."

She took the phone, shoved it back in her pocket and looked around as she shuffled out of the booth.

"How will I contact you guys? It's going to take me a few days to get that kind of money together," I lied, stalling with no intention of transferring anything. "And how do I know that even if I do this, he will keep his word?"

Even though I had no intention of meeting his demands, I was curious what assurances I would be given. After all, only an idiot would hand over a couple of million dollars—it got more ridiculous every time I said it—without something in return. Especially considering he had no dirt on me other than the threat he had friends in "low places." I was a lawyer for fuck's sake, at least a third of the people in my profession dwelled in *low places*.

"I-I don't know," she stammered. "I need to go." She rushed toward the exit before I could say anything more.

I stood, watching her leave, wondering how I was going to use any of it to my advantage when two uniformed LAPD officers entered the coffee shop, stopping her from leaving.

Stefan must have called them. Even though the pre-typed message in my phone had remained unsent, he'd obviously decided to call anyway.

"Something wrong, ma'am?" one of them asked her, her eyes

wide with terror.

She shook her head. "No, nothing. I just need to go." She tried again to maneuver past them only to be stopped a second time.

"Got any ID?" the other inquired, remaining casual.

Dina made a show of shoving her hands into her pockets. "Sorry, I must have left it at home."

"Well, why don't you take a walk outside with us." The first officer held open the door, giving her just enough room to pass.

"No, no, I really must go. I have a child I need to get to," she protested, fidgeting with her coat.

"Yeah, we'll get to all of that in a minute," the second officer assured. "Why don't we get your friend to follow you out as well?" He waved in my direction, beckoning me to approach.

I tossed my phone into my bag and strode to the doorway. "Sure, officer." I complied, not having a reason not to. After all, Stefan would have told them about the note and I'd no doubt have to make a statement, so it was natural they'd want to talk to me.

Dina didn't budge, staying where she was as I walked outside. I half expected to see Stefan out there, ready to read me the riot act but instead was greeted by what I assumed was more plain-clothed police officers. One was a woman who was watching me with particular interest as I approached.

"Maya Zaveri?" she asked, pulling her badge out of her pocket.

"Yes," I answered, confused when I saw Stefan running toward me with a look of concern on his face.

Why was he concerned, wasn't he the one who called them?

My eyes swung back to the officer, the badge she was flashing had a printed identification card with the words FBI above them.

"Maya Zaveri, you have the right to remain silent."

CHAPTER #23

IT HAD TO be a bad joke, or a dream I was going to wake up from, because there was no way any of it could actually be happening.

And yet as they continued to Mirandize me and slip on the cuffs, it became obvious it was very real.

"Maya, what the hell?" Stefan pushed into the fray. "Why are you arresting her?"

"Sir, please step back or you will be charged with impeding a federal investigation." Another plain-clothed officer put his hand out, stopping him from getting any closer while the other hand went to his gun.

"I'm a lawyer," Stefan protested. "I'm *her* lawyer, and I demand to know where you are taking her and on what grounds."

I knew not to say anything, that the *anything you say may be used against you,* wasn't just rhetoric. And despite not knowing what I was being charged with, and that there was no way I could be involved in any crime, I shut my mouth and exercised my 5th Amendment.

They explained to Stefan that Dina and I were being taken to the FBI headquarters in Los Angeles. But other than that, they refused to answer any more questions, telling Stefan he'd have to follow us to the station.

Dina was *not* exercising her right as she continued to protest, being placed in a different car. She had yet to give her name or identify herself, and what she didn't know was they could take her in just for that. Besides, I was positive they knew *exactly* who she was, and her reappearance directly connected to theirs.

We rode in silence, the female FBI agent in my car not bothering to try to get anything out of me. Because, like they knew who Dina was, they also knew I was a lawyer. So they were going to follow protocol and not do anything our side could use later.

My thoughts turned to Alex and I was so conflicted. Part of me desperately wished he wasn't in New York so I could call him to help, and the other part glad he wasn't tainted by the mess. What would he even think? Even though it wasn't my fault, having his girlfriend hauled in by the FBI wouldn't play well to his employers. His friends. His family.

And finally, after all those years, it made sense why my mother left, never remarried, and didn't make many new friends. The embarrassment and the scandal weren't the only reasons she ripped us from the only home we'd ever known, it was to protect those she loved. Us, as well as our friends. Because as much as I thought she had been clueless to everything—she hadn't been.

We didn't go into hiding, instead keeping in plain sight, but at a distance. Where she'd previously stayed home and done the housewife thing, she was suddenly signing up for courses, joining community groups. She told us never to run and hide, to hold our head up high. Make noise, not to be afraid. And like the penny dropping, it made sense. If he wanted to try something, he'd have to do it with a whole lot of witnesses. Little parts of my childhood flashed through my memory, parts I'd clearly forgotten. He had always been vindictive, and shrewd in business. An evil side he kept hidden most of the time except when he got angry. And she knew it eventually would come back to haunt us. And when it did, it would show no mercy in the lives it took with it.

Religion had never played a big part in my life. I wasn't sure there wasn't a higher power any more than I was sure there was one, but in the back of that car, I prayed. Not for myself, because I knew I would be okay. But for the people I loved, and that Alex would take that job in New York and be spared what a lifetime with me might be like.

We arrived at the location and I was helped out of the car. I didn't see Stefan, but I assumed he would have to park elsewhere and come in the front so I hadn't freaked out too much just yet.

My new location was an interrogation room, which was where I would probably stay until they got what they needed. Dina wasn't with us, taken to another room or they were still possibly trying to get her out of the car. But as the door closed behind me, I wasn't sure I'd ever see her again.

"Take a seat." A tall thin man who looked like he hadn't slept in a decade directed me to a chair opposite a table. "We can take the cuffs off, Miles, I don't think Maya is intending to give us any trouble."

My cuffs were removed and I sat down, the guy who seemed to be running the show took a seat opposite me. "My name is Special Agent Francis James. Can I get you anything to drink?"

"No thank you," I answered, rubbing my wrists.

"I assume you have properly been read your rights and understand them."

"Yes." Only giving him the one word in affirmation.

"Good. Now, while you have been read those rights, I want to make you aware that you are not being charged at this time. You are, however, being held for questioning."

All the I's dotted and T's crossed, making it clear that while no charges were being laid, he still had the power to question me.

Hell, he could even hold me indefinitely if the mood took him. All he had to do was cite homeland security and I could sit around for days without any charges.

"Do you understand, Maya?"

"Yes."

He nodded. "Good, want to tell me about the conversation you had with Ms. Dina Stuckey?"

"I maintain my 5th Amendment right and would like to see my attorney," I answered, sitting up straight in my chair and maintaining eye contact.

Stay strong, Maya. You have done nothing wrong.

"You'll be able to see your lawyer in just a minute, not that you need one, right? I mean, you've done nothing wrong." He smiled exposing his teeth that had yellowed from either too much coffee or cigarettes. Maybe both.

"I maintain my 5th Amendment right and would like to see my attorney," I repeated not falling for his *we're all friends* routine.

"Okay, let's just sit here and wait then." He drummed his fingers on the desk and watched me. "Sure I can't get you anything?"

"I maintain my 5th Amendment right and would—"

"*Like to see your lawyer.*" He raised his hand stopping me midsentence. "Yep, I got it. I'm just offering you coffee, making sure you're comfortable. Nothing else."

We sat in the room a little while longer and when there was no sign of Stefan I assumed he was playing *the* game. We both knew he couldn't deny me right to counsel, but there were ways they could drag out the process. Procedures that could take a while, time taken to process someone into the department. And it was night, which obviously meant they weren't operating at full staffing levels. All in the hopes, that while we were waiting, I might give them something usable.

And as long as there wasn't any overt coercion and I was

treated fairly, they were well within their rights to play. All I had to do was sit tight and wait, because whether *Special Agent James* knew it or not, I was not talking.

He looked at his watch as the time ticked on, and while I didn't know for sure, it had to have been at least half an hour.

Still no sign of Stefan.

Still no statement from me.

He stood, stretching his legs as he walked around the room a little before leaning up against the wall. My eyes followed him, maintaining my posture in my chair even though my back was killing me and I wanted answers.

I wondered if they had gotten anything from Dina, if she'd decided to throw my dad under the bus or if she'd been so blindly devoted to him she was willing to take the fall. She'd obviously come out of hiding in an effort to please him by approaching me. My dad, too chicken shit to do it himself, did what he always did, used the people who cared about him without concern for their safety.

Finally there was a knock at the door and it took everything I had not to leap out of my seat and answer it myself. Special Agent James huffed out a breath and then walked to the door and pulled it open.

It wasn't Stefan.

It was Roman, who had a look so pissed even Mr. FBI took a step back.

When he moved into the room, Stefan was standing right behind him, following him in like a proud little puppy.

I could have kissed them both.

"Special Agent James, myself and my co counsel would like some time to confer with our client. I assume since neither of us have been present, she hasn't been questioned?" Roman gave Agent James a death stare that warned him the only right answer would be yes.

Special Agent James, who was tall but at least an inch or two shorter than Roman, coughed as he looked to me. "She hasn't been questioned or said anything."

"Good, then you can leave us." Roman ignored him as he moved closer to me, his eyes on my wrists. They were marked from the cuffs and no doubt would be bruised but I wasn't worried.

Agent James went to the door, holding onto the handle before looking back at us. "I'll be back to ask those questions." He pulled it closed behind him.

I took the first full breath since the coffee shop as he left, letting my body relax in the chair.

"Are you okay?" Roman looked at me, meeting my eyes like he was telepathically telling me he'd know if I was lying.

I nodded, getting out of the chair and hugging him. "I am now, thank you so much for coming."

"Are you kidding me? Jesus, Maya, you're like family, of course I would come." He gently stroked my hair. "But as much as I'd like to take credit—and we know I like credit—I wouldn't have even known about it unless he called me."

I pulled myself away from Roman to see Stefan grinning. "When they kept stonewalling me and not letting me see you, I knew we were going to need to bring out the big guns." He nodded to Roman. "And I know we aren't supposed to know he's Alex's brother, but I figured you'd get over it if you got mad."

"Mad?" I laughed, almost weeping with gratitude. "I can't thank you enough." It was his turn for a hug, my body feeling ten times lighter knowing I had both of them in my corner.

"Okay, we can hug and sing campfire songs later." Roman clapped his hands together as he moved an additional chair to the table for Stefan. "I need both of you to tell me everything. And then we should give Alex a call."

Deep down it felt sort of hypocritical. That, minutes ago I

was glad Alex was miles away from the mess but I was glad his brother had come. And I had no doubt if I'd spoken those words out loud, he'd have felt betrayed. That I somehow thought Roman was a better lawyer, or I trusted him more. But none of that was the truth. It was because I didn't love Roman the way I loved Alex, nor did he love me, at least not in *that* way. Alex would risk everything, even himself, if it came to it. Roman wouldn't. And I couldn't have someone lose anything for me.

I took a breath and everything I hadn't said to Special Agent James flew right out of my mouth, starting with the note on my windshield. My dad had seen the Instagram photo of Alex and I that Astrid had posted and decided that now would be a good opportunity to extort money. I told them about Dina's claim of getting her child back, the phone call, his claims of trying to hurt our families and then pulled out the card with the account number on it, which was where I was instructed to deposit the money. Finishing off with finally being picked up by the cops outside the coffee shop with Dina.

"Did your father say where he was?" Roman asked while Stefan took notes.

"Nope, I always assumed he left the country, but that was never confirmed. He could have made that call from California or Mexico, there is no way to know." I shrugged.

"What kind of man sends his girlfriend?" Stefan asked. "She's wanted for aiding and abetting, not to mention accessory after the fact."

"Yeah, not smart and judging by the quick police response, she'd been under surveillance." Roman tapped his chin, confirming what I'd already suspected. It hadn't been Stefan who'd called the cops. Nope, they'd probably been waiting for us to leave to make their move, possibly even listening in on our exchange.

"Don't think she crossed any borders. Decent fake passports

are hard to come by and I don't think a man who is trying to hit up his kid for cash has the money or the resources to pull it off. They must have been laying low somewhere remote but still in the states," Roman continued, pulling together his version of events.

"So why am I here? Assuming we were under surveillance when we were in the coffee shop, they have to know that I'm not involved. I haven't heard from the man in over ten years and this is the first time since he left that he has tried to contact me."

It didn't make sense but desperate people did desperate things, including the dumbest move of all mankind, which was what my dad had done.

Roman eyed me hard. "There are no charges but they do want information. Anything they can get. Your piece of shit dad has outstanding charges not only from the FBI, but the IRS, FTC and SEC. Are you sure he didn't say anything else?"

"Other than tell me he could make things hard for us?" I offered, the threat so vague I had no idea what it meant.

"You guys make any sex tapes, any suggestive photos?" Roman asked, looking at me calmly like we were *not* discussing my sex life with his brother.

"No," I shot back indignantly. "I'm not an idiot."

He shook his head. "I have to ask, Maya. If there is anything that he'd have as leverage, even if you think it's insignificant, now would be the time to let me know."

There was nothing. I was squeaky clean and I didn't doubt Alex would be any different. "Unless he knows something I don't, there is nothing. He's just trying to scare me, thinking I'm still the same kid he left behind. So let's get this over with." I slammed my hand on the desk not having anything to hide. "He barely said anything to me on the phone but I'll repeat it all."

"Yeah, we will take questions but remember, these guys aren't playing. They need something to take back to their bosses and I know I don't have to go through answering procedure with you."

"Short, concise and not giving them anymore information than they ask for." The rote answer fell from my lips without any effort.

"Always knew you were a superstar." Roman nodded proudly. "Stefan, I want you to see if you can find out anything about Dina. See what her story is and if she's been arrested, and do some digging on this number." He handed him the card. "Judging by the sequence, I'd say it's Cayman Islands but you never know, and he might be stupid enough to have kept an account that is traceable. Oh and one more thing." He put his hands on his hips and shot me a look that said I might not like what I was about to hear. "I want you to dig into both Maya and Alex and see if there is anything that could be used as leverage."

Stefan looked at me, waiting for my consent even though he probably didn't need it. "Just do it, Stefan. Maybe there's something I missed."

"On it." Stefan grabbed the card and his notes, giving me one last look before heading out the door. "Call me if you need *anything*."

I nodded and watched him disappear, leaving me with Roman and no idea on whether I was going to be sleeping in my own bed or in a jail cell. Not sure sleeping was going to happen regardless of the venue.

Special Agent James knocked on the door soon after Stefan left. I assumed he'd been told I was willing to answer some questions and was looking to get started. Federal agents very rarely were patient people, and I had a hunch, given the late hour, he was probably more annoyed than usual.

"So, I trust you have conferred with your client." His eyes went to Roman before swinging back to me. "And I assume you're ready to tell me everything you know."

Roman leveled him with a glare as he moved over to my side

of the table and took a seat. "Let's just stick to the interview and skip the theatrics."

"Sounds good to me." Agent James smiled as he opened a file. "Let's start with what you were doing in that coffee shop."

"I received a note and believed it to be an anonymous tip for a case I was working on," I answered, maintaining eye contact.

"What was the case?"

"Irrelevant," Roman interjected. "Ms. Zaveri's cases are not material to this investigation nor is she at liberty to discuss them."

"Fine." Special Agent James forced the grin. "Have you received a note like that before?"

"Don't answer that." Roman held out his hand. "If you have something specific to ask my client, then ask it. Anything unrelated to this investigation is off limits."

Agent James huffed out a breath of frustration. "Maya, when was the first time you were contacted by your father?"

"The phone call at the coffee shop," I answered.

He looked at me and clarified. "No other time?"

"No."

He continued with the interview.

"What were his exact words?"

"Were there any background sounds?"

"Did he threaten me?"

"Did he say he'd call again?"

Endless questions, which I answered as best I could.

The truth was, I didn't know anything. I didn't believe I was in danger and other than confirming my father was a selfish piece of shit who didn't care for anyone but himself, there was nothing more I could give them.

Having cooperated as best I could, and not having any solid grounds to keep me, they released me with the understanding that I'd make myself available for future questioning. Pretty sure

I wouldn't have any answers for their future questions either, but I wasn't going to make the point as they let me go.

"Stefan's got Alex's car, I'll arrange with him to go back and get his after I drop you off. I think it might be better for you if you stay with me tonight." Roman popped the locks on his retro Ferrari and opened the door. "Lauren's already made up the guestroom."

"You just want to subject me to your tiny terrorist." I tried to laugh as I slipped into the passenger seat.

"That wasn't my motive but since you mention it." He cracked a half smile. "It only seems fair to share the love."

He closed my door and then went around to the other side, hopping in and starting the ignition.

It would have been so easy to take Roman up on his offer and go camp out with him and his family. But I already felt I'd imposed enough and to be honest, wanted some time to process it alone.

Special Agent James had made it clear that it wasn't the end, and I wasn't naïve enough to think just because they'd let me leave, I was free. Nope, it was only the beginning and I needed to go home so I could get my head right and devise some kind of strategy.

"I *really* think you should reconsider and spend the night with us." Roman stopped in front of my apartment building, making it clear he wasn't okay with it.

"Thanks Roman, but I'm fine. I don't think my dad is stupid enough to try anything right now." I opened the door and stepped out onto the sidewalk. "And thank you so much for helping tonight."

"So, if you want to thank me, why don't you come help me with Lucas tonight?" He switched tactics, his tenacity not something that surprised me. "He's adorable, you said so yourself."

"Nice try, but I'm going to pass." My fingers gripped the car door, hesitating.

"I don't remember you being this stubborn." He huffed out a breath, switching off the ignition and exiting the car. "But I'm walking you to your door and checking out your place just in case."

I didn't argue, happy for the compromise as he followed me to my apartment. "Thanks, see all good." I pushed open the door and revealed everything as it should be.

Roman wasn't so sure, continuing into my apartment and systematically checking every room while I waited in the living room.

"Did it pass the test?" I asked when he returned.

He nodded, shoving his hands in his pockets. "From what I can tell, you're good. But keep your phone close to you and call me if you hear, feel, see or smell anything suspect. I mean it, Maya, I don't care what time it is or how insignificant you think it might be."

"I promise, thank you so much." I wrapped my arms around him in a hug. "And if it wouldn't be pushing my luck too far, I need one more tiny favor." I winced, knowing I was probably going to owe Roman for the rest of my life.

"If it's what I'm thinking you're going to ask me, I think it's another bad idea," he warned.

"Just give me twenty-four hours." I tried to reason. "I don't want Alex running back on his white horse. Please, I'll tell him everything and take full responsibility if he's angry."

Roman shook his head. "Yeah, because he is going to listen to *reason* when he finds out. Look, as your attorney you know *I* can't tell him, so anything he finds out is going to have to come from you."

"And it will, as soon as he gets back," I promised.

"Fine." He kissed me gently on the forehead. "I better go, but call me."

He gave me a pointed look, unwrapping his arms and headed out my front door. I waited until he disappeared, the roar of his Ferrari fading just as I closed the door to my apartment. It felt weird to be back, and not just because I hadn't slept there in a while.

After a shower that was probably too hot, I crawled into bed and looked at my phone. It was early morning in New York and Alex had his meeting with the firm, and as tempted as I was to call him, I just couldn't. So instead I shoved it under my pillow and tried to will myself to sleep.

It was going to be a long night.

CHAPTER #24

THERE WAS A missed call from Alex on my phone when I woke in the morning, but I didn't call him back. Not telling him the truth was one thing, but outright lying to him wasn't happening either.

So instead I texted him, told him that I loved him and that I was slammed at work. He texted back that he loved me too and to call him when I could.

Instead of worrying about what I would say when I needed to make that call, I headed to work where Mike was already sitting at his desk. I looked for signs that he knew anything, but he seemed oblivious to what had happened after Stefan and I had left the bar.

"Stefan not here?" I looked around, noticing he wasn't around. I was running later than usual which meant the office was almost full.

Mike leaned back in his chair and anchored his hands behind his neck. "Nah, Leah said he called in sick. I hope it wasn't something he ate last night, you feel okay, right?"

"Yeah, I feel fine," I answered honestly because my bad feelings had nothing to do with food. I had a hunch neither had Stefan's. "Well, hopefully whatever it is, he makes a full recovery soon."

I texted his phone but got no answer, pushing it into the pocket of my jacket to try again later.

Leah wanted to know my findings on yesterday's investigations, and I did my best despite my mind being elsewhere. By noon I decided to come clean, figuring the firm had a right to know what was happening with one of their junior associates. Besides, I didn't know if the FBI was going to come sniffing around while I was at work. That wouldn't have looked good.

She listened, and asked questions, but was sympathetic in response. She not only offered to tell the partners on my behalf but offered me the resources of the firm as well. It was hard not to choke up. I had expected suspicion and possibly even accusation; kindness and understanding were things I still grappled with.

And out of concern instead of punishment, she suggested I take the rest of the day off. I might have argued, but I knew I couldn't perform at a level they deserved so I figured it was for the best. I slipped out before anyone asked me any more questions.

Despite the threats my dad made, I didn't feel he would do anything to *physically* harm me. Call it instinct—or stupidity—but he didn't have the guts. No, his punishment would be something else, much more devious and much more hurtful. Like trying to get me disbarred, or ruin Alex's career. And while I was positive he didn't have that kind of ammunition, I wasn't going to underestimate a man who defrauded millions of dollars from thousands of investors and evaded the FBI for so long.

Without a car—Alex's BMW probably back at his house—I had taken the bus in, which meant a bus back home. It wasn't so bad, the ride giving me time to ponder over everything I'd done since high school which could possibly be inflammatory. Fun times.

So when I finally got home, having walked from the bus stop, I was surprised to see Alex's car parked out front.

There was no one inside—and no notes on the windshield either thank God—and I wondered if Roman hadn't brought it back for me to use until Alex returned. Maybe he put the keys in my mailbox?

I'd just made it into the courtyard when I saw him.

Alex.

He was sitting on the stairs that led up to my apartment, waiting casually, like he *hadn't* been on the other side of the country just that morning.

"You're back?" I asked, trying to stop my feet from running toward him and hugging the life out of him. While my brain had wanted him to be safe in New York, my heart needed him in L.A. and currently my heart was the one running the show. "Oh my God, I've missed you so much." I gave up fighting it, throwing my arms around him.

"I missed you too." He hugged me back, accepting my weight into his strong arms and lifted me off the ground.

I breathed him in, filling my nostrils with his scent to confirm it was him standing in front of me and not some illusion. But it wasn't a trick, his warm body pressed against me as I kissed him. His lips met mine as I pulled him closer, not caring about who was watching, overcome by the need to feel him.

It was while I was kissing him that it occurred to me it was too early for him to be back. His meeting had been set for ten in the morning, which meant he would have hopped on a plane the minute he'd left their office.

"I thought you were going to spend some time with Eric?" I asked, trying not to sound ungrateful.

He pulled his mouth away from mine. "Change of plans, want to go up to your apartment and talk?"

Go up to my apartment and talk did not sound good, especially since he wasn't due back for at least another day. And why had he been waiting on my stairwell? If I hadn't come home early, it would have been hours before I got home.

Shit.

I could barely get the keys in the door my hands were shaking so hard. I had an idea what he was going to say and I was terrified. I didn't even know what I *wanted* him to say, conflicted between thinking it was best if he kept his distance and needing him so much I couldn't bear it if he left.

"You're taking the job?" I closed the door behind us, not being able to take the suspense any more. "You went there and liked it, and you accepted their offer."

He didn't need to say it; I could see from his face I was right. "Maya, I'm sorr—"

"No, please." I pulled him closer. "Please don't apologize to me. This is a good thing; I wanted this for you. Please don't be sorry for doing the right thing."

"Then why does it feel so wrong?" He pulled away, looking at me. "Tell me why I feel like I'm making the biggest mistake of my life?"

Inside, my heart was breaking, desperate to ask him to re-consider. That I needed him, and I couldn't stand the idea of him leaving me. And yet, in the same breath, a sigh of relief. He would be safe, far away from whatever drama my dad had planned, and protected from all of it.

I grabbed the front of his shirt, holding on to him because I knew I'd have to let go soon. "It's not. I promise you, you're going to do great things over there. I wanted this for you."

"And what about *us*, Maya? I told you I'm not going to give you up." He tilted my chin, his thumb tracing my jaw.

"We'll work it out." I shook my head, not sure how exactly. "This is a good thing, Alex. I'm so proud of you."

I meant every single one of those words even if it killed me to say them because I knew there was a chance I'd lose him. And even though it would probably be the best thing for him, I wasn't sure my heart could withstand that kind of trauma a second time.

And yet . . . I had asked for it, pushed him to go because I loved him so much that I'd rather destroy my own happiness than risk his. That was how I knew this was not some childhood infatuation, that it wasn't a crush. And that of all the times I'd thought I'd been in love with a Larsson, there was only *one* I'd willingly cut out my own heart for.

It was hard to stop the tears, the events of the last twenty-four hours flooding me as I wiped my eyes with the pads of my fingers. "Oh my God, I'm being ridiculous." I tried to laugh, hoping he wouldn't see how devastated I was. "They're happy tears, and we should celebrate."

He kissed my wet cheeks. "Yeah, not sure if I believe you, and what are you doing home so early? And why the hell didn't you take my car? I left you the keys."

So many questions and I wasn't sure which one to answer first. "Well." *What did I tell him?* There was no way I could reveal the truth, especially when I had no idea when he'd be leaving. Not to mention I didn't want to guilt him to stay. "I had a headache this morning and didn't think I should drive, and because I couldn't concentrate, they decided to send me home early. Lucky for me, because here you are." I hugged him tight. "And lucky for *you* too or you'd have been sitting on those steps for hours."

"Yeah, I tried to sweet talk Prim into letting me into your apartment but she wasn't biting. She did offer to let me wait in hers until you got home." He shot me a wicked smile. "I politely declined."

I smiled, a little sad to have missed the indecent proposal. "Well, I'm glad you waited."

"So headache, huh?" He scrunched up his nose, probably hoping for sex.

And as much as I wanted to get lost in the sensations that only he could give me, and forget everything for a while, I just didn't have it in me. I wanted to hold him, to commit every single part of his body to memory so I'd never forget it.

"Yeah, but you can lay down with me." I kicked off my shoes and hoped he wouldn't be too disappointed.

He leaned down and kissed me again. "Sounds like an amazing idea."

AT SOME POINT, I fell asleep.

I was still in my work clothes, my arms and legs tangled around Alex as his hand smoothed my hair.

"Hey, feeling better?" Alex asked as I lifted my head to look at him.

I nodded, even though I didn't. "Yeah, still a dull ache, but I'll be okay."

"So you still up for celebrating?"

Oh, yeah.

That.

Hiding the fact my father had tried to extort a couple of million—which I didn't have—out of me, threatened not only my life but the people that I loved, and I was questioned by the FBI was a tall order. But to go out, pretend to be happy and supportive that the greatest love I'd ever had was moving to another city was going to be next to impossible.

"Suuurrrre," I answered cautiously. "What did you have in mind?"

His raised brow told me he didn't buy it. "You don't sound so convinced."

"No, no. We'll celebrate. Just let me shower and get changed." I shuffled off the bed, determined to get my shit together.

"You might want to give Stefan a call, he's called like three times." He picked up my phone that was sitting on the nightstand. "I contemplated answering it but figured if it was important, I'd be required to wake you up. As long as I didn't know context, I had plausible deniability." A wicked grin spread across his lip. "Plus, if it was an *actual* emergency, I'd assume he'd come knock on the door or send someone over."

"You are so smart." I breathed a sigh of relief he hadn't answered. There was no way to be sure Stefan wouldn't talk, probably assuming I'd have told my boyfriend.

I picked up the phone and called, hoping and praying I was going to be able to communicate with single non-descriptive words that wouldn't raise suspicion.

"Hey, what's up?" I tried to sound cheery as he answered the phone.

"*What's up?* What the hell, Maya? I've been trying to call you for an hour. Mike said you left work early." The frustration and concern vibrated in his voice.

"Yeah, I had a headache. Fell asleep." I lifted my hand to my head, rubbing my temples. It might have started as fiction, but I wasn't going to need to fake it much longer.

"We need to meet up with Roman, I think I found something."

"Is it integral to the case?" I was careful to keep my words measured, not arouse suspicion.

"Of course it is. I've already called Roman, and I'm almost at his office. Do you still have Alex's car?"

I paced around the room, keeping my face as impassive as I could when I answered. "That would be a negative. I'm afraid I don't have access to that any more since the original attorney is back and has taken over. Sorry."

"Alex is back?" Stefan sucked in a surprised breath.

"Yes."

"Is he with you right now?"

"Sure is."

"And you *haven't* told him?"

Even one-sided, the phone call sounded like I was setting up a drug deal. I knew I couldn't push it any longer.

"Look, we can discuss that at the sit down. I can probably meet you and the client in the next thirty minutes or so depending on traffic." I continued to pace, deliberately not making eye contact with Alex.

"Okay, whatever." Stefan made it clear that he wasn't going to argue over the phone but it probably was going to be discussed. "Just get to Roman's as soon as you can. See you."

I turned to see Alex was sitting on the edge of the bed, having listened to the whole thing. He pouted in disappointment. "You need to go back to work?"

"I'm sorry, it's an important meeting that I can't miss. But it shouldn't take long." I grimaced, tucking my shirt back into my skirt and smoothing out my hair.

"It's fine. I'm just disappointed we didn't get more time. I'll live." His puppy dog eyes conveyed just how *disappointed* he was. "Why don't I drop you off at the office and then you can let me know when you're done. I wanted to stop by Roman's and give him the good news too."

"No," I almost screamed out, shaking my head as panic bubbled inside of me. Not only could he not drive me to "work"—my destination somewhere else—but he couldn't go visit his brother either. It was like the universe was trying to force my hand to either double down on the lies or come clean once and for all.

"No what? You don't want a ride?" He looked at me confused, wondering why the hell I'd be turning him down. It wasn't like he hadn't driven me to work every single day since I started.

"No, I meant you just got here and you must be tired from the flight." I grabbed his hands, trying to sound less crazy and more concerned for his wellbeing. "The last thing you would want to do is sit in afternoon traffic, there is no way I could ask you to do that."

He shook off my concern and lifted himself off the bed. "You're not asking, I'm *offering*. And you said your meeting is important. Not sure how you're going to get there in thirty minutes if you need to wait for a cab or an Uber."

All excellent points, especially since I hadn't considered my method of transportation, or the time constraints.

"Besides, I told you I'm going to go see Roman. I'll be sitting in traffic either way." He slid on his shoes and pulled his keys out of his pocket.

"Maybe call your mom first and tell Roman later."

Words of a desperate woman, and not very good ones either.

"Why? Is there some reason you don't want me to go see my own brother? What aren't you telling me?" His hands were on my arms, his looming body inches away, and those eyes that I couldn't lie to were looking right into mine.

"Because that's where my meeting is." I couldn't have stopped myself if I tried, my hands automatically grabbing the front of his shirt.

He narrowed his eyes. "Your meeting is with Roman? Why?"

"Because he's my attorney."

He blinked in surprise, his brow scrunching in confusion. "What?"

Keeping it from him was no longer an option, and with the clock ticking I was going to have to talk fast and get to Roman's. "Can we talk in the car? I really do need to go."

"Yeah, okay."

He watched me grab my shoes, my phone and my bag and followed me out, jogging down the stairs to his car parked in front.

I'd barely gotten inside, and he'd already started the ignition, pulling away from the curb and heading onto the main road.

"Okay, now tell me everything." His knuckles white as they gripped the steering wheel.

I tried to be clinical, telling him the details like I was briefing him for a case. No emotions, only facts as I laid out what happened after I left the sports bar with Stefan. His jaw tightened the further into the story we got, grinding those perfect teeth so much I was probably going to be receiving hate mail from his dentist. He didn't ask a single question, listening as he drove until we'd reached the front of Roman's building. Unfortunately the parking gods were not in his favor, his virgin sacrifice expired, with no spots available.

He slammed his hand in frustration against the steering wheel before turning to me. "Are you okay? Physically, did the police or anyone else hurt you?"

I shook my head, glad that the bruises on my wrists weren't obvious and he hadn't had an opportunity to see them. "No, I'm fine."

His eyes moved from me, impatiently scanning the road. "You weren't going to tell me, were you?"

He was right. If there had been a way for him never to have found out, I would have taken it.

"I—" I stalled out.

"Ever?" He probed further, knowing me well enough to know the answer before I said it. "Were you going to let me get on that plane and not tell me at all?" His eyes shot to mine. "Jesus, Maya. You had no intention of telling me at all. What was your plan? Let us drift apart or break up with me before I left?"

Honestly, I had no clue. I just knew I had more baggage than I was willing to saddle him with.

"Alex, I didn't want you to change your mind. You already almost gave up the opportunity for me once; I couldn't be the reason you did it again."

His lips tightened. "Did you ever think maybe I should have some say? Make my own choice? Or that maybe—here's a novel idea—I'd had a right to know that the woman I love was fucking threatened?"

"Please don't be angry." I watched cars zipping by us, flipping us off as we obscured traffic. "I know you think I should have told you, but I swear I had good intentions."

"Fuck good intentions," he yelled, the first time he'd ever raised his voice in anger. "I don't want your fucking good intentions, Maya. I'm going to be fucking miles away and *good intentions* aren't going to cut it. You can't even be honest with me when I'm right here, what the hell is going to happen when I'm on the other side of the country?"

"I didn't lie to you, Alex," I yelled back.

"Don't." He held up a finger and warned. "I went to law school too, know every fucking work around there is. So don't try and tell me that because you didn't say the words, it's a fucking technicality."

A car horn blared from behind us, reminding us that we were sitting in the middle of the street.

"Go." He reached across and popped open my door. "I'll park and be up there in a minute."

"Okay." I grabbed my bag, stepping out of the car and holding the door open as I looked inside. "And for what it's worth I wasn't trying to find a work around, I was trying to spare you. He threatened you too, Alex, and maybe it was all bullshit. Maybe his words were nothing like the empty promises he made to me, my brothers and my mom. But I wasn't going to take that chance. I *will* not take that chance. So if you want to be mad, be mad, but don't ever think for a second it was because I didn't love you or that *you* wouldn't have done the same thing for me."

I didn't give him a chance to respond, closing the door—both metaphorically and physically—as I turned my back and walked into Roman's office building.

My heels echoed off the marble, striding through the foyer feeling pissed off, and hurt, and all kinds of confused. I had no idea what my face looked like, my cheeks flushed hot and my eyes probably wild, so much so that the security guard actually looked afraid of me as he checked my ID.

It was the first time I was visiting a rival firm in L.A. and I didn't even get to enjoy it, pressing the button on the elevator and rolling my hands into fists as we climbed.

God, I hoped Stefan had found something decent. And even if he didn't, I was going to dedicate every free second I had to finding Glenn Zaveri and making his life such a hell on earth that he begged to die.

I may not have started the fight, but since he'd brought it to my doorstep, it was time to end it.

Most of the people from Moss, Byrne & Carter had already left but a kind assistant directed me to where I'd find Roman and his swanky glass corner office most lawyers only dreamt about. Stefan was already there, as was Mike who gave me a look of apology as I walked in.

"Sorry, Maya. I overheard Leah tell the partners, and when Stefan called looking for you . . . well I want in on this."

Even though my heart was being held together by duct tape, it was warmed that so many people who had no vested interest in helping me were ready to roll up their sleeves.

"Thank you." I did my best not to cry and walked over to where they were. There would be a time and place for me to worry about what was going to happen between Alex and me, and it wasn't then.

Roman nodded as I took a seat. "Okay, Stefan, tell us what you've got."

"While I haven't been able to get the details of her interview, I can tell you that Dina and her public defender are talking to the

DA about cutting a deal."

"Well that's not really a surprise," Roman deadpanned as he sifted through papers on his desk. "What else have you got?"

Stefan pulled out a note pad and dumped it on the table. "Halle Washington, Dina and Glenn's daughter. She's living in Portland, Oregon with Dina's parents and has been in their custody since she was three."

The room was still, no one speaking as Roman nodded for him to go on. "She got really sick and I guess Dina couldn't get her the care she needed so brought the kid to her parents. Her folks took Halle to the hospital and promised they wouldn't call the cops if Dina turned herself in. She declined, disappearing from the hospital sometime through the night and there's been no contact since. Grandparents filed for guardianship based on abandonment. Neither Dina nor Glenn have any parental rights and Dina's parents intend to keep it that way. Halle doesn't remember either of them."

"And you know this how?" Roman leaned forward in his chair, asking what we were all thinking.

"Trust me, you don't want to know." Stefan coughed into his hand, eluding that maybe he'd gotten information that wasn't legal.

Roman nodded, the understanding passing between them. "You're right, I don't. Good work. Any leads on the location of Glenn Zaveri or what he might have?"

"Nothing yet. No location and not sure what he might have on Alex or Maya but Mike is helping me go through any possibilities. We figure it might be easier since we know both of them and can get a list of associations, friends, things like that from an interview rather than spending hours on investigation. Then we can see if something doesn't stand out."

"Maya, sit with them and give them everything you can. Any people you've met recently or any interaction that might have seemed suspect, and let's not rule out prior relationships too. Lists

of friends, boyfriends, nail woman who you see at the mall—anyone who you would have had more than a casual conversation."

"I'm assuming you'll want to interview me too?" Alex stood
at the door, his face completely unreadable.

All eyes connected with me before moving to him, but Roman
was the first one to speak. "Alex, back from New York. Take it the
meeting went well?"

Only Roman could carry on a normal conversation when the
rest of us were at Defcon 1.

Alex—clearly possessing the same ability—volleyed back without missing a beat. "It went great, I accepted the position. Moving
there next month and looks like I'm going to need a change."

Every single word pierced my heart like a dagger. He was
mad, and I understood that, but he was very publically taking a
swing. At me? At the situation? At his brother for not breaking
privilege and telling him anyway? Who knew, but he was hurt and
he wanted to hurt back.

I felt the weight of Mike and Stefan's stares, probably wondering if Alex and I were even still together. And to be honest, I
had no idea myself.

"Good, why doesn't Mike interview you and Stefan can take
Maya. There are a few conference rooms down the hall that are
vacant, have my assistant show you the way," Roman directed, not
reacting at all to Alex's little dig.

Mike and Alex left first, the tension in the room so heavy that
it was hard to breathe.

"I take it you told him and it didn't go well." Roman stopped
me at the door before leaving with Stefan.

I shook my head, *not going well* the understatement of the
century. "No, probably compounded by the fact I only told him
because he caught me trying to keep it a secret."

"Yeah, not great circumstances." Roman grimaced, rubbing

the back of his neck. "I'm probably not the best one to ask. But seriously, if it's something you want to fight for, then fight. He'll come around."

I nodded, finding it harder not to cry. "Thanks. Come on Stefan, let's do this."

Blinking back tears, we walked to a conference room at the end of the hall. Thankfully the rooms weren't glass, giving me some privacy while I named everyone I could think of who had been more than a passing acquaintance. Any membership I had, any blog post I followed and freaking page I might have liked on social media, down to the men who had been in my life. That part didn't take long; it was a very short list.

"Okay, well I'll comb through the list and see if we get any hits in public records. See if any of these people have a connection to your dad in any way or the company he used to work for." Stefan tapped on his laptop, working as he spoke. "Mike will do the same thing with Alex, maybe we'll get lucky."

Luck wasn't something I put a lot of faith in. Anything I'd ever achieved hadn't come about by luck, and I didn't expect that to change.

We walked back to Roman's office, who was on the phone calling in a few favors. His wife, Lauren, had a friend who worked for the DA, working that angle as well as trying some other back-end channels.

Alex walked in shortly after, his face no more emotive than when he left, but Mike wasn't with him. "Mike's in the conference room, he wants to compare notes." He tipped his head to Stefan who quickly scurried past him.

And then there were three.

Roman.

Alex.

And me.

"I'm going to go and check in on my mom and brothers." I thumbed over my shoulder to the door, looking for my escape. "Not sure if any of it is going to hit the media, and I'd rather they hear it from me."

Alex's eyes darkened. "Yeah, we wouldn't want that."

Roman rolled his eyes. "Why don't you get out of here too? I'm going to tie up some loose ends with the boys and then head home myself."

"I'd rather stay." Alex strode to a chair near Roman's desk and took a seat.

Well then.

I was not going to cry.

"I'll call you if I get anything else from my mom or brothers." I directed my conversation to Roman, ignoring Alex like he was ignoring me. "And check in with you in the morning."

Roman nodded, handing me a card and scribbling a number on it. "Those are both mine and Lauren's personal numbers. You need anything, call."

"Thanks." I shoved the card into my pocket. "Bye."

It was a general goodbye, spoken to the room but only one of the other occupants acknowledged it. Not wanting to punish myself further, I turned and left the office, closing the door behind me as I stepped into the hall.

While most of the rooms had been empty when I arrived, there were even fewer lights on as Roman's assistant escorted me to the elevator.

"Wait." Alex jogged to the elevator. "I'll give you a ride home."

I was positive he hadn't had a change of heart; his offer to drive me home more likely a very strongly worded suggestion from his brother. "Thanks, but I'm fine. I'm sure you have a lot to talk to Roman about for your upcoming move."

There were two things I didn't want from anyone, especially

not Alex. Pity was one, and obligation was the other, and at that moment, I felt like he was giving me both.

"It can wait."

As the elevator door opened, he stepped inside, giving me the choice to either get in there with him or keep Roman's assistant waiting while I acted like a child. I strode in, pressing the button for the ground floor, watching as the metal doors closed.

"You can tell Roman you drove me, but I'll find my own way home." I lifted my eyes to his.

"Sorry, Maya." His gaze didn't falter. "But I'm not into lying to the people I care about."

"And I'm not getting into the car with you, so it seems like we've reached a stalemate." I put my hand on my hips.

He blew out a frustrated breath, raking his hands through his hair. "You're so fucking frustrating."

"Add it to the list of my defects," I fired back. "And you're not exactly my favorite person either right now."

The icy blue pools of his eyes filled with inky black as he moved closer. "Really? And why would that be? Did you expect me to be ecstatic my girlfriend was keeping things from me? Or that my own brother knew more about it than I did?"

My heartbeat quickened, his body so close we were almost touching. "He was my attorney." The words strangled by my clenched jaw.

"And I was your fucking boyfriend."

Was.

Past tense.

And whether that was the tense he'd meant to choose, it spoke volumes that he didn't correct it.

"Well, lucky for you, you don't have to worry about that anymore." My voice didn't waver, pulling strength I didn't know I had up from the depths of my toes just to get through it.

Like a miracle, the doors opened, allowing me to walk out. Before I could get very far, he grabbed my arm. "I'm always going to worry, whether you like it or not. And I know you don't like being told what to do, but I am driving you home. I'll even let you hate me for it, something you can add to *my* list of defects."

"Fuck you, Alex," I cursed under my breath, my hands balling into fists. And not because I hated him like he assumed, but because I still loved him.

He raised an eyebrow and then pointed to the exit. "Car is this way."

We walked to the car, got in and drove to my apartment without so much as a word between us. I kept my eyes glued to the road outside of his windshield and ignored the sideways glances I felt him throw my way. He wanted to play knight in shining armor and deliver me safe and sound—fine. But I wasn't going to play nice and make conversation like a good girl either.

Fuck.

That.

Instead, when we got to my apartment building, I barely gave him a chance to put the car into park before leaping out of the door and telling him goodbye.

I didn't look back.

Made it all the way to my front door.

And it wasn't until I heard his car drive away that I allowed myself to cry.

CHAPTER #25

MY FIRM HAD generously accepted my request for some personal leave, so I didn't go in, spending my Friday and my weekend in my apartment as I fielded phone calls.

The FBI weren't being forthcoming with information—there was a surprise, *eye roll*—but while I wasn't being charged with anything, the threat my father had issued hung over my head.

I had no idea what would happen or when, or if it was just his parting gift to me, to leave me in a shitty state of limbo for the rest of my life.

My mother had threatened to get on the next plane to L.A., only stopped from booking her ticket by my brother, Jordon, who told her she'd only make things worse. As hard as it was for me, it would be doubly hard for her. She'd gone through hell once already, and if there was any way we could protect her from that again, we would. I promised I would keep her posted, not leaving anything out, and instead Jordon would come, refusing to listen to reason that I was fine.

He arrived Friday afternoon and hugged me so hard at the airport I thought my insides were going to explode. And as much as I thought I was okay on my own, it was really good to have my big brother around.

"You know you are too good for him, right?" Jordon tried—and failed—at making me feel better because I hadn't heard from Alex.

I'd spoken to Roman like five times a day, and even his other brothers had called to check in. But Alex—not a peep.

To be fair, I hadn't called him either so I guess I was partially to blame. He might have taken my dramatic goodbye at the car to mean I didn't want to hear from him, so maybe he was just trying to respect my wishes. Either way, I was annoyed at the lack of contact, and frustrated that Roman, Stefan and Mike had found nothing of substance.

I lolled my head to the side from the couch, looking at my brother burning nachos in the kitchen. "Isn't it a little embarrassing for someone who can perform surgery to be unable to cook the basics?"

"I may not be able to cook, but I also don't get sidetracked by your tactics." He waved a dishcloth in the air trying to disperse the smoke before the alarm went off. "You know, I could talk to him."

"God, please don't," I groaned, hiding my face with a pillow.

Too many people were already involved, I did not need my brother—who currently didn't possess the ability to be impartial—to go have a *chat* with Alex.

I felt him sit beside me, his efforts in the kitchen abandoned. "Well since no one can locate our father, I can't kill him, so I need something to do."

It had been tough for my brothers and mother when I'd told them Dad had resurfaced. The silence on the other end of the phone when I was used to kindhearted teasing, shattered what was left of my heart. But as much as I wanted to protect them, I couldn't keep it from them. I'd tried that with someone else I loved, and it hadn't worked out so well for me.

And I got it, I really did.

Not sure I would be so pleased with someone trying to "protect" me. Which was why moving forward I was going to let everyone make their own decisions on what they wanted to know.

"I really appreciate you coming out here, Jordon." I reached across and gave him a hug. "I know you're busy with work and the kids."

He squeezed me, giving me a hug that only a big brother could. "I'd do anything for you, short stuff. Besides, it gave me the first few nights of uninterrupted sleep in a long time."

"You should have a chat with Roman." I laughed.

"I have. We're going to try and get together after all of this . . ." My brother searched for the words. "Is resolved. As much as I'd love to stay, I need to get back to the hospital."

I knew it was a flying visit, but the reality that in a few hours I'd be alone again, was hard to take. Ben had said he'd come stay for a little, and I'd even gotten similar offers from Jackie and Lisa. But I had no idea how long it would go on. I could literally spend the rest of my life waiting for something—or someone—to burst from the shadows and try to hurt me, and I wasn't going to give that man the power anymore.

So, Monday morning after the cab came to take Jordon to the airport and I waved him goodbye, I decided to call Roman—who surely must be getting sick of hearing from me—and ask him about the files which I'd gone through myself.

"Maya, I get you're frustrated, but I don't have anything new for you. I've got my investigator on it, but it takes time."

God, I was tired of waiting.

"I understand that, but while Astrid's photo of Alex and I might have been the catalyst for all of this, I haven't exactly been living off grid for all these years. He could have found me, through my college registration, through voter records, hell, he could have Googled me and he would have gotten a hit. Something prompted him to take the risk now, I feel like it's right there, staring us right in the face."

Maybe it was my connection with Alex, and his belief I had access to money. Or maybe it was something else.

"What are you thinking?"

"I don't know . . ." I tried to search for something, anything that would give me a clue. "But it's not something your investigator is going to find." Because my additional information had been *so* helpful.

"Well, if you think of something, give me a call. Until then, we'll keep doing what we're doing. He hasn't made any further contact and it's coming up to a week, so maybe it's all smoke. Meanwhile, Dina has been given immunity in return for information. I think she's hoping she might be able to regain custody of her daughter too which has a slim to none chance of happening."

"Has she told them where he is?" I held my breath waiting for the answer.

Roman blew out a breath of frustration. "Not something the FBI or the DA is willing to share but I get the feeling she doesn't know."

My brow scrunched in confusion. "How the hell can she *not* know, wasn't she with him?"

"I don't know, just a feeling. Anyway, hopefully we can find out more through the week." He paused. "Have you spoken to Alex?"

Really? I fought the urge not to glare into the phone.

"You *know* I haven't spoken to him, Roman."

He chuckled. "Yeah, well I'm still hoping one of you comes to your senses."

"He's leaving, there's not much point," I offered, knowing that even if I could speak to Alex, I highly doubted it would change anything.

"This shit was easier when you were both kids and we could

put you in a room until you worked things out."

"We didn't fight when we were kids," I reminded him.

"Are you kidding me?" Roman laughed. "You must have selective memory because I can think of at least two times you weren't speaking to each other. Once when you tried to flush that fucking Ninja Turtle down the toilet, and two when you went out with that guy, Chris. Oh, and let's not forget—"

"What are you talking about?" I cut Roman off, confused about the argument that hadn't happened. "I dated Chris when I was sixteen, it was right before I left. We weren't fighting."

Chris had been one of Alex's friends and the boy who had taken my virginity. It hadn't been terrible, and Chris had been a nice guy, but even if I'd stayed I doubt it would have lasted. Especially since I hadn't given him a second thought once we'd moved to Nevada, and I'd cried about missing Alex every night.

"Then why the hell was he acting like a moody prick and slamming doors, avoiding you the whole time?"

It was amazing how you could freeze a single memory from the past and for that memory to have been distorted. How in all those years I'd always seen our friendship as perfect, and failed to remember us ever fighting. Or that Alex hadn't spoken to me for a week after I'd slept with Chris. And was more detached there after.

Back then I'd assumed it was because Chris had been *his* friend, and he didn't want to be put in the middle if things went bad. But when I'd been forced to move away, none of that mattered, and somehow that painful memory of us not talking had been banished.

Why?

Why had he been so mad?

"You're right. I have to go." I didn't give Roman the chance to respond, killing the call and dialing Alex.

I couldn't breathe as I waited, wondering if he'd even answer and then on the third ring it stopped.

"Maya?"

He sounded surprised, but not upset, and hopefully it would stay that way.

"Why did you stop talking to me when I slept with Chris Banks?" It wasn't my best work, but I was done tiptoeing around anyone.

"I'm sorry, what?"

I sucked in a breath and repeated. "You were fine the whole time Chris and I dated, but after I slept with him, you shut me out? Why?"

"Maya, I'm at work. I really don't have time to discuss something that happened ten years ago."

"Fine, then meet me after work."

I wasn't letting it go. And not because I wanted to know why there'd been a rift between us back then, it was so much more important than that.

"Why? So we can talk about you and Chris Banks? You'll have to excuse my lack of enthusiasm."

"No, so we can discuss *us*, Alex."

My heart pounded in my chest knowing I'd taken a risk. But someone needed to take the first step, and I'd regretted not being that person back then. Maybe if we had been on better terms before I left, things might have been different. And even though this time it was him who was leaving instead of me, I wasn't willing to make the same mistake again.

"Maya . . ." He sighed, and I was sure we'd come to the part where he told me he was done. He didn't have time for my bullshit and he preferred if I stopped calling. After all, that was the speech I had practiced a hundred times on the off chance he'd call me, though I wasn't sure I'd have actually delivered it if he did.

"It's Monday, I have the legal clinic. Were you planning on going?"

I hadn't planned on it but I could.

It wasn't a lot, but it was enough, the door between us opening a slither. "Yeah, sure. You want me to meet you there?" I offered.

"No, I'll leave early, meet you and we can go to your place. Give us more time to talk."

The thought of him in my apartment was almost too much to take. Especially considering the last time he'd been, it was the start of the end. "Are you sure you can sneak out? Won't you get into trouble?"

"What are they going to do, Maya? Fire me? I've already handed in my notice."

Indeed.

I hadn't forgotten he was leaving, but hearing him say he'd put in his notice made it so much more *real*. He'd quit his job and accepted a new one, there was no going back.

"Okay, well. I'm here." I did my best to keep the disappointment out of my voice.

"You're not at work?" He sounded genuinely surprised.

"I took some personal time."

There was a pause, the hesitation making me wonder if he was changing his mind.

"Give me an hour."

"Okay, see you then."

I didn't argue, ending the call before he realized that it was nine a.m. and finishing his workday at ten probably wasn't the smartest move. I was letting people make their own decisions, remember? And he was a grown man who'd demonstrated on more than one occasion he didn't want to be told what to do. So, as I tossed the phone on my coffee table, I took the hour to pull myself together.

I'd waved goodbye to Jordon in sweats and a messy bun, and that wouldn't do when my hot ex—had we ever properly split up?—boyfriend came to *chat*. Not that I had plans of seducing him—the idea of sleeping with him, the furthest from my mind—but I wouldn't be human if I didn't want him to at least have *some* regret.

Tossing out the idea of putting on the dress that made my boobs look good, I instead went for a more casual—jeans, a cute top and pair of Converse—vibe. My hair was brushed out, and I put on some makeup, transforming myself in literally minutes, both mentally and physically. It was amazing how much I thought I was okay not seeing him until I knew I would. I wanted to, even if it was just one last time.

I'd just managed to clean the kitchen—Jordon's attempt at breakfast hadn't gone well—when there was a knock at the door.

It was him.

My body could sense his even without opening the door.

He was standing on the other side in a charcoal suit, black shirt, and a black tie that looked like it had been tugged loose. His blond hair was spiked in a million different directions, the product of raking his hand through it probably a hundred times no doubt. And in the short time since I'd last seen him, he'd somehow gotten better looking.

Because life was cruel that way.

"Hey." His Adam's apple bobbed as he swallowed, stepping inside my apartment and magically taking the air out of the room.

"Hey." I followed him through, hoping we'd be able to graduate to whole sentences soon. "Take a seat, did you want something to drink?"

Bravo, Maya. Bravo.

"No, I'm good." He took my advice and lowered himself to the couch, watching me as I did the same.

It might have been difficult to see him—*God, help me resist the urge to kiss him*—but it wasn't a picnic for him either. His eyes had restlessly swept up and down my body at least three times since he walked in and his hands had formed iron fists as they sat either side of his knees.

"Okay." I figured since I'd called the meeting, I probably should start it. "I was thinking about when we were younger, and how we didn't fight."

Alex narrowed his eyes, probably wondering where I was going with it. "I'm pretty sure we *did* fight, Maya. Everyone fights."

"Yeah. I know. I just blocked it out, wanting the memory of you to be perfect," I started to explain, holding up my hand when he looked like he might speak. "And I know *you're* not. I know *I'm* not. But for some reason, when we're together it's as close to perfection as I ever got. And when my dad called, and this whole mess unraveled, I just wanted to protect you from that. To protect us from that. Not just from my father, but because I didn't want you to feel like you needed to come back and save me. I didn't want to be a burden, even if it wasn't my fault. And as ridiculous as it sounds, I felt like I could control it."

"Maya, you aren't a burden." He shook his head. "And *we* didn't need protecting."

"I know, and I'm sorry." I said the words that had been in my heart. "You're right. I should have told you, given you the choice to make up your own mind. But I guess part of me was scared you wouldn't have chosen me. Or if you did, you had done it for the wrong reasons."

"Is that why you were pushing me to New York? Worried I was staying out of obligation?" He turned facing me, his fists no longer clenched but not reaching for me either.

"Yes. But then . . ." I bit my lip, with the wound open it was harder to keep going.

"Then I proved you right, throwing in the towel the minute it got too hard. And I'd confirmed what you'd always suspected, that you weren't worth it."

Hearing him say those words was like a slap in the face. The initial hit hurt, but its sting seemed to last forever.

I nodded, needing to look him in the eye. "Whether you want to believe me or not, I made my choices because I love you." *Present tense, and it wasn't a mistake.* "But you—"

"I've been in love with you ever since I can remember." He shocked me into silence. "Not just as my *best friend*, but as the only girl I could ever imagine being with." His hand raked through his hair. "You asked me once how long I'd wanted to sleep with you, and I said a while. What I didn't tell you was that it's been since we were fifteen. You were wearing a green top that clung to your tits and a pair of denim shorts. And I wanted in them so badly I jerked off to that memory for an entire year. Yeah, we were friends, but make no mistake, given half a chance I'd have taken so much more from you."

I swallowed, hard, his words of wanting me for so long the last thing I'd been expecting.

"So yeah, when I found out that cocksucker had taken your virginity I was fucking pissed. At you. At him. And at myself because I didn't have the balls to tell you how I felt. I'd wanted it to be me, Maya. I wanted to be your first, and your fucking last. And the thought of him *in* you—of anyone in you—made me want to do things I had no right to do. That's why I stopped talking to you, and why I never spoke to *him* again."

"But, but you slept with Taylor." I vaguely remembered catching them making out and then Taylor telling everyone they'd done it. I had remembered feeling weird, disappointed for some reason, which was when I decided to sleep with Chris.

"No, I didn't fuck anyone until after you left. I dated girls before, kissed them, but I never slept with them."

"Then why?" I had so many questions and not sure which one

of them to ask first.

"Because maybe I had some of my own demons, watching you choose everyone else instead of me. My brothers, Chris— even then I still fucking waited. Hoping. That's why it set me off when you let Roman, Stefan and Mike in but *not* me. Never *me*. I wondered if I was ever going to be your first choice. I love you, Maya. Not because there is no other choice, but because you're my *only* choice. And I'd have preferred to walk away than be your consolation prize."

I couldn't stop myself anymore, throwing my arms around his neck and kissing him. He didn't miss a beat, his hands on me in a second as his lips found my mouth.

"You could never be anyone's consolation prize," I gasped out between kisses.

His hands cupped my chin keeping me from his lips I desperately wanted, his voice raw. "And you could never be anyone's burden. But I need all of you, Maya. The good *and* the bad. I want to be the one you turn to, not my brothers or some other guy. Me. Because you're mine. And I'm fucking yours. You own me. Don't you understand? I had sixteen years with only part of you, but you had all of me."

Oh my God, I was going to die. I was going to wither into dust as my soul left my body, and anything I knew to be true was proven false.

He loved me.

He'd *always* loved me.

And he was just as scared as I was of losing it all.

"You have me, *all* of me."

"I'm sorry, Maya. You hurt my ego, and my heart, but I should never have walked away." He kissed my lips, gently, barely a feather's touch. "You deserved better, and you are worth more than that."

"And you are worth more than that too." I pulled him closer, being unsatisfied with what little contact he was giving me. "We'll both do better."

He pulled me into his lap, pulling off my top as his hips rocked against mine. He was hard, his hands moving at lightning speed as my bra found its way onto the floor.

His mouth dipped to my breasts, kissing them, swirling his tongue around my hardened nipple as I yanked his tie free and unbuttoned his shirt. It wasn't enough, my body arching with each pleasurable tease of his mouth while I tried to get him naked.

With his buttons undone, I helped him shrug off the jacket and then the shirt. His hands had moved to my jeans, working them down while his lips retained their focus.

"Take them off," I groaned, not sure if I meant his pants or my jeans but I wanted something off and I wanted it right now.

Not to disappoint, he eased my jeans off my hips, taking my underwear with them. He didn't get very far, his progress hindered by my need to grind against his hard-on.

I was so turned on, feeling myself get wetter and needing him to fill me.

"Maya, you're going to need to stand." He laughed against my neck. "I can't get them off."

Fuck.

That.

Letting my feet hit the floor, I toed off my Converse, pulled off my socks and pushed my jeans and panties the rest of the way down. He was about to do the same when I pushed him back down, unzipped his pants, put my hand down his boxer briefs and pulled out his cock.

My grip around him tightened, only jerking him off twice before I positioned his blunt head at my entrance and sunk down on him hard.

"Jesus, Maya." He grabbed my hips, fucking me hard as I bucked against him.

It was wild, the fact he was still partially clothed making it hotter because I hadn't been able to wait. I wanted to feel him, needed him inside of me and we'd already wasted too much time. And I didn't mean the few days we'd been fighting, but the *years* in between when we should have been together.

Pleasure built inside of me, my skin tingling as our mouths found each other, sharing the same single breath as I took every inch he had to give me.

It wouldn't last long, the need in me so desperate for release; I didn't have a chance to stop it.

"Fuck me, Maya." He growled in my ear. "Fuck me like I'm *yours*."

That was all it took, the words more freaking erotic than anything he could do to my body as I came in a rush. My body jerked, pulsing around him, taking the pleasure as it taunted him to join me. And he didn't need much encouragement, coming in hard, fast bursts, filling me as he grabbed my hair and rasped, "And you're mine."

No truer words had ever been spoken.

He was mine.

And I was his.

Forever.

CHAPTER #26

SEX IN THE living room had been the appetizer, while moving to the bedroom had been the main course.

I loved having him in my bed, his heavy body pressing down on me, and his hard cock inside of me. And I liked to be on top too, his lips kissing me, playing with my nipples while I rode him.

But more than anything, I loved when it was over how he'd hold me tight and kiss me slow. It was my most favorite thing on earth.

"So we going to talk about the obvious?" His teeth nibbled against my shoulder.

I rolled towards him, smiling. "I'm on the pill, we're okay."

"Not that." He rolled his eyes. "But I want you to know, if I was to ever have kids, I want them with you."

"And if I was to ever have a baby, I'd want it to be yours." I tried to kiss him. "Let's just wait a few years."

"Well." His half-hearted attempts to keep my lips away from his failing as I landed a kiss. "That's going to be pretty easy to do considering I'm going to be in New York."

"Oh. That."

While talking and sex hadn't solved everything, it had gone a long way to heal us. And I knew that as long as we kept talking, and being really honest with each other, there was nothing we couldn't work out. Except for a few thousand miles, which would soon be between us.

"Yeah, baby, *that*." His hand slid down my arm. "I've already given my notice."

"I'll go with you." The words were out of my mouth even before I'd had time to think of them. "Whatever happens, we'll stay together and if you go to New York, I'll go with you."

"But you love L.A., spent years trying to get back."

I shook my head, the point of no return. "No Alex, I'm in love with *you*, and I want to be wherever you are."

I'd have thought leaving would compromise my integrity. I'd given my word to my family, my firm and to myself. But what I didn't realize was giving up my own happiness was a far greater sin than going back on my word. And I wouldn't make myself miserable just to prove a point.

Not for anyone.

Not anymore.

His thumb traced my jaw. "I'm too selfish to ask you if you're sure, Maya. You've said yes, and I'm taking it."

"Good, because I want to be taken," I teased.

L.A. did mean a lot to me and that hadn't changed. But at the end of the day, it was just an address. It wasn't my heart, my soul, or my purpose. Those things were not tied to any one city, which meant neither was I.

With promises to help me break my lease—Prim was going to hate me—and help me find a new job, we jumped out of bed and got into the shower. We were probably acting crazy, but our irresponsibility wasn't going to extend to blowing off the law clinic.

Alex needed to change his clothes, his suit pants requiring some serious dry-cleaning while I needed to get into some professional attire myself. Both of us managed to get ourselves looking like lawyers instead of sex-crazed lunatics and into the car in time so we wouldn't be late.

It was probably the last time either of us would be at the legal clinic, and it honestly made me sad. Those people needed us, which was why it had been important to come even though we'd both wanted to stay in bed.

We sat at our desk like we had the other times, working through the crowd of people until Don called time and shut the doors. It was only after everyone had left that we told him the news that neither of us would be coming back.

"I know you have to do it, and honestly, wish you well." His lips pressed into a tight line. "But it's a big loss."

While his words weren't surprising—I mean, I hadn't expected him to be happy—there was something about them that made me stop.

"It's a big loss."

The voice, the tone, the level of disappointment just triggered something inside me like a forgotten memory.

That sentence.

Don.

When Alex had introduced us, it had been the first time we'd met. But I'd heard his voice before, and it had been in my dad's home office.

Like scattered pieces of a puzzle, it started to take shape.

It had been late, but Alex and I had snuck out and gone to get sundaes at the drive thru and I was trying to stealthily get back in the house without getting grounded again.

And whomever my dad was talking to was agitated, needing to be calmed down. I assumed it was business, thanked my lucky stars for the distraction and got into bed without being detected.

"You, you knew my father." I pointed my finger at Don. "You're the reason."

We're taught in law school to never make an accusation without having a well-formed argument and evidence to prove it. It's not enough to *say* something is true, you need to convince everyone else it is too.

But I had no argument—well formed or otherwise—and no evidence either. Except for the feeling in my gut, and the look on Don's face when I'd said it.

"What are you talking about, Maya?" He tried to laugh it off, looking at Alex for support. "I just met you a few weeks ago, and didn't you say your family is in Nevada? How could I have met any of them, I have never left the state."

"You didn't have to, you came to our house in Encino."

Don eyed the door nervously, looking like he wanted to run. But he didn't. I assumed it was because his body looked like it probably hadn't done cardio in at least a decade, but he may have decided just to do the right thing. After all, it had been ten long years, and his life didn't look like it'd been a bed of roses.

The weight of his secrets was visible on his face, and if I didn't know better, it was something he'd been expecting for a long, long time.

"He's threatened me. Alex. Both our families." I pushed a little further. "He'll hurt everyone. If you have any compassion in your heart, you'll tell us if you know something. Because I assure you, I will spend every single minute investigating until I know the truth."

I could tell his resolve was wearing thin, his heavyset eyes opening and closing as he wrestled with whatever it was that had been tormenting him.

My back straightened, my determination, settling in. "I won't stop. I'll find out even if I have to take you down with him, Don. You have a chance to finally do the right thing."

"Maya, people depend on me. I didn't take a cent of that money."

His plea had been enough to get Alex's attention, who up to that point had been in the dark. "You were involved with Glenn Zaveri?"

"I didn't take the money." Don held up his hands, attempting to prove he wasn't a criminal. "All I did was keep the ledger, the names, the money, and where it all went. Only person I ever met with was Glenn and he paid me cash, I wasn't on the payroll."

"So you knew?" I gasped in disbelief. "You knew all those people were going to lose their money and you did nothing?"

"Maya, what could I have done? Go to the cops? I'd have been implicated. I've spent the rest of my life trying to do right. Look at all the people we've helped, I am not a bad person," he protested, trying to convince us that he'd paid his penance.

Not likely.

I was fairly sure the FBI would feel differently too.

"You still have the information? The ledger, the names, the accounts?" I asked, hoping he did. Even if he didn't, I bet my father assumed he did.

He nodded, scrubbing his face with his hand. "Yes. It's in a safety deposit box. When you came to work here, I thought it might have been a set up. Thought maybe your dad was trying to get it back. So I did some digging."

Well that was a revelation I wasn't expecting.

"You investigated me?" I stared back in shock.

His head bobbed. "Yeah, worked out you were the same Maya Zaveri and waited to see what you would do. Then he called me. Hadn't heard from the man since he left and I could tell he was nervous. Kept asking me about what Alex was doing working for me and if I'd met you. I guess he got nervous or something, figured I'd hand over the ledger. Anyway, I still wasn't sure if you were in on it so I told him that if he wanted the cash, he was going to have to come get it himself and not send his kid."

He was the link, the reason my father would risk his freedom.

Wrongly believing I was after his money and I was trying to get it from Don.

"You spoke to him?" Emotions—ALL of them—surged through me as I waited for his answer.

"Yeah, but it didn't go well, and he didn't tell me where he was. Look, if you do this, Maya. Every single case I've worked will be called into question. Your work might come under scrutiny too, same with Alex. You willing to risk all of that for something neither of us can change?"

And that was it.

The leverage.

"I'd rather never work another case than perpetuate the lie." It wasn't even a choice.

While Alex convinced Don that the best thing to do was turn himself in, I called Roman and the police. It wasn't a good feeling watching Don be led away in cuffs, knowing that because we'd done the right thing, hundreds of other people were going to suffer. The legal clinic, his practice, and all the people he helped were suddenly abandoned. But as shitty as it sounded, you didn't get to pick and choose which laws you got to follow. Don was an accessory at the very least, and quite possibly an accomplice.

Through the night, Roman, Stefan, Mike, Alex and myself sifted through what we knew, and what we'd managed to get from Don before the FBI took him away. It wasn't easy and called for a lot of speculation but we felt confident we had it at least half right. It would take time before we got the full scope of the story but I didn't need an FBI investigation to know that my father had gotten greedy and nervous.

When he'd fled with Dina, he hadn't had time to take the ledger, taking with him only the million he had in cash stashed in a gym bag in our basement. It had been confirmed when Roman was able to get his hands on Dina's interview. We didn't ask questions how he was able to get evidence; just thankful we had at least some of her testimony.

The real money was hidden in offshore accounts, but my dad, too cocky to keep the numbers, had left them behind in his rush to leave. Which meant most of his money—and evidence to provide an ironclad connection to so many felonies he would never see the light of day—was still sitting in the possession of one Donald M. Lamb. And he hadn't done anything with it because he was worried about repercussions from either my dad or the law.

Dear old Dad had probably assumed Don had turned, testified and the money had been seized by the authorities; it's what *should* have happened but didn't. Instead, it was right where he'd left it—my father completely unaware it was still in play until his phone call.

The irony was that my dad hadn't even been after the money—probably reasoning it was long gone. Instead he got worried about the connection, something he discovered around the same time he found out that Alex and I were dating. Which Astrid so *helpfully* provided.

#ThanksALotAstrid

#NotSoHotWhenYouBringTheDevilBackIntoMyLife

Then we assumed he did what every felon on the run does when he finds out his daughter is shacked up with a decent man whose last name is famous. Yep, the internet had a lot to answer for. All he had to do was Google Alex and see his name listed with Don's legal clinic. Donating his time and expertise since college, Alex's name was on the website and in their records.

I'd have loved to seen his face while he built up his version of reality.

Of course, it had been wrong but ego will convince you of almost anything.

Then like the jackpot, he got two for the price of one;

information and then money.

Not sure if he still would have extorted money from me simply because I was with Alex or if he was worried I was going to get my hands on the evidence. It was something we may never know. But one thing was for sure, in all those years he was willing to risk everything and manipulate anyone for greed.

Either way, he either had to run for the rest of his life—without his precious money—or wait until the authorities found him in whatever snake hole he'd been hiding. And at least part of the money was recovered—sitting in the Cayman's just like Roman suspected—able to give some of the people compensation.

The legal mess was intense too, but that was something for the California bar to sort out. Thankfully because Alex had been unaware of the connection and the clinic had been legitimate, it was unlikely any of his cases would be threatened. It was a very small consolation.

It was late by the time we got back to Alex's house, both of us clumsily stripping down and climbing into bed. We didn't make love, preferring to hold each other and trading soft kisses that I wanted to last forever.

"I love you," Alex whispered in the dark. "We were always meant to be together."

"Such a shame it took us this long to work out," I whispered back.

His lips brushed against my forehead. "I don't care how long it took, I'm just glad I didn't lose you. I'm never taking that risk again."

"You won't lose me." My hands moved against his back, getting as close as I could to him. "But just so you know, my mother is probably going to freak when I tell her I'm moving to New York. Probably the only thing that is going to calm her down will be that she knows I'll be with you."

Alex laughed. "Well how about we make her really happy and

tell her you'll be my wife."

My heart shuttered, skipping a few beats like the wiring was all wrong. We had joked before, but I wasn't sure if that was one of them. "Are you serious?"

Both myself and my heart couldn't take the risk. I needed to know.

His hand cupped my chin, raising it so I could just make him out in the shadows. "I'm going to give you a proper proposal but I've waited my whole life for you, Maya. I'm not going to waste another second."

"Yes," I answered without hesitation. "Yes now, and yes for forever."

He kissed me softly, slowly, drawing it out because he knew it drove me crazy.

"Good, going to make those plans for world domination a hell of a lot easier with you as my wife."

My smile spread across my lips in the darkness. "We've been training for this our whole lives."

EPILOGUE

"I SWEAR IF you hadn't married the man, I'd have married him myself." Jackie pulled me in for a hug, welcoming me back having just arrived from our honeymoon.

"She means because she is grateful for him bringing you home to us." Lisa elbowed Jackie before taking her turn at hugging me. "And we are eternally grateful."

"No, I mean because he is hot and insanely good in a courtroom." Jackie smirked. "Are you sure there aren't any more of *him* laying around waiting to be snatched up. Older, younger, as long as they're legal, I'm not fussy."

"Sorry, I got the last one." I tapped her hand, trying to sound sorry. "Better luck next time."

Alex and I had picked out an engagement ring the first week we'd been in New York. Then, because he liked to torture me, he waited a whole two weeks before he proposed again and let me wear it. I might have waited a few minutes before saying "yes" for the second time, because I liked to torture him too.

I closed the chapter on Prim and my apartment, paying out the remaining months in full, which finalized the end of my lease without me breaking my contract. Prim was only too happy for the money, and I'm sure she had no trouble finding a replacement tenant. The jizz in the pool was now their problem. And Palmer and Loft had reluctantly accepted my resignation. It had been bittersweet leaving, sad to say goodbye to my two new friends, but excited for new possibilities.

We'd found an apartment in the East Village, and Alex's new firm suddenly had a vacancy for a new associate. I had a hunch Alex had lobbied on my behalf to get me an interview, but it had been my resume and enthusiasm which had landed me the job. Not only was I being mentored by a partner but I'd also earned their respect. And because it was New York, no one gave a rat's ass about my last name or my family connection.

As Alex had anticipated, news of a wedding made it easier for my mother to adjust to me leaving yet again. And a year later, she got to walk me down the aisle herself as I married the man of my dreams. I think between my mother and Kate, Kleenex saw a spike in share prices. And—Lord help us all—they'd already started an extended family group chat thread that gave me hives every time I saw the bubble with a billion unread messages.

Life was perfect, or as close to it as it got.

"Fine." Jackie sighed dramatically. "I'll take that guy, who worked with you when you were being a traitor, Stefan."

I laughed, my short stint in California still not forgiven. "He's still going out with Astrid, it's looking serious too. Not anything I'd have predicted."

Astrid and Stefan were an anomaly, but somehow it worked. He dug her "influencing" and she loved his attention, and somewhere along the line, the two of them actually started liking *each other*. She'd even posted pictures of herself on Instagram wearing conservative Chanel suits, her subtle hint that she was done with her partying lifestyle.

We still saw them whenever we visited Los Angeles, and they'd both been at our wedding, along with Mike who was still stead fast in his resolve not to date lawyers. His current girlfriend was a schoolteacher from Torrance.

"Maya isn't here to help you find a boyfriend, we're here to celebrate her triumphant return from her honeymoon. Tell us all about Europe, did you love it?" Lisa yanked on my arm.

"Every country was stunning, the food, the people—I just couldn't pick a favorite. But I'm really glad to not to have to live out of a suitcase anymore, and it feels good to be back and know I'm not going to be moving around for a while."

It had been a really long time since I'd put down any permanent roots, but finally I desperately wanted to. It hadn't been in the city I'd anticipated, but sometimes life has a way of changing things and giving you more than you asked. And regardless of where we lived, it was absolutely with the *right* person.

The girls and I shared breakfast mimosas and pastries at an adorable little café we'd discovered not far from where I lived. It was different to L.A., but I was slowly starting to fall in love with the city.

We chatted a little more about my trip, and then I enjoyed finding out what I'd missed out on during the three weeks while I was gone. I'd never get tired of listening to their craziness, and really glad my change in plans had enabled me to see them almost every day for lunch. Their firm was less than a block from ours.

It had been an hour into our celebratory brunch that my phone buzzed with an incoming message, Alex, telling me he needed to talk as soon as possible.

"Are you kidding me?" Jackie pointed accusingly at my phone. "He had you alone for three freaking weeks. Screwing each other's brains out in different romantic cities. It's enough to make me sick."

She made fake gagging noises while Lisa and I both laughed.

"It might be important." I played with my phone, a little embarrassed at how much I'd missed him. It had only been a few hours, but truly I was pathetic. Not sure in what world I'd believed I could have ever been away from him—completely and utterly delusional.

Lisa's eyes flicked with concern as they dropped to my phone. "You think it's about your dad?"

"Oh shit, Maya. I'm sorry." Jackie's hand grabbed mine. "I was joking."

"Don't," I warned them, smiling at my dear friends whom I loved so much. "Don't you dare apologize for being you."

While Dina had provided information for the FBI's inquiry, my dad had remained elusive. Not sure why anyone was surprised, running out on his family after he made a mess, was his thing. About a month after he called me, they thought they'd tracked him down to a small town on the Californian/Mexican border but he'd already left and been a ghost since.

The authorities had assumed news of my wedding might have flushed him out but I knew that it wouldn't. I was only useful to him when he had something to gain, and that ship had sailed when Don Lamb was arrested and charged. With all of Glenn Zaveri's dirty secrets, along with the money trail, handed over to the authorities, the only thing left for him to lose was his freedom. But whether we'd ever hear from him again remained to be seen. It would have been awesome for him to be found, to have tied it up in a lovely bow. But life doesn't always work out like that, and ends sometimes have to stay unraveled.

A beat passed, neither Jackie or Lisa saying anything before I cracked. "I mean it. Besides, if anything it's me who should be concerned for you. I'm married to the *hot guy who's insanely good in a courtroom* and working at an amazing firm in New York. As far as fairytales, I'm pretty much living it."

"Yeah, yeah." A smile crept across Jackie's lips. "Rub our noses in it why don't you, and you might as well just call him if you're going to sit there and be smug." And with that, any tension about my father or my past disappeared.

"Sounds like good advice." I picked up my phone and did what I'd been dying to do, my heartbeat still skipping a beat whenever I heard his voice.

Or saw him.

Or kissed him.

Seriously, I had major issues.

"Having fun?" He chuckled, his voice sending a shiver down my spine.

I bit my lip, trying hard not to smile like a lunatic. "Yes, so what's so important you need to speak to me?"

"Can't I just miss my wife and want to hear her sexy voice?"

My skin heated, even when he wasn't in the room, he could make me blush. "Yes, but I *know* you and I know that isn't the reason."

He took a breath, and it worried me for about a second.

And then I remembered, no time, no distance, no catastrophe, could ever take him away from me. We would always find our way back.

"Okay, so Mike called. They have finally set the date to reopen the legal clinic in Lynwood. And he wanted to know if we'd go back for the grand opening. I know we *just* got back but—"

"Tell him yes." I answered without hesitation.

It hadn't been immediately, but Mike and Stefan had taken up the fight and gotten the legal clinic back up and running. With the backing of my old firm—Palmer and Loft—and Astrid's social influence, they were not only able to help, but upgrade from the old hotel function room and set up a dedicated building. It would be staffed by volunteers with funding through fundraising efforts. And even though our contribution wouldn't be huge, we promised to go out at least once a month and help when we could. It also gave me an extra excuse to see my many nieces and nephews and extremely large extended family.

"I knew there was a reason why I married you."

"Why?" I laughed. "Because I'm so easy to convince?"

"No, because you have an amazing heart. I love you, baby. Enjoy your time with the girls and see you when you get home."

Lisa and Jackie both wore matching grins, clutching their hands to their chests like they were watching a bunch of puppies.

"Stop it." I laughed, putting my phone away. "It's rude to listen into people's phone conversations."

"Yeah, well too bad because we're rude people." Jackie scoffed, picking up her mimosa and taking a sip. "And judging by the look on your face things are going to get very *rude* when you get home."

And I didn't disagree.

It was so easy to fall in love with a Larsson—all of them beautiful, kind and successful. And I had been in love with each of them through the years in my own special way. But there was only one who had been my best friend, and who I'd given my entire heart. I'd waited, keeping it from him because I was scared about giving it away. Because you can't live without your heart.

I needn't have worried though.

Because I had his.

THE END

ACKNOWLEDGEMENTS

THANK YOU TO my loves—Gep, Jenna, Liam and Woodley. As always, your support and love mean everything to me.

Big thanks to my family and friends who have overlooked insanity and no longer bat an eye when I start a sentence with "So, I have this idea . . ." Instead—for better or worse—they cheer me on.

Thanks to the team at Brower Literary and Management—Kimberly, Aimee and Caroline.

Thank you to Nichole Strauss, from Insight Editing. No point hiding it, you love my ridiculous. Thanks for the oodles of work through all the projects! Here we are wrapping up another series together. Buckle in for the next one.

Thanks to the amazing MK! You had questions; I hope I answered them. I love your beautiful brain and eyes all over my words, it honestly makes me a better writer.

Christine Borgford from Type A Formatting, OMG it's our last one. It's been a privilege and an honor. Thank you for making my pages look so stunning.

Thank you to the best cover designer in the world, Hang Le. There's no one I'd rather be in the stock trenches with, you continue to astound me with your work. Don't ever leave me or I will find you LOL.

Thank you to my amazing proofreaders Lisa B, Jackie R and Rosa! You are an invaluable part of the process and I adore you.

Thank you to my author peeps—you know who you are! I have mad love and bucket loads of respect for all of you.

A huge thank you and shout out to all the bloggers, reviewers and promoters who read, promote, review, and share my work There are so many amazing authors and books out there, and it's an honor to be included in reading piles.

Thanks to KP, Jessica and Team InkSlinger!

Thank you Liz, MJ and Jillian at 1001 Dark Nights.

THANK YOU to the T Gephart Review Crew and Entourage. SENDING YOU ALL THE LOVE AND THANKS! Shout caps necessary!!! Thanks to Michelle Clay and Annette Brignac who wrangle the review crew and put in so much hard work.

And MASSIVE thank you goes out to YOU. Thanks for reading, enjoying, reviewing, sharing, and following my crazy journey. It would be the same without you, and if you're game, we'll keep doing this a little longer.

What do you say? You ready?

ABOUT THE AUTHOR

T GEPHART IS a USA Today and International bestselling author from Melbourne, Australia.

With an approach to life that is somewhat unconventional, she prefers to fly by the seat of her pants rather than adhere to some rigid roadmap. Her lack of "plan" has resulted in a rather interesting and eclectic resume, which reads more like the fiction she writes than an actual employment history. She'd tell you all about it, but the statute of limitations hasn't expired yet. But all those crazy twists and turns have led her to a career she loves—writing romantic comedy.

When she isn't filling pages with sassy and sexy characters with attitude, she's living her own reality show in the 'burbs of Melbourne with her American husband, two teenage children, and her fur child—Woodley.

She loves adventure, to laugh, travel, and strives to live her life to the fullest.

CONNECT WITH T

www.tgephart.com
Facebook
Goodreads
Twitter

BOOKS BY
THIS AUTHOR

The Lexi Series

Lexi

A Twist of Fate

Twisted Views: Fate's Companion

A Leap of Faith

A Time for Hope

The Power Station Series

High Strung

Crash Ride

Back Stage

The Black Addiction Series

Slide

Sticks

Stand

#1 Series

#1 Crush

#1 Player

#1 Rival

#1 Lie

#1 Muse

#1 Love

Collision Series
Train Wreck
Car Crash

Standalones
The Fall
One-Night Stand-In (rereleasing soon)

www.ingramcontent.com/pod-product-compliance
Lightning Source LLC
Chambersburg PA
CBHW030623110726